CW01433131

A WOMAN OF FORTUNE

Also by Val Wood

THE HUNGRY TIDE
ANNIE
CHILDREN OF THE TIDE
THE GYPSY GIRL
EMILY
GOING HOME
ROSA'S ISLAND
THE DOORSTEP GIRLS
FAR FROM HOME
THE KITCHEN MAID
THE SONGBIRD
NOBODY'S CHILD
FALLEN ANGELS
THE LONG WALK HOME
RICH GIRL, POOR GIRL
HOMECOMING GIRLS
THE HARBOUR GIRL
THE INNKEEPER'S DAUGHTER
HIS BROTHER'S WIFE
EVERY MOTHER'S SON
LITTLE GIRL LOST
NO PLACE FOR A WOMAN
A MOTHER'S CHOICE
A PLACE TO CALL HOME
FOUR SISTERS
THE LONELY WIFE
CHILDREN OF FORTUNE
WINTER'S DAUGHTER
FOSTER'S MILL

A WOMAN OF FORTUNE

Val Wood

bantam

TRANSWORLD PUBLISHERS

UK | USA | Canada | Ireland | Australia
India | New Zealand | South Africa

Transworld is part of the Penguin Random House group of companies
whose addresses can be found at global.penguinrandomhouse.com.

Penguin Random House UK, One Embassy Gardens, 8 Viaduct Gardens, London SW11 7BW

penguin.co.uk

First published in Great Britain in 2025 by Bantam
an imprint of Transworld Publishers

001

Typeset in 11.85/16 pt New Baskerville by Falcon Oast Graphic Art Ltd
Printed and bound in Great Britain by Clays Ltd, Elcograf S.p.A.

The authorized representative in the EEA is Penguin Random House Ireland,
Morrison Chambers, 32 Nassau Street, Dublin D02 YH68

A CIP catalogue record for this book is available from the British Library.

ISBN 9780857507181

To my family with love,
and for Peter as always.

CHAPTER ONE

1860

Lydia stood dutifully by the front door, holding Nicholas's top hat and mentally counting to ten while he put on his top-coat, took the hat without looking at her and adjusted it in the mirror, giving it a final tap with his forefinger. Then he turned, smiled, and gave her a peck on the cheek.

'I hope you have a good day, m'dear. I'll see you at about five.'

She smiled and nodded. How surprised I'd be if you didn't arrive until half-past, she thought. Why, the heavens might fall. You're just like Papa. She recalled seeing her father go through the same ritual with her mother as her childhood self watched from the stairs. Was that why Papa introduced us? Did he recognize something of himself in his new employee? Nicholas had applied for a post as a legal secretary with her father and came with excellent references: he was bound for great things, her father enthused, and invited him for supper especially to meet his daughter. Her mother was charmed by him, her father thought he had great potential, and somehow, Lydia mused, I was swept along in their wake.

She waited now in the doorway, saw the hired hackney roll up, and watched her husband routinely greet the driver, step inside the carriage and lift his hand to her as the driver raised his whip to touch the horse's flank and away they went. Turning from the door and closing it behind her, she emitted a deep sigh of discontent as she did every weekday. On Saturdays and Sundays Nicholas had a different routine. *I think I've made a big mistake.*

'I'm going out,' she said out loud. 'I'm bored, and I'm not staying in all day.' Lydia had developed the art of talking to herself if Maggie, the maid of all work, and Cook were not there, not that either had many conversational skills when they were. This morning Maggie, who had flexible hours and was paid accordingly, had not yet arrived, though as Lydia moved away from the front door she realized that Cook was already in the kitchen, preparing food for the day. Anything left over for the next would be put in the cold larder, which had a wire mesh meat safe where normally a window would be. The former residents had had it fitted. Such a clever idea, Lydia had thought when they first came to view the house. It keeps the flies out and the food cold.

When Lydia and Nicholas had married almost three years before they had moved straight into this pretty three-bedroomed cottage, a wedding present from her parents. It was a mile away from the nearest village and on the outskirts of the old market town of Beverley, where she had been born. Used to a much larger family home, Lydia had decided that life in such a restricted space wasn't conducive to having live-in servants; she would have been too tempted to chat to them as she had done in her parents' house.

'I'll drive to see Emily,' she said. 'She's due to give birth very soon, or so she said, so she might be glad of company.' Lydia didn't mind being alone, but she had enjoyed her time at boarding school and missed the company of friends. She had considered that she would make local ones; but there were few residents in this quiet hamlet and so she was pleased to be able to visit Emily, who was only a short journey away.

She changed now into a plain grey silk dress that reached her ankles with a slight fullness, sought out a smart red velvet waistcoat and a matching bonnet of the same material to cover her ears, and completed her outfit with a woollen cape, as the March weather was still rather unpredictable.

Her mother had advised her on her marriage that during the day she should wear a lace cap at home so that she was tidy in case anyone should call. Lydia had nodded and murmured, but completely ignored her mother's advice. She did not, she considered, want to wear anything that was fashionable; I am my own person and will not follow a trend of what others might be doing.

She was about to go towards the stable block at the rear of the cottage to bring out Frisky the pony and let his donkey companion, Janet, into the paddock where she could safely roam while they were away when Maggie came rushing through the gate. 'Sorry, ma'am,' she said breathlessly. 'I can't believe that I overslept. I've never done that afore in my *life*.'

'It's allowed, Maggie,' Lydia said mildly. 'That's why we agreed on flexible hours. You do look a little tired, though;

do some dusting and sweeping and leave the laundry for another day.'

'Thank you, ma'am. Thank you.' Maggie gave a nod in lieu of a dip of her knee, as Lydia had advised, saying there was no need for it every time they spoke – especially, she had thought, considering the maid's arthritic knees.

The journey to Bishop Burton, where Emily and her family lived, took a mere twenty minutes in the trap, and she enjoyed the drive. She was pleased that she had insisted on having her own transport. At first Nicholas had raised some objections to her driving alone, but she had promised she would not drive the trap after dark, and he had eventually agreed.

The weather was sunny, though with a crisp breeze, when she reached the ancient village, where, it was said, an Archbishop of York had lived aeons ago, so giving it its name.

She pulled up at the front of the house, which was much larger and grander than hers and Nicholas's. A young lad working on one of the flower beds came to her aid, tipping his cap, and led the pony and trap away to be tethered. She looked up and saw that one of the front bedrooms had its curtains partly open. That was Emily's room, she was quite sure, and she went up the stone steps to the door. It was open, so she knocked and stepped inside.

Jane, Emily's personal maid, called out from a lower staircase. Lydia could just see the top of her head. 'Go on up, Mrs Mercer,' the girl called. 'We're not standing on ceremony today. I'll bring tea up shortly.'

Lydia smiled and walked across the hall to mount the

wide oak staircase. This was why she loved coming here. The Horners' household was never stuffy and starchy or conventional, and they were always welcoming.

'Twins!' Lydia gazed in astonishment at her friend, in bed after the birth of two babies the evening before, both now tucked up one at each end of the cot, and clasped her hands together. 'Both boys! Oh, Emily. They are darlings! But you, you poor dear. Was it really dreadful? But worth the trauma!' she added hastily.

Emily sighed and remarked languidly, 'Well, I have done this before, if you recall?'

'But not two at the same time!' Lydia exclaimed. 'At least there was a year between Simon and Edwin. You had time to recover.' Lydia actually had no idea how long it took to recover from childbirth, but thought that a year sounded all right. 'What names will you give them? Or perhaps Gideon will choose – has chosen?'

'Mm, no, I doubt that very much. In any case, he hasn't seen them yet and doesn't know that there are two.'

'Doesn't know! Is he away? Couldn't someone have telegraphed on your behalf?'

Emily nodded slowly, and yawned. 'I suppose, but there's no hurry, and in any case he couldn't have rushed home. He's in York on business. Something to do with cattle.' She stretched, lazily. 'I'm a farmer's daughter, don't forget; I don't actually need him here. He'll know that I'm all right.' She gave another huge yawn. 'Although I am exhausted. You'd have thought the doctor would have known, wouldn't you? The midwife did; she said weeks ago that there were two and

Dr Tennyson disputed it. So, have *you* had a word with Mrs Bower yet?'

'No! Nor have I told Nicholas that I was going to speak to her.' Lydia looked away, gazing towards the window rather than facing Emily. 'There's nothing to discuss in any case. I'm rather embarrassed.' She looked back, pink-faced. 'He'd be embarrassed too, I think.'

Emily smiled. 'Surely you're not serious? You've been married for – what, two years? Nearly three? Ring the bell please, will you, there's a dear. I'm gasping for water, or tea – anything!'

'I'll go down for it.' Lydia got to her feet and went to open the bedroom door, revealing Jane, with a tray in her hand, about to reach for the doorknob. 'Shall I take that?'

'No you will not, ma'am, thank you. We don't want this lot spilling over.'

The maid headed towards a round table by the window and poured two cups of tea from a large teapot, added milk and two sugar lumps to one cup and stirred it, and carried it over to her mistress. She placed the cup and saucer on a small chest by the bed and took a shawl from the top drawer.

'Now, ma'am, let's have you up a bit. No, not too much,' she added, hooking Emily under her arms and gently bringing her to a sitting position, whereupon Emily groaned and wrapped the shawl about her shoulders. 'There,' Jane murmured, handing her the tea. 'A cup that cheers. Midwife's having a cup down in 'kitchen; she says she'll be off as you're all right, and she'll be here again in 'morning, unless you need her for owt meantime, when of course you must send for her.' She lifted her head and listened; a door had opened and closed. 'That'll be Mr Horner – sounds like his tread.' She smiled broadly. 'I wonder what he'll say to having two more lads, eh?'

'Don't tell him, Jane!' Emily warned. 'I'm going to surprise him.'

'He can have my cup,' Lydia said quickly. 'I'll come down and have one with you, Jane.' She didn't want to intrude on the moment that Emily's husband discovered that he had two more sons.

She was still on the landing when the large form of Gideon Horner loomed in front of her at the top of the staircase and huffed out a breath. He's not very fit, she thought.

'Now then, my dear,' he puffed. 'How are you? It's Mrs Brown, isn't it?'

'Erm, n-no,' she stammered, and shook her head as a vision of Gideon Horner in his nightshirt climbing into bed alongside Emily floated in front of her. 'It's – it's Lydia Mercer.'

'Of course it is, of course. Been to welcome the new baby, have you? Has it arrived? Another little Horner, eh!'

She smiled and nodded. Best not to speak, she thought, I'll probably give the game away; and immediately burst out that Emily looked very well – considering.

'Oh, she's a game girl,' he said heartily. 'Comes from good stock. And how's your husband? Jonathan, isn't it?'

She opened her mouth to say, no, his name is Nicholas, but the men had only met a couple of times so the mistake was excusable, she thought. Before she could say anything Jane came out from Emily's bedroom and greeted her employer.

'Mrs Horner is having a cup of tea, sir. There's one already poured, if you'd like it, and I'll bring up another pot.'

'Yes, thank you, Jane, just the thing, and a little cake or something, if Cook has anything handy.'

'I'm sure she will have, sir.' Jane dipped her knee and she and Lydia hovered on the top step, waiting for the bedroom door to close. Almost immediately, a great roar echoed behind it and they both smiled, Lydia holding her hand over her mouth to stifle her laughter as they heard '*Good God, woman, we could start our own army! Whatever were you thinking of?*'.

They didn't stay to hear Emily's reply but hurried down the stairs. 'I'll join you in the kitchen, Jane, if Cook doesn't mind.' Lydia gave a chuckle. 'A quick cup of tea and then I'll be going; I'll come back another day. Will you tell Mrs Horner?'

'Yes, ma'am, and Cook won't mind at all. I'm sorry I didn't bring tea up earlier. I wasn't expecting Mr Horner just yet.'

Lydia noticed that Jane's lips were quivering and her voice was wavery as she opened the door to the kitchen, and began to laugh herself in order to allow Jane to do the same.

Whatever was she thinking of? Did he – surely he doesn't think – yes, he must; he thinks that it's the mother can choose if her child will be male or female. What? As if we women can decide on anything!

She glanced at Jane, who was wiping her eyes, then at Cook who was gazing at first one and then the other with an enquiring frown above her eyebrows, and finally at the midwife, Mrs Bower, who was shrugging into her coat, a half-drunk cup of tea going cold on the table.

'We're laughing at something Mr Horner said,' Lydia explained. 'He's so very jolly, isn't he?' She knew it would be perfectly acceptable for her to mention Mr Horner's misconception but not for Jane, who was in his employ; or at least, she thought, not in front of a visitor.

Jane took a breath and wiped her eyes on her apron again; and then her nose on a clean handkerchief she'd taken from her pocket. 'Yes, indeed, ma'am, he is. Very jolly. Mr Horner's requested cake, Cook,' she added with a little hiccup, 'to have with his cup of tea.'

Cook bustled to the kettle, shook it gently and then put it back on the stove. 'I'll make a fresh pot, Mrs Mercer, if you'd like to take a seat? Kettle won't tek long to boil. Will you have another, Mrs Bower?'

'No, no, thank you,' the midwife replied, picking up her large leather bag. 'Must be off. I have another mother to see to. Mrs Wade,' she explained, turning to Lydia. 'You'll no doubt know her? Good day, Mrs Mercer.' She nodded, and Lydia was quite sure that her eyes roved all over her, from shoulders to toes.

Lydia drank her tea for politeness' sake as much as anything, but it was hot and strong and rejuvenating and she thanked Jane and Cook sincerely before leaving by the kitchen door. The pony in his harness was cropping on a patch of grass close by the yard.

She turned him gently round by the bit and then, hitching up her skirts, climbed into the cart, shook the reins and trundled down the long drive, sorry to leave so soon after arriving. When she reached the gate to the lane, she turned and looked back at the lovely old house, its mullioned windows reflecting back the bright sun.

Emily had married money, although her father, a gentleman

farmer who worked the land alongside his farm workers, was not without wealth himself. He it was who had decided that the house they lived in was too big for him and his wife now that their children had left home, and had handed it over to Emily and her husband when they married, whilst he and Emily's mother moved to a smaller, more convenient residence. Convenient, that was, for him with his few wants, but not for his wife, who had liked to entertain.

Lydia was the only daughter of a professional lawyer with a practice in Beverley, and her mother came from highborn though penniless gentlefolk in a western county. Lydia was born in a town house on the edge of Beverley and had lived there until her marriage to Nicholas, who had a keen brain but not much personality and little charisma, deficiencies which she had somehow missed before agreeing to marry him.

Remarkably, as she and Emily were born in the same area, they had first met at a ladies' college in Herefordshire, where they had been sent at seventeen after home schooling. Both were eager to be independent and free of male domination, but their subsequent marriages had scotched that idea completely. They had, though, remained firm friends.

The babies are lovely, Lydia pondered as she took the green and narrow lanes towards home. Would I like children? she thought. Are they essential to married life? They keep a woman in her place, her place being at home. Emily will be happy and satisfied, for despite our youthful discussions about being equal to any man it plainly isn't true, and just considering a profession or occupation would be impossible even if it were. At least Emily knew that by marrying the benevolent Gideon Horner she would face no difficulties whatsoever in ordering her household exactly as she wished.

But Lydia, who still longed for independence, realized that for her it would never be quite the same; and besides, she thought, Nicholas doesn't seem to be in the least interested in begetting children, which is an extremely difficult subject to discuss with him, for although he occasionally comes to my bed he offers nothing but a chaste kiss before returning to his own, and I am left thinking that he does not desire me in the least.

She reached the short narrow track off to her right that led down to the Wade family's cottage, less than half a mile from her own. As the midwife had reminded her, Mrs Wade, when Lydia had last seen her, was heavily pregnant; her husband was a carpenter working for a local company and had done a few tasks for the Mercers when they'd first moved into the cottage. Lydia often wondered how the family survived, for he couldn't have been earning much; his employer wasn't known for his generosity, and would certainly not pay a wage that would be enough to feed all their young children and another to come.

She turned to drive down the track. There was nothing urgent waiting for her at home, and although Matthew Wade seemed disinclined for small talk, and rarely greeted her with anything but a nod and a finger-tap to his forehead if he happened to be at home when she called, Mrs Wade was very pleasant, even though she often looked weary.

She pulled in near the gate and saw the midwife's dog cart at the door. She climbed down from the trap just as a stream of children rushed out of the house, almost falling over each other; the youngest of them, still an infant, was being carried by the eldest girl and was opening her rosebud mouth as if about to cry when she saw Lydia and stopped.

'Hello!' Lydia smiled at them; they were very attractive children despite their hair being tangled in unruly curls, and the two boys muddied to the knees. They all stared at her, and then the eldest girl dipped her knee. Alice, Lydia remembered.

'Ma's having a bairn,' Alice said, though Lydia hadn't asked. 'She can't come down. Midwife's here.'

'Yes, I recognized her pony. Is your father home?'

Alice shook her head. 'He's working fer 'gaffer today; he'll be home at teatime.'

'Oh! So who is looking after you?'

They all turned their eyes towards her, then one of the boys spoke up: 'We can look after us selves,' he maintained. He must have been all of seven, or eight at most, Lydia considered.

'Me. I look after 'em.' This was Alice again. 'I'm 'eldest, so Ma said I could be in charge.'

'Ah, of course. You're Alice, aren't you?'

Alice bobbed her knee again. 'Yes'm,' she mumbled. 'I saw you 'last time you come.'

'I remember,' Lydia said. 'Alice, if I hold the baby, could you call up to Mrs Bower and tell her that Mrs Mercer is here and wants to know if there's anything that I can do for her?'

Alice hesitated. 'Baby Mary needs changing; she's a bit smelly. I don't think you'd like it. Ben can hold her.'

'Aw!' This was the boy who said they could look after themselves. 'Do I have to? She's right stinky.'

'Tell you what, I'll go in,' Lydia said decisively. 'I don't think your mother would mind.' She strode off into the house and looking up saw a short stairway leading up to what must be the bedroom, for she could clearly hear Mrs Bower's voice. To her right was a room with a low fire burning.

She called up. 'Mrs Bower, it's Lydia Mercer. I'm on my way home but called to ask if there's anything I can do to help?'

Mrs Bower came out of a doorway and silently shook her head. 'You could fetch Mr Wade home if you know where to find him, or drive to 'doctor's house on 'top road and ask him to come.' She lowered her voice. 'It's urgent.'

'I know them both,' Lydia murmured. 'Mr Wade works for Stephenson, doesn't he?'

Mrs Bower nodded and returned to the bedroom, and Lydia went back outside to speak to the children. 'I'm going to drive to fetch the doctor and pick up your father. I'd like Ben to come with me, if you wouldn't mind, Ben. You could show me the way.'

Ben's mouth formed a startled *oh*, but she guessed he would be pleased, and she thought that perhaps Alice might be able to handle the younger ones better without him there getting into mischief. She could certainly see mischief written all over him.

'Are we going in 'pony'n'trap?'

'We are, so are you ready? We'd better be off.'

With a quick glance at Alice for approval he jumped into the trap and grabbed the reins, which Lydia firmly took from him. 'You can drive part of the way when we come back, Ben, but right now we have to hurry and fetch the doctor to look at your mama.'

'My ma? She's onny having a babby, she's not poorly.'

'Who said so?'

'Ma did.' He looked up at her and blinked, his lips parted. 'She's used to having bairns; there'll be six of us wi' next little un. I counted,' he said. 'I'm second. Our Alice was 'first, an' then me. Charlie and Lily are next, cos they came on 'same day, and then it's Mary. She's still onny a babby; she's not got any ears yet, I don't fink.'

'Not got any years, do you mean? She does have ears.'

'Yeh, that's what I said.'

She smiled. 'So Charlie and Lily are twins, are they? I didn't realize that.' Lydia urged the pony on with a flick of the reins.

'I fink so,' he answered, folding his arms. 'They came out of 'same egg. Have you ever seen a double yolker? From a chicken, I mean?'

'Erm . . .' Her voice quivered as she hid a smile and thought she'd never again feel the same about eating a double-yolked egg for her breakfast. 'Yes, I have.'

They hadn't travelled very far when Ben called out, 'Look!' He stood up and pointed at someone coming towards them. 'That's my da.'

'Please sit down, Ben; you'll disturb the pony if you move around in the trap.'

'But it's Da,' he said, and waved his arms. 'What's he doing coming home now?'

'I don't know, but do keep still, or I'll have to stop.'

He sat down again and folded his arms in front of him as his father approached. 'Da,' he shouted. 'We're coming to fetch you.'

Matthew Wade came to Lydia's side of the trap. 'What's up? Where're you going wi' Ben?' He sounded angry.

'I – I was coming to fetch you; Mrs Bower asked me to. Then I'm going on to ask the doctor to call. Your wife is unwell, Mr Wade. I brought Ben with me so that Alice could manage the other children.'

He stared at her. 'Tek Ben wi' you to fetch 'doctor, Mrs Mercer, if you will, please. I'll be off home.' He threw his rucksack into the back of the trap and set off at a run.

He'll probably be there faster than I can drive. She pondered for a minute, then shook the reins and went on as quickly as she considered safe, hoping very much that she would find the doctor at home. When they reached the house, she gave Ben strict instructions to stand by the pony's head and keep him calm before going up the steps and knocking the shiny brass knocker on the heavy oak door. To her relief, Dr Tennyson opened the door himself. 'Mrs Mercer! Good day to you. How can I help you?'

Explaining the situation, Lydia thought she saw some disquiet in the doctor's expression. 'Have you seen Mrs Wade yourself to ascertain her condition?' he asked.

She shook her head. 'It was Mrs Bower who asked if I could fetch you. She intimated that it was urgent, so I've alerted Mr Wade and he's on his way home.'

'Mm,' he said. 'Well, the child is early, and Mrs Wade is not in good health. If you could go back now, Mrs Mercer, to entertain the children, I'll saddle up and overtake you.'

'Very well, doctor,' she said, and went back down the steps. Gathering up the reins, she showed Ben how to turn the pony round, and within a few minutes the doctor cantered past on his way to the Wades'. It seems as if it is very urgent, she pondered as she watched him ride by, but there's nothing more I can do; Mrs Bower and the doctor are in charge.

'Come on, Ben.' She gave him the reins. 'You can drive for some of the way.'

The boy beamed. 'Giddy up,' he called to the pony. 'Let's head home.'

CHAPTER TWO

When Lydia and Ben arrived back at the Wades' house, the children were playing outside and the doctor's horse was tied up to the fence. Ben jumped down and ran to his sisters and brother, calling out in excitement, 'I drove 'pony! By myself, not wi 'missus helping me.'

The younger children looked up with interest; Alice was sitting on a wooden stool with Baby Mary on her knee. 'Clever boy,' she murmured lethargically. 'Well done. Da's home.'

'I know that,' Ben said excitedly. 'I saw him first; we'd have been home afore him, but we had to go and fetch 'doctor.' He turned for the door. 'I'm going in to see Da and tell him I drove 'pony on 'way back.'

'We've not to go in yet.' Alice roused herself. 'He's talking to 'doctor.'

'So why can't we go in?'

'Cos Da said so,' she answered crossly. 'Just shut up a bit, will you? They're talking!'

Ben gave an exaggerated sigh and began walking about, kicking at stones with the toes of his boots.

'Ben, come here a minute. Ben!' Lydia leaned on the trap. I really should be going home, she thought. I think I've missed lunch. I wonder if the baby has been delivered? Mrs Bower must have gone; her dog cart's not here. 'Your father will say when you can go inside,' she said calmly when Ben came unwillingly towards her, but she had the uneasy feeling that all was not well.

The door opened and Dr Tennyson came out, closely followed by Matthew Wade. 'Here's Mrs Mercer,' the doctor said. 'Perhaps she will know of someone.'

Lydia glanced at Matthew Wade. His face was grey, and his hair was standing on end as if he'd been running his fingers through it. 'I doubt it,' he said, his voice cracking as if he could barely get any words out. 'We'll leave it to 'midwife. Reckon she'll know if anybody does.'

'Know what?' Lydia asked.

Mr Wade licked his lips. 'Of a wet nurse; somebody who's mebbe just had a new-born and has milk to spare.'

For a minute, she didn't understand what he meant, too uninformed regarding pregnancy, birthing and everything that went with it to construe his words into something she could understand. *Can Mrs Wade not feed the child herself?* She went hot with the embarrassment of even thinking of such things with Mr Wade standing there staring at her, let alone the doctor, pondering with his chin in his hand.

'You'll have to give him a bottle if we don't find anyone,' Dr Tennyson said suddenly. 'Warm boiled water will do for now. Mrs Bower will show you what to do; she said she was coming back.'

Matthew Wade nodded; he seemed to be in a daze. 'I know what to do,' he mumbled. 'I've got five other bairns.'

Lydia stood up straight. 'Could – erm, could you tell me what's happening? I'll have to get home soon, so if I'm not needed here . . . ?' She glanced at the doctor, who stared silently back at her, and then looked to Matthew Wade, who also seemed to be struck dumb. At last, the doctor spoke.

'The child was safely delivered,' he murmured, 'but I'm sorry to say that Mrs Wade didn't survive.'

Didn't survive? Meaning . . . Lydia felt faint and hung on to the side of the trap; she glanced at Alice, who was frowning and staring at her father as if she didn't know him. Baby Mary was wriggling, trying to get out of her grip. Suddenly reality sank in and Lydia stepped forward. 'Give Mary to me, Alice. Your father needs you now.'

The baby looked at Lydia in astonishment as Alice handed her over, and reached for the feather in her hat. Seeing her playing with it contentedly, Alice slowly went to her father, and he put his arms out to pull her close to him.

Lydia had never seen such a show of affection from father to child as she saw now, although no words were spoken between them. Alice appeared to understand what had happened to her mother, and her father was comforting her, his cheek on the top of her head. Lydia felt a tug on her coat, and looking down she saw that Ben was holding on to it. He too was watching his father, but the twins were playing their own game of pat-a-cake and seemed unconcerned.

The rattle of a cart stirred everyone and Dr Tennyson looked up. 'Ah!' he said, and his relief was palpable. 'Mrs Bower. You're back! Any luck?'

The midwife came through the gate. 'Yes, I think so, sir,' she said, catching the tail end of his question. 'A young woman in yon village. She said she'd come; she's just waiting on her ma to bring her in 'cart. Too far for her to walk; she's onny just a week from childbed herself, but she has plenty o' milk to feed two.'

Lydia had the sense that she had arrived in an unknown world. Surely the young woman should be resting at home, not traipsing out to feed someone else's child as well as her own? She swallowed hard. *But what do I know? Nothing, and I can't help anyone.*

Mrs Bower was still talking in a low voice. 'Undertaker will be here in an hour, sir,' she was saying. 'He said he'd be quick as he can.'

'Did he say how much?' Matthew mumbled.

'He said not to worry about it for now,' Mrs Bower murmured. Lydia felt she was in a bad dream and wanted to wake up and be gone, but she couldn't: she was glued to the spot.

'Mrs Mercer.' Matthew Wade had come up to her and was taking Baby Mary from her arms. 'I'm sorry you've come at this difficult time,' he said quietly. 'Please leave if you wish, and I thank you for your kind assistance.'

She felt tears trickling down her face and found she couldn't speak immediately. 'I'm so very sorry for your loss, Mr Wade,' she gulped, her voice cracking. 'Is there anything I can do? Could I perhaps take some of the children to stay with my husband and me for a while?'

He gave a sad smile and shook his head. 'No, thank you. We'll stay together as a family and welcome 'new babby; and 'children, or some of them, must say goodbye to their mother – Alice, and perhaps Ben, so they will see that she's onny sleeping, and can tell the younger ones so.'

CHAPTER THREE

Nicholas was at home when Lydia arrived back at the house, exhausted and tearful. She left the pony hooked up near the gate, still harnessed to the trap, and stumbled towards the front door. She felt she had left the Wades too soon, yet there was nothing she could have offered, apart from the suggestion that she should take the children; no other proposal of assistance, for what else could she have done? She had no personal experience of such a dreadful occurrence, no understanding of death; only the passing of one of her mother's aunts whom she had never met.

'Wherever have you been?' Nicholas sounded piqued and querulous as he met her at the door. 'Do you know what time it is?'

She shook her head; she had no idea at all. Mid afternoon, perhaps? Time seemed to have no meaning; all she could think of was Matthew Wade's haunted look as he had gazed at his children, and Alice, who instinctively knew that her mother was gone and had moved towards her father to both give and receive comfort. *Poor child.* Lydia took an intake of breath, a sob that couldn't be contained. Even young Ben seemed to know that something beyond his understanding had happened and came to her, an adult, for protection.

She walked past her husband and sat down on the sofa, not even taking off her coat or gloves.

'What is it, Lydia? What has happened?' Nicholas came to sit beside her, reaching for her hand and taking off the glove. She reached up with her other hand and removed her hat, tossing it on to the floor.

'Mr Wade's wife died giving birth to another child,' she whispered. 'I saw the midwife whilst visiting Emily, and then . . . and then on the way home I saw her dog cart at the Wades' cottage and decided I'd call to ask how she was.'

'How who was? The midwife?'

'No,' she said sharply. 'Mrs Wade!'

'Wade the carpenter, is that who you're talking about?' He frowned. 'Do you know them?'

'A little. I've seen Mrs Wade sometimes when I've been visiting Emily. She's been delivered safely of twin boys,' she added.

'Who has?' he said, exasperated. 'Lydia! Tell me what you mean. You're not making sense!'

She told him about Emily, reminding him that she already had two boys, and then got to her feet, saying that she'd ask Cook to bring him a pot of tea. 'I'm going upstairs,' she added. 'I'm feeling unwell.'

She went to see Cook about the tea first, as she knew she would be waiting for instructions. Like Maggie, she didn't live in, but came in every day to prepare the meals, sometimes leaving something ready for Lydia to cook after she had left. Lydia asked her now if she had time to bake a cake, one that would keep well in a tin; and maybe a few biscuits. 'My mother is coming for tea tomorrow,' she added appealingly.

Cook sighed. She wasn't easily persuadable, but she had met Mrs Mercer's mother and knew what a stickler she was, and nodded. 'Very well. I'll mix 'cake now, ma'am, and perhaps you could bake it later? I'll write down instructions for how long, and how hot 'oven should be, so that by tomorrow it'll be cool and ready for slicing.'

'Thank you, Cook. Perhaps my mother will think I've made it,' she said weakly, but a frown on Cook's forehead warned her that she'd said the wrong thing. 'I'm joking,' she added hastily. 'My mother will know without any doubt that I haven't.' Her eyes filled with tears. How could she even have thought of joking after such a terrible tragedy had occurred?

'Perhaps I'll teach you one day, ma'am,' Cook offered, mollified. 'If you really want to learn.'

Lydia drew in a breath; Cook rarely chatted about anything, and she was astonished. 'Thank you,' she said. 'Baking is one of the most desirable skills that anyone could wish to have, but it has never been suggested that I should learn, and even my mother has never been taught. Yet all women are expected to marry and keep house and put food on the table, whilst men come home at the end of the day and simply expect to be fed.'

'Not all of them, ma'am,' Cook replied stoically. 'Some men have to learn if they're left without a wife or a daughter or some other obliging female relative. My pa learned when my ma died. I was seven and we learned together.' She gave a rare smile. 'His Yorkshire puddings were allus better than mine.'

At this, Lydia burst into tears and told her what had happened to the Wades.

'Do you know them well, ma'am?'

'Hardly at all.' Lydia reached into her pocket for a handkerchief. 'I've met Mrs Wade and the children before – in passing, you know – but I don't really know Mr Wade. He certainly seems to dote on his children, but I do wonder how he will manage to look after them all.'

'There'll be others who'll grieve with him over 'loss of his wife, I dare say. I've heard she was an amiable woman. Perhaps if you were to call from time to time, tek a cake or something for 'bairns? But he wouldn't want charity, that's for certain.' She filled the kettle with water as she spoke and put it on the range, and Lydia suddenly remembered that she had told Nicholas she would ask Cook to make a pot of tea. She'd completely forgotten about it.

'I'm sorry to take up your time, Cook,' she said, 'but will you make a cup of tea for Mr Mercer, please? And have I mentioned that Mrs Horner has given birth to twin boys? That's where I was earlier.' She knew that Cook had worked for the Horners on the occasion of their marriage, when they had given a big celebration party and taken on temporary local kitchen staff.

'Well, I never,' Cook exclaimed. 'Am I mistaken or do they already have two young bairns?'

'They do,' Lydia agreed, 'two boys.'

'Then there might be some baby clothes that they've grown out of,' Cook said astutely. 'Boys and girls are dressed up just 'same when they're little.'

'Are they?' Lydia said vaguely. 'I didn't know.'

'Oh, aye, nightgowns and such. Boys don't get breeched

until they're three, or four, sometimes five. Mebbe ask Mrs Horner if she has anything her bairns have grown out of that you could give to 'new motherless babby at 'Wades'. She wouldn't mind, I'm sure.'

Lydia nodded. *She won't, I'm quite sure of it. Emily's very generous. I'll call again. Oh! Not tomorrow, as Mama is coming; drat! Emily and I had so little time today. I'll drop a card to ask if I may come later in the week.*

Cook said she'd make a cup of tea for Mr Mercer and take it in to him before she left, but she didn't offer to make one for Lydia. I can hardly expect her to, Lydia thought as she went up to the bedroom, took off her coat and hung it up in the wardrobe; she's a cook, not a maid.

She stretched out on the bed. *I feel so useless, not knowing what to do; as an unmarried young woman I knew nothing of real life, nor heard anything of real people and their struggles.* She paused to recall the look of love that Matthew Wade had given his eldest daughter, who though still a child herself already had responsibilities, and now the new baby would add to them. Perhaps there were grandparents who might help her, but if there weren't what would she do?

Nicholas tentatively opened the bedroom door. 'Is it safe to come in?' he asked. 'Will I disturb you? Cook's gone.'

He had such an anxious look on his face that she couldn't help but smile. 'You won't disturb me,' she said softly. 'I'm so sorry, it's just that I was so upset about Mrs Wade and I couldn't do anything to help, except drive for the doctor, who couldn't save her in any case.'

Nicholas sat on the side of the bed. 'You drove to fetch the doctor?'

'Yes. The midwife asked me to. I took young Ben with me,' she added. 'He's so full of mischief I thought it best for Alice to have fewer children to look after.'

'And Alice is? A friend? A neighbour?'

She shook her head. 'The eldest girl. She's about ten or so, I think. There are twins, too, and a little girl – I don't know, eighteen months, or two years or something!'

She heard Nicholas give an exclamation beneath his breath. He got up and looked out of the window. After a moment, he turned round. 'It seems to me, Lydia, that you were very helpful, despite the doctor's not being able to do anything. You might have given the poor woman a chance by going to fetch him; it wasn't your fault that he wasn't able to save her. She must have been worn out, with so many children.'

'I don't know,' she said. 'I'm so ignorant about these matters. I know nothing. Absolutely nothing!'

His eyebrows lifted, as did his lips. 'I don't know much either,' he said, 'certainly not about babies.' He unbuckled her shoes and slipped them off, then reached to unroll her stockings and murmured, 'Unless you have any books on your bookshelf?'

'Nicholas,' she breathed. 'We've been married for nearly three years; we should know about procreation. Emily has been married for the same length of time and has four children already. It's ignorance of life that I'm talking about. I've never been expected to know how other people live, or understand how they survive.'

He's not listening, she thought as he stretched out beside her, his eyes closed and his hand on her thigh. If I need to know about life, and I do, I'll have to find out for myself.

CHAPTER FOUR

Lydia's mother was due to arrive by hackney carriage at two the following afternoon, and was being collected at three thirty; she often said that no one could ever accuse her of overstaying her welcome. The length of a visit to her only daughter was never more than two hours, to friends and confidantes no longer than half that, depending on how well she knew or for how long she could tolerate them.

Lydia had given Cook's cake mixture another stir and baked it in the side oven as instructed; when it had cooled she had sliced it in two and filled the middle with buttercream.

'There,' she muttered to herself. 'If Mama thinks I've made it, she's sure to find something wrong, like not enough butter in the mix, or she'll tell me it's a little sad, so should I say that Cook made it and let her say it's not up to her usual standard? Do I care enough either way?' But she knew that she did care; to receive the smallest compliment from her mother would be rather nice, and quite unprecedented.

She prepared a table between two easy chairs near the front window and put a small bowl of spring flowers, snowdrops and sprigs of winter jasmine on the wide windowsill, taking care to leave enough room for a tray of tea and crockery. Maggie had cleaned the hearth, given the brass fender a rub and polished the furniture that morning, and there was a cosy smell of wax polish and a warm flickering fire of wood and coal. Lydia plumped up the cushions and put a few more pieces of coal from the copper hod on the fire. 'There,' she murmured, glancing around. 'I can do no more. It's a cosy little house and I'm rather fond of it.'

When she looked up, she saw the hackney draw up at the gate and her mother alight from it, not waiting for the driver to help her down. She's quite agile, Lydia thought as she went outside to meet her, but so she should be – she's only forty-five.

She greeted her mother warmly. 'You look nice,' she said. 'A new hat?'

'Yes, indeed.' Her mother patted her head. 'A new shop in Beverley. I thought that as spring is almost here I would take a look and I saw this. I love the colour; what do you think?'

Lydia was astonished that her mother would ask her opinion; had she at last realized that her daughter was a grown-up? 'It's delightful,' she declared. 'The colour suits you very well.' The felt hat, which had just a short cream veil, was a very pale shade of green that lifted the grey of her mother's cape. 'Come along in, do; don't catch a chill. It's still quite cold.' She took the cape from her mother's shoulders and hung it up, then opened the door into the warm front room.

'It's rather a charming little house, isn't it?' her mother said, looking around. 'I don't suppose you miss having more bedrooms, and at least you have a separate dining room.

It's fine for the time being.' She left a short, significant gap, which Lydia instantly filled.

'Three bedrooms are quite sufficient,' she said, 'considering we have a large bathroom *and* a separate water closet.' Which her parents didn't have, in spite of their much larger house. 'Perhaps you might consider converting your small bedroom too, if you could persuade Papa,' she added, knowing that would be like a red flag to a bull.

'Oh, I can do as I wish,' her mother told her. 'Your father doesn't take any interest in how things are, as long as he's comfortable.' She paused for a moment. 'He's had some thoughts, though. Shall we have tea first, dear? I'll then enlighten you on something.'

'Of course.' Lydia rose from her chair. 'The kettle is on low, and you might like to try my cake.' Her mother's eyebrows rose as Lydia left the room.

Whatever does Mama mean to tell me? Lydia wondered as she waited for the kettle to come to a full boil. She enjoyed making tea, and coffee too; she had only learned how to do it since coming to live in this cottage. Then she brought the cake out of the larder, where she had put it in the meat safe away from flies, and having sliced it carefully put it on a pretty plate and carried the tray into the dining room. 'There, Mama,' she said, putting down the tray and offering her a slice of cake. 'What do you think of that?'

'I'm astonished!' her mother exclaimed. 'Did you really make it?'

'Well,' she prevaricated, 'most of it. I asked Cook to mix it for me, because the balance of ingredients is so important, but I gave it a stir and put the tin in the oven to bake.

The proof will be in the eating, of course.' She watched her mother choose a small slice and take a bite, and felt like a child again waiting for her approval.

Her mother chewed and swallowed, and then looked at her. 'I'm astonished!' she said again. 'It's lovely, my dear. Whoever would have thought it?'

'Not I,' Lydia admitted, thinking that it wasn't much in the scheme of things, and probably nowhere near what the child Alice could achieve under far more difficult circumstances.

They both began to speak at the same time, and Lydia laughed. 'You first, Mama,' she said, fingering a spot of cream from her lips and transferring it to her tongue. 'About Father?'

Her mother took a sip of tea, and then sighed. 'Yes, your father. He's considering retirement.'

'Retirement! But he's not yet fifty. Surely—'

'I know, and he'd be under my feet all day. He'd want to know where I was going and what I was doing; I'd have to be pandering to his needs all day.'

Lydia nodded. It was true, she would; but what would it mean for Nicholas? He wasn't yet qualified to take over the practice, but would he wish to work for anyone else?

'Why?' she asked. 'I thought he enjoyed his role, especially now he has Nicholas to assist him – and Nicholas will be taking more exams later this year. Surely Papa won't give up the practice altogether? Not yet, at least. Later he will be able to leave Nicholas in charge.'

'I don't know what he intends to do. He won't discuss it with me; he says that it's men's business and I won't understand it.'

'That's very demeaning,' Lydia replied, annoyed.

'I suppose he's right, though,' her mother admitted. 'I wouldn't. Why should I take an interest in something as dry as law?'

'Because it affects all of us, Mama, not only men.'

'Not me it doesn't,' her mother replied petulantly. 'Your father looks after everything important. I don't have the bother, except of course the household requirements – the servants, the groceries and so on, you know.'

Lydia sighed. 'Yes, Mother,' she said, 'that really must tax you.'

'It does,' her mother said, and reached delicately for another slice of cake. 'Men just don't realize how much women have to do. Is there more tea?' she added.

Lydia got to her feet. 'I'll make another pot.'

'You really should have another maid,' her mother called after her. 'For when you have visitors, you know.' She didn't hear Lydia's sigh, or her mutter of 'You're my *mother*, not a visitor!'

They had run out of conversation by three o'clock, and her mother began to gather her things together. 'I'd better be off,' she said. 'Your father might be home early and wonder where I am.'

'Did you not mention that you were visiting me?'

'No, I didn't. He's not interested in my day.'

'But what about the carriage? What time did you tell the driver?'

'Oh, I think I said half past three. Ah! Here he is.' She was looking out of the window. 'What excellent timing. He's very good, you know – you might try him sometime.'

'I can hardly do that when he's based in Beverley,' Lydia murmured. She saw the carriage waiting outside the gate and went to fetch her mother's cape. 'And you forget, I have my own transport.' Even if it is only a pony and trap, she thought. It suits me very well, and I think I'll use it again today.

When her mother had gone she quickly cleared away the tea tray, then ran upstairs to take her long navy coat from her wardrobe and change her slippers for outdoor shoes. Picking up a navy and grey hat, a pair of gloves and a handbag, she was ready, running lightly downstairs and wondering whether she should, or should not, take the remains of the cake.

No, she decided. The Wades' neighbours would surely take essentials to them. They would know the family much better than she did, even though the few cottages nearby were not exactly next door to one another.

Frisky, when she took him from the field behind their house, lived up to his name and was ready for some exercise; the trap was lightweight and easy for him to pull, and he never objected to it. She locked the house and set off on her mission, which was to find out when Mrs Wade's funeral would take place.

Pulling up outside the Wades' cottage, she saw that the door was open and could hear the sound of children's voices. Assuming that they were under the care of a neighbour, she was tying Frisky to the fence when Ben came racing outside. He stopped when he saw her and stared for a minute before lifting his voice and calling out, 'Da, Da! Missus is here. Can I go wi' her?'

As driving young Ben wasn't her intention, she shook

her head, and stepped through the gate, closing it carefully behind her. 'Is your father at home, Ben?'

'Yeh, he is. He's not going to work today – 'gaffer said—'

'That's enough, Ben. Go inside.'

Matthew Wade's voice was firm and brooked no nonsense, even when Ben said, 'Aww, can't I give 'pony a bit of apple?'

'No! You shouldn't feed other people's animals. Now go inside, please. I'm sorry, Mrs Mercer,' he went on. 'Ben's a handful. Allus wants to know 'far end of everything.'

Lydia smiled. 'He's lovely,' she said, and meant it. 'I don't mean to disturb you, Mr Wade; you must be overrun with things to do. I really came to ask – erm . . .' She hesitated. *Will it seem like an imposition? Am I pushing my nose into something I shouldn't?* 'Erm, when will – when will Mrs Wade's funeral be, and would you mind if I came? I have met your wife a few times since we came to live here,' she excused herself.

'Of course you can come!' he said warmly. 'I'd be pleased if you would. You were very helpful,' he added on a sigh. 'I'm not sure I thanked you – I was in shock, I think.'

'So unexpected,' she murmured. 'But I did very little. There's no need for thanks.'

'My fault,' he said softly. He blinked, his eyes misty. 'Too many children in too short a time.'

There was no answer she could give, except to murmur, 'You loved your wife. No fault or blame can be attached to that.'

Without conscious thought, she held out her hand. He took it, and bending his head he turned it over and kissed her palm. She drew in her breath, but didn't pull back. His grip was strong, and she thought it felt as if he needed something to stop him falling.

'I wanted to say . . .' his voice was thin, and wavered as he formed the words he needed. 'When I saw you wi' Ben, when you were going to fetch 'doctor, I'd just been given notice. I was late into work and 'gaffer said it was happening too often. I told him I allus made up 'hours, and that I had to get 'bairns up and mek breakfast for 'em cos Mary was unwell. He said he didn't give a toss, put his hand in his pocket and gave me my dues, not including that morning. That's why I was so foul-tempered, and' – he pulled in a breath – 'abrupt.'

'Mr Wade . . . you don't need to explain. I guessed that something worrying had happened. How will you manage?'

She recalled the way he had turned after she had spoken to him and begun to run home, swift as a rabbit that had seen a fox. He had lost his job and then his wife in one day; how *would* he manage? How would they live, and how would he earn a living with five children and a new baby to look after?

He shook his head. 'I'm not going to think about it until after 'funeral.'

'Where and when will it be?' she asked softly.

Gently he dropped her hand. He seemed bewildered, as if he didn't know what he was doing, and put his hand to his head. 'Erm, Etton. Chapel, not 'church. Mary was born in Etton and we were married in 'chapel. It's onny fitting that she'll be laid to rest there. Next Friday,' he added. 'Two o'clock.'

'I'll be there,' she said softly. 'Is there anything I can do for you meanwhile?'

'Nothing, ma'am.' He gave a thin smile that barely lifted his lips. 'Thank you.' Then he added, 'You seem to turn up in my hour of need,' and gave her a wider smile. 'Ben thinks you're his personal adviser and guide – he calls you his missus.'

She tried to smile back. 'Will the children be there at the chapel?'

'Alice, and possibly Ben, but not 'young uns. They don't understand why their mother isn't here. I've sent a letter to a niece of mine in Driffield to ask if she can come over. She's good wi' bairns, has two of her own. They'll be all right wi' her, if she can come.'

She left then, saying she knew where the chapel was, and feeling sad for him and his children, especially Alice.

Before going home, she called again to see Emily; she was out of bed but still in her bedroom, and fretting over it. 'I'm not used to sitting around,' she complained. 'Being idle. Tomorrow, come what may, I will be going downstairs. I have other babies to attend to, poor little mites; I hear them crying for me.'

'Can you not bring them in here? Perhaps they'd like to see their brothers?'

'That's what I said when Jane told me Edwin's almost walking. I must see that, my poor little ones.' Her voice cracked and tears ran down her cheeks. 'Go and fetch them for me, Lydia. Please! Bring the nursery maid back with you.'

I'm surrounded by children, Lydia thought as she opened the door to what she thought was the nursery, yet none of them are mine. I think I'm better with children at arms' length. I don't think I'd cope, though it's all right for Emily, with a large house and servants to help her. I'm not a bit jealous of her at all.

She picked up one of the infants, and the nursery maid, who introduced herself as Lizzie, carried the other as they took them to their mother. 'You're holding Edwin, ma'am,' Lizzie told her, 'and I've got Simon. Don't think 'new babbies have been named yet.'

'No, I don't think they have,' Lydia said, making sure she was holding Edwin securely before she opened the door to Emily's room. Emily gave a cry of delight, and immediately put out her arms to greet her older babies. 'May I go down and order tea for you, Emily?' Lydia asked.

'Ring the bell, dear,' Emily said, happy now with all her children around her. 'No need to bother yourself.'

'No, I'll pop down, give Jane a break.'

She hovered on the top step. Motherhood must be hard work without servants to look after your needs, she thought. Poor Mrs Wade – and poor Matthew Wade, so full of guilt and sorrow, and no money coming in. How would he pay his rent? Was there anything anyone could do, without it seeming like charity? Was he competent enough to start his own joiner's shop and if he was, how would he fund it?

She went downstairs to order the tea, then sat down on the bottom step, pondering, until the front door crashed open and Gideon Horner all but fell in. 'Damn and blast it!' he said, before spotting Lydia. 'I beg your pardon, Mrs . . . ?'

'Lydia,' she offered, thinking he might remember a first name more easily than a label.

'Of course! Emily's friend. Damned nuisance, isn't it, having to observe distinctions.' He sat next to her on the step, which fortunately was a wide one; it was a very grand staircase, Lydia considered.

He gave a great sigh. 'I've had a bothersome sort of day, Lydia, and I apologize for the words I used when I tripped over the step. Had I known I was in the presence of a lady then I would have chosen a different description entirely.'

'It's your house, Mr Horner,' she laughed. 'You can say whatever you like.'

'That's true, I can, except that by default the house really belongs to Emily.'

'So what has bothered you today?' she asked.

'Well, two of my cows are sick,' he said. 'My foreman has been off with some malady or other and one of the fences round the pastureland has fallen down and I've no one to fix it.'

'What is needed to fix it?'

'Just somebody who knows how to use a hammer and has a bag of nails handy.'

'I know of someone like that,' she hustled in before he could say anything else.

'Do you?' He looked at her, astonished. 'Who's that, then?'

'A neighbour of mine. He's a joiner.' She wasn't sure of the difference between a joiner and a carpenter, but thought maybe it didn't matter too much; after all, they weren't talking about furniture or craftsmanship.

'He's probably too busy to bother about a broken fence.'

'I don't think he is; in fact I know that he's not. His wife has just died, and Stephenson has sacked him for taking time off to look after his children.'

'Stephenson!' Gideon roared. 'Nobody wants to work for him; he's a b—' He stopped himself just in time. Fortunately, Lydia knew already that he was very much a gentleman and wouldn't normally use any kind of expression that might distress a lady.

'I'll be passing Mr Wade's door on the way home,' she said. 'Would you like me to ask him?'

'Dear lady,' he said, 'you're an angel.'

CHAPTER FIVE

Lydia had asked Jane if she'd take the tea up to her mistress. 'Would you tell her that I've had to dash away on an errand and that I'll call again as soon as I can?'

Emily wouldn't miss her, not now she had her older babies to play with whilst the twins slept soundly in their crib. I'd love to see them awake, she thought as she flicked the whip gently above Frisky's ears. I've never seen tiny infants so close; I wonder if they are identical. She laughed to herself as she thought of young Ben's double-yolked egg.

As she approached the Wade cottage she saw a spiral of smoke issuing from the chimney and was pleased that the family did at least have some warmth and a fire to cook on. What would they have, she pondered; a stew, maybe of onions or potatoes? Does Mr Wade grow them himself? Or perhaps he traps rabbits? She herself had a regular order for vegetables delivered every week, and hadn't previously considered that some people might not be able to afford to buy such food and must turn over their flower gardens to vegetable plots and rabbit traps.

She saw some of the children outside; playing, she thought, until she saw Ben hauling a long branch towards the shed door. Behind him was his younger brother, Charlie, trying to hold together a bunch of kindling in both arms and dropping bits with every step.

For a second she paused outside the gate, considering the young age of the children already helping with the household chores, and then she saw Alice with a basket full of wet washing, reaching up to hang it on a line at the side of the cottage. She was about to call to her when Matthew Wade came out of the house and she beckoned to him instead. 'Mr Wade, can you go to Bishop Burton? Are you able to leave the children?'

He frowned. 'For what reason, Mrs Mercer?'

'A farmer I know urgently needs someone to repair a fence. I don't know whether it's large or small, but he has no one on hand to mend it. It's Mr Horner – his wife is a friend of mine.'

Matthew Wade seemed to draw in a breath, as if reasoning or planning. 'Yes,' he said. 'I know him, or of him at least.' He rubbed his chin. 'If I went now, I could perhaps make it safe for 'time being and then go back tomorrow to finish it.' He wasn't asking her opinion, just pondering his options. He looked across at her. 'Wet nurse is here. I *could* go now.'

'Would you like to take the pony and trap? I can walk home, and you could bring them over later.'

He looked towards Frisky and the trap and then shook his head. 'Thank you, Mrs Mercer, but no; I can get there much quicker if I run over 'fields.'

She nodded. He could; she'd seen him.

'I'll fetch my workbag,' he said, and turned for the house,

then glanced back at her. 'I'm in your debt once more. Thank you.'

Within two minutes he came out with a bag strapped on his back, had a quick word with Alice and set off at a run up the lane. Lydia turned her head to watch until he jumped a fence and cut across a field path and was gone from view. When she turned back Alice was standing beside the fence. 'Is someone in trouble, Mrs Mercer?' the girl asked tremulously.

Lydia smiled. 'Not trouble such as you have endured, Alice,' she said quietly. 'It's a job of work that has come up and your father has gone to do it.' This child is grieving and trying not to show it, she reflected. Stepping down from the trap, she hooked the reins over the fence post. 'Do you think I might take a look at your new baby?'

Alice nodded. 'He's a boy, but we haven't named him yet. Wet nurse is here – I'll ask her.'

How perceptive of the child, Lydia thought; what good parenting she has had, being taught to respect others. 'If it's an intrusion, Alice, will you tell her that I'll wait until another time?' She followed Alice to the door and waited outside, hearing the cracking of twigs and the sound of small children's voices coming from the shed.

'Yes'm.' Alice had come back out. 'She said it's all right to go in.'

'What is her name?' Lydia whispered.

'Lottie Evans,' Alice whispered back, and invited Lydia inside.

Lydia was shocked to see a very young woman sitting in a chair close to the fire with a baby in her lap, her breast modestly covered by a towel; Lydia thought she couldn't be more than seventeen or eighteen years old. Beside her in a cane chair with a pillow beneath him or her was another baby closely wrapped in a blanket.

'Hello,' Lydia said softly. 'Is this Mrs Wade's new baby?'

'Yes, mum,' the young mother replied quietly. 'Other one is mine. She's a girl.'

Lydia took a peep at both babies and then backed away, murmuring goodbye to the young mother. Outside again, she asked, 'Is everything all right, Alice? I don't think your father will be long. Is there anything you need, or that I can help you with?'

Alice dipped her knee. 'No thank you,' she said in a low voice. 'Lottie said she'd stay until Da comes back 'n' he said he wouldn't be long.'

'Do you know where I live?'

Alice nodded. 'Yes. In 'house with 'apple tree in 'front garden.'

'That's right.' Lydia smiled. 'I just wanted to say that if there is ever anything you need whilst your papa – I mean your father is out, you can come to me at any time.'

'Thank you.' The child dipped again and pressed her lips together. 'Thank you,' she repeated. 'Da said we hadn't to be a bother to you and I had to watch that Ben doesn't run off.'

'Shall I have a word with him? Ben, I mean?'

'Yes please,' the girl said shyly. 'He don't allus listen to me.'

She led the way towards the shed, and once inside Lydia saw that it was larger than it appeared from outside. She found Ben and Charlie breaking the sticks and twigs into smaller pieces of kindling and dropping them into a sack; Charlie was dropping more on the ground than he was putting into the sack, and his twin sister was sitting on top of a heap of logs watching them.

They all looked up when Alice and Lydia came through the door. 'We're doing this *himportant* job,' Ben announced. 'And I've to mek sure that Charlie does it right cos he's onny little.'

'I'm not little,' Charlie said indignantly, 'I'm five and nearly growed up, aren't I, Alice? And Lily is as well, cos she's 'same as me.'

Alice went up to him and patted him on the shoulder. 'Yes, you are, Charlie. You'll soon be a big boy like Ben.'

Lydia hid a smile as both boys stood up straighter. 'What I really want to do is saw up that big branch that I brought in this morning, cos it's mine really,' Charlie said proudly. 'I found it.'

'Are you going to be a carpenter, like your father?' Lydia asked.

'Yes, I am. I'm nearly a carpenter now. I've just got to learn how to saw, and then I'll be ready.'

'Goodness,' Lydia exclaimed. 'Well done! Your father will be a good teacher, so you'll watch him carefully, won't you?' Having looked around, she had already seen that saws, planes and hammers, and various other tools guaranteed to take off small fingers or do some other injury, were placed on hooks and shelves well out of reach of eager little hands.

The shed was well set out, she could see; probably a place that a joiner could work in, with a heavy table – or a bench, she thought, would better describe it – and what she thought was a saw horse. Perhaps Mr Wade did odd jobs for home or neighbours, she conjectured.

An idea floated into her mind, one of her dreamings as

Nicholas would say, but she dismissed it. She had a few words with Ben about not leaving the house and garden whilst his father was out and looking after his sisters and brother until he came home, and then set off for home herself; she had to change for their evening meal and hoped that Cook had baked a meat pie, as she'd asked in the note she had left for her.

When she returned from the stable block she was surprised to see Nicholas descending from a hackney at the front gate, and wondered what had brought him back from the office so soon. 'Hello,' she called. 'You're early?'

He lifted a finger to the driver in thanks and took Lydia's arm, but didn't reply to her implied question. 'And where have you been?' he asked instead.

'I went to see Emily. But she was busy with babies, and then Gideon came home, so I didn't stay long.'

He opened the door and she went in first. 'I've decided to go to Mrs Wade's funeral,' she told him. 'It's on Friday, at Etton chapel.'

He turned to look at her, frowning, and then took her coat and hung it on a peg on the coat stand. Tossing his top hat on to one of the hooks, he turned back to her. 'Why? That's hardly etiquette that you need to follow. It won't be expected of you; you hardly knew her.'

'She was a neighbour,' she answered briefly; 'and I want to. Those children have lost their mother.'

'They won't be there!' He was abrupt. 'It's no place for children.'

'Two of them will be,' she said stubbornly. 'The eldest girl, and possibly her next brother.' She didn't say that Ben was only about seven, and added, 'I know them and they know me.'

'Lydia!' He reached out a detaining hand, but she turned away.

'Don't try to dissuade me, Nicholas,' she said. 'I intend to be there; I don't know if there are grandparents or other relatives – I've never seen any – but if there are I won't intervene, and if there aren't I will be there for those children if they are distressed, particularly the eldest girl. Etiquette or not,' she added.

He shrugged and muttered something she couldn't hear.

'So why *are* you home early?' she asked.

'Your father,' he said briskly. 'He mentioned taking on another partner, but he's also spoken of retirement, so I asked him where that left me and he didn't seem to know. I said I was hoping for a partnership later this year; I'd thought that was the plan, but he said we'd discuss it at some other time, so I thought I'd let him stew and came home!'

'Go up and change,' she suggested, 'and I'll make some tea and we can discuss it. It's just some whim he's come up with. He's told Mama about it too, and she does *not* want him home all day.'

'I'm sure she doesn't!' He headed for the stairs to change out of his striped trousers and short black wool coat, and came down less than ten minutes later in more casual clothes as Lydia emerged from the kitchen with a tray of tea things and a plate of biscuits. 'When I'm fully qualified and gain my partnership,' he went on as if there had been no break in the conversation, 'that is, if your pa hasn't changed his mind, we could perhaps move to a bigger house and employ more staff.'

'I don't mind making tea,' she said. 'It's hardly hard work

and I'm happy with the arrangement with Cook and Maggie; they're both trustworthy, and if we move house and I suggest them living in they would both leave! They have homes of their own.'

He sighed. 'It seems as if I can't make any suggestions at all. I'm totally in the wrong; you won't compromise about the funeral – and I wonder what your mother will say when she hears about *that* – and I offer you a grander house than this little cottage and you don't want that either!'

She handed him a cup and saucer and put the plate of biscuits on a small table close to his chair. 'No,' she said calmly. 'I don't. I like it here. We could perhaps have an additional bedroom built on if you think it too small.' She sipped her tea for a few minutes, then remarked, 'You could come with me to the funeral if you think I'm defying the rules of etiquette by attending alone. If you were with me I might escape the stigma of committing a social solecism by attending a funeral unaccompanied by a man!'

'You're being ridiculous, Lydia, and you know it. I have never met Mrs Wade and have only seen her husband perhaps once or twice. He would not expect me.'

'This might be an opportune time, then,' she snapped. 'It would be a neighbourly thing to do – and it would also show that you are not bound by convention,' she added slyly.

'What time is the funeral?' he said wearily. 'Would you prefer it if I came with you?'

She smiled. 'Two o'clock in the afternoon. It would be so thoughtful and kind if you showed sympathy for their loss.' She leaned forward and kissed his cheek. 'Yes, I would.'

'All right,' he said resignedly. 'I'll take the afternoon off and your father will have to manage without me. Shall I arrange for a cab to take us to Etton?'

She shook her head. 'No. We'll take the pony and trap; more fitting, I think, not ostentatious. We'll be amongst country folk.'

'As you wish.' He looked at her. 'I thought I was marrying a demure and mild young woman, one who would only care to do my bidding and want to follow my every whim.'

'No, you did not! That might have been what my father told you about me, and if you recall . . .' she paused whilst topping up his teacup, 'I said you mustn't believe a word that my parents said about me, particularly not the picture they painted of the obedient wife I would be. I think they were glad to be rid of me. I wasn't following the pattern that they expected. That's why they packed me off to boarding school.'

'So I was swindled,' he said, raising a finger. 'But be sure, my dear, the funeral is an exception. You will have to change your ways; when I have a senior position to uphold, you will – indeed, you must – conform to what is expected of you and behave as the wife of a professional man should.'

But even as she smiled and nodded, she wondered. *Is he joking or being serious?* She didn't always understand him. He had many big ideas, but she knew her father didn't pay a large salary to his employees, so who was going to meet the expenses of a bigger house if they bought one? Was he expecting to have shares in the practice, or would he use her dowry? From his wry expression, she really couldn't be sure.

CHAPTER SIX

Lydia dressed in a slate-grey wool dress and wore a matching sleeveless waistcoat over it. Dark enough, she thought, for a funeral of a friend or acquaintance; better than all black. She took a black straw hat out of the wardrobe and then reached to the back of the shelf and brought out her jewellery box.

She chose two pieces of jewellery, one a jet brooch, the other a brooch made of silver with a jet centre; she wrapped the latter in a lacy handkerchief and placed it carefully inside her handbag. The jet brooch she pinned to her waistcoat.

Nicholas arrived home at a quarter past twelve, and as he was already wearing his dark business suit he simply changed his top hat for a shorter beaver one. 'What's the plan?' he asked mildly.

'I don't know,' Lydia confessed. 'I thought if we set off now we would pass the Wades' house, and if they haven't yet left we could follow them. What do you think?'

She knew he didn't want to be there, but he nodded and went out to bring the pony and trap from the stable to the front. Lydia followed him out of the house carrying a basket containing a cake tin, and locked the door after her. 'Cook made a cake,' she said diffidently. 'She thought perhaps the children would like it; wasn't that kind of her?' She put the basket carefully in the back of the trap and covered it with a towel, and then sat next to Nicholas on the bench seat.

'Were you thinking of staying after the service?' He flicked the reins and they moved off.

'I don't know what to expect,' she said. 'Let's just see what happens, shall we?'

'If there's a gathering afterwards, I don't want to stay for it,' he muttered. 'We won't know anyone—'

She interrupted him. 'I doubt there will be one. There won't be any money for food or drink – he's just lost his job.'

He turned to look at her. 'He's lost his job? How? Why?'

'The day his wife died,' she murmured, 'except I didn't know then what had happened. I was driving to fetch the doctor at the request of the midwife and saw him heading for home.'

'I see,' he murmured. 'I didn't realize.'

Did I not mention it? she considered. Maybe I didn't, the day was a blur. But perhaps you weren't listening to what I was saying, Nicholas, as so often you don't.

'There's the undertaker's carriage,' he broke in on her thoughts as they approached the Wades' dwelling. Slowing Frisky, he held back. 'Shall we follow or go ahead?'

Lydia took in a breath. She hadn't known what to expect. The hearse in front was an open one, and she could see that it held a simple wicker coffin that had daffodils and wild flowers all around and over it. 'I don't – let's wait a minute. I think – yes, I believe Mr Wade will follow on foot.'

She had seen Matthew Wade come out of the cottage door wearing a black bowler, followed by Alice and Ben, hand in hand; Ben had a black armband over his sleeve and Alice a wisp of something black on her head. The twins stood in the doorway behind them, both weeping copiously.

Matthew saw the Mercers waiting and as if on impulse hurried towards them. Touching his hat to Nicholas, he nodded at Lydia. 'Mrs Mercer,' he murmured. 'It's kind of you to come.' He hesitated, and then glanced at Nicholas again. 'Would it be a burden to ask if 'twins might ride with you? My niece hasn't arrived – too short a notice, perhaps. The bairns have been crying all 'morning since they heard they couldn't come with us; it's over a mile, so too far for them to walk. They'd slow us up, and 'young nurse might not be able to manage them as well as two babies and Baby Mary, if they're unhappy. They don't understand what's happening or why their mother isn't here. Coming home I'll carry them on my back in turn.'

'Yes,' Nicholas said instantly. 'Of course the children can ride with us, and we'll wait and bring them home again.'

Lydia felt such emotion in her heart that she wanted to weep. She had all but forgotten about little Mary until Matthew had mentioned three babies. However was he going to manage without some help? She lifted the latch on the door of the trap and stood up. 'I'll tell the twins,' she said quietly. 'You get up with my husband, Mr Wade; we'll join you in a minute!'

Matthew Wade sat on the driving seat alongside Nicholas for part of the journey, with Charlie next to him and Lily on his knee, but as they approached the village he set them both gently behind him and jumped down to walk behind the coffin with Alice and Ben. Nicholas drove slowly until they reached the chapel, and then turned to Lydia. 'What now?' he said.

'We wait,' she replied in a low voice and turned to the twins, who had been sitting quietly in the back of the trap but now kneeled up eagerly to look for their father. 'Your da will be here in a minute,' she said. 'You've been very good. Today is a very special day, so we must all be as quiet as mice.' She remembered how chatty Charlie had been when he was breaking up twigs, and she was sure he would give a wave if he saw anyone he knew. Lily had remained sitting quietly and not saying a word.

Alice came towards the trap and spoke to the twins. 'Da said we all have to walk behind him when we go into 'chapel, and not talk at all. If you're very good we can have cake later.'

'Ooh.' Charlie beamed. 'What kind of cake?'

'I don't know,' Alice said crossly. 'We'll have to wait and see.'

Nicholas moved the pony and trap on to the grassy verge where it wouldn't be in the way and the twins jumped down and followed Alice, while Nicholas took Lydia's arm. 'Shall we go inside and wait? Is that the tradition?'

She shook her head; she didn't know. But then she saw a carriage approaching; it was the doctor's, and trotting behind it was a man on horseback.

'That's the doctor driving the carriage,' she told Nicholas, 'and look, Gideon Horner behind. Emily's husband.'

'So it is!' Nicholas touched his hat to Gideon when he looked their way. 'I wonder how he knows the Wade family?'

'He'll know everybody, I should think,' Lydia observed. 'Probably had work done by Mr Wade,' she added, sure that Matthew would have fixed Gideon's fence by now.

'Ah, of course. Shall we wait and follow them?'

Lydia knew by Nicholas's voice that he was relieved to see someone they knew. She took his arm. 'Let's follow the doctor,' she said quietly. 'He probably attends many funerals of different denominations, and will know just what to do.'

She heard the flatness of his agreement. Nicholas was not a religious man by any means, but she was grateful that he had agreed to come at all. They moved forward, for now the plain coffin was being carried towards the chapel door by Matthew and the undertakers, all dressed simply in dark clothing without any of the ostentation of white plumes or feathers which she had occasionally seen in Beverley as she'd passed other funeral processions.

A small crowd of villagers was now filing in; Lydia recognized some of the women, but none of the men; perhaps, she thought, they had been Matthew's workmates at Stephenson's and had left their benches to be here as a mark of respect.

It was a brief and simple service. Few words were said and only one hymn sung, and there was a short silence for private prayer. The children behaved beautifully, and stood waiting by the church door as their father followed the coffin to the graveyard for the committal.

'Can we go now?' Nicholas asked quietly. 'Others are leaving.'

'We should wait until Mr Wade returns. You did say that we'd take the children home.'

'Ah, yes, I did.' Nicholas turned his head. 'I'll just have

a word with Horner.' He strode off to where Emily's husband was chatting to the doctor, and Lydia stayed near the Wade children, watching as some of the congregation talked among themselves, and then began to move away. She felt a small hand in hers and looking down saw Ben standing close, pressing his lips together with a frown on his face.

'Where's my ma?' he said. 'I thought she was coming back today.'

'I did too,' Charlie broke in.

'No,' Lily interrupted. 'Today she's gone to heaven to live with 'angels. Da said so.'

Lydia glanced at Alice. She was standing a little apart from the others, as still as stone but blinking furiously as if trying to keep tears away. She, Lydia thought, of all the children would feel the sorrow most. Being the eldest, she had known her mother longest and would remember this day of sadness more clearly, Lydia knew. She opened her handbag and brought out the brooch wrapped in the lacy handkerchief.

'Alice.' She gently released her hand from Ben's and went towards her, holding out her hand. 'I have something for you to keep as a remembrance of your mother.'

Alice looked at her, her lips slightly apart as she looked down at the brooch glittering in Lydia's hand. 'For me?' she murmured.

'Yes, for being so brave and taking such care of your brothers and sisters, but most of all to remind you how much your mother loved you.' She pinned the brooch securely on Alice's cotton dress and saw the emotion on the girl's face. 'Next time I go into Beverley, perhaps you'd like to come with me and we'll have a safety chain fitted to keep it secure?'

'I've never been to Beverley,' Alice breathed. 'I don't think Ma did either. I'll tell her when I say my prayers tonight.'

Lydia felt her throat tighten and tears wash her eyes, so that for a moment she couldn't speak. 'Yes,' she said at last. 'She will be so pleased for you.'

Looking up, she saw Matthew Wade coming from the chapel garden and going up to the doctor, Gideon and Nicholas, holding out his hand to shake theirs and, Lydia supposed, thanking them for coming. He turned then to those of the congregation who were left and spoke to the women. One of them said something to him and he stepped back as if startled, then turned to the doctor and Nicholas, and all three turned with one accord to head for their vehicles. Three of the women, all carrying baskets, stepped into the doctor's carriage and Alice looked up as her father signalled to her.

'Doctor has kindly offered you a ride home in his carriage,' he told her, 'and these good women, kind friends, have brought food for a repast,' he added with a catch in his voice. 'Alice, will you go with them to arrange 'table?'

'Yes, Da,' she said, and bent her knee to the doctor, who patted her shoulder. 'I can't stay long,' he murmured. 'But I can see you safely home, and these good people too.'

Nicholas came back to the trap. Ben and Charlie had climbed into the back with Lily, and their father came up to them. 'Thank you again for your kindness,' he said to Lydia. 'Those dear neighbours have brought food and apple wine.'

She nodded. 'And we have brought cake; Ben and Charlie are watching it carefully. There is still room for you – I can sit in the back with—'

'No! No, thank you. It's kind of you,' he added, 'but I'm going to run home. I need to – to . . .' He paused, and squeezed his eyes shut tight. 'I need to shake off—'

'You don't need to explain,' she broke in on a whisper. 'Go! Go now.'

And turning, he did as he was bid and began to run, as he had done previously when she had told him that he was needed urgently at home. That time, he was running to be there in time, but also to shake off his anger at losing his job; now he was running, she thought, to come to terms with the loss of his wife and to find a way of caring for his children too.

CHAPTER SEVEN

The Wades' cottage was crowded when the occupants of the doctor's carriage and the trap arrived back, and by the time Alice had spread a clean and crisply ironed tablecloth on the table and laid it with mismatched crockery, the women had put out the food – freshly baked bread, potted meat, slices of ham, pickles and chutney, cheese and scones and jam and cake – and the kettle was steaming on the fire. Matthew Wade had arrived home and put his head under the water pump outside in the back yard, and shaken himself like a dog.

He rubbed his hair on a towel and went across to the young woman who had been feeding his new child, lifted the infant up into his arms and kissed his forehead. 'Welcome, little baby,' he whispered. 'I'm sorry you won't ever meet your ma, though I'm sure she would have kissed you goodbye and blessed you, knowing we will do our very best for you.'

He turned to the small crowd of neighbours and held the child up high. 'This is my new son, who will never know his mother, but we will tell him about her so that he can be sure he was born of love. His name is Aaron. The name, meaning strength, was chosen by his mother; perhaps she knew that he would need it in life.'

The other children came across to kiss the baby on his forehead too, and Baby Mary, no longer the youngest child, tottered across and put out her arms to give him a hug as if he were a new toy.

Lydia persuaded Nicholas to stay for half an hour. The doctor had left as soon as he had helped the women down from his carriage, brought out the baskets of food and made his farewells, and Nicholas soon became fidgety and wanted to leave too, but Lydia insisted on having a cup of tea and a slice of cake before they went. She really wanted to stay and ask the women how they thought Matthew Wade would manage, but perhaps, she considered, that wouldn't be appropriate just now, and certainly not anything to do with her. However, before she and Nicholas finally took their leave, she did tell them how pleased she was to have met them, despite the sorry circumstances; but she was aware of their constraint and did not press them to respond, contenting herself with saying casually, 'If ever you are nearby, do feel you can call at my house for a chat or a cup of tea.'

They nodded and thanked her and some of the younger ones dipped their knee, but she knew they wouldn't come; there was a divide between them like a prickly hawthorn hedge, and she knew no way of breaking through it.

Nicholas let out a deep breath as they drove away. 'Well, thank goodness that's over! I felt like a fish out of water; I'm extremely sorry for Wade's position, but I can't think that our being there has helped in the least – possibly worsened it, in fact, by drawing attention to our differences.'

'Differences?' she said sharply. 'I thought it showed our similarity. We're all the same when it comes to birth and death; we all share the same emotions, no matter the gulf between our circumstances.'

She didn't speak to him again until they arrived home, when he manoeuvred the trap into the outhouse, released Frisky into the paddock with the donkey, and went up to his room to change into casual clothes. Lydia changed into her house gown and put on her indoor slippers, then sat down to ponder some of the very real differences that set her and Nicholas apart from their nearest neighbours.

For a start, she thought, those women have more worries than I do: finding the rent for their homes, making ends meet if their husbands don't have jobs and there's no money coming in . . . and what about schooling? Is there any? Who teaches their children? It isn't compulsory to send young children to school; I was taught at home, first by a nursery teacher and then by a tutor. These people I met today couldn't possibly afford to employ anyone, yet surely some education is absolutely necessary? How can children make progress if they can't read or write?

She gave a sigh and got to her feet. *I'll make tea. I can at least do that.*

Nicholas was reading the newspaper in the sitting room, his slippered feet stretched out across the sofa. 'I've been thinking,' he said, rising to take the tray from her and putting it on a side table. Lydia had set a plate of shortbread biscuits on the tray and he took one and nibbled on it, but left the pouring of tea to her and sat down again. 'I'm going to speak to your father and tell him that when I'm finished with exams, which will be sometime in October, I would like him to consider me as a future partner in the practice. I have my law degree already, and some experience of court procedure, and we could put some money into the practice if necessary. How do you think he will react?'

She sat at the table and poured the tea, taking a sliver of lemon for his cup and adding milk to hers. 'If he's in an amiable state of mind, I think he'll agree,' she said, handing him his cup and saucer and offering him another biscuit. 'But please don't *tell* him, *ask* him. I think he might be pleased; he seems to be tired. Mama said he's behaving oddly, and has been talking about retirement. I might have told you that already – I have had such a lot on my mind. I want to ask *you* something too, but that can wait . . . so, Papa? Yes, prepare him, and why not suggest he takes a short holiday before thinking of retirement?'

'Good idea,' he agreed. 'He has been busy. He had that big court case recently as well as everyday business, and if he does take some time off I'll have a chance to find out what it takes to run a law practice.'

But is he ready, she wondered. Nicholas hadn't often been at court to watch and listen to procedure, and they hadn't had such a conversation in a long time. *Can it mean that at last Nicholas is including and not excluding me from that part of his life? Unlike my father, who seems to think that my mother is incapable of understanding what he does in his professional life. How belittling is that?*

She put a meat pie that Cook had prepared into the oven and considered. She was out of kilter, she thought. *There will be many who would disagree with me; but people just need a chance to succeed, an opportunity that they recognize when they see it.*

Something else swirled around in her head; a germ of an idea that had come to her earlier but she hadn't quite been able to grasp; it was something to do with Matthew Wade. There were two things, in fact, that she hadn't quite formulated either separately or together. She would sleep on them, she decided, and work out a plan.

She and Nicholas had separate bedrooms, though sometimes, as now, Nicholas would climb into her bed and immediately fall asleep. Finger to lips and eyebrows raised, Emily had once confided to her that she and Gideon had separate bedrooms because he snored, and Lydia had laughed and told her she was not a chatterbox and would tell no tales. Yet they have still managed to have four children, she considered, whilst we have none.

So what was that brilliant notion that I couldn't quite pin down? she asked herself as she lay with a pillow behind her head and an open book by her side, whilst Nicholas, so handsome and peaceable in his slumber, lay facing her, his arm across her waist and a hand on her hip as if steadying himself – or perhaps, she thought now, anchoring her down.

She closed the book and looked towards the window; a misty silver moonlight shone through the partially open curtain. *Another week and we will be into spring.* Clumps of daffodils were already in flower; their yellow heads had been bobbing by the chapel door today, and beneath the apple tree in their front garden were the ones she had planted when they first came to live here.

It was of Matthew Wade she had been thinking: his task of

bringing up his children, buying food for them, or perhaps growing vegetables in his long garden. Had she glimpsed a glasshouse there? But it was the woodshed she was remembering, and Ben and Charlie breaking up sticks, and young Ben saying he was nearly ready to be a carpenter.

The ideas swirled around in her head, somehow sparked by Nicholas's saying he was going to ask her father about his prospects, and suddenly she knew what she wanted to suggest to Matthew. But would he laugh at such a suggestion from a woman he barely knew but must have guessed was unversed in real life? And Nicholas – what would he say to her, a wife who didn't conform in the least to what was expected of someone married to a professional up and coming lawyer?

But why should men make all the decisions when they affect women too? she thought; and then, well, there was another thing to be considered as well.

CHAPTER EIGHT

It was a week later and Lydia watched Nicholas in his nightshirt through half-closed eyes as he stood looking out through the open curtains, but she lay still, savouring the last half-hour of drowsiness. *It's Saturday, I think; that's why he's not yet dressed.*

He turned. She closed her eyes. 'I was working out what day it is,' he said. 'I think it's Saturday.' She nodded but didn't answer, and turned over, tucking one hand beneath her cheek. 'There are some yellow flowers beneath the apple tree,' he continued. 'Daffodils? No, smaller than that.'

She nodded again. 'Crocus now,' she said thickly. 'Good. I've been waiting for them.'

'I thought I might drive over to Beverley and see your father,' he murmured, getting back into bed and snuggling down to her warmth.

'You saw him yesterday,' she muttered. 'Surely you don't need to see him again until Monday?'

'I do. I've got a bee under my hat regarding the partnership issue I discussed with you. I barely slept for thinking about it.'

Not true, she contemplated. You were sound asleep.

'I thought that if I discussed my situation with him he could think about it over the weekend.'

'And ruin it for him?' she offered. 'He's probably been looking forward to a couple of peaceful days.' She pushed herself up on to the pillows, knowing there was no chance of more sleep. 'It's not so urgent. You are fully qualified, aren't you?'

'Mm . . .' He hesitated. 'I still need your pa's approval before a partnership can be set in stone. He'll want to know that everything will run along in the same way as always.'

'That's a bit tricky, isn't it? He's such a stickler for procedure.'

'I know. We have to be in our profession. That's why I want to talk to him and get everything settled.'

Wondering if she really had married just another version of her father, she slid down between the sheets again. I suppose it's no bad thing, she considered. I do at least know what to expect from him.

She knew she wouldn't sleep again, so she got out of bed, reached for her dressing gown and went downstairs to make coffee whilst Nicholas washed and dressed. By the time she took the tray of coffee into the dining room the sun was shining through the windows, and she went to fetch the newspaper that was showing through the letter box.

'Do you know, Nicholas,' she began, giving him the paper, 'I think it might be rather nice to build an annexe here at this side of the house; the sun is glorious this morning. If we had another room added on, perhaps a dining room with two windows, think how lovely it would be.'

'We already have a dining room,' he said. 'We have breakfast in here.'

'I was thinking of something more casual,' she said. 'Less formal, like a summer room. It would catch the sun for most of the day.'

'Hmm.' He sipped his coffee as he read the headlines, and she didn't rush him.

'We could use a local builder.'

'We don't know one,' he said, reaching for the jug to top up his coffee.

'Gideon Horner would know. He knows just about everyone!'

'Hmm,' he said again. 'His family have been around the area for a long time, haven't they? And *he* would probably have the money to pay for one,' he added.

'Yes, that's true, I suppose. But this cottage was a gift, wasn't it? Remember how we loved the cosiness of it?' She looked around. 'But it is a little cramped sometimes, don't you think?'

He looked up from the newspaper. 'Is it?'

'Why yes,' she said, surprised. 'For instance, if Maggie is having a good turn-out in the sitting room, I have to sit in the dining room to do my sewing or whatever until she's finished.'

'Yes, but didn't you just say that this side of the house catches the sun? As it is doing now, in fact.'

'Exactly!' she said joyously. 'That's just my point! If we added on a small annexe with a lot more glass . . . have you seen those buildings with tall windows that reach right up like a glass doorway? We would also be able to get straight out into the garden!'

He put his cup down and folded his arms across his chest, abandoning the newspaper to look across at her. 'Why do I get the feeling that this is leading up to something? Pass the coffee jug, will you?'

'I can't imagine what you mean!' She frowned as she returned his gaze and gave a little shrug. 'It was just an idea, that's all, though I suppose it might increase the value. Might I have some coffee too, please?'

'Oh, sorry.' He poured her coffee and sat back on his chair.

'I'll just have this,' she said, 'and then make breakfast before you go out. Will you take the trap, or will you walk?'

'What?'

'Didn't you say you were going to see my father? Though he does sleep in sometimes at the weekend, or so my mother says.'

He scratched his head. 'Erm, yes, I did say that. I'll take the trap, I think.'

After they'd had breakfast he left, calling out that he wouldn't be long, and she replying that he needn't hurry, as she would take a walk whilst the weather was so lovely. But she took her umbrella in case of rain when she walked away from the house to admire the crocus under the apple tree and the daffodils growing along the green verge, the young leaves showing in abundance on the ash trees and the rowan trees bursting with buds.

It's so lovely here. The birdsong is glorious, and I can hear rustling in the hedgerows. A rabbit shot across the road in front of her, and then another. Ahead of her she could see smoke issuing from the Wades' chimney and smell the scent of burning applewood. I wonder if I should call, she pondered. I wonder how Matthew is coping with the children? Poor little Alice. She's far too young to manage without her mother.

She slowed her steps as she approached the cottage. The yard in front of the house was neat and tidily swept and the door to the wooden hut was firmly closed. Then the cottage door opened and Ben rushed out.

'Missus,' he called. 'Are you coming to see us?'

She smiled. 'I'm taking a walk as it's such a lovely day,' she called back. 'You can come if you'd like to— *Wait!*' He had nothing on his feet and was wearing a thin shirt with short sleeves. It was a bright day but still rather chilly, and he was about to dash towards her far too lightly clad. 'You must ask your father first.'

'He won't mind.'

'Ask him first,' she repeated, and he went back inside. A few minutes later Matthew Wade came out, carrying the baby Aaron wrapped in a warm blanket.

'I think you might want to choose a different route in future, Mrs Mercer. Ben is constantly on 'lookout for you.'

'That's all right,' she said, drawing nearer to the gate. 'He's very good company.'

'He tends to chatter too much. But I haven't seen you pass lately,' he added.

'Oh, I've been busy with household things, that's all; and I didn't want to get in the way of whatever you might be doing.' She paused for a moment. 'But I have been wondering how you were coping. Is the young nurse still able to come?'

He nodded. 'Yes, but not for much longer. Aaron will have to have a bottle. I need to speak to 'midwife about it.'

Ben came outside again wearing a warm jumper that came down to his knees over his shirt; on his feet he wore a pair of boots without laces.

His father gave a short, exasperated groan. 'If you're walking out with a lady, Ben, we'll have to find laces to fit those boots, or you'll fall over.'

'I'll go ass over tip, won't I, Da?' Ben said cheekily, but then saw the expression on his father's face. 'Sorry,' he grinned, and Lydia tried not to laugh. What a handful of mischief he must be, she thought, and told him she would wait until he found some bootlaces. He disappeared, and Matthew invited her to wait inside.

Alice was in the scullery washing up in the sink, but immediately stopped what she was doing and turned to dip her knee to Lydia. Lydia smiled at her and saw she was wearing the brooch she had given her on the day of the funeral, and remembered that she had promised to take her to Beverley to buy a safety chain for it. Charlie and Lily were sitting at the table with crayons, Lily colouring in a passable drawing of a donkey with a tree in the background, and Charlie, obviously bored, scribbling shapes in different colours.

'That's interesting, Charlie,' she said, looking over his shoulder. 'Very modern. Can I see mountains and rivers in there? Or perhaps it might be showing the end of the war in France? I was in Paris many years after the Revolution ended and there was still a great deal of damage.'

She realized she was speaking about things he would not understand, but thought there was no harm in that until Charlie turned to her and mumbled, 'I don't know what Paris is. I've just drawed boxes and piled 'em on top of one another then coloured 'em in different colours.'

This was a different Charlie from the one who had chatted to her as he was breaking twigs with his brother. Bored, she thought, with nothing to occupy him. 'Would you like to come for a walk with me? Ben's coming.' She saw Ben frown, but she felt it important to include his brother in the invitation. He shook his head, and she looked at Lily. 'What about you, Lily?'

'No fank you.' Lily shook her head too. 'I've got to finish this. It's for my ma.'

'Of course; another time, perhaps? It's a lovely picture.'

Lily nodded. 'I know. Ma will like it. She allus likes my dror-rings.'

Interesting, Lydia thought; she speaks of her mother as if she's still here. She looked up as Matthew, having put baby Aaron in a wooden cot, emerged triumphantly from a deep drawer in a pine cupboard with a pair of black bootlaces in his hand.

'I knew we'd have some somewhere. These cupboards need clearing out, Alice. There's stuff in them that we'll never use.'

Lydia saw Alice nod her head. 'Yes, Da,' she said steadily. What is happening to her childhood, Lydia wondered. She's so young.

'I haven't forgotten that we're going to Beverley, aren't we, Alice?' she said, and saw the girl's face light up. 'We're going to get a chain for your brooch. That's all right, isn't it, Mr Wade? Alice and I are going out for a treat.'

'Me too,' Charlie and Lily chorused, but their father frowned at them. He gazed steadily at Lydia. 'That's kind of you, Mrs Mercer, but we don't want to be a bother. I'm sure you have a busy life without tending to us.'

She gave a deep sigh. 'You would be astonished at how non-busy I am, Mr Wade, and how much I long for some useful employment. Alas, there are few openings for "privileged" married women like me.'

He looked away and sat down next to Ben. 'Foot!' he ordered, and Ben put up his booted foot so that his father could thread in the first lace. 'I know the situation well,' Matthew muttered.

'You have an empty shed, I observed,' she said. 'Could that not be utilized for employment?' She chose her words carefully, aware of the small ears listening in.

'I only rent,' he said abruptly. 'It's not my property.'

'I see. Would the owner raise objections?'

There was no immediate answer, and then he said, 'I haven't thought of asking. The question hasn't come up before, but 'shed is mine. I built that.'

He remained silent for a moment or two and Ben jiggled his other foot in front of him. 'Da!'

He gave himself a shake, and then said, 'Sorry, Ben,' and laced the other boot. 'Now then,' he added, 'best behaviour, or you won't be invited again.' He smiled at Lydia. 'Thank you, Mrs Mercer. I'm very much obliged to you for your kindness. Ben is generally well behaved, but sometimes he gets over-energetic. Please feel free to chastise him.'

'I won't need to do that. I'm completely against smacking children.'

'I wasn't suggesting that,' he said, startled. 'Verbally, I meant.'

She smiled. 'I realize that. He needs to let off steam sometimes, I'd guess. He's very energetic, and that energy has to go somewhere.'

He shook his head and sighed. 'I just wish I had half of it.'

'Do the children go to school?'

'No, because most of the schools are shut – no teachers, or at any rate a shortage of them. My wife taught Alice to read when she was little, but the others have never learned.'

'I see.' She nodded. 'I just wondered.'

But only wondered, she thought as she and Ben set off up the lane. I have no picture of the kind of life that the Wade family leads, except that it is very different from mine. She and Ben continued their walk, and he chattered away and told her which birds were singing and whistling. 'Listen,' he said. 'That's a throstle!'

'A throstle?' she queried. 'A thrush? Is throstle a country name?'

'I don't know,' he said. 'It's what my da calls 'em so it must be right. They've got spots on their chests and they sing all sorts of songs, not 'same one all 'time. Did you know that?'

'I confess I didn't.' She shook her head.

'My da says it's a medley. I fink that means a lot of different songs.'

'And what do they eat, these throstles? Berries?'

'Yeh, and snails and worms as well. I once saw a throstle swallow a whole worm, and they don't have any teeth, you know. Not like we do. I wouldn't want to eat a worm, would you, missus?'

'I would not, Ben, not at all. Do you think you could call me Mrs Mercer instead of missus?'

He looked up at her and nodded. 'What does it mean?'

'Mercer? Originally it was a French name which meant merchant, and a merchant was someone who dealt in cloth.'

'And d'you know what my name means?'

'Benjamin, do you mean, or Wade?'

'Wade. My da says it means to go over water, like crossing a ford. You know when there's been a lot o' rain and 'river gets high and you've gotta cross at 'lowest point? That's what's called a ford. You have to *wade* across it to get to 'other side.'

She looked down at him, astonished. *He maybe can't read or write correctly, but he's a proper country lad and knows about the important things. He's gleaned so much information.* 'How old are you, Ben?'

'I'm nearly seven. Charlie and Lily are only five.'

'Nearly seven's a good age to be. Have you ever been to school?'

'No. I wasn't old enough at first, and then, when I was, 'school shut cos they couldn't get a teacher.'

'That's a pity. Were you disappointed?'

'Yeh; I wanted to learn to read. Alice used to read to us, but she's allus busy now helpin' our da to cook an' that, an' looking after Aaron.'

'Yes, of course,' she murmured, and thought how unfair life was for some.

CHAPTER NINE

They walked for almost an hour, with Ben telling her many things about the plants they saw, and stopping her occasionally by holding up a hand when he heard a trilling in the trees and whispering what he thought it was. She stopped and listened too, and wondered if she would remember the sound if she heard it again.

'Who taught you all the bird songs?' she asked as they turned about to make their way back to the Wade cottage.

'My da,' Ben told her. 'He knows all 'birds, and *his* da larnt him. My ma knows 'em as well, but not as many as Da does.'

Like Lily, he spoke of his mother as if she were still there, and she thought that it would be wrong to negate that understanding; eventually, she thought, he would realize that she had gone and acceptance would come more easily.

'We have had a lovely walk,' she told his father, who was sweeping up outside when they eventually arrived back at the cottage, and Ben dashed into the house to tell the others where he had been and what he had seen and heard. 'Ben has such a great knowledge of country matters.' She smiled.

'I've learned what a throstle is, and I know the name of many more trees than I did before.'

He leaned on a yard-brush handle and nodded; the shed doors were wide open and he had obviously been having a good clear-out in there. 'He's a bright lad; he should be at school. He'd catch up in no time once he learned to read and write.'

She spoke quickly and earnestly, the words rushing out before she had even formed them in her head. 'I'll teach him – and the others too. Is it all right if I take Alice to Beverley for our day out first?'

'Yes – I told her she could go with you.' He hesitated. 'You – you don't have to teach them, Mrs Mercer. Please, don't do it because you pity them for not having a mother any longer. We'll cope; they'll find it easier after a while.'

His eyes were a soft brown – hazel, she thought – and appealing for understanding as he looked at her.

'I'm not doing it because I feel sorry for them,' she said abruptly, unnerved by his gaze. 'I'm offering because they're intelligent children and deserve to be allowed to learn; and also . . .' she hesitated, and took a deep breath, 'and also because I feel useless too, a grown woman with energy and intellect that is going to waste. I'm not saying that I could be a schoolteacher, although lately that has crossed my mind, but because I am a married woman and therefore precluded – barred – from using my brain and must pretend a lack of interest in world affairs and have conversations only about the latest fashions – which interest me not a jot – or who amongst my circle is doing what – or not! And I won't have it!' Her voice had risen. 'I just won't!'

She saw his lips twitch, and then he let the brush fall, and taking her hand pulled her gently towards the shed. 'The children will think we are quarrelling,' he said softly, taking her other hand too, and for a breathless moment she thought he was going to kiss it as he had once before, but he simply gazed at her.

'You're a very passionate lady,' he murmured, 'and I thank you for 'interest you've shown in my children.' He let go of one of her hands and gently touched her cheek. 'I'd be glad and honoured if you would teach them to read and write. Just Alice and Ben for now, and I shall be extremely grateful.'

She swallowed. I almost made a fool of myself, she thought. How did that happen? Frustration, she decided. Not enough to do, or at least nothing that I would like to do. But now I do have something in mind; I will turn someone's life around, even if it's not my own.

'Thank you,' she whispered. 'I'll buy paper and pencils and rulers and exercise books when Alice and I go to Beverley.' She put up her hands as she saw objections coming. 'And erasers and all the things we will need,' she added before he could speak. 'Please! Let me do this.'

He nodded slowly, his eyes fixed on hers. 'What would my wife say, do you think?'

'I didn't know her well enough to guess, but in her place I would be glad that my children were being given the chance to flourish. As for Charlie and Lily, they can entertain themselves for now – I've seen that they can – but at the end of each afternoon I'll read to them, or tell them a story.'

He nodded. 'Thank you.' He looked away from her around the building they were standing in. 'You've given me hope,

Mrs Mercer,' he said, and she wished that he could use her first name, but convention dictated otherwise, and he changed the subject.

'When we were speaking earlier, you asked me whether the shed could be used for employment.' He swallowed, and she guessed that whatever he was thinking, he hadn't yet worked out a plan. She hoped that it was similar to hers.

'Yes, I recall.' She didn't want to suggest her idea if he already had one of his own. 'And have you thought of something that might work? Setting up to work for yourself, perhaps, so that you would always be here for the children? You have two little ones who will need constant attention, three more who will be dependent upon you for some time yet, and Alice, who for all her capability and the knowledge she gained from her mother will need her father by her side for several more years before she grows into womanhood.'

She stopped speaking, and he looked at her for a moment. 'Have you time to come inside whilst I outline what I have in mind?' he asked hesitatingly. 'Sometimes talking about an idea can be helpful.'

'Yes,' she said, 'I have. Nicholas has driven into Beverley.'

'Are you sure? We've taken up too much of your time already.'

She shooed away that suggestion with a flap of her hand, and followed him into the house. Charlie and Lily were curled up together on a small sofa with a picture book between them. Baby Mary was on the floor cuddling a toy and crooning to herself, whilst Aaron was in his crib fast asleep.

'Such sweet harmony,' she said softly, 'but there are two missing!'

'Alice is upstairs,' Matthew told her. 'She has a cupboard of a room that is entirely her own, and Ben will be entertaining himself somewhere. He's never short of something to do.'

'So – your plans, Matthew.' She took a chance in using his given name; she thought convention forbade it, though she wished it otherwise. 'Have you thought of something?'

'Yes.' He gave a brief, sardonic laugh. 'Staring me in 'face,' he said, 'and I didn't think of it until you mentioned 'shed. But it might not work immediately, as it will need money, which I haven't got.'

She wasn't going to suggest lending him any; she was sure that he wasn't the sort of man who would accept a loan from a woman.

'So what I thought I would do,' he continued, 'is put a sign up at 'gate and another at 'end of 'lane. "*Wade, Joinery. Fences, kennels, hen houses*" . . . summat like that.' He grinned, as if speaking about it was actually making it happen. 'I've enough timber to make the signs, and if I carve small things first – like a crib, for instance, or a rocking horse with wood that I have already and they sell, then I'd buy more.'

'Excellent!' Lydia clapped her hands. 'But wouldn't the timber suppliers sell you wood on credit? They'll know you already, won't they?'

'No,' he said with vigour. 'They know me only as a carpenter who worked for Stephenson, and he could have told them any old tale about why he sacked me.'

'Oh – of course.' She frowned. *What do I know about the carpentry trade, or any kind of business, come to that? I have ideas, but no real skills to impart, only suggestions, leaving those with abilities and talent to carry through my concepts.*

'I know who would put the word about,' she said. 'My friends the Horners; rocking horses and toys sound just the kinds of things they would like.' She picked up her gloves. 'I haven't time to call on them today, but I owe them a visit, as Emily can't go anywhere for a week or so. Oh, that reminds me – would you be offended if I asked if she had any spare clothing her older children have grown out of that would fit Baby Mary?'

He gave a dry laugh. 'I'm long past being offended by 'offer of hand-me-downs. If anyone is kind enough to pass any on, then yes please.'

CHAPTER TEN

She told Nicholas that Matthew Wade was going to start his own business, but hadn't any money to start him off. Nicholas laughed.

'Brave fellow,' he said, 'though a little foolhardy. There won't be many passers-by to see a sign at his gate! He needs some leaflets or cards to leave at the village shops. There's one in Cherry Burton, for instance; that's close to home. Bishop Burton, too – it's a busy village.'

'That's a good idea,' she agreed. 'I'll suggest it when I next come across him.' She didn't want to give the impression that she saw Matthew Wade every day – that wouldn't do. There I go again, she thought: I am definitely becoming my mother. Why can't women have friendships with men, other than their fathers or potential husbands?

'If he sets something out, we could probably ask the print shop that we use to run some copies off for him.' Nicholas's suggestion broke into her thoughts. 'It would look more professional than a handwritten sign. Hannah could see to it. Check it for errors, you know: spelling and so on, maybe do a little drawing or something; she's quite good at that.'

Hannah had been the secretary at her father's office for several years, taking notes and writing letters in her clear, strong handwriting. She was unmarried and in her middle thirties, and apparently able to do such work without eyebrows being raised. She arrived early every morning to open up before the solicitors or their clerks came in, and took exactly half an hour for her lunch break. She brought her own food, which she ate sitting on a bench on the green and lovely Westwood pastures when fair weather permitted; if it was raining or cold she would slip into a small café and have tea or coffee there and charge it up to expenses.

So if Hannah, Lydia had mused, can do such work without the lift of an eyebrow, I don't see why I shouldn't teach children to read. But perhaps I won't mention that just yet; I'll let it evolve. She decided to visit Emily the next day; she must surely be downstairs by now. *I would be dying of boredom if I were confined to my bedroom for so long.*

Yes, Emily was up, though not yet dressed. Still in her dressing gown, she greeted Lydia warmly. 'I'm dying for conversation that isn't about babies,' she said, putting out her arms to give her friend a hug in the Emily way. 'I adore my baby boys, they're so sweet, and I don't know how I'll ever tell them apart. Simon and Edwin love them too. I thought they might be jealous, but they're not in the least. We've decided to name the twins Roderick and Maxwell. Roderick is Gideon's middle name and his father's name is Maxwell.'

'Roddy and Max?' Lydia said, peering over the cot. 'I think I can tell them apart, though I don't know which is which;

look, this one' – she pointed to the baby at the top of the cot – 'has a freckle at the corner of his eye.'

Emily peered at the baby. 'So he has! That one is Roddy – look, I've tied ribbons on their ankles. The red one is Roddy, and the blue one is Max. They're already looking around and I think they're smiling, though the midwife says it's wind. Gideon is going up into the loft soon to bring down the other cot.'

Lydia laughed. 'How many cots have you got?'

'Only one other. We bought it for Simon after I had Edwin so that he didn't squash him. Now they share a bed; they seem to prefer it.'

'That reminds me. Matthew Wade is setting up his own joinery business; he's going to make rocking horses and toys and cots and such, as well as things like fences and dog kennels.'

'Oh, really? That's definitely a useful trade. Cook said she could use another cupboard to store her jams and marmalades; perhaps he could do that for us? Gideon was really pleased when he fixed the fence in the bottom meadow. I saw him from the bedroom window on the day he came,' she added girlishly. 'He's handsome, isn't he, in a virile sort of way? You'd want to turn and look at him if you thought no one would notice!'

'Emily!'

Emily shrugged and laughed. 'Well, being married to someone like Gideon, I'm something of an observer of handsome men,' she said. 'Don't tell me that you aren't, Lydia, even though you haven't been married for as long as I have, or spent most of that time having babies!'

Lydia put a hand over her mouth to hide a smile. Typical

Emily, she thought. She was the one at school who could tell any innocent girl the facts of life, simply because she was a farmer's daughter and anything to do with procreation was to her an everyday matter.

'He'll not stay a widower for long, you mark my words, except that a houseful of children might put some women out of the running,' Emily added.

I hadn't thought of that, Lydia considered. Another woman would have to be very special, because she would have to love his children too. They were all delightful, but there were a lot of them.

She also told Emily that Matthew needed to find a new milk nurse for Aaron, as the present one would soon have to give up. 'I can't believe I'm talking about such things,' she giggled into her handkerchief. 'My mother would faint clean away if she heard me.'

'For heaven's sake!' Emily poured the tea that Jane had brought upstairs for them, along with a plate of Cook's shortbread biscuits fresh from the oven. 'It's life, Lydia. We all do it once we have children, or at least most of us do, though some "ladies" bring in a wet nurse, of course; they think it's not the done thing to feed their babies themselves, despite its being the most natural occurrence in the world for both animals and humans!'

Lydia swallowed. 'I suppose it is,' she murmured. 'I hadn't really thought about it.'

'Oh, heavens,' Emily sighed. 'I think I might start giving lectures on procreation and the hazards of childbirth and the understanding of both!'

'You'd never get an audience!' Lydia wondered how they

had arrived at this subject. '*Young* women wouldn't be allowed to come – their mothers would forbid them – and they'd remain in complete ignorance until their wedding night. Which, when you think about it, is *so* unfair.'

'So what about you, Lydia?' Emily gave a complicit grin. 'Who told you about the facts of life?'

'Apart from you, do you mean?' Lydia laughed. 'Why, books, of course! I bought them on the sly. Mother once asked me what was I reading and was it a romance. I said it was a sort of romance and she asked if she would like it; I said that she might and then conveniently lost it!'

'She might find it and be shocked,' Emily suggested.

'I don't think so,' Lydia said. 'I've tucked it in a drawer under the winter long johns I bought for Nicholas. She'd never look there, and neither would Nicholas!'

They both laughed until each had a stitch and Emily said they must stop at once or they'd frighten the babies. 'But it's so ridiculous,' she cried. 'I can't believe that young married women should have to go to such lengths to talk of such normal events.'

'That's because you're a farmer's daughter and now a farmer's wife.' Lydia wiped tears from her eyes. 'Whereas I am – was – an innocent.'

'But not any longer,' Emily remarked, 'with a handsome neighbour to keep your imagination busy.'

'Emily!' Lydia was rather shocked. 'He's a widower – shattered after losing his wife and terribly anxious about having to care for his children as well as finding work to pay his rent and buy food. None of the children are old enough to work – even the eldest is still a child, and yet she does the laundry and helps with the cooking and cleans the cottage, which is spotless. I feel so sad for them all. The oldest boy, Ben, has rather taken to me; he calls me *missus.*'

'Oh, I didn't mean to be flippant,' Emily said forlornly. 'You know how I am: speak first and think second. So, what can we do for them? Baby clothes – we've plenty of those that no longer fit Simon or Edwin, and Roddy and Max won't need anything else just yet. And when Gideon brings the other cot down – what is the new Wade baby called? Aaron? Yes? Well, he can have the one the twins are using now if Mr Wade would like it.'

She gave a big smile, and Lydia thought how lovely it would be to be Emily, who solved problems so quickly. Every young woman needed a friend like Emily, especially to teach them the facts of life, about which, sadly, she hadn't quite gained all the knowledge herself, in spite of what Emily seemed to think.

CHAPTER ELEVEN

The day had arrived when Lydia was taking Alice for a jaunt into Beverley. It was sunny, with a breeze but no rain. Lydia took Frisky from the stable and hitched him up to a post where he could graze on a patch of grass, and then went indoors to change into a warmer dress and a long woollen coat.

Alice arrived on the stroke of ten o'clock, dressed in a summer frock and wearing a straw hat that had seen better days. Over the dress she wore a pale blue knitted jacket with white edging around the neck and buttonholes.

'Alice! Do come in,' Lydia called when she knocked on the open door. 'I'm almost ready. I think it's going to remain fine, don't you?'

Alice stepped inside. 'Yes, Da said it was. He's usually right about 'weather,' she added shyly. 'Allus seems to know when we should take a gamp.'

'Oh, that's very useful,' Lydia said, looking in the hall mirror to put on her own blue straw. 'Let me look at you.' She took a step back, and exclaimed, 'You look lovely! What a very nice jacket.' She bent down to look closer. 'That is *charming,*' she enthused. 'I love the pattern, and the contrasting edging. Is it hand knitted? You must tell me who made it!'

'Yes,' Alice answered shyly, and then put her hand over her mouth to hide her smile. 'You're standing right next to her,' she said daringly.

'No! I was going to ask if your mama had knitted it.' Lydia fingered the sleeve.

'My ma said I was as good as she was, if not better.'

She was pressing her lips together and Lydia wondered if she'd gone too far with her probing. 'Well, it really is lovely,' she said. 'Did you work out the pattern yourself?'

'Yes. When I first learned to knit, Ma showed me how to count the lines and stitches evenly, so when I wanted this cardy I could picture just what I needed to do.'

'Really? I almost can't believe it,' Lydia said. 'How clever you must be. Do you enjoy doing it? It's not a chore?'

Alice shook her head. 'Ma used to say I'd be able to make my living as a knitter.' She looked a little sad. 'But I don't have a lot of time now that Ma isn't here, cos 'children have to be looked after and I'm 'eldest. Da can't look after them all 'time cos he has to make a living.' She said the last words parrot-fashion, as if she'd heard the phrase several times, and gave a little sigh. 'But he said 'other day that things were looking up, and our fortunes might be changing for 'better,' she added, and Lydia's heart went out to this brave little girl who was taking on a grown-up's role.

'I think your father is absolutely right,' she said softly. 'And I also think I know several people who might like to buy your knitwear. Can you knit baby clothes as well, or are they too small and fiddly?'

'No!' Alice laughed. 'Ma showed me how to knit for 'twins when I could onny use big needles, but then Baby Mary came and she needed a lot of little jackets cos she grew out of them so quickly, so now I can make all sizes. Oh, and I nearly forgot. Mrs Horner – she's your friend, isn't she? – she's sent a cot for Aaron and loads of things that she says don't fit their older babies, and if we don't need them we're to give 'em away to someone who does. We've kept some for Aaron for when he's grown a bit, and we've given some of them to Lottie, 'milk nurse, to thank her for feeding him. She's run out of milk now, so we'll have to give him a bottle. Da said he'd feed him today whilst I'm out with you, and then later I can sort out some of 'other clothes for him. They'll be too big for him just now, but I expect they'll come in useful soon.'

'How lovely of Mrs Horner to think of you,' Lydia said, dizzy with the prospect of possibilities for this clever little girl, with expectations beyond her years. 'Now, come along – it's time we were leaving. We can discuss as we drive how we're going to make your fortune when you become the best-known knitter in the area!'

She's so young to be thinking of such things, she pondered, yet I've heard of other places, mainly in the south of England – well, say Nottingham, for instance – where children much younger than Alice are taught to make lace, and work all day; and although I can't bear to think of it I believe small boys might still be sent down the coal mines in West Yorkshire. I really should know. She sighed. In the countryside it was accepted that at harvest time children would be expected to work in the fields alongside their parents in order to earn money for the family's finances – their education wasn't considered to be as important as bringing food to the table – but Lydia knew that too many children were being forced by unscrupulous business owners to work in such dangerous environments as cotton mills and coal mines.

They drove along the quiet lane until they reached the top road that led to Beverley. There was a little more traffic here, mainly traders driving small carts full of sacks and boxes piled high with eggs, potatoes and vegetables, and buckets holding bunches of fragrant flowers.

It was a lovely day to be out; the blossom on the privet and hawthorn hedges was at its prettiest, and full of rustling and the twittering of birdlife.

'There are two markets in Beverley,' Lydia told her companion, 'Saturday Market and Wednesday Market, and today is . . . ?'

'Wednesday!' Alice squeaked in excitement. 'Which is best?'

'Saturday Market is bigger and busier but they're much the same, really,' Lydia told her. 'When we get to the town we'll be driving under what is called North Bar, which is ancient, and once had a gate on it to keep out any enemies.' She glanced down at Alice, who seemed really excited, with her bright eyes and eager expression, and went on, 'Then further along we'll pass a beautiful church called St Mary's and a very old inn called the Beverley Arms, and come to Saturday Market. There's a splendid Market Cross where people often gather for a chat; sometimes a brass band plays there too. There are lots of shops for us to look at as well as the jeweller's where we'll have a chain put on your brooch to keep it safe, but first we'll leave the pony and trap in the yard behind my father's office and find somewhere to have a pot of coffee, or lemonade if you'd rather, and maybe a slice of cake or a scone. How does that sound?'

'Very exciting,' Alice said, her eyes shining.

'Wednesday Market is farther along. There'll be flowers on sale there, and stalls where we might find knitting wool for you. If you'd like that,' she added hastily, not wanting to seem pushy, for this was Alice's treat after all.

She waved to Hannah through the office window as she unhooked Frisky from the shafts of the trap, to let her know who was using their private yard, and turned to Alice with a smile. 'First the jewellers, I think,' she said as they walked down a narrow passage into the market area. 'We might have to leave the brooch; I expect they'll be busy today.'

Alice nodded and fingered it. 'They'll look after it, won't they?' she murmured.

'Oh, yes, indeed they will,' Lydia assured her as they crossed over to the other side. 'This is the shop. Look at the beautiful things in the window!'

Alice's eyes opened wide. Lydia guessed that she wouldn't have seen such splendid jewellery before, and reminded herself that her companion was still a child. I mustn't spoil her, she thought, or give her too many expectations.

The jewellers were busy and asked if Mrs Mercer could leave the brooch for an hour. They remarked on how lovely it was, and they didn't recall seeing it before. 'I hope it is insured, madam?' the jeweller commented. 'Perhaps you'd like me to arrange that for you?'

'My young friend here is a minor. Could you perhaps put it in her father's name, in case of mishap?'

'I will look into that for you when I have arranged a valuation.'

'What did he mean, Mrs Mercer?' Alice asked as they left the shop, the jeweller opening the door and bowing to them both as he did so, and Alice giving a little dip of her knee in return.

'Oh – he meant that he will find out how much the brooch is worth, and I shall give him some money, and then should the brooch be lost or stolen he will give me back enough money to replace it.'

'Oh, I shall never lose it, Mrs Mercer, never ever in my whole life!' Alice said sincerely. 'I'll onny wear it on special occasions and I'll *always* fasten 'pin.'

Lydia took her hand and gave it an affectionate squeeze. 'I want you to wear it and enjoy wearing it,' she said softly. 'It's yours, and you mustn't worry about losing it.'

'All right,' Alice agreed, 'but I won't wear it every day, not when I'm doing jobs in 'house, or working outside,' she said earnestly.

'That's very sensible,' Lydia said, determining to buy her something bright and cheerful that she could wear every day and not be afraid of losing.

They were almost in Wednesday Market, close to a café she knew, when they heard someone calling, 'Lydia! Good heavens, it's Lydia!' Who knew her well enough to call her by her first name?

A dark-haired young woman wearing a feathered hat was coming towards her, waving. 'Lydia Davenport! It *is* you! Such a long time! Edwina Rogers – now Selby. Don't you recognize me? We were such good friends at school.'

'Were we?' *Why don't I remember?*

'I'm Lydia Mercer now,' she said, aware that Alice was giggling as she raised her eyebrows. A vague memory returned. 'Oh, of course. Eddie, didn't everyone call you?'

'Oh, they did! So tiresome! But look at you – married and with a nearly grown-up daughter!'

'Erm, no, this is my good friend, Miss Alice Wade.' Alice gave the newcomer a wobbly bend of her knee and tried to keep a straight face.

'Oh, how sweet,' Edwina purred. 'I have a boy and a girl.' She mentioned two names, which Lydia promptly forgot. 'Do you still live in Beverley?'

'Erm, yes . . . well, no, just nearby.' *Please don't ask me to call. I haven't got time, and I don't want to anyway.*

'We're in Woodmansey village, and I'm heading to Saturday Market now,' Edwina said. 'I'm meeting Pamela Brown for coffee. Do you recall her? It would be lovely if you would join us – and – of course . . .' She smiled down at Alice.

'Oh, I'm so sorry, but we have an appointment in five minutes, and must dash along. Always so much to do, isn't there? Some other time, perhaps, but lovely to see you after so long. So good to meet again. Do give my kindest regards to Paula.' She began to move away.

'Pamela,' Edwina called after her. 'Brown,' she clarified. 'She's still unmarried, and such an attractive young woman . . . I adore your little coat,' she added to Alice, who gave another dip of her knee. 'I'd love something similar for my little girl. She's three now – doesn't time fly? Yes, yes indeed,' she agreed with herself as Lydia began to edge away. 'Goodbye then, Lydia.'

'I'm so sorry, we're going to be late – well, you know how it is, never enough time – look as if we're hurrying,' she muttered to Alice as she waved goodbye. 'That's it, up to the top of the market, a quick swing round' – she took hold of Alice's arm – 'and in here.' She ducked quickly into the café, and glancing up saw Edwina's feathered head disappearing in the opposite direction.

'Let's sit further in so no one can see us from outside,' she whispered, and saw Alice's face light up in a smile. 'Then we can have a cosy chat. Now, what shall we have?' She picked up a menu, and put it down again. 'But here's Nancy to advise us.'

The owner came across to them, wearing a long white apron over her dark gown. 'Good morning, Mrs Mercer. How are you today? And you've brought a friend along to see us!' She smiled down at Alice. 'I love your jacket, miss, such a pretty design.' She bent towards Alice to admire it. 'Beautifully knitted. I used to knit,' she went on, stepping back, 'but there's never enough time since we took on the café. We're always busy. It's cake and scones and biscuits and what not or knitting, so baking wins.' She shrugged her shoulders and gave a merry grimace.

'I don't know how to bake yet,' Alice told her, 'but I do like knitting.'

'Well, you might like to try my chocolate cake? I'll bring you a sample and a piece of scone and you can choose. Or have them both if you can manage them?'

Alice giggled. 'I don't want to be greedy!'

'You can have them both if you'd like to,' Lydia told her. 'I'm going to have a piece of chocolate-topped shortbread.

It's a speciality of Nancy's – in fact, bring a selection, if you will, Nancy.' She turned to Alice. 'And what we don't eat you can take home and share with your sisters and brothers. Does Baby Mary eat cake?'

Alice's eyes grew wide and she laughed. 'She hasn't eaten any yet,' she said, but then her expression changed. 'Ma allus made a Christmas cake, but it didn't last very long, and I don't know how to make another one.'

'Well,' Lydia shook a finger, 'I have some recipe books. Why don't we have a look through them one day, then buy the ingredients and bake one together? Because, if I'm honest, I don't really know how to bake either, and here I am, a grown woman making that admission!'

As it was nearly lunchtime, Lydia suggested that perhaps they could have a light meal of cold meat and salad whilst they were there, and as there was a sponge pudding on the menu they had that too, with custard, and Nancy packed them a bag full of various cakes to take home as well as bringing small samples for them to try with their coffee or tea.

'Will it be all right to take one of these little cakes for Ben?' Alice whispered. 'It was his birthday the other day, and this would be a treat for him.'

'Oh, I'm so sorry I missed it!' Lydia said. 'Ben told me he was seven. We must buy him a little present.'

Alice decided she would have coffee with her lunch as she had never tried it before, and she declared that her shortbread sample was the best she had ever had. When they had finished, Lydia suggested they looked around the market stalls to see if they could find a treat for Alice and something for Ben as a late birthday present, and reminded herself that she had also meant to buy crayons and notebooks and pencils and such for the younger ones. Alice found a bead necklace she loved, and Lydia spotted a similar bracelet and bought that too, thinking that all little girls should have a pretty jangly bracelet at some time in their lives.

Then, in the middle of the market area, there was a stall selling children's clothes: boys' trousers and short heavy cotton coats – denim, Lydia thought the fabric was called – and girls' cardigans, none of them as nice as the one Alice was wearing.

The stallholder came across to them as they riffled through the piles. 'Nice little jacket 'young lady's wearing, ma'am,' she said to Lydia. 'Looks like a handmade, not one o' them foreign un's that's coming in from abroad.'

'You're quite right,' Lydia told her, 'it is locally made, and beautifully knitted.'

'How much did that cost then, if you don't mind me askin', ma'am?'

'I'm afraid I don't know,' Lydia said. 'I didn't buy it. How much do you think it would sell for?'

The woman scratched her head. 'I reckon I could buy at three and sell at five,' she said.

'Shillings, are you saying? I can enquire for you if you wish? It was given to me by a friend who knows the knitter and undoubtedly she would be able to find out.' Lydia smiled brightly at the stallholder. 'Is it the kind of thing you could sell?'

'Aye. I'd like to sell summat better'n second hand, especially new. Summat that would appeal to better-off folk; you'll know what I mean, ma'am.'

Lydia wasn't sure she did know what the woman meant, but she nodded. 'And sizes? For older children?'

'Oh aye,' the woman agreed, 'or bigger, for young ladies, mebbe? I think they'd sell all right.'

'Next time I'm in Beverley I'll call to see you,' Lydia said agreeably. 'I'll let you know what I've found out. Goodbye.'

They walked back towards Saturday Market, and Lydia was glad to see that Alice had a little smile on her face. 'Did you understand all of that conversation?' she asked, taking the girl's arm and tucking it under her own. 'The stallholder was very interested in your jacket.'

'Did she want to buy it to sell on, Mrs Mercer?'

'I think she did, or one similar. Your mother was right, don't you think? You *could* make a living from knitting.'

'Yes – yes, she was. Wouldn't she be pleased!'

'I'm sure she would have been delighted. So what other clever things can you do? Next on the agenda would be . . . baking?'

'We wouldn't be able to sell what I baked, though,' Alice said, breaking into a grin. 'We'd eat it all first!'

'You're right,' Lydia admitted. 'And anyway, most young women know how to bake. They're not all as deficient as I am when it comes to household tasks.'

Alice turned to her. 'What does that mean, Mrs Mercer?' she said in a small voice. 'I don't know the word deefishunt. And you said ajender – I don't know that word either. What do they mean?'

'Ah!' Lydia was stumped. *Of course she doesn't. She's a child without schooling. Whatever am I thinking?*

CHAPTER TWELVE

Lydia bought exercise books, pencils and crayons, rulers and erasers, several copies of the same story books – for she thought that as well as Alice and Ben, Charlie and Lily would probably join them – and even if Baby Mary was not yet two she could look at a children's book made from cotton that wouldn't tear filled with pictures of cats, dogs, chickens and rabbits. She had also bought slates and chalk, and story books for slightly older children that could be read aloud. Matthew would have to make his own arrangements for baby Aaron.

What she had not yet done was consider a way to break the news to Nicholas that she was going to teach the Wade children to read and that they were coming to their house for their first lesson the very next Monday morning.

They were due to arrive at ten o'clock; she would pause at noon and give them lunch – a sandwich and a warm or cold drink depending on the weather – start again at one o'clock and finish at three, when she would take them home in the trap. She would then be free to heat the meal that Cook had prepared and left ready in the meat safe before Nicholas arrived home.

On Sunday evening she piled all the books on a chair in the dining room and put the slates, pencils and crayons and other items in a bag on the floor next to them, so that he would be sure to see them when they sat down for supper and enquire what they were. She would then express surprise, and say that she thought she had mentioned the plan previously.

He surely won't mind; why would he? I'm just helping a friend; he couldn't object to that, and why should it matter if the friend is male? He's someone who needs help, and I'm someone who needs to feel useful.

Nothing was said; it seemed as if Nicholas hadn't noticed the bag or the books, which was surprising, but then he didn't always draw her into a discussion, she reflected; he hadn't even referred to her visit to the office the previous Wednesday, which Hannah would surely have mentioned.

She was quite nervous over breakfast on the Monday morning, as they still hadn't discussed the subject. He was generally preoccupied on Mondays and spoke little during breakfast, so she topped up his coffee cup without asking if he would like more. He just looked up and nodded, murmuring 'Thank you'.

When he left the house, he gave her the usual kiss on the cheek, but sighed as he did so. 'I've got a headache coming on, right behind my eyes.'

'Oh, no. Won't you take something? Aspirin perhaps?'

'It will go, I expect.' He kissed her again. 'I hope you have a good day.'

'Oh,' she began, 'I forgot to mention—' but she was cut off from confessing as the hansom drew up at the gate.

'Got to go,' he said. 'See you at five.'

She let out a breath. 'Yes,' she said quietly, and, 'I expect you will.'

Maggie came out of the dining room with a tray of used crockery. 'Shall I polish 'furniture in 'dining room, ma'am? I onny dusted it yesterday; didn't use polish.'

'Erm, no, leave it for today, Maggie. I'm expecting the Wade children at ten o'clock. I'm, erm, looking after them this morning and tomorrow, and – and Wednesday too, as it happens; I said that I would, just to help Mr Wade out. He's . . . well, he's got rather a lot on his plate at the moment.'

Maggie stared at her open-mouthed, then closed and opened it again before she said, 'That doesn't surprise me at all, ma'am. He'll have plenty to deal with. Lost his job is what I heard. Nobody's got a good word for Stephenson. Talk about kicking a man when he's down.' She tutted, and then asked, 'Does that mean 'latest babby as well?'

'No, no! I don't think I could manage that,' she stammered. 'I said I would read to the older children; teach them their letters, you know.'

Maggie nodded. 'Very generous of you, ma'am. I'm sure your kindness will be appreciated. I did wonder why there were so many children's books in there.'

'Small gifts,' she said. 'Something to occupy them.'

'Aye,' Maggie answered approvingly. 'Some of 'em should be at school, I reckon, if there was one handy. Leconfield's 'nearest that's open, so I'm told. It's not right. Every child should be taught to read and write without having to pay for it, in my opinion.' She hitched the tray a little higher. 'So not worth polishing in there, ma'am? There'll be sticky fingerprints everywhere. I'll do it tomorrow morning.'

Maggie went off to continue her chores, and Lydia found a large cotton sheet and spread it over the table. Then she set the slates out, and the books of children's stories; then the pencils, chalk and crayons and a stock of plain paper too. She was looking forward to her morning, but Maggie's comment about free schooling slightly bothered her. *Does she think I'm charging a fee? Surely not!*

They arrived exactly on time, Ben and Charlie racing to be the first to the gate, Matthew holding on to Baby Mary's ankles as she perched on his shoulders, and Alice holding hands with Lily, who was complaining that she didn't want to come.

'You'll love it, Lily,' she was saying as Lydia walked down to the gate to greet them.

'Will there be cake?' the child persisted. 'I'll stay if there's cake.'

'You'll stay if there isn't cake,' Matthew said firmly, 'and you'll behave for Mrs Mercer or I'll want to know the reason for it – *and*,' he continued, 'you will not be allowed to come again – ever!'

Lily looked up at her father and scowled, but she remained silent, as if she was trying to work out what her father would want to know. Lydia smiled. She was almost on the point of whispering that there would be cake, but then thought better of it, not wanting to usurp Matthew's authority. 'Good morning,' she called instead. 'How are you all today?'

Lily put her head down and pouted; the others shouted out that they were very well thank you.

Lydia looked up at Baby Mary on Matthew's shoulder; was he going to leave her too? She hoped not. Mary was a sweet little girl, and would listen to a story, but she was too young to manage a pencil.

'I've asked Lottie if she'd come to look after Aaron and Baby Mary at home,' Matthew told her; he must have noticed her questioning glance. 'She said she'll make Aaron a bottle and prepare vegetables for tonight's dinner, and give Baby Mary something to eat too.' He looked down at Lily, who was still pouting. 'Now then, young miss, are you coming back wi' me to stay wi' babbies?'

'Can I draw an' paint?' she said eagerly.

'No!' There was no compromise. 'You can dust and help Lottie, and mebbe peel taties.'

'Oh, I hadn't realized you weren't staying,' Lydia broke in, comprehending that Lily was being awkward. 'I've bought lots of paint and colouring books and heaps of paper to draw on. Charlie is good at painting, isn't he?'

'He's not as good as me. I'm much better than he is!'

'Well, you'd have to stay to prove it,' her father interrupted. 'But still, never mind. Come along, if you've made up your mind. You can sweep out 'stall instead. I've had 'promise of a loan of an owd hoss,' he murmured to Lydia. 'He's seen better days, so he can't be sold, but he's fit enough to trundle a small cart, an' that'll be enough for me.'

'Have you got work, Matthew? That *is* good news.'

'Yes,' he said. 'Thanks to your intervention regarding his fence, Mrs Mercer, Mr Horner has put me on his list of employable team members, and although there's nothing he needs doing at 'minute, apart from mekking a cupboard for Mrs Horner's kitchen, he's told me I'll be 'first on 'list if he needs a joiner in the future.'

'That's wonderful,' Lydia said. 'Well done!' She thought of Emily's remarks about Matthew Wade and guessed that it was she who had suggested that he be put on Gideon's list of reliable workers. She'll pop down to the kitchen while he's fitting the cupboard, I don't doubt at all, she thought, and hid her smile.

'Come along then, children,' she called, turning for the door. 'Alice, will you lead the way? Let's get started; there's lots to do! Are you sure you won't join us, Lily? I was really looking forward to seeing what you could do with a paint-brush; it's very disappointing. Perhaps another time?'

'Thank you, Mrs Mercer.' Matthew watched the children heading for the house, only Lily refusing to move, and Alice looking anxious as she stood waiting for her little sister.

'Lily!' Charlie was hesitating on the doorstep, calling to his twin. 'Please come.' He seemed quite upset, and Lily glanced up at her father, pressing her lips together. Matthew did nothing to persuade her but stood still, waiting for her to decide.

'Come on, then,' he said at last. 'I have jobs to do. Let's go home.'

Everyone except Charlie had gone into the house; only Charlie stood forlornly, one foot blocking the door. 'See you soon, Lily,' he said plaintively.

Lily took a breath. 'Wait! Wait, Charlie! I'm coming. Da,' she called, but her father kept on walking down the drive and unlatched the gate. 'Da, I'm going in!'

He turned briefly and looked at her. 'Off you go then. Next time I won't wait.'

She ran inside, and Lydia, watching through the window, heaved a breath. *How old are they? Nearly six? Learning about life and life's rules. Is Lily struggling without her mother's direction? She only has her father's now, and he's struggling too.* She turned towards the group gathered around the dining-room door. 'Come in and find a chair, everyone, do.' She chose a high-backed seat for herself and drew Lily closer, putting an arm round her. 'I'm so glad you all came; we're going to have such fun. I thought that as this is your first time we'd start with a glass of lemonade and a biscuit, and we'll have a little chat to get to know each other. Alice, would you be kind enough to pass the glasses round, please?'

Alice did as she was bid, then handed the plate of biscuits round too. Lily bit her lip, uncertain whether to take one, and Lydia realized that the child wasn't quite as bold as she tried to appear. She had dug herself into a hole and had had no idea how to get out of it until her father came to the rescue.

CHAPTER THIRTEEN

Lydia read the children a story about a family out on a picnic, when everyone fell asleep in a meadow and woke up to find themselves in a wood full of strange and fascinating creatures. One of the animals was a lion with two tails, one of which was longer than the other so the lion kept falling over it. Another was a tiny mouse that lived on top of a peacock, and every time the peacock spread its magnificent tail feathers the little mouse fell off and had to scoot after the bird and take a flying leap to get back up again.

Alice gave a polite little yawn. The story was far too young for her, but the letters were large and easy for her to follow. Ben and Charlie leaned on their elbows as they listened and laughed as chickens came into the story, but Lily picked up her colouring pencils and began to draw a blue sky and a yellow sun and a hen house with white eggs and one brown one in a little basket. 'It's just like our hen house,' she said to no one in particular. 'We sometimes get brown eggs as well as white ones. Why is that? Why are they sometimes white and sometimes brown, and sometimes speckled, like this?' She quickly drew an oval shape on the sheet of white paper she was using and coloured in several brown spots.

Lydia didn't know, but covered up her lack of knowledge by saying, 'It's something called pigment!' but then wished she hadn't, because Ben and Charlie asked in unison, 'Do they come from pigs, then?'

'No.' She laughed. 'I'll ask a farmer about it when I next see one.'

'That's silly,' Lily said, not even lifting her head as she continued with her picture. 'Pigs don't have feathers, and they have little piglets, not eggs. I've seen 'em.'

'Brown eggs come from brown hens,' Alice said, 'and white eggs from white hens.'

'I'm sure that's exactly right,' Lydia said. 'Well done, Alice. Now, what I'd like everyone to do is write the words "egg" and "chicken" on your slates. Let's see who can finish first. Do you all know the alphabet?' Alice nodded her head, but Ben, Charlie and Lily all shook theirs.

'Well, while we're in class I would like all of you to answer with a polite "Yes, Mrs Mercer" or "No, Mrs Mercer",' Lydia told them, determined to speak to them as their teacher, and not in this instance as a friend. 'One at a time,' she added, 'not all together. Alice, will you show everyone what I mean, please?'

Alice stood up. 'Yes, Mrs Mercer, I *do* know 'alphabet, cos my mother telled – taught me,' she said politely, and then sat down again, her cheeks flushed.

Ben got up next and put his hands behind his back. 'No, Mrs Mercer, I don't know 'alphabet, cos nobody learned me.'

He sat down with a great beam on his face, and Charlie

got up next, but only to say, 'You can go before me if you like, Lily.'

Lily put down her colouring pencil and stood up. 'I don't know what 'alphabet is, Mrs Mercer, so I don't *fink* I know it. Charlie might, but he's never telled me, and usually he does cos he finks he knows everyfink, so I 'spect he don't.'

I need tea, Lydia thought as Charlie called out that he didn't, but would ask his da when he got home. 'You may ask me,' she told him. 'This is why I wanted you all to come here today.'

Or maybe a strong coffee, she decided; I need a stimulant. This is *not* going to be easy. Alice has had a good start, but what a struggle it must have been for her poor mother to take care of them all and teach them too. I'm sure that Matthew would have done what he could when he wasn't at work, but with no one to help cook or clean, and being with child so often – well, my goodness, *how* would she have had time to teach them all the alphabet, let alone any lessons?

By break time, they were chanting the first seven letters of the alphabet in a sing-song manner, which they thought was great fun; and then, after each of them had had a glass of milk or lemonade and a biscuit, they mastered up to M, then to T, and finally the last six letters as they came up to lunchtime. Lydia was delighted.

'Children,' she said, 'you have all done very well. Now you can take a little break outside, but don't go near the animals, please; the pony will shy away, and sometimes the donkey kicks. Then come inside and wash your hands and we shall have lunch.'

Everyone but Alice gave a cheer and headed for the door.

'I wondered if I could do anything for you, Mrs Mercer?' the older girl said quietly when they had gone.

'No, thank you, Alice. You've worked very hard all morning,' Lydia told her. 'Why not have a wander outside and take a breath of fresh air before we start again?'

'All right,' Alice said softly, and Lydia wondered if her father had told her to be ready to help if necessary, or take charge of the younger children. But she does enough, Lydia thought; she's still a child herself and shouldn't always be responsible for her brothers and sisters. She wondered, too, what Alice had thought of the lessons, which Lydia had meant to be appropriate for the younger children; there was nothing to tax Alice, so was she wasting the girl's time? She watched her wander outside and be immediately surrounded by her siblings, Lily even taking hold of her hand. Such obligations, Lydia thought. She's taking on the role of their mother and she's far too young for that. The sudden thought came into her head that in another year or so Alice would be entering puberty. Had she been told the facts of life, as they were somewhat obliquely known? Lydia rather thought not. So who was going to tell her?

Instantly she had a name in her head, but should she first ask Alice's father? It wasn't her place, but what if Matthew hadn't thought of it? It was too far away for him to have even considered, and after the trauma of losing his wife he really wouldn't want the worry.

But Emily would know how to explain everything about the begetting of babies without any mortification at all, unlike me, Lydia pondered. I would die with embarrassment. I am still living in the shadow of my mother and *her* mother, who both held that such personal subjects shouldn't be discussed under *any* circumstances. None whatsoever.

I really must speak to Emily. Alice is motherless and vulnerable and must be given time to be a child before the chance slips away. In fact I'll ask Emily if I can bring Alice to see her as soon as she's recovered after the birth of the twins.

After they had finished lunch she began teaching the children about numbers, adding up and taking away, and it went very well; Ben in particular could add and subtract without any problem, and Charlie was not far behind. Lily wasn't at all interested and continued with her drawing and colouring, until Lydia asked her how many eggs she had crayoned in the basket. She immediately counted them, and reported that there were four white and three brown, which made seven in total. Alice was very quick, and pointed out that her mother had taught her to count stitches when she was learning to knit.

I've been no help at all, Lydia considered. These children are managing perfectly well without my assistance. They are able to cope with their lives; they have had the great gift of loving parents who have taught them what is important and what is not. What is missing now is their mother, and I can't replace her, but although they don't realize it yet, their father is gently closing up that gap, for the time being at least.

She walked them home rather than taking the trap; the children skipped and ran and Ben pointed out different birds, recognizing their song, and Alice saw a squirrel as it dashed from one wood to another across the lane. Lydia asked them the names of the trees they passed on their walk and Ben and Alice and Lily knew each one.

'Blackthorn shows its blossom afore 'leaves uncurl,' Alice pointed out, 'and hawthorn—' 'is called May,' Lily and Charlie shouted in unison. 'And that's 'tree children dance round on May Day,' Lily added. 'Ma said it was, so . . .' Her steps slowed and her voice faltered. 'And – I don't want to dance round it again.'

'I don't either.' Charlie came to her side and took her hand, and Alice went to her other side and put her arm round her shoulders. Ben, who was running ahead of them down the lane, began to slow his steps as if he guessed that something was not quite right.

They are still grieving, after all, Lydia reflected. They haven't forgotten anything, not even the maypole dance, which was almost a year ago, and even though they can laugh and play the grief is still there, and will be for some time to come.

And it seems to me that occupying them with stories and teaching them to read might be the only help I can provide, and I only hope it may distract them a little; give them things to do that will fill their days and begin to plug the huge gap that has opened in their lives.

CHAPTER FOURTEEN

Matthew Wade was in the shed working at his bench when they got back. He didn't have the anxious, worried expression he'd worn previously, and although he didn't exactly look happy he seemed much brighter as he greeted his children heartily and asked what they had been up to. They besieged him with descriptions of what they had been doing, the boys telling him what they had had to eat as if it were the most important thing of the day, and Lily interrupting them to say that she had been colouring in a picture. 'It's for you, Da, when it's finished.'

'Really?' Matthew picked her up and swung her round until she screeched.

'I might go again,' she told him when he put her back on her feet.

'And is that all right with Mrs Mercer? Did you thank her for today's lesson?'

They all were silent for a moment, then Lily spoke up. 'Was it a lesson? I didn't know. I fort we were playing.'

Lydia smiled broadly and gave a small sigh. Success, she thought. I'm so pleased.

'Mrs Mercer has given up her time to be with you today,' Matthew told them. 'Wasn't that kind of her?'

Alice spoke up boldly. 'It was very kind of you, Mrs Mercer. Thank you.'

'It was my pleasure, Alice. I enjoyed our time together too.' Lydia smiled as if they were sharing a secret.

'Fank you, Mrs Mercer,' Lily piped up, copying her sister. 'It was very kind of you.' The boys thanked her too, and then the children rushed into the house to see Baby Mary and Aaron, who were being looked after by Lottie.

'I'm so grateful.' Matthew turned to Lydia. 'I can't tell you what a difference it has made to my day. Lottie has been more than useful, and her mother came with her this morning and offered to do some cleaning and maybe scrub 'vegetables to make soup; she said that if I could afford to give her a copper or two she would use it to buy essentials for her grandchild. It seems she and her husband have been very supportive of Lottie,' he went on, 'and understand 'position she's in.' He rubbed his bristly chin and looked away as he spoke. 'There's many would've thrown her out, but 'lad who's 'father of her bairn wants to marry her all right. Unfortunately he has no job or money to support her.'

'And presumably nowhere to live, either?'

He shook his head. 'No. But I've had a good day, Mrs Mercer,' he added. 'Your friend Mr Horner paid me for 'repairs of his fence, and I fixed a wonky gate that I'd noticed. He said he'd recommend me to other folk in 'district, and I've almost finished the cupboard for their kitchen.'

Lydia smiled. She'd thought as much: Emily had had a finger in the pie. She almost laughed aloud when he added,

'And their cook happened to be baking a meat pie and said there was enough meat for two, and she's baked us an apple pie as well, with apples from last year's crop.'

'How lovely,' Lydia said. 'The Horners are very generous people.'

He nodded in agreement. 'I've also been asked if I can build a small shed for somebody in Cherry Burton. They'd seen the sign near our gate. I'll go and look tomorrow and find out what he wants and measure up, but I've told 'em that I'll need a deposit to pay for 'timber.'

'Incredible!' she said, and thought how quickly he had put up the signs near the fence and at the end of the lane with an arrow on them pointing to his cottage, so that orders were now coming in without any other advertising. 'I can't believe how fast things are changing for you; you just seized an opportunity and doors started to open. That's wonderful. And,' she added, 'it's very wise to ask for a deposit.'

He laughed. 'It's all been down to you, Mrs Mercer, and if it were not for young Lottie being in 'house at present I'd like to swing you off your feet, just as I did Lily.'

Her eyes widened. 'Oh! Well, perhaps another time,' she gasped. 'I wouldn't want you to get a reputation with the ladies of the area. I know them,' she added slyly. 'They'd be queuing up at the gate!'

'Seriously?' he said, though he gave a broad grin. 'But I am truly grateful, and I'm aware that we're taking up your time.'

She looked at him for a moment. He had lost the down-cast, worried expression he had worn previously; he must have been overcome with grief and worry over his children and what would happen to them if he couldn't find enough work to fund the essentials such as food and a place to live.

'Matthew,' she murmured, and swallowed hard. 'I *love* your children. They are so bright and merry and caring, and although I know they're missing their mother they rely on you now, trust you for their security, their protection; and . . . and your steadfast love for them is so obvious that even though they wouldn't know how to put it into words they're just *sure* of it.' She felt so roused, so strung up with passion for his motherless children, that tears gathered and she had to blink them away.

He noticed, and reached for her hands, stroking them gently with his thumbs. He isn't afraid to show emotion either, she thought. He's not like most men; certainly not men of his generation, or my father's generation. Neither my father nor Nicholas would be able to express themselves in such a manner.

Not the done thing, you know; she could almost hear her father's voice. *One doesn't express feelings, especially not when ladies are about. No, no – wouldn't do at all, you know.*

He walked her to the gate. 'Will you be all right walking home alone?'

'I will.' She smiled. 'I'm practising becoming a country-woman, no longer a "townie".'

'It suits you, Mrs Mercer.' He smiled. 'Lydia.'

'Goodness.' She looked up at him. 'At last! Was that very difficult?'

He laughed, putting his head back. 'Very. It goes beyond what I have been taught. To "know my place in society".'

'What tosh!' she responded bluntly. 'Whoever taught you that?'

'Would you believe – my father? He always tipped a finger to his brow whenever he met his "betters".' His face creased into a grin. 'Lads at school taught me to do 'same when I was six or seven, onny not in exactly 'same way, and then my da caught me and I was given a leathering so I never did it again.'

'And that's why I was always Mrs Mercer?' She shook her head and unlatched the gate. 'I don't believe a word of it.'

'Every word is true.' He covered her hand on the latch with his. 'But it didn't apply to friends.'

She put her other hand over his and took a breath. 'That's all right, then.'

'I reckon it is,' he smiled, and they parted company. She looked back after she'd taken a few steps just as he did the same, and they both lifted a hand.

A friend, she pondered as she walked. A true friend: it is possible after all. To be friends with men, able to converse with them in the way we do with women. Well, not exactly the same, perhaps; there are personal subjects we wouldn't discuss, but it *is* possible to share conversation or a joke. We can be on level terms with them. They're not a different species, though perhaps some of them might seem to be: the older generation, perhaps, who have been brought up in a different way. Could I teach the children that? I don't see why not, but I'd need to understand how others might feel about the subject. She sighed. I would dearly like to show the way.

She was home, and the door was partly open; Nicholas must be back already. *I wonder why? Has there been some magnetic shift of the planet? Has a star fallen out of the sky? Has the moon turned green?* 'Hello,' she called as she entered. 'Did you get time off for good behaviour? Or are the law-abiding people of Beverley not in need of legal advice?'

Nicholas appeared at the living-room door and leaned against the jamb. 'Where've you been?' He didn't respond to her flippant comment, nor look her in the eye as he added, 'We've been invaded by a host of children, judging by the number of crayons and colouring books scattered about.'

'Oh, yes. I was going to tidy up, but decided to make the most of the weather. It's been a lovely day; quite unexpected.'

She was a little unnerved by his manner: there was something amiss, but she couldn't put her finger on it. Why was he home so early? Her father was a stickler for time-keeping and continuity in his staff.

'So who was here?' he went on. 'No, let me guess! Those children from down the lane – the joiner's children? Don't tell me you've been child-minding.' This time his eyes bored steadily into hers.

She lifted her chin and stared back at him; then spun round and took off her hat and threw it on to a chair. She hadn't picked up her coat when she and the children had left the house, but only a shawl and the hat. 'No,' she told him, 'not child-minding. I've been teaching the Wade children to read. They picked it up very quickly – they are such intelligent children.'

'So why aren't they at school, if they're so clever?'

'Nicholas!' she said irritably. 'What is this? Why are you home so early? Has something happened?'

'Yes, as a matter of fact, it has, if you're interested.'

'Of course I'm interested! My father isn't unwell, is he?'

'No, why would he be?'

'I don't know, except that he's coming up to the age where he might be. So if it isn't Father, what *has* brought you home so early? I'll make a pot of tea, and you can tell me what it is and I'll help if I can.'

He humphed and muttered something and she turned towards the door. He was definitely avoiding her gaze, but why? Was it because she had invited the children here? But why would he object? In the kitchen she put more wood in the range and lifted the half-filled kettle on to the hot-plate; Cook had left the teapot and two teacups and saucers on a tray as she always did, with two plates and the biscuit tin close by.

Nicholas followed her into the kitchen, something he rarely did, and never if Cook or Maggie were there. 'I'm sorry,' he mumbled, standing behind her and folding his arms. 'Something ridiculous occurred and your father took umbrage. He's such a martinet sometimes – always sees the serious side of a situation even when there is none.'

Lydia frowned. *He's making light of something, or at least trying to. I wonder what it is?* She turned to him. 'Perhaps you'd like to tell me, if you think it might help. But it's of no use arguing about my father with me if it's an office situation. Shall we sit?' She pointed back to the living room.

He shook his head. 'I'd rather stand,' he said, but she ignored him and marched back into the living room and sat down.

'Go ahead,' she said, when he followed her. 'I'd rather sit, as it sounds like a life or death situation.'

'Don't be ridiculous, Lydia! It's nothing that can't be explained.'

She didn't answer, but sat with her ankles crossed and her hands in her lap.

'You know that walk-in cupboard we have in the rear office, the one where we keep the clients' files?'

'Y-yes.' She knew it was there, though she wasn't familiar with the rear office or the front one either if it came to it, except that there were three desks and some filing cabinets.

'Well,' he began, and she saw colour rise on his cheeks and neck. 'I'd gone in there to check on a file . . .'

'In the cupboard?'

'Yes, of course,' he said irritably. 'That's what I said!'

She lifted her eyebrows but said nothing, though she felt slightly uneasy. His manner was odd.

'And Hannah was already in there looking for a file too.'

'Yes?' she murmured. 'And . . . ?'

'Well, your father came in and thought we were up to something,' he said quickly.

She breathed deeply. 'And were you?'

'No, of course not! Nothing that wasn't acceptable to her, at least.'

'So you were?'

'Look, there's not much room in there, not for two people anyway, and she was wearing one of those long-sleeved blouses with a low neck – quite provocative, really, and totally unsuitable for office wear – and all I did was—'

'Spare me the detail, please,' she interrupted. 'Was she upset? Angry?'

'Hannah? No, not at all. She didn't mind, and really all I did was . . . sort of nuzzle into her ear. She was wearing a nice fragrance, as she always does.'

'And you admired her blouse, no doubt,' Lydia muttered. 'And then, presumably, my father also chose to come in, and caught you.'

'Yes. And told me to go home, like a naughty schoolboy,' he added sarcastically.

'Instead of treating you like a man of the world,' she mocked. 'You're his son-in-law, for heaven's sake! He has to make an example of you, or how are the rest of the men going to behave?'

'It meant nothing, just a bit of fun.'

'And was it fun for Hannah to be accosted in that way? Did *she* think it was fun?'

He bit his lip. 'I don't know,' he admitted. 'I, erm, I saw her when I was looking for a cab. I don't know what your father had said to her, but she was heading down past Market Cross, away from the office. Erm . . . this week is crucial for me, as it happens, and if your father should choose to make an issue of this incident it could ruin my future career.'

'This *incident*! *Your father*! My father happens to be your employer. This *incident*, as you call it, has nothing to do with my parentage, and might well cost Hannah her situation. Have you thought of that?'

He gave a shrug. 'She should have pushed me away, then.'

Lydia got up without looking at him and walked straight past him. 'Make your own tea,' she snapped and went out of the room, up the stairs and into her bedroom, slamming the door behind her.

CHAPTER FIFTEEN

Lydia eased off her shoes, climbed on to the bed, and put her head back against the pillow, the better to think. What a stupid thing for Nicholas to do. Why didn't he think of the consequences? Didn't he consider his standing in the office as the husband of his employer's daughter; probably the man next in the line of succession? Going up the ladder to the top?

True, he had further to go in experience to achieve his prospective role, but her father had believed in him well before regarding him as a potential son-in-law. He had invited Nicholas to supper one evening close to Christmas four years before, not long after the young man had been invited to 'join the team', as Thomas Davenport described it, and he had seen the spark that flashed between his only daughter and his latest recruit. He had, after all, to consider a successor to his successful law practice.

Lydia had objected at first; she had no intention of allowing her parents to choose her life partner. She was perfectly capable of doing that for herself, she had told Emily, who was busying herself with plans for her own wedding to Gideon Horner. And somehow, with wedding bells ringing in her ears and the excitement of being asked to be Emily's chief bridesmaid so intense, somehow the passion had rubbed off on her. Nicholas was very personable, after all, and funny and clever, and after a few invitations to supper and charity balls she found they had some compatibility. But I never thought of him as a philanderer, she mused now; too strait-laced, or was that because my father was also his employer?

Nicholas had explained that he had come to Yorkshire after finishing a London-based education which had earned him excellent recommendations. He had formed the intention of working in the north, but avoided industrial cities like Manchester, with its towering factories and cotton mills, or Leeds, the dominant 'capital' of Yorkshire, and instead searched the smaller towns for legal opportunities and a foothold in the county's prospects. He had no family, he had explained, his parents having died when he was young, so he saw a future in law that he was building for himself.

I suppose this is how marriages are arranged for people like us, Lydia had considered, with introductions to like-minded people; unlike, say, Matthew Wade and his Mary, who could just meet someone and fall in love and get married.

Now, Nicholas cautiously opened the bedroom door as if he was expecting a tirade of abuse or something more solid – a shoe, or a book, say – to come flying in his direction.

'Blithering idiot,' she muttered.

'What do you want to do?' Nicholas asked, hovering at the end of the bed. 'You can't divorce me. Women can't divorce their husbands – and besides, I didn't do anything.'

'I know – I'm not a lawyer's daughter for nothing! And every woman of means who marries is aware of that. She has no rights, although I think she's allowed the house contents. How marvellous! The husband can do as he wishes and the wife is left with a sofa, a pair of curtains and a cupboard full of mismatched crockery!'

'You're being ridiculous,' Nicholas snapped. 'What do you want to do?'

'I want *you* to apologize to Hannah. You might have cost her her employment – her livelihood, remember – and she needs it. She lives with her widowed mother; it might be their only income.'

Nicholas scratched his chin. 'I'm sorry; I was out of order. Men.' He grimaced. 'Hannah said we're not fit to be let out on our own.'

Lydia frowned. 'Has it happened before? Should I know anything else?'

'No, of course not.' He shrugged. 'Well, maybe when I was a very young man – but long before I met you,' he added hastily. He sat on the edge of the bed and reached for her hand. 'I'm truly sorry, Lydia. I'd never knowingly hurt you. I was just caught in the moment.'

For a brief moment she held her breath. She had had her hand held recently by someone who wasn't her husband, and *she* had been caught up by a strong emotion that she had found both endearing and acceptable.

'Will you speak to my father about Hannah?' she asked more reasonably. 'Ask him not to dismiss her? Tell him that it wasn't her fault.'

For a second she thought he was going to refuse, to retreat

from making such an admission, and if he had done that she wouldn't have been able to forgive him, but he nodded. 'Yes. Whether he will agree, or even allow either of us back . . .' He shrugged. 'And if he doesn't I'm scuppered.'

'And so is she,' she added sharply, 'and it isn't her fault.'

'I'll go and talk to your father now. Should we both go?'

'What time does he leave the office? Is it still his old time of four o'clock?'

'Yes,' he muttered. 'He'll be home now.'

'All right, let's go now and get it over with, or we'll never sleep tonight, and neither will he.' She swung herself off the bed and reached for her shoes. 'Mother will be having a fit if he's told her. She hates anything unsavoury.'

He sighed as they went downstairs into the hall. 'He doesn't have to tell her.'

'You chose to tell me,' she pointed out.

'That's different. You had to know in case there were consequences; Hannah might have said . . .' He paused for a moment. 'Shall we eat out? We could book a table at the Beverley Arms.'

'I'm not dressed for dining out,' she said grumpily. 'We might see someone we know.' He gave a little laugh, which she thought sounded disparaging. 'We're hardly celebrating anything,' she said sharply. 'It's a matter of appeasement! Besides, all the local farmers will be there at this time. They won't want us littering up the place and taking their tables.'

He sighed. 'Whatever you say. You're the local.' From the coat stand he took a grey top hat, shorter than the usual one that he wore for his journey to the office, and offered her his arm. She gave a slight shake of her head. He'll have forgotten all about it in a couple of days, she mused; it will be a matter of no consequence.

Lydia drove, with Nicholas beside her mumbling something about getting a new pony and a bigger carriage, with a hood. She knew that he would prefer something smarter, such as a brougham or a two-wheeled chaise that he could drive with style, measuring up to his own estimation of his standing, but she was happy with the pony and trap for her shopping, or, she thought now, an occasional child or three.

Unusually, Lydia's mother opened the door to them when they arrived; she had heard the wheels on the drive, seen them from the front window, and forestalled their live-in maid, Dilys, whose duty it normally was.

'We just came out for a breath of air and thought we would drop in, Mama,' Lydia said, presenting her cheek for a brief kiss. 'It's such a lovely evening. We're not interrupting anything, are we?'

'Not at all.' Her mother leaned towards Nicholas, who bent down to take her hand and brush her cheek with a kiss. 'Come in, come in. Your papa is having a glass of sherry in the sitting room before supper. Will you join him?'

'Not for me, thank you,' Lydia said swiftly. 'Nicholas would like to, perhaps?'

'Thank you; I shall.'

He's always so kind with Mother, Lydia thought; such a charmer. She gave him a little nudge with her elbow. 'You wanted a word with Papa in any case, didn't you?'

'Oh, yes – yes, of course I did. Shall I . . .' He put out his hand towards the drawing-room door.

'Do go through, Nicholas. Lydia and I will bring the

sherry – or would you prefer tea, dear?' she asked as Lydia followed her through to the dining room.

'Yes, tea, please. Nicholas remembered he had a work matter to discuss with Papa, so I suggested we come out for a drive and call in.'

'He's so conscientious, isn't he?' Mrs Davenport lowered her voice. 'I do like to see that in a young man.'

Lydia nodded. 'Indeed,' she agreed. 'Yes, indeed.'

They stayed just long enough for Nicholas to drink a small glass of sherry with his father-in-law and Lydia her tea. As she rose to leave she raised her eyebrows in Nicholas's direction, and caught a subtle nod in return. 'I'll drive,' she told him as they waved goodbye. 'I think Frisky prefers it; he's used to me.' She paused for a moment before flicking the reins above the pony and moving on. 'So what did Papa say?'

'He said he didn't think that Hannah should have taken offence the way she did when he told her she mustn't give men any encouragement.'

'For heaven's sake! But he didn't tell her to leave immediately?'

'Apparently not, but he said she stormed out anyway. The thing is, he can't manage without her; none of us can. She knows where everything is.'

'You mean where the coffee and tea are kept, and so on?' she said sarcastically.

'No!' he said emphatically. 'She doesn't do any of that. The clerks have to do it themselves.'

'Poor things,' she scoffed, and then, instead of turning left for the road home, she turned right, towards the centre of the town.

'Where are you going?'

'We're going to see Hannah. We might as well get everything dealt with now, and be sure that she'll come back to the office tomorrow.'

'Oh, we could let her stew for a couple of days—'

'You won't say that if she doesn't turn up in the morning and goes looking for a more suitable position!' Lydia sounded furious. 'One where she's *appreciated*.'

'Do you even know where she lives?'

'Not exactly, but it's one of the houses in High Street, close to the Minster. Someone will know her.'

'I'll wait in the trap for you,' he mumbled, and Lydia, glancing at him, said coldly, 'No, you won't. You'll show yourself as a perfect gentleman who almost went astray.'

She pulled up in front of one of the terraced houses in High Street, got down from the trap, and fastened a long leading rein around the nearest lamppost. 'Come on,' she said to Nicholas. 'Let's knock on doors.'

He gave a reluctant sigh and she hid a smile and thought of young Ben, who did the same sometimes when he was asked to do something he didn't want to do.

She knocked on the nearest door and a young maid answered. 'I beg your pardon,' Lydia said. 'I'm looking for Miss Hannah Pearson. Have I come to the right house?'

The maid bobbed her knee. 'Next door, ma'am.'

'Thank you.' Lydia smiled. 'I'm sorry to have bothered you.'

'No bother at all, ma'am.' The maid bobbed again.

Lydia moved to the next door and rang the brass bell. 'Come on,' she whispered sharply to Nicholas. 'Look humble!'

He fixed her with a glance that she couldn't interpret, so she raised enquiring eyebrows at him.

'You're loving this, aren't you?' he hissed between clenched teeth as he came towards her.

'Actually, yes,' she murmured. 'The feeling of power is wonderful, isn't it? And to think that men have it all the time.'

He was unable to raise a reply, as the door was slowly opening to reveal a white-haired elderly woman. Nicholas took off his top hat and gave a short bow, and Lydia bent her knee. 'Good afternoon, Mrs Pearson,' she said. 'I'm sorry to intrude on your time, but my name is Lydia Mercer, and this is my husband Nicholas. I wonder if Miss Pearson is at home?'

'She is indeed.' Mrs Pearson smiled as if delighted to be greeting someone. 'She isn't usually at this hour, but she is today. Won't you come in?'

'Who is it, Mother?' a voice, unmistakably Hannah's, called from an inner room. 'Don't be inviting anyone in.'

'It's Lydia and Nicholas Mercer,' Lydia called. 'We won't keep you long.'

Hannah came through to greet them. 'I'm sorry,' she said. 'It's just that Mother invites everyone in. The butcher's boy was here one day when I arrived home, and he was on his second cup of tea with a slice of cake!'

'He was so delighted,' her mother interrupted. 'He said no one had ever invited him into their home before.'

'Well that's as may be, Mother, but he was delivering supplies, not visiting for afternoon tea.' She affectionately patted her mother's arm. 'But do come in, Lydia, and you too, Mr Mercer.' She glanced at her mother. 'Mr Mercer is here on a business matter. I'll see him in the sitting room.'

'Very well, dear, I'll be in the kitchen if you need me. Will you be having a pot of tea or a glass of sherry?'

'No thank you, Mrs Pearson,' Lydia swiftly answered for them all. 'It's very kind of you, but we're on our way home, so we won't detain you too long.' She followed Hannah and an uneasy-looking Nicholas into the room nearest the front door; a window covered by a lace curtain and hung with long heavy draperies at the sides overlooked the narrow street.

Two dining chairs were placed close to a small mahogany table near the window which was covered by a chenille-fringed cloth with a paraffin lamp in its centre, leaving space for an upright piano against the wall next to the door. A horsehair sofa and matching chair stood near the fire, which was unlit but held wood and coal laid ready for lighting.

'What a charming room,' Lydia commented. 'So cosy!'

Hannah Pearson nodded. 'Mother's doing. She's lived here most of her life, since her marriage to Papa.'

And here you live too, Lydia supposed. I wonder why. Clever, attractive, Hannah must have caught many a male eye. Did she choose her occupation; living at the beck and call of men? Do they pay her enough to make it worthwhile?

Nicholas cleared his throat. 'Hannah,' he said. 'I've come to apologize for the misunderstanding at the office.'

Hannah raised her eyebrows and glanced at Lydia, giving a slight shrug. 'What do I say?' she asked. 'Have you come to support your erring husband – make an excuse for his behaviour?'

Lydia considered for a second, and then said, 'No, neither of those things. But I am curious enough to ask if that kind of behaviour occurs often?'

'Not too often; not at the office, at least. I laid down a set of rules when I first joined your father's company. Sometimes older men are worse than younger ones.' She looked meaningfully at Lydia, who drew in a breath. Not Papa, surely! 'I was surprised, though, when Nicholas kissed my cheek,' Hannah went on frankly, 'though in all honesty I could have ended it with just a sharp word of admonishment if Mr Davenport hadn't come in and made such a fuss, and blamed *me*!'

Nicholas cleared his throat. 'I'm so sorry,' he said. 'Really sorry, Hannah, but self-control in the company of attractive young women is sometimes extremely difficult.'

'And you think it isn't the same for women when a handsome man is around?' Lydia broke in. 'Do you think that we don't notice men with charm and good looks?'

'We are more in control, obviously,' Hannah murmured, and both women laughed, leaving Nicholas totally confused. 'Shall we forget it ever happened?' Hannah asked him. 'Though perhaps you might warn the other men in the office that I am a woman to be reckoned with and don't give my favours to everyone.'

'Yes please,' he said fervently.

A few minutes later both Lydia and Nicholas sighed in relief as they got back into the trap. 'She certainly is a woman to be reckoned with,' Lydia commented. 'She's right – it would be as well to let the other men know.'

'I reckon they are in the picture already,' Nicholas said lightly. 'As is your father.'

Mm, Lydia considered. I think that if Papa hadn't made such a fuss, Hannah would indeed have dealt with it herself and no harm done, but oh dear, what a to-do when men and women have to be so careful of one another. She smiled a little to herself that she had conquered her own particular battle and negotiated a truce over her friendship with Matthew Wade. She was delighted that she had done it, for she valued his company immensely.

CHAPTER SIXTEEN

Nicholas was whistling the next morning; Lydia could hear him from downstairs as she made coffee whilst Cook was frying bacon and eggs. She went into the hall and called up to tell him breakfast was almost ready.

He's in a good mood this morning, she thought as they sat together in the sunny dining room; quite different from how he'd been yesterday. He'd talked to her father to sort out the misdemeanour of the day, and it seemed that her father hadn't taken the incident quite as seriously as Nicholas had reckoned. Lydia guessed that the blame had been laid firmly at Hannah's door, which she considered quite unfair.

'Don't worry about it,' Nicholas had said airily as they'd trotted home after talking to Hannah. 'Hannah knows how to look after herself,' which had aroused Lydia's suspicions once again.

He left at his usual time and she saw him off at the door as always; she put their breakfast dishes on a tray for Maggie to take away and then prepared the table for the children as before, by setting out books, slates, pencils and chalk, pots of water and large sheets of thicker paper in preparation for painting and crayoning. Maggie put her head round the door and said she would change the bedsheets upstairs and leave them for the laundry woman, clean the bathroom, then tidy and dust the bedrooms. Lydia nodded her agreement.

Matthew brought the children as he had done the day before, only this time they arrived in a small wagon, driven by the *owd hoss* he had previously described; he carried Baby Mary on his shoulders but left Aaron asleep and wrapped up in a basket in the wagon, because Lottie hadn't yet arrived.

'Would you like to leave Mary here?' Lydia asked. 'I'm sure we'll manage. I have some books she can look at.' He agreed, and said he would come back for her after he'd been to see the man who wanted a shed.

'If you're all really good and eager to listen and learn,' Lydia told the children after Matthew had gone, 'I'll ask your father if I can arrange a treat for you.'

Hands were raised with questions of what the treat would be, especially from Lily, but Lydia wouldn't be drawn to tell, instead asking them to concentrate really hard and recite the alphabet to her before they began any reading. They were quite excited at the prospect of reading a story, which seemed to be their favourite lesson of all.

They had a break at mid-morning, and at lunchtime she asked them to straighten up their work very neatly and leave it on the table. Alice and Lily spread a tablecloth outside on the grass and Ben and Charlie went into the kitchen to fetch cutlery, plates, and coloured paper table napkins which Lydia had bought specially for them.

Cook had made flans and Lydia had mixed a salad – of

which only the tomatoes were eaten – and then there was cake, as well as scones and lemonade.

Alice sat Baby Mary on her knee and fed her with small pieces of bread and butter, giving her sips of milk from a glass. She also offered her some cold crushed boiled egg, which she immediately spat out. Lydia took the child from her so that Alice could eat unimpeded. 'How old is Mary now?' she asked.

Lily and Charlie looked up. '*Baby* Mary,' Lily responded. 'Our ma was Mary.'

'But she's growing very fast, isn't she? She can walk and chatter now, and you have Aaron who *is* still a baby.' She paused. 'Perhaps she would like to be just Mary now that she's bigger, do you think? She must be nearly two – she's a proper little girl.' Lydia teased her fingers through Mary's reddish curls. 'Do you think she would like a pretty dress?'

Baby Mary was still wearing the other children's hand-me-downs: mainly bloomers that were always falling down, but also a short-sleeved vest and woolly jacket that Lydia guessed had been knitted by her mother or Alice.

'Yes, she would.' Ben answered for everybody. 'She's one and a half years old, I fink. Them clothes she's wearing used to be mine, and then Lily and Charlie had 'em after me.'

'In that case, I think we'll have to go shopping.' Lydia smiled at Alice and lifted her eyebrows in Lily's direction.

'I don't want to go shopping,' Ben said quickly. 'I'm going to be very busy.'

'I am too,' said Charlie. 'I'm going to help Da saw some wood for that shed, if he gets 'job.'

'Well, young ladies,' Lydia smiled at Alice and Lily, 'it looks like an outing just for us, but not today,' she added hastily. 'Does Mary have a perambulator, or a chair with wheels that we could take? She's too heavy to carry and it will be too far for her to walk.'

The girls were silent. Lily wore a puzzled frown, and Alice shook her head. 'No, Mrs Mercer, we don't. We've never had need of one afore.'

Which means that they haven't been anywhere, Lydia pondered, or if they have the youngest has always been carried. Would these children be considered to have been deprived? They seem to be well rounded, intelligent and bright, even though they have spent most of their lives in their own home and garden. I think that could be why Ben is always so eager to ride in the trap with me, and Alice was so thrilled to go to Beverley. 'Well, we don't need one today,' she said, 'as we aren't going anywhere, but I might know someone who could help us out in future.' Once more she had her sights fixed on Emily.

Matthew came back to collect Mary with a huge beam on his face. He gave a thumbs-up when Lydia asked him whether he had spoken to the people who wanted a shed. 'They're new to 'village – Cherry Burton, I mean. They've onny just moved in so will want shelves and cupboards for their kitchen; he wants the shed cos he's setting up as a gardener – veg and stuff, not cutting grass – though I'm guessing he'll do that whilst he's waiting for his crops to grow.'

'Is he young, then, if he's only just starting up?'

'In his early thirties, I'd guess. He's inherited some money, apparently, and always wanted to be a gardener, so he and his wife bought a plot o' land, though 'cottage is rented.' He rubbed his bristly beard. 'I'm going to suggest that Lottie's young fellow goes to see him to ask if there's a chance of a job.'

Lydia smiled and nodded; she was always intrigued by the way that opportunities opened up in the country villages: there was always someone who knew someone who could offer an advantage they had been waiting for.

'I'd like to take the children to Bishop Burton to meet the Horners' babies,' she told him. 'We'll take Mary too, if you can spare her. It will give them a chance to mix with other children, though yours are older, of course, and I'm going to ask if we might borrow a perambulator.'

'A perambulator!' he repeated. 'Whatever for?'

'*Whoever* for,' she corrected him, with a sly smile. 'Your daughters and I are going shopping in Beverley on Saturday, and I thought we'd take Mary. Ben and Charlie don't want to come.'

Lydia saw his raised eyebrows. 'Well no, of course not,' he said. 'They wouldn't want to unless there was ice cream or cake.'

'We'll bring them something back,' she said. 'We're going to buy Mary a dress. Baby Mary,' she added swiftly, seeing a slight shadow cross his face. 'Is that all right? She's wearing hand-me-downs and they're far too big for her.'

'She's been neglected,' he said thickly, as if his throat had closed up.

'She hasn't been neglected in the slightest,' Lydia countered. 'She's had lots of love and she's happy with her sisters and brothers close by. It's just that she needs some clothes of her own; those she's wearing are not suitable for her. Don't worry,' she said quickly, seeing the gloom on his face. 'She doesn't care and she won't remember, but she'll look so sweet in a dress of her own – and Alice has knitted some woolly jumpers to sell, which she says will pay for clothes for Mary; we know where we can find bargains.'

She felt that Matthew wouldn't want her to buy practical things such as clothes for his children, and she didn't want to demean him by offering; it had been Alice's idea that they should call on the stallholder in Wednesday Market who had been interested in her knitting, and Alice had been very industrious since their last visit.

Matthew gave a suspicious frown. 'You're not turning my daughters into businesswomen, are you?'

'Would I do such a thing, Mr Wade?' she parried. 'Certainly not. Well, maybe just Alice! She has a lot of talent; but I will ensure she's not exploited. She does her knitting in her own time and at her own pace.'

'All right,' he said. 'I trust you to keep them safe.'

Lydia nodded; how hard it must be for him to put his trust in someone who wasn't family, and not to put pressure on his eldest daughter to watch over the other children when she was still a child herself.

'So is it all right if I take the children to see the Horners and their children on Friday? I won't, if you don't agree.'

'Of course you can. I wouldn't trust anyone else as much as I do you. I'm conscious, though, that we are taking up your precious time.'

'I offered, Matthew, it isn't as if you asked me. Besides, they are such a joy to be with, and I'm sure they will love the Horner family, who are free and easy with everyone.'

'That's true, they are, but will you remind Ben and Charlie to touch their fore'eads?' he said, a huge grin on his face.

'Of course,' she said, adding, tongue in cheek, 'and ask the girls to dip their knees; it goes without saying that we'll all do that!'

He spread the fingers of his right hand and held it towards her and she did the same with her left. Their fingertips touched briefly; Lydia felt a tingle that resonated through her arm, and she dropped her hand and laughed. 'Promise,' she said.

His eyes are definitely hazel, she thought as they shared a glance.

'Pact,' he said in return.

CHAPTER SEVENTEEN

Lydia called to the boys to put blankets and cushions in the trap for them all to sit on, and suggested to Alice that she take the seat beside her with Mary on her knee. She had brought exercise books and pencils for them, too, in case they saw anything interesting and would like to write it down.

'Yes,' Ben said excitedly. 'I'll write down 'names of any birds we see; there might be different ones where we're goin' to 'ones we have at home.'

'That's very true, Ben,' Lydia agreed. 'Shall I tell you where we're going, or would you like a surprise?'

They all agreed that they would like to know, except for Mary, who clapped her hands when the others cheered on hearing they were going to see some children in Bishop Burton.

'Are they 'bishop's children?' Lily asked. 'Is he like a chapel parson person?'

'No.' Lydia smiled as she waited for Charlie to fasten the gate behind them and scramble aboard. 'They are a farmer's children,' she went on, 'and the farmer's wife is a friend of mine. There used to be a bishop in the village once upon a time, but in the very distant past.'

'What does that mean?' Lily asked.

'Distant past? It means much longer ago than anyone remembers.'

'So how does anybody know?' Lily was curious.

'It would have been written down,' Lydia told her. 'That's why it's so important to learn to read; memories are very precious, and writing them down means that they will always be there for other people to read after the writer has died.'

Lily leaned towards her. 'So if I write down that we've travelled in a horse and trap for 'first time, somebody might see it in a book after I've died and gone to heaven, in a million years or somefink!'

'Some*thing*,' Lydia emphasized. 'Not *think*. Yes, that's right, Lily. Well done.'

'And if I write down that our ma died and went to heaven and then if I have some children when I'm big, they'd be able to read about her?'

'Yes, exactly, Lily,' Lydia said as they trotted on, 'and although you will always remember her' – she took a deep breath – 'as will Charlie and Ben and Alice, because you are all old enough to store your memories, Baby Mary . . .' she paused; it seemed appropriate in this instance to give the little girl back the name she had been generally known by, 'and Baby Aaron won't be able to, because they're too young to remember. But they'll get to know her through what you write.'

They drove on at a slow trot as they discussed memories, and then Alice cleared her throat, and when Lydia turned towards her she saw the slow trickle of tears on the child's cheek as she bent her head to brush them away on the top of Mary's bonnet. 'So, will you help us, Mrs Mercer?' Alice gulped. 'Would you help us to write a memory of our ma?'

'Of course I will, Alice,' she said gently. 'I would be delighted to. Writing a memory would be a lovely thing to do. Perhaps over the weekend you might all like to think of the happy things you remember about her – because you will all have different memories – and then we'll write them down on Monday when you have your next lesson.'

'I want to join in too,' Charlie broke in, 'but I'm not very good at writing yet.'

'We'll do it together, Charlie,' Lydia told him. 'You can think of the best things you remember and I'll help you choose the words you like best.'

'When?' Lily asked eagerly. 'When can we start?'

'As soon as you like, Lily. Just write little stories as you remember them, in any order, and we'll begin on Monday. Tomorrow we are going out shopping – and here we are at the Horners' farm!'

A pair of small children staggered towards them across the lawn with the nursemaid hurrying after them. 'Boys,' she called. 'Wait. Stop!'

But the very small boys had no intention of stopping after seeing a trap full of possible playmates, so Lydia reined in and called to them. 'Simon! Edwin! Hello! Where's Mama?' Of course, they can't talk yet, she told herself, or maybe the elder one can, but I don't know which one he is. She turned to take Mary from Alice's arms so that she could help the other children down from the trap, but they jumped down anyway, Lily landing unsteadily on her knees but getting up again and not crying in spite of falling on gravel.

'We'll wash that off in a minute, Lily,' she told her. 'And no tears! How brave you are!'

Lizzie caught hold of the two boys and turned to Lydia. 'Beg pardon, ma'am. We'd only just come out when they heard the trap wheels. They're such a handful; they go off in different directions and I can't allus catch 'em.'

Lydia laughed and turned to Charlie and Lily. 'Can you remember when you were that age?' she asked. 'And just learning to walk?'

The twins shook their heads. 'No,' they said in unison, and Charlie added, 'They're like a double-yolked egg, aren't they, Mrs Mercer? Like Ben said.'

Lizzie looked up in astonishment. 'I've never heard them called that afore,' she said.

'Charlie and his sister are twins,' Lydia explained, watching the pair making friends with Simon and Edwin. 'I do believe Charlie thinks that all babies arrive in pairs, complete with shell!'

'Well, these two would have broken theirs on arrival,' Lizzie said. 'I've never known a child get into as much mischief as they do, and I've looked after a few!'

'They're not twins, Charlie,' Lydia informed him. 'They're just over a year apart, but they do look alike, don't they?'

'If you're visiting Mrs Horner, ma'am, she's in 'nursery with 'twins, just settling them down for an afternoon nap,' Lizzie called over her shoulder as she rushed to grab one of the escaping boys.

'We'll wait,' Lydia said, and asked her if she'd bring a wet flannel for Lily's knee while she watched over the children. Lily gazed at the toddlers as they ran about the lawn, with Ben and Charlie chasing after them and Alice looking on, holding Mary in her arms. Lydia felt a slight pang of loneliness drift over her and gave herself a reminder that although she did love being with the Wade children, she also enjoyed her freedom.

'Lydia! How lovely to see you.' Emily came down the steps to greet her. 'I thought you'd gone off somewhere today?' They touched cheeks. 'Come and sit down. It's a lovely day.' She led the way to a table on the lawn with a parasol over it and several chairs set around it, and Lydia followed.

'Jane's bringing tea,' Emily went on, 'and cake too, I expect. I told her we had company.'

'I thought I'd bring my pupils.' Lydia laughed. 'I'm giving them a change of location. I don't think they ever go far from their own garden; I hope you don't mind?'

'Not a bit. They'll be new faces for Simon and Edwin, who must get bored with my company all the time, even though Jane and Cook as well as Lizzie spend ages playing with them. I'm very lucky; I'd never cope on my own.'

Alice came across to them. 'Can I give Mary to you, Mrs Mercer, so I can keep an eye on 'children?' Though she was speaking to Lydia, she dipped her knee first to Emily.

Lydia took Mary from her, and Emily reached for the girl's hand and drew her towards her. 'I've heard about you,' she said. 'You're Alice, aren't you? The knitter?'

'Yes'm,' Alice answered shyly.

'Tomorrow, Alice and Lily and I are going to Beverley Market,' Lydia told Emily, 'and Alice is hoping to sell some of her knitted baby garments to one of the stallholders. *And* we're going to buy Mary a new dress.'

'Oh, I'll buy some baby clothes from you, Alice,' Emily broke in eagerly. 'We'll certainly need some warm jumpers for Simon and Edwin before winter, they're growing so fast.'

'I'll knit some for them, Mrs Horner,' Alice said shyly, 'but perhaps wait for a bit because they'll be bigger by then?'

'How very sensible you are,' Emily said admiringly. 'I'll take your advice, Alice. I was never very practical. And I suppose I'd better order something for the twins, too, and maybe some cot blankets for when they have separate cots? And what about . . .'

Emily went on at length until Alice drifted away on the pretext of looking after the children, who were wandering off in various directions, and then turned to Lydia. 'They'll be all right,' she told her. 'They won't come to any harm; we've no ponds for them to fall into, or barbed wire on the fences, or anything like that.'

'They're a worry when they're not your own children!' Lydia commented. 'Tell me, what did you mean when you said you thought I'd gone off somewhere?'

'Oh, erm . . .' Emily hesitated. 'Gideon went to Beverley railway station this morning to collect a parcel and thought he saw you and Nicholas boarding a Hull train – I wondered if you were having a day out somewhere?'

'No, he went off to the office as usual. If he was going to Hull on office business, I wouldn't have gone with him. Some of those meetings can drag on for hours.'

'It was about nine-ish, I think Gideon said – he thought that you were probably going shopping.'

'Alice,' Lydia called. 'Tell Ben and Charlie not to climb that tree.' She turned to Emily. 'Why would Gideon think that? You say he thought he'd seen me?'

Emily turned pink. 'It was probably someone who got on the train in front of Nicholas.'

'Who knows? But no, it wasn't me. I do take the train in to Hull sometimes, for a new hat, or maybe shoes . . .' She was rambling. 'But Beverley generally suits me for most purposes.'

Emily agreed, but somehow their conversation was stilted.

The children had a picnic on the grass. Lizzie produced a woollen blanket for them all to sit on and Jane brought out sandwiches and cake and lemonade, and then as a special treat she presented everyone with a bowl of ice cream. The Wade children's eyes opened wide when it was offered. 'When I'm rich,' Ben pronounced, licking his lips as he tasted it, 'I'm going to have ice cream every day!'

When they drove home later, Charlie said solemnly that this had been the best day of his life. Lily gazed at him but made no reply. She was the more thoughtful of the two; Charlie made snap decisions or came to instant conclusions, but Lily took her time to decide before she made any judgement. It was fascinating, Lydia thought. How was it that children's personalities could differ so much when they had been brought up by the same parents and lived in the same household? But even as she was analysing the children's disposition, she was aware that she was avoiding the subject of Gideon Horner's saying that he had seen Nicholas at the train station.

It was quite possible that he had caught a train into Hull to meet a client, but who was the woman Gideon had mentioned? Had Nicholas simply stepped back to allow a woman to enter the carriage first? That was the kind of thing he would do, as most gentlemen would. But a picture of Hannah came into her mind. She was taller than Lydia herself was, that was true, but only by an inch or two, and her hair was as dark as her own; from the rear they could have been mistaken for each other. But why, she asked herself, would her father's secretary be catching a train on a workday? Surely Gideon was mistaken. He was a charming, personable man who greeted everyone with the same bonhomie but, as she knew well, was incapable of remembering who was who, or where and when he had met them before. He used a different name for the household staff each day, according to Emily, and they answered to any designation he gave them.

That's it, she breathed, as later they drew up at the Wade cottage and Matthew came out of his workshop door. Gideon simply concluded, on recognizing Nicholas, that the woman in front of him would be me.

CHAPTER EIGHTEEN

'So there you are!' Matthew pretended to be stunned by their arrival. 'I thought that someone had stolen my children.' He let his lips quiver and took Mary into his arms.

'No. No!' The children raised their voices, all exclaiming that they had been out for a picnic and that they'd been to see the farmer's children. 'They're onny babbies, Da, not big like us,' Ben proclaimed. 'They kept running off and Charlie and me ran after 'em to bring 'em back. They've got a great big field to play in,' he added, talking about the Horners' lawn.

'They're bigger than Mary.' Charlie wanted to give his pennyworth of explanation too. 'Is it all right to call her Mary now she's walking? Mrs Mercer said it was.'

He looked quickly at Lydia, as if unsure who had the authority to make the decision, but she smiled and nodded at him. 'Of course,' his father said. 'She's growing faster every day – a proper little girl, isn't she? Not so much of a baby any more.'

Lily, not to be outdone, put in her piece about the new babies who were twins like her and Charlie. 'But they're both boys, Da, and look exactly 'same. They were asleep in their cot, one at each end.'

'Like peas in a pod, hey?' their father joked. Charlie seemed confused, chewing on his bottom lip and looking at Ben, which made Lydia laugh as she thought of them possibly comparing peas with the double-yolked eggs.

'It's good to see you laugh, Lydia,' Matthew said, his use of her name coming more easily to him now. 'I thought you seemed rather tense as you came in.' He handed Mary over to Alice, who said she would change her, and gave both Alice and Mary a kiss on their cheeks.

'I was – I am a little,' she murmured. 'But nothing to do with the children or the day; we've had a lovely time, haven't we, Lily? And . . .' She hesitated. Was she making plans without asking permission first? '. . . if it's all right by you, Mr Wade, arrangements are currently being made to go shopping in Beverley tomorrow. Only the girls, though.' She smiled. 'The boys don't want to come as seemingly they're very busy, but we could take Aaron if you can spare him; we have the use of a perambulator that Mr Horner will drop off here later today.'

'Oh, yes. I nearly forgot.' Lily jumped up and down. 'Da, we're going to Beverley tomorrow to buy Ba— Mary a new dress, so that she doesn't have to wear our old clouts.'

'Oh.' Matthew's face crumpled. 'Oh, my poor baby. She's been neglected, wearing cast-offs.'

'She hasn't been neglected in the least,' Lydia said indignantly. 'She's known an abundance of love, and that's worth far more than new clothes. But she will need them now that she's growing so quickly.'

Lily looked up, first at Lydia and then at her father. 'Will you come shopping with us one day, Da? Have you ever been to Beverley? It's not very far,' she said knowledgeably. 'Alice said it wasn't.'

'Yes, I do know Beverley. I've bought boots, shirts, trousers and a jacket there. Only not recently,' he added. He didn't say that he might go with them, but watched as Ben and Charlie slid away.

'When?' Lydia asked. 'When did you last visit Beverley?'

'Twelve years ago or thereabouts,' he answered wryly. 'To buy new clouts for a wedding.' He looked at her. 'Clothes in your language, Mrs Mercer. There was no need to visit trade places – I was working for someone else then, not for myself. The dream of being self-employed had not yet been born. But I do need more tools.' He gave her what she thought was a winsome smile. 'Maybe we'll all come with you one day.'

She hesitated, and then said softly, 'But might that upset the apple cart, Mr Wade?'

'Ah!' His face cleared. 'Of course. I was forgetting. For you, at least. I beg your pardon.'

'Take the boys with you to buy tools,' she suggested. 'Give them a dream they can follow.'

'Wade and Sons?'

'Charlie, for certain,' she agreed. 'Not sure about Ben – he might be looking in a different direction. His love of nature, especially birds, is striking. He'd need a good education, but he could learn and earn in a country house, or a stately home, perhaps? I think he's bound for something else: to study bird life or plants; be a naturalist.

'And then there's Aaron,' she went on, 'and you have Alice,

Lily and Mary to take care of you in your old age. But you will allow them to follow their own dreams and aspirations, won't you, Matthew? Allow your daughters to choose an occupation for themselves if they don't want to travel the long road of marriage and children? Lily could be an artist, and Alice *definitely* a designer of fashion – and who knows what Mary might do when the time comes for her to choose?'

He gazed at her, his eyebrows creased into a frown as he listened. 'Do you think I wouldn't?'

'I don't know,' she admitted. 'I only know that women and girls must be enabled to reach their full potential.' She sighed. 'I know it's a relatively new concept, but it is worthy, and I believe that many women are already making their own choices despite opposition.' She gave herself a shake. 'I'm sorry. I'm in my soapbox mood. My life might have changed somewhat today,' she added. 'We'll see.'

The children were drifting away, Lily towards the cottage door and Ben and Charlie racing for the joiner's shop, as it was now officially named. Matthew raised his voice. 'Don't touch anything!' Each boy lifted a thumb, and Matthew gave a broad smile. 'So what might have changed?' he asked, turning back to her.

'I have reason to think that my husband might not come home tonight!'

Matthew frowned. 'Is there a reason why you'd think that?'

Lydia shook her head. 'If he follows his usual routine he will come home.' She paused. 'But if for some reason he has decided to take another path . . .' she breathed deeply, 'then he won't.' She gazed into the middle distance, over the fence and down the road, not the way she would drive home. 'But nothing in life is set in stone, and if I'm honest . . .' her voice dropped to barely a whisper, and Matthew frowned as he listened but didn't speak, 'if I'm truly honest, I'm not entirely sure that I care.'

'What?'

'It's true there might have been a mistake,' she murmured, 'so I should perhaps go home and view the situation as I find it and then act accordingly.' She lifted the silver watch which was firmly clasped on her jacket lapel to look at the time, and gave a small sigh. Her mouth drooped.

'Shall I come with you?'

'No. No, thank you!' She blinked rapidly at his offer. 'This is something – or nothing – that I must do alone. I'll come for the girls in the morning.'

He shook his head. 'I'll bring them to you,' he said, 'and Mary and Aaron too if Horner brings the perambulator and it's not asking too much of you?'

'It isn't – not at all.'

When she arrived home and stepped down to open the gate, everything seemed to be as she had left it. There was no smoke from the chimney, no windows open, and the door was closed. The house seemed abandoned.

She led Frisky through the gate, and the donkey came up to the fence and began braying noisily. Frisky responded, whinnying happily. 'Well, that's good,' she said out loud as she unhitched the pony from the trap and opened the field gate to let him join his companion. 'I'm glad that at least there are two creatures here happy to welcome one another.'

She lifted the brick under which they kept the front door

keys and brought hers out, giving a small sigh as she unlocked the door and breathed in the lingering aroma of newly baked bread and wax polish. She thanked her lucky stars that she was fortunate enough to be able to afford domestic help. If Nicholas ever left – and why do I think that, she wondered, when I have no reason to assume anything just because Gideon Horner mentioned seeing him at the train station – but if it were so, well, what then?

She walked through the hall and into the kitchen, and it was as tidy as always; she could smell bread, and there on the table were golden loaves and 'bread cakes', as Cook called the soft buns with the golden-brown crusty tops, sitting on a wire tray with a white tea towel covering them.

I wonder how Nicholas would let me know if he was going to be late tonight, or held up with business, or – perhaps not coming home? He would have to tell me sooner or later.

She unbuttoned her jacket and returned to the hall to hang it on the coat stand, but left her hat on. She looked in the hall mirror, moving her head from side to side. Yes, it suits me, she thought.

Back in the kitchen, she shrugged her shoulders, thinking it wasn't as warm as usual, and opening the fire grate on the range she picked up the tongs and dropped in a few large pieces of coke and then two lumps of coal. This hasn't been mended since this morning, she thought. Luckily it hasn't burned out.

She half-filled the kettle and put it back on the hob, knowing she would have to wait quite a while before the water boiled. Emily's cook had packed her a bag of leftover sandwiches and she'd meant to leave them with the Wades, but she had forgotten that they were in the back of the trap and had brought them back with the rest of the bits and pieces they had taken to the Horners'. I haven't the energy to walk back to the Wades', she decided, so I'll eat them now. By tomorrow they'll be stale.

She took a cup, saucer and plate from the cupboard and placed them on a tray, leaving the teapot on the hob to warm. When the kettle whistled she made a pot of tea and sat on a kitchen stool to eat and drink, deciding that if Nicholas didn't come home she would skip a cooked meal. *I'm not hungry, and I'm sure Cook will have left either scones or biscuits in the larder.*

Maybe I might have become a lawyer had I been a man, she considered as she drank her tea, her mind drifting off at a tangent; some women study law for interest, though rarely for occupation. It is a long and hard road to follow with male opposition, and women can't gain a degree as men can. But, she reflected, I was always more inclined towards being a good listener rather than an achiever. What a good thing I had a rich papa, and have never had to earn a living, as some women are obliged to. Teaching, though, might have appealed, and would have been achievable had Nicholas not come along when he did.

I'm still wearing my hat. She got up from the stool and wandered back into the hall and up the stairs to her bedroom. Having flicked her hat on to the top of her wardrobe, she walked across the landing to the other bedroom and gazed about her. The window was slightly open, the bed neatly made; Maggie had plumped up the pillows and shaken the eiderdown and, she thought, dusted the top of the chest of drawers, where Lydia now saw a sealed envelope lying on top of a book.

Oh, please don't say she's leaving was her first thought as she picked up the envelope, but on turning it over she saw Maggie's scrawl on the back: *Found this on the bed, ma'am, on one of the pillows. Maggie.* 'What on earth was he thinking?' she said aloud. Leaving a note where the servants could see it! She was astonished at his indiscretion; surely he knew that Maggie made the beds and would have to move the envelope from the pillow to do so.

No paper knife lay handy, so she slit it open with a fingernail and read the contents. *Probably late home. In York. Lots on today, might stay over if we're late.*

What did that mean? More to do than usual? She scanned down the single sheet, feeling a slight sense of release, considering, as she had told Matthew, that she wasn't sure if she cared whether Nicholas came home or not. Clearly she did care, but there was nothing in the note she held that could not have been discussed when he'd arrived home the previous evening.

He often did tell her things that had occurred at the office, or were about to, and she was always interested in the day-to-day dealings of the law, just as she had been when her father had spoken of such things to her uninterested mother, whilst she as a young girl listened with flapping ears, eager for knowledge.

'Not even a full sheet of notepaper,' she huffed. 'Done in haste?' She glanced at the clock beside the bed; a quarter past six. She couldn't recall any of the train times from Hull, which would have been his penultimate stop no matter where he had been, but she thought there would be several at this time of day. It's not late in the scheme of things; people do get held up with last-minute discussions and so on – it's what happens. 'And who is we?' she mumbled. 'Does he mean if the meeting is late or if others from the office might be?'

She wandered downstairs again and into the living room; Maggie, who had still been here when she had left with the children, had been the last person in there and all was exactly as she would have left it. She sighed. She was prevaricating, she knew that. Why wasn't she worried about her husband's absence? If Emily hadn't mentioned Gideon's visit to the train station and the possible sighting of Nicholas, would she be concerned? Six twenty; still not late, but if Nicholas was going to a business meeting in York that might overrun, why didn't he mention it before he left this morning? Why write a note?

She stared out of the window, the envelope in her hand. He could have said something at breakfast. There was every opportunity, though he did seem to rush his porridge and said he didn't need anything more than that; no bacon or eggs, kippers or toast. The hackney driver was early too, so he had to dash away so as not to keep him waiting. He had dropped a brief kiss on the top of her head, murmuring, 'Must rush; lots on today.'

So do I expect him until I see him? What else can I do? Do I lock up for the evening? He hasn't actually said that he won't be home, just that he might be late. It's six thirty.

'Oh, jigger it,' she said out loud, turning away from the window. 'I'm going to lock up. He can knock if he comes, although I'll hear the hackney, I expect. I'll put on my house robe. No one will be calling at this time and it doesn't matter if anyone should. I'm perfectly decent. It's a lovely evening,' she went on, mumbling to herself. 'I might just step outside and enjoy the rest of the day. No, I won't. I'll warm some milk and put a drop of brandy in it and take a book upstairs. It's been a busy day with the children; they can be exhausting. I'll sleep well. Oh, no, Frisky and donkey Janet! They're still outside.' She grabbed the old coat that she wore in the garden and put it on, giving a big sigh. 'Stupid woman. What's wrong with you?'

She opened up the stable and took out feed for the animals, and then brought them in. 'Sorry,' she said, giving them both a pat before she left. 'I'm not at my best just now. I don't know why but I feel like crying, and yet I've had a lovely day.' Back indoors, she locked up again, put the fireguard in front of the fire, turned out the lights and went upstairs.

'Goodnight, house,' she murmured on a sigh.

CHAPTER NINETEEN

She read for a while, adjusting her pillows to support her neck and moving the oil lamp further away from the bed so that she didn't accidentally knock it over. Oil or candles, both were dangerous; in the winter a fire was lit in the grate so that there was more light as well as heat. In the streets of the old market town of Beverley, gas lamps had been installed for decades to keep the streets safe for pedestrians and other road users, but here in the country districts people out after darkness often carried an oil lamp or a slow-burning branch of wood to see their way down the lanes. Those of a nervous disposition only travelled when there was moonlight.

Tonight, a full moon with a pale pink glow was rising in the darkening sky and shining in through the gap in her curtains, which she had pulled apart to give her extra light as well as to show Nicholas, if he should come home, that she was awake; but it was now nine o'clock and he had not appeared and at this late hour she no longer expected him.

Am I anxious? she considered. No, not so much anxious as annoyed; has he given any thought to how I might feel? I could be nervous being alone at night. I'm not, she assured herself, but does Nicholas know that?

Did I lock both doors? She sat up and tried to remember. *I came in through the front door and locked it behind me.* Yes, I'm sure I did, she reassured herself, and I didn't go out at the back . . . did I? to top up the hay bags? No, of course not, I did that when I brought the animals in. And I locked the door again behind me.

But she was disturbed. *Perhaps I'll check. I must get into a routine of locking doors.*

She slid out of bed, picked up her dressing gown and put it on, pulling the hood over her head. I don't need a candle, she told herself; moonlight from the side window near the landing will show me the way down. She trod carefully in her bare feet, clutching the stair rail until she reached the hall floor. How lovely, she thought. Moonlight shone through the glass panel at the top of the front door and from the living-room window, glinting on various pieces of furniture, whilst outside apple tree branches swayed gently, their leafy tendrils shadow-dancing on the glass.

'I knew it,' she breathed as she checked the kitchen door. 'I had locked up; why did I think that I could have forgetten?' Usually, Nicholas locked the outer doors on retiring at night, but she always listened to hear the click of each lock.

She wandered into the living room and plumped up the cushions on the sofa, sighing softly. It was a lovely room, cosy and comfortable. Then she crossed the hall into the dining room. The silver candlesticks on the dining table had been a wedding present to her parents from Lydia's grandmother, and subsequently from her parents to herself and Nicholas, and were much cherished. Now they sat in the dark, and Lydia moved to open the curtains and let in a sliver of light to see them glint.

'Yes,' she sighed. 'I like it here.'

She turned down the oil lamp and listened to it pop-pop-popping, then climbed back into bed and fell asleep almost immediately. She woke at seven to the sound of birds chirping on the roof top. 'Ah,' she said aloud. 'It's Saturday, and we're going to Beverley. I'll write a note and leave it on the table for Nicholas in case he should deign to come home.'

I won't think of what I might do if he doesn't, she told herself as she made breakfast, boiling an egg and slicing bread for toasting. In fact I don't know why I should imagine that he won't, except that, in three years of marriage, never have I been unaware of where he was or might be. Is he still in York now, if in fact he went there at all? Papa might know – perhaps I'll call in on the way home. Would they want to see the children? Or not?

She took a breath and sighed it out. They won't approve, of course, and will wonder why I brought them into town. They'll be well behaved, 'the children, I mean,' she mumbled out loud. 'Alice is always polite; Lily will be curious and might ask questions, but it doesn't matter if she does.'

Matthew had said he'd bring the children to the house for nine o'clock, so she scurried about, clearing away her breakfast crockery and putting the dishes in a bowl of water in the sink to wash on her return.

I'll wear sensible boots, something comfortable, and though it isn't cold, perhaps I'll take a wool scarf with me. I wonder what Lily will wear. Alice has a coat, but I've never seen Lily in one; I'll take two scarves, three perhaps, just in case there's a chill breeze. She sighed again. 'What do I know of the wants of children?'

She was slipping into her coat when she heard the trundle of wagon wheels and opened the door to see Ben opening the gate to let Alice and Lily through; out in the lane Matthew was dropping down the tailgate of the wagon and sliding the perambulator wheels down what looked like two floorboards. Mm, she thought, I would never have thought of that.

'Good morning, Mrs Mercer,' Matthew called. 'You haven't changed your mind, have you?'

She stepped outside. 'No! Why would I?'

He walked towards her, pushing the baby carriage with Aaron propped up on a pillow and looking about him, and Mary sitting opposite him. 'Because it's quite a challenge,' he said, lowering his voice, 'to take on the care of someone else's children.'

She laughed. 'I think you're the one who might be nervous of letting them out of your sight, Mr Wade.'

He nodded and frowned, pinching his lips together. 'I think you might be right,' he muttered.

'I've had them in my care before, remember,' she assured him. 'There's nothing different about today. You needn't worry, and they're good children, they don't misbehave.'

She smiled at Alice, who she noticed was wearing her brooch fastened to her coat and clutching a very large and full bag, whilst Lily was hopping from one foot to another. 'We're going to have a lovely time, aren't we?'

They both nodded, Alice dipping her knee, and Mary from the pram gave a big shout of 'Dada'.

'Will you help me to put the pram in the trap, Matthew? And can we borrow those pieces of planking to slide it down? That way Alice and I will be able to manage getting it in and out again quite well.'

'You will,' he agreed. 'Alice has already had a practice run with it.'

'There's nothing that young lady can't do,' Lydia said approvingly. 'She is exceedingly capable.'

'She is,' he agreed. 'Come and help me get Mrs Mercer's pony and trap from the stable, Alice, and I'll show you how to handle the traces.'

Mary put her arms up to Lydia, indicating that she wanted lifting out of the pram, and as she obliged Lydia could smell soap on her skin and hair that told her the little girl had been bathed that morning. 'Mm, she smells nice,' she said to Lily. 'Come here. Do you smell lovely too?'

'Yes.' Lily came up to her and stood on tiptoe so that Lydia could sniff her hair. 'We all had a bath last night so's we'd smell nice for this morning.'

'Goodness, that must have taken ages! All of you?'

'Not Ben or Charlie,' Lily said. 'Da said that they could wait for another day, cos he'd have to pump out another bucket full o' water, and it takes ages to heat up on 'fire!'

'Of course it does,' Lydia agreed. *Every day I realize how lucky I am to have these so-called luxuries, which should be available to everyone.*

Alice held the pony's reins as she walked back leading Frisky. The donkey looked over the fence and watched them.

'Oh, poor donkey,' Lily said. 'I fink he wants to come wiv us.'

'Well, she can't,' Lydia said firmly, stressing the s. 'She

would hate it. A donkey does not like shopping. She'll be quite happy here as long as she's got her hay and barley straw.'

Matthew watched as Lydia and Alice pushed the pram up the homemade ramp and gave a thumbs-up signal to them. 'Well done,' he said. 'Pushing it up is the hardest; you won't have a problem bringing it down as long as there's only one child in it – then it's not too heavy.'

He's nervous, Lydia thought, and of course he is, letting his children go off with someone who hasn't had children of her own. I suppose it was easier with just Alice, but now, with two babies and Lily as well, indeed I'm an absolute beginner. Have I taken on more than I can manage?

Alice sat in the trap with the pram, Mary sitting on her knee, and Lily sat on the driver's seat next to Lydia and waved to her twin and her father as they set off, leaving them to close Lydia's gate and wave goodbye.

'I'm really excited,' Lily said. 'It's an adventure, isn't it?'

'Yes, I suppose it is,' Lydia agreed, 'if it's something you haven't done before.'

'I wish Charlie had come,' Lily said seriously. 'He'll be wishing he'd come. He likes to be wiv me.'

'I understand, Lily,' Lydia said. 'But sometimes it's nice to do different things and then you can tell each other about them; and would Charlie really like shopping?'

'No, he wouldn't. He'll like to be wiv Ben and our da cos they're going to make fings, and he would be bored wiv us. That's what he said, anyway.'

Lydia laughed silently. So that's the difference between male and female: the male likes to be doing, making his mark, and women do too but don't always have the opportunity. She marvelled at this little girl sitting beside her, who was able to articulate with reasoning exactly the difference between them.

She decided not to leave the trap in her father's office yard. There was no lock on the gate and the office would be empty on a Saturday. There'd be no one there to watch the pony and trap, and though Beverley was a safe town she would worry about leaving them. I'll drive into the yard at the Beverley Arms, she decided. My father is known there and I'm sure they'll find a stable for Frisky.

A stable hand who had worked there for years remembered her. 'Miss Davenport,' he greeted her. 'Oh, no! Of course not! Now what was it – Mrs . . . erm . . . my memory is not what it was!'

'Mercer,' she reminded him with a smile.

'Of course, of course, and this is your pony . . .'

'Not the same one, Harry,' she said, remembering the man's name just in time. 'This one is Frisky, by name and nature. And don't be thinking these are all my children.' She laughed gaily. 'I've borrowed them from a friend.'

Lily looked up. 'I'm Lily,' she said, 'and I'm a twin. My bruvver's called Charlie.'

'And this is Alice and Mary and Aaron,' Lydia told him, 'and we're going shopping, so may we leave Frisky in your care, please? We'll come back for lunch later on and collect him.'

He touched his cap. 'Of course,' he said. 'Anything for 'Davenports. How is your mother? I haven't seen her lately.'

After a few minutes of small talk he helped them down with the pram and they went on their way, Lydia holding Lily's hand and Alice pushing the pram, which now held Alice's large bag as well as Aaron and Mary. They continued down the busy Saturday Market, where crowds of shoppers were heading for the stalls where all manner of goods were being sold, from socks and shoes to cheese and jam.

'I'm assuming, Alice, that this bag contains your knitted goods?'

'Yes, Mrs Mercer. I've brought baby jackets and matching bloomers that I thought would suit baby boys. I measured Aaron, and made some a bit bigger as well.'

'Is Aaron wearing one of yours? And Mary too? That looks *very* sweet. I am most impressed, Alice. And what a good idea to dress them both to show off your work.'

'I'm wearing one as well,' Lily burst in, not wanting to be left out of the discussion. 'Mine's a cardy. Look, it's got pink flowers and a little pocket where I can put my handkerchief!'

'My word, Alice,' Lydia said admiringly. 'How clever you are.' The market stalls in Wednesday Market were just ahead. 'So are you ready to sell? Do you know your prices?'

Alice pressed her lips together. 'Yes, Mrs Mercer. Da worked out 'prices with me, taking what I'd spent on wool into account. And he said not to tell anyone that it's my work, or somebody might try to – erm – barter me down. That means to sell it to them cheaper, he said.'

'He's quite right, Alice. Exactly what I would have said. And because we're partners now, I think you may all call me Miss Lydia. Right. Let's go and see what we can sell!'

They found the stall immediately, and it was the same stall-holder. She recognized them at once.

'Oh,' she exclaimed. 'I'm really glad to see you! Have you brought any woollens?'

'We have,' Lydia said. 'Our friend the knitter has packed them all in this bag for you to look at.' Alice lifted the bag on to the counter and began to lay out the knitwear on the stall. 'As you will see,' Lydia continued, 'these rather special ones are being worn by the children: our baby, our toddler and our smart young lady here.' Lily looked up at the stallholder and held out her arms so that the cardigan she was wearing could be seen properly, and then turned round to show the back, which made Lydia smile.

The stallholder gave a small gasp. 'I won't be able to afford all of 'em,' she said. 'Not all at once.'

Lydia nodded. 'I do understand, but the knitter has a family to support too.' She appeared to consider. 'For a small deposit, I'm sure she would keep some garments on one side for you.'

The woman nodded, then turned, put two fingers to her lips, and whistled. Lydia glanced at Alice for approval, and Alice nodded and gave a little smile.

A man came rushing up. 'What's up,' he said brusquely. He was thickset and carried a canvas bag over his shoulder, and Lydia guessed that he might be in charge of the takings.

'Nowt up,' the woman said, 'but I need some money. I telled you, do you remember, that I'd be buying some woollen goods?'

The fellow looked at the clothes laid out on the stall and rubbed his chin as if assessing their worth. ''Ow much?'

Alice took a slip of notepaper from her coat pocket. 'They vary,' she said quietly. Her voice strengthened as her confidence grew. 'Some of 'garments are more difficult to knit, 'knitter said, and so they tek longer to make. But she's written down all of 'costings so you can see.'

'An 'ave all these been made specially for us?' The man frowned.

'Oh, no sir. She wouldn't expect . . .' She looked up at the woman who was watching her keenly. 'Mrs . . . ?'

'May,' the woman said. 'Mrs May.'

'There are others who are interested, Mrs May,' Lydia interrupted. 'Shopkeepers, not stallholders like yourself, but the knitter suggested we approach you first as you were among the first to ask about them.'

'Who else, then?' the fellow interrupted.

'I'm afraid I'm not privy to that,' Lydia said haughtily; 'and if I were I wouldn't discuss other people's business matters. That really would be beyond the pale!'

'Aye, all right then. 'Ave a look, Mrs May, and see what you can sell. Don't get owt too fancy – folks come 'ere for bargains, not fancy stuff.' He wandered off to stand outside an alehouse and took a pipe out of his pocket, but without filling it with tobacco and lighting it he just chewed on the stem as he watched them.

Lily stood on tiptoe and pulled on Lydia's coat. 'I don't like him,' she whispered. 'He's not very nice.'

Lydia nodded in agreement, and put her finger over her lips to whisper, 'I don't either, but he's watching over Mrs May to make sure that no one robs her.'

Lily inhaled. 'Oh! Is someone going to?'

Lydia shook her head. 'Not while he's there!'

Mrs May chose the garments that she knew would sell and

seemed happy with the price, though she had to whistle the man over again to ask for the money. He gave a sharp exclamation when she told him how much she wanted, but he handed it over.

'You'd better sell 'em,' he said brusquely, '*and* make a profit.'

'I will, Mr May,' the woman said, and gave Alice a sideways glance and a wink, which Alice didn't understand at all. 'I'll buy some more in a fortnight if I sell these,' she said in a low voice to Lydia as the transaction took place. 'Mebbe a couple o' cardies like 'little lass is wearing. I'm looking to upgrade, y'see, rather than sell second-hand; I'd like to buy new, cos young mothers that can afford 'em will definitely want them for their babbies.'

'I quite understand, Mrs May. I'll pass on your intentions to my knitter friend.'

They left the stall, and Lydia led them towards the café where she had taken Alice last time. 'Let's go for a cup of chocolate, shall we, and celebrate your success, and then we'll buy Mary a new dress and petticoat.'

Lydia lifted Mary from the pram and put her to the ground, Lily put her hand out to steady her, then Aaron too was picked up and handed to Alice, and Lydia manoeuvred the pram close to the window and put on the brake.

'Sit at the table in the window,' she said to Alice, 'then we can watch over the pram. You go inside too, Lily, with Mary if you can manage her, and choose a chair.' She didn't want the risk of anyone's stealing the pram; it was an expensive-looking one and rather desirable. With that in mind, she lifted out the bag with the remaining knitted garments and took them with her into the café. I'm exhausted, she thought. Child-minding is not for the faint-hearted. She sat down next to Lily, picked up Mary, and put her on her knee. A waitress came across to her. 'We have a nursery chair, Mrs Mercer. Shall I bring it over?'

'Oh yes, please, if you would.' She didn't know the young woman, but had seen Nancy, the owner, at the back of the café, and guessed that she had sent the young maid over to assist.

They manoeuvred Mary into the chair and the young maid gave her a wooden spoon, which the baby immediately began to bang on the tray. 'It's what my ma allus does,' the assistant said by way of explanation. 'She says it keeps 'em happy without mekkin' too much noise.'

'It's a wonderful idea,' Lydia responded, picking up a menu. 'For me a very large pot of tea, please, and for— Oh! Could you give us a moment, please?' She'd glanced towards Alice, who was sitting with her back to the window with Aaron on her knee. Outside, through the glass, were plant and flower stalls, with many people gathered about them and forming queues. One of the women in a queue was Mrs Pearson, and behind her was Hannah, who was looking straight across at Lydia and on catching her eye gave a big smile and waved her hand. Lydia saw her speak to her mother, who also looked at Lydia and gave her a wave. Then Hannah left the queue and came inside.

She came up close to the table and bent towards Lydia. 'I'm pleased that I've seen you, Mrs Mercer. Is Mr Mercer with you?'

'Wh-what? Nicholas? No. He's still away, isn't he?'

'Away where?' Hannah frowned.

'York, wasn't it?' Lydia began to feel uneasy. 'Didn't he go to York for a meeting yesterday?'

Straightening up, Hannah looked down at Lydia and shook her head. 'Not as far as I know,' she murmured, and then cast her eyes to where her mother was handing money to the stallkeeper. 'I have to take Mother home,' she said. 'Could I come back in about half an hour? If you haven't finished I'll wait for you.'

'Yes,' Lydia breathed. 'Of course.'

By the time they had ordered what they wanted with their tea and lemonade and milk for Aaron and Mary, half an hour had gone and Hannah was back. Lydia wanted to take the remaining woollies to a shop she thought might buy some of them, and also to look for a new dress for Mary, so Hannah said she would walk along with them.

'What's this about Nicholas being in York?' she asked. 'A meeting, you said?'

'That's what I understood. A friend of mine said he saw Nicholas boarding a train to Hull.' She didn't mention that there was possibly a woman with him.

'Why did you think he'd gone to York?'

Lydia was confused, but didn't want to admit that Nicholas hadn't told her anything in person, but had left a note. 'Erm, I thought that was what he said. Perhaps I misheard. Where else might he have gone?'

'I've no idea.' Hannah shook her head. 'We have no appointments out of town, apart from Hull, for at least another three weeks. And he can't have been attending at court; not on his own, at least.'

'Why not?' Lydia was uneasy.

'Because, erm, because he's not yet qualified to do so.'

Lydia gazed at her. 'I thought . . .' What was it that Nicholas had said – something about it being a crucial time for him? *I should have listened more closely*. 'Something else then,' she said lightheartedly, which wasn't at all how she was feeling. 'I'll have to wait for his return to find out.'

Hannah nodded. 'Indeed. Do let me know if there's a problem, Lydia. I can always speak to your father first if you'd like me to – break the ice, you know!'

'Yes, thank you. I am rather confused about it all.' She gave herself a mental shake. 'Here's the shop we want, Alice,' she said brightly, giving Hannah a cheery smile. 'We're shopping for a new dress for this lovely lady,' she added, bending to give Mary a tickle on her neck. 'I'll let you know what's happened as soon as Nicholas is back.' Hannah nodded and about-turned to walk back the way she'd come, and simply waved.

CHAPTER TWENTY

Lydia and the children called in at the children's clothes shop, and although Lydia was feeling decidedly confused, they chose a pretty dress for Mary with a little short-sleeved jacket to match it, and then they showed Alice's woollens and sold them all, to Alice's amazement.

They walked on then to the Beverley Arms and ate a light lunch of soup and sandwiches, after which Lily and Alice had a dish of ice cream, Alice looking about her at the old inn with great excitement and awe. They collected the pony and trap, and a young stable lad – not Harry, who was dealing with someone else – pushed the babies' pram up the ramp and into the trap with ease.

'Are you going to sit with me, Lily?' Lydia asked. 'You can wrap this blanket over your knees to keep you warm.'

Lily climbed up and leaned against her. 'I've had such a lovely day, Miss Lydia, 'best one I can remember, 'cept when my ma was here.'

Lydia stroked Lily's cheek: it was soft and warm. 'Your ma

would be so pleased that you were enjoying yourself, wouldn't she?'

Lily nodded as they trundled out of the yard. 'I fink so. She said she liked to hear us laugh. I haven't started my memory book yet – I might start it when we get home. I'll write down that we've had ice cream – will Ma ever have had ice cream, do you fink?'

'Oh yes, I expect so, but perhaps not very often, as it was expensive and not everyone could afford it.'

'Maybe the Queen could, and 'princesses, and people like that?'

'Yes! Exactly. And then more and more people liked it and wanted it and eventually it became more available because it was cheaper.' Lydia knew she was speaking above Lily's understanding, but thought that it did no harm if it increased her knowledge of words.

They turned towards their lane, driving past Lydia's house. There was no smoke issuing from the chimney; no one was at home.

'Has all gone well?' Matthew asked as he opened the gate for them on their return, leading Frisky in and unfastening the tailgate. 'Lydia, are you all right?'

'Oh, yes, indeed!' she said forcefully, although in truth she was feeling rather unsteady, which had nothing to do with the shopping, the selling or the buying of clothes for the children – which Alice had insisted that they do with the money she had made – and new socks and a bag of sweets each for Ben and Charlie.

'I think I'm rich, Miss Lydia, but I don't know what to buy

Da,' Alice had said plaintively as they'd sat in the inn's restaurant. 'And what can I buy for Aaron? He already has lots of wool jumpers.'

'A box of handkerchiefs for your father,' Lydia had suggested. 'Men are difficult to buy for. Or chocolate, maybe? And Aaron won't know about presents yet, but maybe something in cotton that can be easily washed?'

'Shall we go inside and you can tell me all about it,' Matthew said now. 'We've been busy too, haven't we, lads?' Both boys nodded, but they were keeping an eye open for what was in the shopping bag. Alice lifted it on to the table, and Lydia unclasped her handbag, took out an envelope and handed it to Alice. 'I think I'll trot along home,' she said, 'if you don't mind. I've got a headache hovering.'

'Oh, please stay,' Alice implored. 'Just until we've told Da about selling our woollens.'

'You sold some?' Matthew raised his eyebrows. 'Really? In Saturday Market?'

Lydia sat back. She didn't really have a headache but wanted to go home to think, for she had much to consider.

'Wednesday Market,' Alice said excitedly. 'There are two markets open on a Saturday. The lady at one of 'stalls said she'd been waiting for us to come and she bought some jumpers and baby cardies, and then we went into a shop that Miss Lydia knew, where they sold ladies' dresses and children's clothes so we bought things for Mary, and then they bought some of my little jumpers and paid more than 'lady on 'market stall.'

'Good heavens!' he exclaimed, and sat down to wait for more.

'There was a man there who was in charge of 'money,' Lily piped up. 'I didn't like him, but he gave Mrs May some money to pay Alice for 'fings that she'd knitted, and then Alice said she wanted to buy our lunch instead of letting Miss Lydia buy it like she wanted to.'

'Lunch!' Matthew exclaimed. 'Not dinner, then?'

Lily frowned. 'It was like dinner, 'cept that 'lady called it lunch. It was very nice,' she added. 'We had ice cream.'

'Oh!' Both boys gasped at having missed out on a treat.

'Next time,' Alice promised, 'you can come with us.'

'There'll be a next time?' Matthew murmured, glancing at Lydia.

'Seemingly so.' Lydia too spoke quietly. 'But we must be careful that Alice doesn't overdo things. She loves to knit, but it shouldn't become a chore.' She raised her voice. 'Are you going to show your father the contents of the envelope, Alice?'

Alice beamed, and handed the heavy envelope over to him. 'It's for you, Da, to buy things we need.'

Matt glanced at Lydia, weighing the envelope in his hand, and then looked back at Alice, slowly shaking his head as he opened it. 'It's your work, Alice, so it's your money, not mine.' He looked inside, looked up and blinked, and looked again. 'They gave you all this for your knitting?' He glanced at Alice and turned to murmur to Lydia, 'There's a week's wages in here!'

Alice nodded. 'Yes. And Mrs May wants more in two or three weeks if 'knitter can manage. We told her that she was very busy just now.' She giggled. 'Or Mrs Mercer did.'

Lydia nodded. 'I don't like to teach children or young

people subterfuge.' She lowered her voice. 'So on this occasion – well, I thought it best coming from me, and the knitter is busy, it's true, and she must have time for childhood.'

'I'm eleven, Miss Lydia.' Alice had heard her. 'I'm nearly grown up.'

'We've been very busy as well,' Charlie piped up. 'Haven't we, Ben?'

'Yeh, but we onny had time for some bread and dripping. We didn't have ice cream'n that,' Ben muttered.

'Another time, then,' Lydia agreed, and raised an eyebrow at Alice, who gasped, 'Oh, I nearly forgot.'

She delved into the shopping bag and brought out several parcels, one of which she carefully put on a plate, and then she gave each boy a paper bag. Ben opened his first. 'Chocolate drops,' he said, his eyes opened wide.

'Pear drops!' Charlie said, looking into his bag. 'And socks.'

'And cake,' Alice squealed, opening the bag on the plate, then handed a chocolate bar to her father. 'And that's for you, Da.'

'My word,' her father said, and Lydia thought that his eyes were moist. 'Riches, Alice. How very generous of you.'

'And – and what about Miss Lydia?' Charlie said. 'Has she got anyfink?'

'Yes.' Lydia smiled at this little boy who didn't want to see anyone left out of this conferring of gifts. 'Alice insisted on buying our lunch. She is a very kind and generous young lady. I think we should give her a big cheer.'

And that was what they did, and then Lily got up from her stool and gave her sister a kiss on her cheek and then Ben and Charlie too, and their father put out his arms and Alice slid into them. Lydia saw Alice's shoulders shaking and knew she should leave. This would be the most poignant time in the family's life since their mother had died. Perhaps Lily and Charlie wouldn't understand the significance of the moment, but Ben might, and Alice would certainly have memories sweeping across her as she entered a new world from which her mother was absent.

She picked up her bag and hat and slipped out of the room, turning slightly and touching her fingers to her lips as she went out of the door. She led the pony out of the yard and into the lane where she climbed into the trap, not looking back and therefore not seeing Matthew standing on the step watching her as she left.

Her thoughts were tangled and she was in a complete turmoil as she drove away, and had been since leaving Beverley. Now that she was alone she remembered more clearly just what had happened when Hannah had appeared in the Beverley Arms just as she and the children were finishing their lunch. 'I see you're very busy with your young friends,' she'd murmured, 'but may I have another quick word?' Lydia was surprised, but had asked Alice to stay with the children for a few minutes while she stepped outside with Hannah. 'Forgive me for this second intrusion, but we had been wondering, at the office,' Hannah had begun, 'if perhaps Nicholas was unwell.'

'Unwell?'

'His absence from his desk yesterday? Although I said that I thought you would have informed Mr Davenport if that were the case.'

'I – I understood that he might have had to stay over in York; something about the meeting overrunning? Something like that? I'm assuming that he'll be home today.'

Hannah had frowned. 'I make all the business appointments,' she said. 'As I told you, there were no appointments in York on Friday, or any day last week for that matter.'

'Oh! Would – could Nicholas have made an appointment himself with a client he was dealing with?' Lydia stammered.

Hannah shook her head. 'No, only through me,' she said steadily. 'That's the way we work. I make the appointments with the clients to free up the solicitors or clerks. Nicholas doesn't have individual appointments, only those with the solicitors when he sits in with them.'

'I don't understand,' Lydia murmured. 'He left me a note to say that he might be late, or maybe even stay over in York.' She struggled to recall what exactly Nicholas had said. 'I thought it might have been a company meeting?'

'No,' Hannah replied, frowning. 'I would have known. Nicholas didn't come in at all yesterday, and he left early on Thursday. That's why there was the worry that perhaps he was unwell.'

'He was not unwell when he left home yesterday morning,' Lydia said shakily. 'He was up early and his driver was early too, at least fifteen minutes earlier than usual. I was going out myself to visit a friend, and it wasn't until my return in the afternoon that I discovered the note he had left to say he might be late home.'

At first Hannah made no response, and then said quietly, 'I'm sorry, Lydia, but there's nothing I can possibly say to alleviate your anxiety. I don't understand why Nicholas would behave in such a way, and the only thing I can suggest is that you speak to Mr Davenport, who perhaps could throw light on the matter.'

My father is the last man I would speak to about a personal matter, Lydia thought now. He is always on the straight and narrow path. He knows nothing whatsoever about subterfuge, which, I fear, is what this is. Except – she drew in a sudden breath. Perhaps Hannah is referring to something else entirely, and that's why she is drawing away from the matter. Some kind of duplicity? Dishonesty? Surely the company doesn't deal in money. But finance, possibly?

No, she thought. Surely not!

CHAPTER TWENTY-ONE

She took Frisky into the stable and put him into his stall and then called to the donkey, who was at the furthest edge of the field and ignored her completely, so she trod slowly back to the house.

Bending to pick up her door key from its hiding place, she saw that Nicholas's key was still there so picked that up too. Clearly, he wasn't coming back today – or, if he did, then she'd respond to his knock and greet him as if he were a stranger.

When she opened the door it seemed as if everything was as she had left it, except for the smell of furniture polish, and a ham simmering in a large saucepan on a low heat in the kitchen. I'm not hungry, she thought, taking a cloth to lift the pan lid and seeing the water trembling, but I might be later.

She unfastened her coat and took off her hat and went back into the hall to hang both up. There was post trapped in the letter box.

Two envelopes: one she recognized immediately as a bill from the coal merchant and the other, unmistakably, was in

Nicholas's bold handwriting. Her name was scrawled in large dashing letters, proclaiming who had sent the letter.

'I can't deal with this right now,' she muttered. 'I've had a long day with the children and I don't want any more bad news, thank you very much.'

She threw the envelope on to the hall table and went upstairs to change into a house dress and slippers before going to stand looking out of the front window. A late afternoon sun was casting a rosy glow over the fields and woods opposite, and she could hear wood pigeons calling and birds chattering in the eaves.

'No matter what the letter contains, I'm not moving from here,' she muttered, and thought that she must check with her father about her status regarding the house if Nicholas was considering leaving. *But why am I thinking this? I'm becoming paranoid, but I know that something is not right.* There have been great strides in women's privileges, she pondered, her mind blundering from one thought to another, and here I am professing to be a worldly woman.

I might be totally wrong in my thinking, of course, she considered, my imagination perhaps getting the better of me; but I do know that a woman's position is tenuous if she is left or divorced. Why, though, hasn't Nicholas discussed any issues with me? Why is he keeping me in the dark as to where he is, and why he hasn't been into the office?

She jumped as the doorbell jangled. She hadn't heard the gate squeak as it usually did when it was opened.

She paused at the bottom of the stairs; it was still light, but who was outside?

'Hello!' she called. 'One moment please,' and waited.

'Mrs Mercer! It's Matthew Wade. I'm calling about that job you mentioned.'

She smiled. He was being cautious in case Nicholas was home. I've never mentioned a job of work. She unlocked the door and opened it; she trusted him completely.

He touched his forehead. 'Sorry to bother you, ma'am,' he said, looking over the top of her head and down the hall.

'Do come in, Mr Wade,' she said, seeing that Charlie was by his side. He's taking precautions by bringing a child with him, so there's no compromise, she realized. 'There's no one else at home. Won't you come through into the kitchen and have a cup of tea?'

He shook his head. 'Thank you, but no. I just wondered if you had arrived safely home after leaving us.'

'Of course. Perfectly safely, but thank you for your concern.'

'You're on edge, I think?' A small frown appeared just above his nose.

She nodded in agreement. She was; she couldn't deny it. 'Charlie?' She turned to the boy. 'There are some biscuits in a tin in the larder. Will you bring the tin out and put it on the kitchen table and we'll find a bag for you to take some biscuits home? You know which is the larder, don't you?'

'Yes, Miss Lydia,' he said eagerly, and shot off to the kitchen.

She turned to Matthew. 'I *am* in a state of unease. Nicholas has been away from home – I thought on business matters, but I discovered today that that isn't the case. I don't know where he is, but I found a letter awaiting me when I got home just now. I haven't yet opened it.' She pointed to the hall table. 'It's there, waiting for when I'm feeling brave enough to read the contents.'

'I see. I thought you were rather distracted.' He rubbed his short beard. 'Are you thinking it might be bad news?'

She swallowed. 'I don't know. I don't understand why Nicholas didn't tell me why he was going to York – for I understood that was where he had gone – and now I hear that he hasn't been into the office since leaving early on Thursday.'

His eyes narrowed. 'How do you know this?'

'I met my father's secretary in Beverley today and she asked me where he was, and was he ill. I hadn't an answer for either of those questions. I do know, however, that he was seen boarding a train yesterday morning at Beverley station.'

'Did the person who saw him know him well enough to recognize him?'

'It was Gideon Horner. He told Emily – Mrs Horner – that he'd seen Nicholas boarding the train . . . and . . . and he thought that I was with him because there was a woman quite near him.'

'It could have been another passenger, Lydia,' he murmured. 'Don't jump to conclusions.'

She nodded and took a breath. 'I did, of course, but now I realize that Gideon might have been mistaken; it could have been anyone, and some women do travel alone nowadays. The days of always having to travel with a companion or a maid are happily disappearing.'

He nodded. 'At last,' he agreed. 'But there are some who were always brave enough to defy convention, even though there were frowns of disapproval.'

'Would Mary have dared?'

'Mary had more freedom than ladies of your class, but she would never have gone on a train! She would have been afeared to do it, even if she could have afforded 'fare,' he added with a wistful smile.

'Of course.' Train travel was for everyone, but not always affordable, and the Wades had little money, as she had gathered as soon as she had met them. Things were looking up for the family, but sadly not for poor Mary.

'Would you – would you mind waiting whilst I open the letter?' she murmured as Charlie appeared with the biscuit tin clutched in his arms. 'Please do come through,' she added, rescuing the tin from Charlie as she saw it beginning to slip. 'Let's find a paper bag, Charlie. Look in the bottom drawer on the right, please.'

Matthew followed her into the kitchen and she slid the kettle back on to the hob. 'I will have a pot of tea after all,' she murmured. 'I might need it to give me strength once I've read this.'

Matthew picked up the kettle and poured a little hot water into the teapot, swirled it around and threw the water into the sink, then put the kettle back on the heat and reached up to take the tea caddy down from a shelf above.

'How did you know to do that?' She had never seen a man make tea before.

'What?' He grinned. 'Make tea? It's essential!'

'No, put hot water in the teapot.'

'You can't make a good cup o' tea without warming 'pot, Mrs Mercer. Everybody knows that, don't they, Charlie?'

Charlie nodded. ''Cept that I can't do it 'til I'm eight. That's 'magic number so's I don't scald myself!'

'Ah, of course,' Lydia agreed. 'I recall it well.' Which was a complete untruth, as she had never made tea until she was at least fourteen. Her mother wouldn't allow it.

Matthew held out the envelope that he'd picked up from the hall table and handed it to her. 'Your post, ma'am. Shall I make 'tea while you open it?'

A positive action on his part, and in any case she had asked him to wait, thinking that perhaps she might be glad that someone understood her position and would have some consideration for her if the contents of the letter were disturbing. I should just get on with it, she reflected. Why am I dithering? It's just a piece of paper with thoughts turned into words and might be innocuous after all. With the nail of her forefinger, she tore it open.

Matthew made the tea and waited a moment before stirring it and then pouring her a cup. He added milk and pushed it towards her, then joined Charlie by the open drawer to find a clean paper bag for the biscuits. 'Don't take them all,' he murmured to the boy. 'Just enough for one each, so how many is that?'

Charlie counted on his fingers. 'Alice, Ben, me and Lily and Mary and you, Da. That's six.' He peered into the tin and counted the biscuits. 'One left,' he cheered. 'That's for Miss Lydia.'

'Good lad,' his father said. Glancing up, he saw Lydia's lips moving as she read the letter. 'But I don't want one, thank you, so leave that for Miss Lydia for her morning cup.' Father and son stood up, and Charlie went to stand by the biscuit tin. His father handed him a paper bag. 'Put 'biscuits in 'bag, put 'tin away, and wait for me by 'front door,' he murmured. Charlie nodded, and with the empty biscuit tin in his hand went back to the larder to put the tin back on the shelf, carefully closing the door and locking it with the large iron key when he came out. He touched his forehead before opening the door into the hall. 'G'night, Miss Lydia,' he murmured, 'thank you for 'biscuits,' and backed out towards the front door.

'Well,' Lydia breathed, gazing at the letter. 'This could be life-changing.'

'The biscuits?'

She gave a weak smile, then shook her head. 'You need to go home, Matthew. Your children are waiting for you.'

'Can you cope?'

'For tonight, yes,' she told him. 'Tomorrow is another day and I'll need to speak to my father.'

'You know where I am if you need me, if there is anything I can do for you.'

'Yes,' she whispered, 'I know.' She seemed to be on the verge of saying more, but glanced towards the door into the hall and shook her head. 'Tomorrow,' she said. 'I don't want to rush into anything.'

He nodded. 'Wait for me at 'gate, Charlie. I'll onny be a minute.' He watched from the window as Charlie pulled over the catch on the gate and stood on the bottom rung to swing to and fro, then he turned to Lydia and took both of her hands in his, his thumbs gently stroking her skin. 'Lydia,' he said softly, 'I want you to know that I'm your friend. I hold you in 'greatest esteem and must tell you, if you don't already know, that you can trust me with any confidence . . .' he took a shallow breath, 'and with your life.' He bent his head and kissed her cheek. 'I ask for nothing from you, but I'm here if you need me.'

CHAPTER TWENTY-TWO

She didn't expect to sleep well, and she was right. She had climbed into bed with a cup of warm milk – into which she had slipped a teaspoon of brandy – but still she didn't sleep, and at midnight she read the letter once again.

Nicholas is leaving, but doesn't say why or what he expects me to do. He is suggesting that we live apart for six months, but doesn't say why or where. She gave a cynical humph. Well, I'm not going anywhere!

She looked at the letter again. He doesn't mention divorce. I'm so angry – I will have to speak to my father, even though I don't want to. I need to know my rights. I need to know about money, although I'm fairly sure he will have to support me. I wonder how that will work? I don't know – I don't know anything!

She had eventually fallen asleep, her nightlight melting away into a pool of wax in its deep container, and woken up at almost eight o'clock on Sunday morning. She slipped into her dressing gown and went downstairs to make a pot of coffee, carrying it back upstairs on a tray with a deep cup so that it didn't spill and placing it on the small table by the window. Sitting down, she wrapped a shawl around her shoulders and watched the day emerge from a blue sky partly covered with fluffy white cumulus cloud into golden sunshine.

'I'll drive to see Father today,' she murmured. 'No time like the present, even though he'll be furious with Nicholas. It doesn't seem as if he gave them any notice.' Surely Nicholas wouldn't just leave. He held a position of some standing; her father wouldn't give him a reference without knowing his reason for going.

Feeling restless, she climbed back into bed, taking the coffee cup with her, and nibbled on the biscuit that Charlie had left for her, smiling at the memory of the boy carefully counting them out so that everyone should receive one.

Then her mind drifted back to Matthew's calm words on leaving. It had taken all her strength not to slip into his arms to receive the comfort she knew he would give: comfort and strength, but nothing more; he would not presume. Yet she knew that if he had, undoubtedly she would have been tempted.

After a light breakfast she dressed in a smart blue dress with a long coat reaching her ankles, and searched in her wardrobe for a matching hat. 'And here we are,' she murmured. 'Pale grey with blue flowers on the brim, and the obligatory short veil.'

She turned her head this way and that and thought the hat looked appropriate – not too outlandish for a morning visit, but smart enough to show some boldness – then slipped on a pair of low-heeled boots and thought that anyone seeing her would never guess that she was seething with nerves just thinking of her father's reaction to her news.

She had opened the stable door earlier and pulled out the trap, and now she opened the gate to the field so that the donkey could wander in, whilst Frisky waited patiently for her to come back. I must find a lad to help me, she considered, gazing at the animals, who she thought needed grooming. Nicholas did it when he remembered, but was mostly unenthusiastic. She needed someone to fill the coal hod and stack the firewood, too. Maggie often filled the coal hod if she saw that it was nearly empty, but the task wasn't expected of her: not her role at all.

I might possibly have to think of some way to occupy myself. I'm teaching the lovely Wade children, but I will need more. I must begin to think of my future if it does not lie with Nicholas.

She locked the front door and pocketed both keys so that there was no entry to the house if Nicholas should return – unless, she thought, he had a spare. He could have had one cut unbeknown to her.

What am I thinking? she asked herself as she drove out of the gate and into the lane. He was entitled to come into the home they had shared for three years. She shook the reins. 'Trot on,' she called to Frisky, the one command that the pony obeyed instantly.

At least, I think he is. Her mind was churning. I don't know my rights; I thought I did but I have had no reason to question them until now. Papa will know: he drew up the paperwork relating to the house. On the other hand, her thought continued, what if Nicholas intends to come back? His letter was so vague.

As she approached the old town, she heard the bells of St Mary's, and then the Minster bells too. I love to hear them, she mused. Such a joyful sound, harmoniously blending, calling the parishioners to prayer. Mama might be at St Mary's service – I might find my father at home alone. He would not like to be disturbed, but it would be a good opportunity for a conversation.

The front door was unlocked and she stepped inside, calling, 'Papa, are you here?'

He came out of the sitting room in his slippers, a newspaper in his hand. 'Hm,' he grunted. 'I thought you'd call today. I said as much to your mother, and suggested she took herself off to church with some of her friends as I needed to talk to you.' He gave a big sigh. 'You'd better come through; I've asked for coffee. It will be here in a minute.'

She was surprised. She hadn't thought that her father would be so ready to talk to her alone, but she was grateful for it. If her mother knew what had happened, she would try to suggest ways of putting things right between her and Nicholas, whereas her father would tell her her options directly.

She took off her coat and draped it over a chair by the window. 'Does Mama know that Nicholas is away?'

'No.' He settled himself back into his chair. 'I felt there was no need to bother her.'

Didn't want to listen to her queries, he means. He's only interested in business matters at the office, and certainly not in any innuendo or gossip which is probably circulating among the staff. Nothing, she knew, would escape his eagle eye or ear, and nothing would slip through those impregnable walls to the outside world without risk of dismissal.

The housekeeper brought in a tray bearing a coffee pot and accoutrements ready for Lydia to pour, dipped her knee, and left, closing the door behind her.

'How've you been?' Mr Davenport asked abruptly. Lydia was taken by surprise, and paused in pouring the coffee. Her father rarely asked about her well-being.

'I'm well, thank you, Father. I hope you are too?'

'I'm a bit out of sorts over this dilemma, I must admit! It's not something I'm used to, a member of staff taking off without as much as – er – as a "do you mind, sir",' he added sharply. 'Just what is he up to?'

'I wish I knew,' she answered with the same irritability. 'I know nothing – *knew* nothing,' she emphasized, 'until a friend of mine said Nicholas was seen getting on to a Hull train on Friday! I discovered later that there was no business meeting in York on that day.'

'I know,' he said more quietly. 'I was informed. And have you heard anything since then?'

'I've received a letter.' She too lowered her voice, although it was unlikely that anyone else in the house could overhear their conversation. 'I've brought it with me.' She reached for her handbag. 'Nicholas has suggested that we live apart for a while – six months, he proposed.'

'What? I've never heard of such a thing! Are you having disagreements? Every married couple has them at some time, you know; it's part of getting to know each other.' He frowned, and added as she handed the letter to him, 'Though you're hardly newlyweds, are you?'

'No, we are not, but perhaps we are incompatible. We are not always in agreement over some matters.'

'What sort of matters?' he grunted as he began to read the single page. 'Personal, do you mean? If that's the case then you must speak of it – to each other, I mean,' he added hastily. 'Not to anyone else.'

'We would not in any event discuss personal matters with anyone else, even if we had them, which we have not,' she answered abruptly. 'At least I haven't, and Nicholas has never suggested that he has either.' She clamped her lips together. How ridiculous, she thought. What a ridiculous notion – that we might discuss personal matters with anyone else. We never would, and *never* with our parents, if that's what's worrying him. Heaven forbid!

'It will be up to you to agree with his suggestions, of course, whatever they are. Or at least, in most instances between man and wife the woman must defer to her husband; men have more understanding of life than women have. Unless, of course,' he humphed, clearing his throat, 'what he suggests is something abhorrent to you.'

'Because women have smaller brains, is that it, Father?' she said mockingly. 'I have read that comment in a comic paper.' Her father looked at her, a frown above his shaggy eyebrows, not sure if she was joking or not, which she wasn't.

'Well,' she went on, taking a sip of coffee. 'If *you* haven't any idea of where he is, and I haven't in the least, I might as well go home and see what happens next. I'm assuming that you will dismiss him if he does return.'

'Well, probably, unless he has a good reason for not saying where he has been, such as, say, a medical problem that rendered him too ill to return to the office.'

'But you would assume that if that were the case someone

would have informed me, his wife, so that I would know where he was? But it still doesn't explain why he left the house *and* the office without telling either of us.' She took the letter from him and began to read it aloud. '"My dear Lydia, I'm so sorry I haven't been in touch for a few days, but important matters have occurred of which I cannot speak. I suggest we take a six-month break from each other's company until they have been resolved." I have no idea what these important matters are,' she told her father, 'but I would like to know what I should do about them. Might I lose the house if he leaves me?'

'No,' he said firmly. 'There's no fear of that. The house is in your mother's name, so he has no influence there.' She gave a relieved sigh; that had been her one great fear.

'And our joint bank account?'

'Draw out your own money and put it under your bed, or in your handbag, and spend his. That is the law: he must maintain you even if he leaves you, which he hasn't; he is temporarily away from home. Hm,' he grunted disparagingly. 'Some senior lawyer he'd make, forgetting about something as simple as that.'

'So, if I want to employ someone to help in the garden, say, or on other work, I can use his money to pay them, and other everyday matters? If there is any money,' she added.

'Yes, but be careful not to bankrupt him! There won't be any salary going into the account. Does he have another source of income?'

'I wouldn't know. I'm just a woman – "I don't know about money matters,"' she simpered sarcastically. '"My brain is much smaller than his."'

Her father looked at her and frowned. 'If ever Hannah should leave her position in my office I'd employ you, Lydia, but doubt if I would have as much control over you as I do over Hannah.'

She almost laughed. That was the funniest remark she had heard in an age. Would she share it with Hannah the next time she saw her? I'm not sure, she thought, and then considered that Hannah was clever enough to manipulate the men in the office, including her employer, without their knowing; she also knew that Hannah was sufficiently sharp never to let her fellow workers know that she was aware that she was much more intelligent than they gave her credit for, and was paid well for it.

CHAPTER TWENTY-THREE

Lydia felt reassured after speaking to her father, by actually having a proper conversation with him about the rights that women did and didn't have once they married. Best of all was knowing that she wouldn't lose the house. But her father had more to say.

'However, I will need to question why Mercer – erm, Nicholas has taken leave of absence from my employ without so much as a word; if everyone acted in such a manner the company would collapse. I must have trust in my employees – which is what he is, regardless of marrying into my family. I will not make any exceptions.' He tapped his fingers around his mouth, a clear sign to Lydia that he hadn't yet finished. 'Do you think . . . well, it seems preposterous, but is it possible that he has had his head turned by some pretty little woman? Though I wouldn't know when he might have had the opportunity.' He cleared his throat. 'Unfortunately, I'm not sure your mother could advise you on such matters; on the whole she has lived a sheltered life, I'm happy to say.'

She felt a fondness overcoming her for both him and her

mother. They were far from being old, but they had been brought up by their parents to believe in dignity and grace and would never accept misconduct in anyone within their family or circle of friends; and yet, she considered, her father had thrown the ball back into the lap of some 'pretty little woman', as if the man concerned were incapable of breaking the rules of etiquette himself.

She got up to leave. 'I won't wait for Mama.' She dropped a kiss on his forehead. 'I'll call again to see her. Thank you, Papa. I feel much easier in my mind after listening to your advice. I'll give Nicholas time to come home and explain where he has been; perhaps he has had something bothering him which he didn't feel he could share with either of us. I won't rush into anything.'

Which is a complete lie, she thought as her father rose from his chair and she picked up her handbag to leave. For I will call in to see our bank manager next week and ask to see our account. I'll then transfer my share to another bank – one which doesn't know Nicholas. There are several in Beverley that I might use.

Her father came out to close the gate behind her as she turned the pony's head towards the town. There were no shops or banks open as it was Sunday, but as she passed beneath North Bar and neared St Mary's church she saw her mother and two other ladies crossing the road and heading towards the Beverley Arms. She gave a little chuckle. Coffee and cake, she thought. Her mother would enjoy that, in fact she probably suggested it, as she was leading the way up the steps to the hotel entrance. Her mother knew what she liked. She had no ambition as her daughter had of making her mark on the world. She was content with what she had, and Lydia's father was exactly the right husband for her.

Lydia sighed. Why wasn't she like her mother, or any of those chattering ladies who went through those doors, content to enjoy the smaller things of life such as good company and laughter. Is that what some husbands offered? Had she somehow taken the wrong direction by wanting more out of life? Nicholas obviously didn't understand her. So is that my fault, or his, or perhaps neither of us – or, she thought for a second, perhaps we are totally wrong for one another. Did we rush into marriage? I hadn't thought so, but perhaps he thought I was a good catch as my father was in the same profession. Had he spotted a swift way up the ladder?

She dismissed her thoughts and urged the pony on, heading towards the Minster, not for morning service, which would be over, but to call once again on Hannah. She might be at church, she thought, or perhaps walking with her mother, but we'll see. She is someone I can speak to, Lydia considered. A few years older than I am, and I'd guess with more knowledge of the world than I have. Perhaps a better education, too.

Hannah opened the door to her ring. She was wearing her outdoor coat, but on the point of taking it off. 'Come in, come in,' she said warmly. 'I have this minute returned from collecting Mother from church. I give her time to chat to her friends there, for she's been attending Sunday service since time immemorial.'

'It's very easy walking distance.'

'It is. I believe that is why my parents bought this cottage!' Hannah led the way into the sitting room Lydia had previously admired. 'Father wasn't a regular attendee, but Mother always has been.' She raised her eyebrows. 'I rarely atend myself, although I like to go at Christmas. I've been invited to join the choir, but I didn't want the commitment.' Shrugging off her coat, she said, 'Do take a seat and I'll make coffee. Mother baked earlier this morning and made scones, which I can heartily recommend.'

Lydia smiled. 'Thank you, you're very kind. I don't want to intrude on your Sunday but thought I'd put you in the picture regarding Nicholas. I've had a letter from him, and I've just come from speaking to my father.'

Hannah nodded. 'Then do please take a seat. The Sunday newspapers are there, if you'd like to trawl through them, and I expect Mother will join you.' She smiled, and Lydia thought how attractive she was when she did, which wasn't often; whenever they had met Hannah had been mostly solemn. *Perhaps because we meet only rarely – and she works for my father.*

Mrs Pearson came in and greeted Lydia warmly. 'No, please don't get up! These chairs are very deep, aren't they? I often have difficulty getting out of them.' She sat down herself, facing Lydia. 'Hannah and I generally have coffee at this time, after she collects me from church.' She leaned forward. 'Sometimes I have a sherry too,' she confided, as if it were a treat she shouldn't speak about. 'Perhaps you might join me. It's rather nice with coffee, and you're going to try my scones, I hear.'

'I'm looking forward to trying your scones, Mrs Pearson,' Lydia replied, 'but I won't have sherry, thank you. I'm driving the pony, and although I'm sure he knows the way home, he just might take short cuts if he thinks he's in charge!'

'Have you ever travelled by train, Miss Davenport?' Mrs Pearson began, and then stopped short. 'Oh – I do beg your pardon. You are not Miss Davenport, are you? You are . . . I forget sometimes when young ladies grow up, I'm afraid. I recall your wedding day. Not so long ago, is it, since you married that nice young man? Hannah took me to the church to see you – she knows I like to watch a wedding.'

Hannah pushed the door open with her foot and Lydia got up to help her, clearing a small table of a vase of flowers so that she could put the tray down. 'I was just saying, Hannah,' said her mother, 'we went to see a bride at St Mary's a year or two ago, didn't we? I can't remember whose wedding it was. Was it someone we knew?'

'We've seen a few, Mother,' Hannah said, straightening up. 'Practically all the weddings at the Minster!' She smiled at Lydia. 'We're usually there before the bride, or Mother is,' she said. 'She does love a wedding, although her only daughter doesn't!' She laughed, but not unkindly. 'We can hear the bells of St Mary's from here, you see, so it's hat and coat on and off we go to watch it, no matter who it is.'

'I think perhaps you were talking about mine, Mrs Pearson,' Lydia said, 'to Nicholas Mercer. You did meet him briefly when we called one day.'

'Oh, did I? Well, it was very nice of you both to call. We don't have a lot of visitors, but I'm able to watch people go by. Many of them visit the Minster: it's a very fine building.'

She sipped on her coffee, and Hannah broke in to ask Lydia if there was any news to impart. 'You had received a letter, I believe you said. Did that throw any light on where the writer might be?'

Lydia acknowledged Hannah's avoidance of mentioning Nicholas's name with a nod. Second nature, she imagined, considering the work ethic in a professional company. 'None,' she said. 'Except that it was posted in York. That city keeps cropping up.'

'A fine city,' Hannah responded. 'I lived there for a while. I attended Bedford College in London and then applied to teach in a York school. I was there for two years, but then,' she lowered her voice, 'my father became ill and I was needed at home, and coincidently the position of secretary came up at Davenport's and as my father knew yours' – her eyebrows rose – 'I applied and was accepted. I organized the office and took on more duties; I'm very methodical, and I earned a much better salary, so I was able to look after both my parents. Sadly, my father died the following year, but I was here for Mother.'

Lydia glanced at Mrs Pearson, who was looking out of the window, now and again raising a hand to a passer-by. 'You haven't regretted it?' she questioned in a low voice.

'Sometimes I do. But there are snags in every industry or profession, aren't there? I did love to teach. There's so much pleasure in teaching a child and seeing the light of understanding shining in their eyes.'

Lydia nodded, a germ of an idea hovering in her subconscious. 'Yes,' she agreed. 'The children you saw with me in Beverley yesterday – my neighbour's – I've been teaching them to read.' She lowered her voice. 'Their mother died in childbirth not long ago. She used to read to them, I understand; they are incredible children. There are six of them, but two are still babies – or at least the new one is – but the local school is closed and their father is trying to make a living as a joiner. I just wanted to help if I could. I'm not a trained teacher,' she added, 'but I have always liked to read and I thought it might occupy them – take away some of the sadness. The eldest daughter, as you saw, is still a child herself, but she looks after her siblings, and does some of the housework too. She is very talented, and never complains about the chores.'

'Poor things,' Hannah murmured. 'That is so very sad. What does Mr Mercer think about you teaching them?'

'I don't know. I didn't actually ask him,' Lydia confessed. 'Should I have done? I still have my own mind *despite* being married.'

Hannah laughed. 'Some women I know always ask their husbands' advice before making a decision! It's not funny, I know, but I realized what was expected of me when I had a suitor. He didn't stay around very long after I had explained what I wanted. It didn't match his picture of the ideal woman!'

CHAPTER TWENTY-FOUR

When Lydia gave serious thought to the problem of Nicholas, she was still unsure of how to proceed even after talking to her father and Hannah. Hannah was a woman who did exactly what she wanted. She told Lydia that she often travelled alone, mainly to Paris or Rome but to Austria and Germany too. 'Discoveries' was how she described the excursions: not holidays, but tours of historical sites, castles and art galleries, mountains and rivers, not stays in places where one was expected to laze under a parasol. Nor did she take the waters of a spa, or chat to strangers about the weather.

She confessed that she avoided people as much as she could, unless she found a companion with similar tastes, but she wasn't one for idle chatter and didn't mind being alone. 'I come back completely refreshed,' she'd said. Her mother's sister would come to stay whilst she was away and they ate out every day, sometimes at the Beverley Arms or a local café. They visited the Minster and St Mary's church, and if the weather was clement they took short walks on Westwood Common, wearing rubber boots to avoid the cattle pats, for the beasts there had right of way over people on foot, or driving drays or carriages.

'I'm not brave enough to travel alone,' Lydia had confessed. 'Too sheltered as a child. Yet I feel like an independent woman, or at least I did until I married Nicholas. Now I'm unsure.'

Lydia pondered on this as she made her way home, and mused that she herself wouldn't be able to do everything alone. She had faithful help in the house, but would need assistance for the menial labours that Nicholas had always taken care of – grudgingly, perhaps, and with a bad grace sometimes, as he organized workmen for outside, grass cutting in the paddock, ordering feed for the animals and so on. I'm sinking, she thought. What am I to do?

I'll ask Matthew, she thought; he'll know of someone. Will he think I'm a nuisance? But above all, I must make myself useful, prove myself in some way. I'll continue teaching the children to read if Matthew would like me to. There's still nothing happening with the closed schools – and what was it that Hannah said? Something that struck a chord. She had been a teacher, a fully trained teacher. Lydia sighed. Not like me, she thought, trained for nothing. My education was a waste of time and energy. I'm hardly going to make my mark in any capacity, and yet I want to.

She let the pony into the paddock and noted that he needed a good brush to brighten up his coat, which was matted in places where he had been rolling in the grass. She hadn't groomed either of the animals for several days, and she chastised herself for the neglect. I will change my coat and boots and go now to talk to Matthew, she decided. No time like the present.

She had reached the door with the keys in her hand when she heard the crunch of gravel. She pulled in a breath, and turned quickly. 'Matthew!' she said. He had Ben by his side. 'And Ben! How lovely. I was about to come and see you all.'

'I wanted to ask you sumfink, Miss Lydia,' Ben burst out, and she wanted to gather him up and give him a hug, but his father wagged a finger at him.

'Manners,' he said, but mildly, and Ben drew himself up.

'We wanted to ask if you have any jobs we could do for you. Me and Charlie, but mainly me cos I'm older than Charlie. It's a change from reading.' Lydia's eyebrows rose and she put her head on one side in a query. Matthew mouthed something to Ben, who took a breath and said, 'I mean – in *hexchange* for reading.'

'Ah, I see! Of course,' she smiled. 'In exchange for teaching you to read? Well, that's *very* kind of you to offer, Ben. Thank you. I'm sure there might be something; as a matter of fact' – she glanced at Matthew – 'I was about to walk down to your house to discuss the very same subject. Perhaps if you'd like to come in whilst I change my footwear and my coat . . . or you could take a look around outside,' she said, looking at Ben. 'See if there's anything that you think needs doing, and that you could manage.'

'I'll have a look,' the boy said, standing tall. 'See if there's owt I can tackle,' and he marched off towards the stable.

'I think he's already bored with joinery.' Matthew had lifted his battered hat in greeting, and now gave a broad smile. 'He asked if he could come and see you to ask if there was anything he could do for you, because you lived alone.' She looked up sharply, and he shook his head. 'That didn't come from me, Lydia; but possibly from Alice or Lily?'

She gave a slight nod. They were very bright little girls; had they overheard some of the conversation between herself and Hannah? Something about Nicholas not being at home? It was possible, she thought, but of no matter. Neither child would understand the significance of the discussion.

'Do come in, Matthew. There was – is – something I'd like to discuss with you. Once again I need your advice – and Ben's too, it seems!' She hung up her coat and led the way into the kitchen, where she reached for the kettle and pulled out a chair at the table. Matthew could sit whilst she asked him for advice.

'I've realized that whilst I am temporarily without a husband' – she kept her voice light, yet not flippant – 'and have no idea when Nicholas might return, I cannot fulfil all the tasks that need to be done by myself. The household chores are not a problem, as I have a cook and a housemaid, but I really need someone to fill the coal buckets and bring them inside, to scythe the grass in the paddock, and not least to groom Frisky and Janet and clean out the stable.'

She began to feel overwhelmed as she made a mental list of all the tasks that needed attention, including cleaning the outside windows, and many more. Maggie was willing, but Lydia didn't want to overwork her and so maybe lose her. Who was the man who used to come and clean their windows?

Matthew raised his hands. 'I know how much needs doing in a household,' he said placatingly, 'and I'd guess that Mr Mercer would probably have brought people in to do a lot of it.'

And he did, she thought, but I don't recall any names. We used to have a lad from one of the villages. What happened to him?

'I'll ask around,' Matthew went on. 'I can't think of anyone in our small hamlet, but mebbe your friend in Bishop Burton might know of someone. Meanwhile, are you still keen to teach my children to read?'

'Yes, I am,' she answered at once. 'I need to do something. I can't just sit at home all day; I need something to occupy my mind before it goes stale.' She gave herself a shake. 'Do you think the children are benefiting from it, or do you think it's not enough, which of course it isn't,' she confessed. 'They need more stimulation, and teaching on other subjects too, which sadly I can't give them. They have brothers and sisters, but they also need the company of other children, and the schools are still closed because there aren't enough teachers.'

He sighed. 'They're country children. In a few years' time they will be working on farms, helping with 'harvest and earning a copper or two, the lads at least, and mebbe Alice too. It's what country children do. It's what I did; it's what is expected of us.'

'But don't you want more for them?' She dropped her voice as she heard the front door latch open.

'In here, Ben,' Matthew called, before returning to his conversation with Lydia. 'Yes, I do, I sincerely do, but how? I've heard that Leconfield might be opening again. I could take them now that I've got a hoss and cart; I'd fit them in between jobs, which I'm pleased to say are increasing.'

Lydia was about to answer when Ben came in and put his

hand on his father's arm. 'Da, there's a blackbird's nest in 'hedge at 'back of missus's garden. There're three eggs in it. Isn't it a bit late for hatching?'

'No. Spring to July, but this might be 'last,' his father told him. 'You'll mebbe have to bring some bits of apple or dig up some worms to help them out.'

'Can I do that, Miss Lydia, please? You'll be able to watch 'young birds fly from this window when they're fledged.'

'I will, won't I?' she said. 'I'd like that. There aren't any cats about, are there?'

'No,' Ben said, 'but you'll have to watch out for sparrowhawks and magpies as well. You can generally hear 'magpies coming, but sparrowhawks swoop down and you can barely hear 'em 'cept for 'swoosh of their wings, and they'll catch little birds.'

'We don't want that, do we? So I'll watch out for them,' she promised. 'Did you find anything that you could do here?'

'Yes, I fink so,' he nodded, and she thought he looked so much like his father, with his sincere expression. 'I can sweep out 'stable and chuck out some of 'old straw bedding. We'll have to order more, though; 'pony won't want to lie on 'brick.'

'I'll see to it immediately,' she promised. 'Thank you very much, Ben. It's *very* kind of you to think of me.'

'We can get 'straw bedding, Ben,' Matthew said. 'It'll save Mrs Mercer 'bother. We'll see to it first thing tomorrow with a farmer I know, and mebbe you can start tomorrow afternoon? Will you want Charlie to give you a hand?'

Ben chewed on his lip. 'Mm, not sure,' he said. 'Sometimes he messes about.'

'He's not as old as you,' his father said in mitigation. 'But he does like to help.'

'Do you not want a reading practice tomorrow?' Lydia asked. She was intrigued by the way Matthew held conversations with his children, giving them the opportunity to make decisions and yet guiding them in the right direction.

'Could I come in 'morning for reading and I'll do other jobs in 'afternoon?' Ben directed the question at Lydia, but glanced at his father for approval.

They both nodded. Lydia didn't comment, but a vague idea was swirling about in her head. She was thinking of what Matthew had said about country children working on farms during harvest time. That would mean they would miss even more schooling. Would they ever catch up on their education? And what about city and town children? How would they ever learn? Or perhaps they wouldn't. Of course, some town children could go to the Ragged Schools if their parents could afford it. Those schools were set up in particular for town children living in poverty, but even if there were no fees, what if they hadn't shoes for their feet, or coats for their backs? And would their parents consider it more important that they worked and brought money home for food than learned to read or write?

Something must be done – surely will *be done. Can I help in even a small way? I don't really have the expertise to teach, having had no training, and besides, married women are not allowed to teach in a school. Jobs must only be offered to men or single women, not women who have a husband to support them.*

She glanced at Matthew, who was looking at her from over his cup. Should she run her crazy idea past him or let it simmer for a while? She was capable, she was sure, and she had some money to spare; maybe could even obtain a grant. What else could she do with her life?

CHAPTER TWENTY-FIVE

Am I clutching at straws? Am I capable of doing this? It's a huge project. Who can I consult? I'll need to speak to the bank – and my father too, to ask if he thinks it feasible. I don't think he'll approve.

Once again Lydia hadn't slept, and now she was wishing that she had run her idea past Matthew. But I must get up, she thought; Maggie and Cook will be here before long, and I don't want to be found in my night clothes. And the children will be coming, and I'm not prepared! How can I consider organizing a huge project when I can't get myself up in a morning?

Hurriedly, she washed and dressed and went downstairs to unlock the front door before Maggie and Cook arrived. She made tea and toast, both of which took a long time as the fire in the range was very low. She picked up the tongs and opened the range door to replenish the fire with coke and coal so that the oven would be hot when Cook came in. 'I'll ask her to bake scones and I'll have one for breakfast,' she muttered, 'and this afternoon, after the children have gone home, I'll drive into Beverley and speak to the bank manager.'

She outlined in her head the programme she was planning, for she would have to discuss it with Dawson. *I'll ask him for his approval; he has generally accepted my suggestions, and I'll move my dowry so that it will earn more interest than it does now. Nicholas always said leave it where it is in case we need it. But what did we ever need it for? We've never touched it. But I might need to touch it now. It might be of great use, and besides, it's mine.*

Matthew brought the children, carrying Aaron and with Mary on his shoulders. The toddler walked unsteadily when following the other children, trying to catch up and wanting to be with them, particularly trailing Alice, who always took her hand.

'Matthew,' she said as she greeted him, 'I have to finish a little earlier today; I need to drive into Beverley. Do you mind?'

'Of course I don't mind; you're doing me a huge favour by having 'children here. I'll collect them a bit earlier. Can I help you with anything?'

She hesitated. 'Erm, yes, but not just now. Maybe later when I'm back from Beverley. I might need your straightforward thinking.'

He nodded. 'Any news?'

'Not since the last message; that's one of the reasons why I'm going into Beverley.'

'Quite right. The not knowing has gone on long enough.' He frowned. 'You need to bring the matter to a head, not be dangling on a string! Maybe see a solicitor – ah, of course! Sorry, I was forgetting.'

'He's aware, but I don't want him involved. It doesn't seem right and he wouldn't like it; he would think it disgraceful – which it is. He would consider it as a slur on the family.'

'But not one of your making!'

'Nicholas married into our family,' she murmured, 'so the shadow has fallen on all of us, and ultimately some blame will land on me, even though I am the innocent party; that much I *do* know,' she clarified bitterly. Her parents would be horrified if Nicholas divorced her on whatever charge he might conjure up. They would consider it a complete disgrace and disaster.

'It would be better if he just went to live in another country if he doesn't want to be with me,' she muttered. 'No one knows where he is.'

'But what would your life be like if he went elsewhere?'

She shook her head. 'I don't know. I've never considered such a dilemma – why would I? But how I am expected to continue with my life in such a predicament escapes me.'

'Perhaps report him missing?'

'But he isn't.' She moved to hold Aaron as Matthew bent to let Mary down from his shoulders, and the little girl tottered off to join her siblings. 'He wouldn't have sent the letter if he wanted us to think he was gone for good, would he?' She could feel the anger building up at being put in such an untenable position, but she also felt defenceless and vulnerable.

Matthew changed the subject, deliberately, she thought. 'I'll pick 'bairns up at twelve; is that all right? Lottie and her mother are coming to my house this morning; Lottie will look after Aaron and her ma is coming to tidy round and do some washing.'

She smiled and nodded. 'You're managing,' she murmured. 'I'm so pleased, Matthew.'

He gently touched her cheek. His fingers were surprisingly soft, though firm. 'My thanks are due to you,' he said in a low voice. 'You've been my good luck charm.'

'I'm happy to know I can please someone,' she whispered, 'and I can't think of a more deserving person.'

She watched him as he went off at a fast walk, holding Aaron firmly and nuzzling into his neck; she could see Aaron waving his hands as if he was chortling. How quickly time is passing, she thought, and how much has changed! But I've come closer to the Wade children, who are such a delight, even while growing away from my own husband and he from me.

'Children,' she called, 'let's go inside. Shall we write in our memory book this morning, and then perhaps have a glass of milk or lemonade and a biscuit before your father comes for you at twelve?'

'Oh,' Ben said. 'I wanted to tell you that I saw two little owls last night.'

'Did you? Well, in that case we'll stop ten minutes before twelve so that you can tell us all about it; how exciting!'

'It's not *very* exciting,' Lily said contrarily. 'Owls always come out at night.'

'Well, it wasn't dark,' Ben argued, 'and Da said they were quite rare, and there were two of 'em. I reckon they were mates.'

'You mean mating,' Lily said.

'No I don't! I know what mating means and you don't,' Ben insisted, and Lydia hustled them inside.

'No arguing, please,' she said. 'We'll discuss this on another day. Go inside and find your places.'

They took their usual seats at the table, and Alice put her hand up. 'Miss Lydia,' she said quietly, 'is it all right if I knit while we're talking? I want to finish this cardy for Miss Lottie's little baby. She's going to need it now that 'weather's colder.' She lifted her pink knitting.

'That's so pretty, Alice. Of course you may. Ben, Lily and Charlie, please get out your memory books.'

'Baby Mary hasn't got one, Miss Lydia,' Charlie piped up.

'No, I realize that, Charlie, thank you. Mary has a colouring book instead.'

I can feel a headache coming on, she fretted. I should have cancelled this morning's lesson, but then if I were doing this for a living – she sighed – which I have to consider, then I couldn't just drop everything. Oh, heavens. What a dilemma.

Alice started them off by saying that she remembered sitting on the stairs with her father and Ben when her mother was giving birth to the twins. 'She'd had one of them,' she said, 'and Da went to 'bedroom door and Mrs Bower shouted at him to go away, but he wouldn't and went inside.' She giggled. 'And 'next thing was that we heard another babby cry. Do you remember that, Ben? You might not have – you were only little.'

Ben shook his head. 'No, I don't remember.' He gave a big sigh. 'But I knew they'd be trouble.'

Lydia hid a smile. She just loved these children, each separate personality so easy to see.

Maggie tapped on the door and opened it a crack. 'A visitor, ma'am.'

'Oh, not my mother,' Lydia breathed, and Maggie whispered, though there was no need, 'It's Mrs Horner, ma'am. Shall I invite her in? She has two little ones wi' her.'

'Yes, please, if you would; and could you bring some milk and lemonade and biscuits for everyone?' She turned back to the children. 'Whilst you are writing or drawing your thoughts, Maggie will bring you milk or lemonade, and I must speak to someone.'

'Is it our da?' Lily said, and Lydia put her finger to her lips and shook her head, intimating that she mustn't ask questions, and Lily looked sheepish and bent her head.

'Lydia,' Emily said, when she went through to greet her, 'I'm so sorry. I'd forgotten about the children being here.' Emily was holding her own older children, one in each arm, and Lydia laughed.

'Look at you,' she said. 'Motherhood really does become you.'

'Does it?' Emily said. 'I feel a wreck, but the nursemaid has a dreadful cold, so I sent her home. The other babes are fast asleep and I said I wouldn't be long; someone will hear them if they wake. How crazy are we with four young babies! I needed a break, so I thought I'd come and see if you're all right.'

'Well, no, I'm not, actually.' Lydia thought there was no point in prevaricating. 'Nicholas is still away.'

'Away where?' Emily asked. 'On business?'

'I don't know. Emily, can I come over to talk to you? I only have the children here until noon, and then I must drive to Beverley, but there's something I'd like to discuss with you. But not today. Could I come over tomorrow afternoon?'

'You're worn out!' Emily said consolingly. 'I'll come to you, today or tomorrow.'

'Tomorrow then, please, if I'm not being a nuisance.'

'You're not a nuisance at all. I'll leave you now; I can see you're busy with those dear children. I'll be so happy when mine are that age and I can play with them. Do take it easy, darling Lydia. Will Nicholas be home again soon?'

Lydia shook her head. 'I honestly can't say, Em. I don't know where he is – or even if he *is* coming back.'

Emily stared at her. 'What? Whatever do you mean, you don't know if he's coming back? Have you checked his wardrobe?'

Lydia stared back; she hadn't thought of that. Numbly, she shook her head. 'No!'

One of the boys began to wriggle and try to get out of his mother's arm. Emily shook her head. 'Then go now and check. I'll come again tomorrow afternoon. Go on, up with you. You need to know.' She blew a kiss and turned to leave just as Matthew arrived at the door to collect the children. Was it already twelve o'clock? Lydia wondered. Surely not.

'Come in, Matthew,' she called weakly. 'I must just slip upstairs for something.' She waved to Emily and turned to run upstairs, lifting her skirt and holding on to the banister rail, and headed towards Nicholas's bedroom. Did it seem like prying? she thought. But no, sometimes she looked to see if everything was tidy or if the window was open or closed. The room was tidy; Maggie had dusted in there when the envelope had been found. There would have been no need for her to go in again.

Slowly she pulled open the wardrobe door and looked inside. Pushed in as a bundle on the top shelf were a pair of casual narrow trousers and a wool jumper that he used for jobs outside; a cord waistcoat that had seen better days, and one of his two much-worn beaver hats. There were no tailed suits or silk top hats, no shirts, no plain daily wear or office clothing hanging on the rail, and no smart clothing either. The wardrobe was practically empty.

CHAPTER TWENTY-SIX

Lydia walked out of the bedroom in a daze, and stood at the top of the stairs holding on to the newel post. She could hear the chatter of the children talking to their father and his voice answering them, but didn't hear what they were saying. She felt weak-kneed and slightly dizzy.

This must mean that he's left for good, she thought. Was I supposed to look in there after reading the letter? I must read it again – I'm sure he didn't hint that that was what I should do. Where is it? Where is the letter? What did I do with it? I'm such a scatterbrain, I can't recall.

Matthew came out of the schoolroom, which was how she now thought of it, and looked up. 'The children are just collecting their belongings and we'll be off.' He paused. 'Are you all right?'

She stared down at him. 'I – I, erm, I'm not sure. I'm not ill, but I've had a shock.'

'Yes?' He put a foot on the bottom step. 'Can you come down? Hold on to 'banister rail and step down on to 'first step. That's it. Now wait a second. Tek a deep breath. Breathe in. Now let it out. That's it. Now tek another, breathe in, breathe out. Tek another breath and step down; lift the hem of your dress. Can you manage some more steps? Nice and easy; don't rush.'

Ben came out into the hall and stopped, watching, and then Alice, holding Mary by the hand, appeared and looked up. She reached for Ben and put Mary's hand in his before taking the bottom step up towards Lydia, glancing first at her father. Then another step, and another.

He nodded. 'Nice and easy,' he murmured. 'Don't rush.'

Lydia felt as if she were sleepwalking, but suddenly she took a breath and shrugged her shoulders and gave a shudder. 'Oh!' she breathed, and reached out for Alice's outstretched hand. 'I'm – so sorry. I don't know what came over me.' She put her other hand on the banister and together they slowly trod down the stairs until they reached the hall floor.

'Alice,' Matthew said quietly, 'would you bring Miss Lydia a glass of water, please? You know where things are kept. Lydia, sit down on 'stairs for a minute.'

She did as he said, and Ben sat down beside her and put his hand on hers. 'I'm being very silly, Ben,' she murmured. 'I'm sorry; I didn't mean to startle you.'

Charlie and Lily came out into the hall and stood looking at her. 'Don't you feel very well, Miss Lydia?' Lily asked. 'Sometimes I don't feel very well and want my ma, so I hold Charlie's hand and then I feel better.'

'You can hold it if you want, Miss Lydia,' Charlie said. 'Like Lily sez, she feels better when she does.' He stepped forward and held out his hand, and Lydia didn't know whether to laugh or cry. She reached out to him and took his hand in hers.

'Thank you very much, Charlie. I feel much better already for your kindness. Yours too, Ben and Alice,' she said as Alice came back with a glass of water. She took a sip and then looked up at Matthew. 'It looks like abandonment after all,' she said quietly, knowing that the children, except perhaps Alice, wouldn't understand what she meant. She took another sip of water. And nor did Matthew understand, for he frowned and put his head to one side. 'Have you received further correspondence?'

'No!' She gave a grunt of disgust. 'Just an empty wardrobe. What a farce! I could almost laugh, except it's not funny.' She handed the glass back to Alice and smiled at her. 'Thank you, Alice. What a reassuring person you are. Your manner is so comforting!'

Alice took the glass back into the kitchen, and Ben followed her. Lydia murmured to Matthew that she'd opened Nicholas's wardrobe and it was almost empty. 'I think he's left. Why else would he take all his clothes and a suitcase to carry them in?' She saw his lips move as he assimilated what she had said. 'He must have packed whilst I was asleep,' she went on. 'Perhaps left the case by the front door.'

'And you heard nothing?' His eyes roved the top of the stairs.

She breathed deeply, and wondered what he would think when she answered. 'We have separate bedrooms.'

'Ah! I see.'

He showed no emotion, no surprise, no raised eyebrows, just a slight nod of his head. 'Well, we'd better get out of your way, if you still intend driving to Beverley.'

'I do,' she said unsteadily. 'I must.' She swallowed. 'I – I would like to discuss something with you; a project, nothing to do with any other subject, except possibly a connection to what I have told you regarding a missing person.' Her eyes caught those of Alice, who was trying to put Mary's arm into the sleeve of her coat, but Alice dropped her gaze to her little sister.

'Curl up your fingers, Mary,' she said. 'Come on, stir up.'

Matthew hurried the children outside. 'Come along, come along. Miss Lydia is wanting to go out. Ben, come with me. We'll get the pony out and you can hitch him to the trap to save Miss Lydia a job.' He glanced up at the top window as they came back from the stables, and saw Lydia's arm reach out to close it.

Upstairs, Lydia sat down on her bed. Should I go to Beverley, or wait until I'm in a better frame of mind, she thought. But if I don't speak to Dawson today, then anything could happen. If Nicholas should happen to be in Beverley – or anywhere for that matter – would he have access to funds from our joint bank account, perhaps via telegraph? I don't know. There is only one way of finding out, so yes, I must go.

Quickly, she changed into a buttoned jacket and ankle-length skirt and took out of her cupboard a plain velvet hat with a low brim, which she thought looked very businesslike but also hid her face, which she was sure was showing her anxiety.

Locking the front door behind her, she unhooked Frisky's reins from the fence where Matthew had fastened them and climbed into the trap, driving out and leaving the gate open. She huffed out a breath. Will Dawson discuss banking matters with me? she wondered. Will he treat me like a little woman who knows nothing? Should I really talk to my father first? she pondered. He would advise, but would he approve of my scheme?

I know of only two people who would listen without prejudice: one is Emily, the other is Matthew, she realized. Perhaps I should speak to them both. Emily would speak from her heart, Matthew from practicality and caution, I'm sure of it. But he would encourage me if he thought the project would work. But it would need considerable planning; am I capable of that? I am full of ideas, but can I carry them through?

She drove into her father's office yard and unhooked the trap, then led the pony into a stable and closed the bottom door. Her father would know it was Frisky, and no one else to her knowledge used the stables. She thought she would go to the bank and see Dawson first, and then speak to her father when she came back. She looked through the office window as she passed but no one looked up, and she didn't see anyone she knew; the clerks were mostly strangers to her and she to them, and they were all engrossed in whatever they were doing.

The door of the bank was open when she arrived, and she stepped inside. Approaching the desk, she greeted the teller. 'Mrs Nicholas Mercer,' she told him. 'Is Mr Dawson available? I have something important to ask him.'

'I will enquire, Mrs Mercer. Would you care to take a seat whilst I find him?' He smiled, and, encouraged, she took a seat and tried to quell her anxiety. The teller came back almost immediately and, bowing politely, said, 'Mr Dawson will be with you in a matter of minutes, Mrs Mercer.' She thanked him gratefully.

She took off her gloves and put them into her handbag, feeling the need to have something to do, and glanced around. There was only one other person waiting, a man who stood near the desk, drumming on it with his fingers. Behind the desk a door opened and Dawson came out, caught sight of her and smiled, and came towards her.

'How very nice to see you, Mrs Mercer. I hope you are well?'

'Very well.' She smiled back. 'But in need of some advice.'

'Then you've come to the right place.' He gave a short bow. 'Do come along into my office. May I offer you coffee, or some other refreshment?'

She went through the door he indicated, saying, 'A glass of water would be most acceptable, thank you.' Her throat was dry and parched.

He drew out a chair for her and poured a glass of water from a covered jug. 'It's not often we see you, Mrs Mercer. We see Mr Mercer from time to time, though not recently.'

'He is away on business at present,' she murmured, and wondered why she was lying for him.

'We saw your father this morning. He looks very well.'

'I believe he is; he keeps in good health,' she replied, and wondered if there would be an end of the platitudes, and how she could begin to explain her reason for being here.

'Yes, indeed.' He took a breath and cleared his throat. 'He, erm, mentioned Mr Mercer, as a matter of fact, querying if we had seen him lately, but we hadn't. Not that we ever discuss our clients, except in general terms, of course.'

She nodded. 'My father is also very discreet,' she said. 'But occasionally he, erm . . .' She ran out of words; her father must be very anxious about her monetary predicament to have mentioned Nicholas here. 'Mr Dawson,' she said. 'May I speak frankly?'

'Of course,' he said. 'Whatever we discuss remains with me.' Seeing her hesitation, he added, 'Mr Davenport—' he cleared his throat, 'your father has told me of your husband's temporary absence and his own concern for your well-being.'

Dear Papa, she thought. I should have known that he would take steps to protect me, but I don't know if he can. I believe that what is mine is Nicholas's too, and I can do nothing at all about that. Except – perhaps I can. My father doesn't know everything about me.

'It is true that my husband has chosen to be out of reach for the time being. I have no fear for his safety; I believe this absence to be deliberate on his part. I am here today to ask your advice on two issues. One, has my husband moved any monies from our joint account to one in his own name only, and the other, can I move my dowry from that account to another in *my* name only?'

'There has been no movement on the account recently, Mrs Mercer, but as to your second question, no, you can't as things stand, but it does depend on the original arrangements, which I will look into. A dowry is a gift, in fact, intended to be shared between husband and wife in their new household. That is my understanding, but your father would know more about that, as well as exactly what was agreed at the time of your marriage. But to give you confidence that the money in your joint account won't all be removed or spent without your knowledge, we can create a new one under another name. Have you a need for an appreciable amount of money?'

She swallowed. 'I wouldn't wish to deprive my husband of his fair share if he is entitled to it, but yes, I do possibly need a considerable sum as security for a large project I have in mind, so should be grateful if you would create a new account.'

Dawson picked up a notepad and pen and drew an inkwell towards him. 'And what name shall we give this account, Mrs Mercer?'

She hesitated. *I haven't discussed this with anyone. Am I sure about it? Will it work?*

'As I said, I have a particular project in mind, Mr Dawson,' she told him. 'Something very dear to my heart. In short, I wish to open a dame school.' She took a short breath when she realized that this was the first time she had spoken of it. 'As yet I have no clear plan, but I wish to employ trained teachers, mainly married women, who are at present barred from teaching due to their marital status.'

Dawson nodded his head, pursing his lips, she thought, in interest and approval, and dipped his pen into the inkwell. 'And the name of the new account, Mrs Mercer?'

She took a deep breath. *Am I a complete idiot? Can I do this? Am I capable?* 'The Children's Academy, Mr Dawson, if you please.'

CHAPTER TWENTY-SEVEN

She walked out of the bank in a daze and along Toll Gavel, the ancient street where tolls were once collected from the market traders, and without looking left or right headed towards a coffee shop, not her usual one in Butcher Row as she didn't want to speak to anyone and the owner there was always very chatty, but a smaller one, tucked away in an out-of-the-way court that not everyone knew about.

'A cup of coffee, please, strong if you will,' she ordered as she took a seat in the empty café. However do they make a living? she wondered, but she was glad that it was quiet. She wanted to think, and contemplate the step she had just taken.

'Would you like cake, ma'am, freshly baked this morning?'

'Yes please,' she said, and wondered if she had had breakfast or lunch; maybe not, she thought. *Matthew brought the children early, and then – then stupidly I looked in the wardrobe in Nicholas's bedroom as Emily suggested, which completely wrecked my morning.*

She took a deep breath and sighed it out. Have I done the right thing? she wondered, the thoughts coming thick and fast. It's what I wanted, but can I manage it alone? I will have to ask for help; I'll need to add an extension on to the dining room, which is what I always wanted, so that the sunlight comes in to brighten it even more. Will Matthew know a builder? He must do, surely. He could perhaps do the window frames and fittings in the room. We'll need small desks and chairs, too. How many children am I considering? How much will it cost? Can I get sponsors? I'll need sufficient money to pay the teachers; they won't teach for nothing as I have been doing, but then I'm not trained. Reading to children and teaching them to read is not sufficient to call yourself a teacher.

'Thank you,' she murmured to the server who brought the coffee and a slice of sponge cake. I'm an innovator, she thought. I'm not a businesswoman – why did I think I was? I'll need someone to advise me on so many matters. I'm bursting with ideas, but—

'Hello!' A voice broke in on her thoughts as she put the cup to her lips. 'Good morning! I haven't seen you in here before.' She spilt coffee into the saucer as she hurriedly put the cup down.

'Oh, I'm sorry,' Hannah said, standing over her. 'I startled you. Are you having a quiet morning, or may I join you?'

'Oh, please do.' She removed her handbag from the other chair. 'This isn't my usual place, you're quite right, though I have been in a few times before. There's nothing I need from the Wednesday Market end, and as I've just been into the bank I thought I'd call in here before turning for home. I've left Frisky and the trap in the office yard. Are you here on office business?'

'No, I just felt as if I needed a break. We've had a hectic morning and your father disappeared for half an hour or so, so I thought I would too as soon as he returned.' She leaned back towards the kitchen to indicate with her hand that she was ready to order. She was obviously a regular here, for the young server nodded immediately and went back into the kitchen without asking what she wanted.

Lydia smiled. It was quite clear to her who ran her father's office so efficiently. She wondered whether to confide in Hannah regarding the project she had just begun, but then thought not; she would wait until she could discuss the matter with her father.

'Have you had any further news from Nicholas?' Hannah asked. The use of his first name came easily to her, Lydia noticed.

She shook her head; there was no point in talking about it. 'No. Have you? Are you likely to? No letter, or notification of absence?'

'No, nothing,' Hannah told her. 'But I hardly expect to. He'll surely know that your father won't want him back in the office after being absent without any warning. Neither,' she went on, lowering her voice, though there was no one else in the café, 'and you might know this already, will he receive any salary. I know that for a fact, Lydia, for I sign off the salary receipts. There will be nothing going into his account.'

Of course, Lydia thought. I should have known that my father wouldn't continue to pay him, especially as Nicholas didn't give him any notice. She gave a sigh. How glad she was that she had changed the name of the joint account, for it could otherwise have gone down very rapidly had Nicholas tried to withdraw any funds.

'I'm sorry, Lydia,' Hannah murmured. 'This must be a hard blow for you.'

'It is indeed,' she answered, but not really wanting to discuss it. 'He might turn up when he's had a think about his options.'

Hannah shrugged. 'He will have fewer options now that he's left the office, unless he finds another position, but even so,' she said thoughtfully, 'any other professional company worth its salt will want to see evidence of former employment before taking him on.'

Lydia nodded. She had already thought of that, but what Hannah didn't know was that Nicholas had suggested a short separation, and she wasn't going to tell her that. She didn't know her well enough to be perfectly sure of her discretion.

After a few minutes of small talk, and as Hannah sipped her black coffee, Lydia gathered her things together. 'I'd best be off,' she said. 'I'll pop into the office and say hello to my father before I drive home.'

'I'll get these,' Hannah told her, indicating both coffee cups. 'Don't tell your father you've seen me,' she said, smiling ruefully. 'He'll say I'm time-wasting – I'm joking,' she offered, but Lydia knew that she wasn't.

I mustn't stay long talking to Papa, she thought as she hurried back; dusk comes down so quickly. I'll just tell him briefly what I've arranged with Dawson. We can have a discussion about my project some other time.

As she walked she saw that the street lights were already lit; Beverley was lucky enough to be one of the first towns to be lit at dusk. The tall, stately and mostly green ironwork was an asset to the town, but the privilege didn't extend to the villages yet, although promises had been made.

She opened the door to her father's office and the clerks all stood up. 'Good afternoon, Mrs Mercer,' one said – she recognized the senior clerk, Mason – and the others nodded, then sat back down at their desks again. Mason remained standing.

'My father? Is he . . . ?'

'He won't be a moment, ma'am. He's just in the cupboard looking for something.'

Ah, the cupboard, she thought, and Hannah isn't here to look for him.

'May I go through?' She indicated the inner door. 'I only want to have a word.'

'By all means. Please come this way.' She followed him through the door, and there was her father in front of her, holding a folder.

'Lydia! What are you doing here?'

'Just want a word, Papa.' She dropped her voice as the clerk backed out. 'I need to speak to you – not for long as I must get home before dark, but I wanted to tell you that I've changed the name of the account containing the dowry money. I spoke to Dawson and we agreed this was the best way to keep it secure.'

'What do you mean? It was secure. And – Dawson! He agreed to this, did he?'

'Yes. I told him it might be needed as security for a project I have in mind. I'll tell you about that another time.'

'And he agreed? When you were there alone? You should have asked me to be present, as Nicholas is – erm . . .' He humphed. 'Well, someone, at least.'

'I am perfectly able to have a business discussion on my own, Father. I know what I'm doing, and I didn't want to risk Nicholas drawing on it without advising me beforehand.'

'But that's what *you've* done,' her father spluttered.

She shook her head. 'No, I haven't. I've simply put it under another name and if Nicholas needs any of it he can discuss it with me first.'

She saw he was lost for words, so she clutched his arm. 'I must go, Papa. I don't want to drive in the dark. There are no street lights once I'm out of town, as you know, so I mustn't linger.'

'Of course. But drive steadily. The pony will know its way, so let it lead. You must be careful, now. I don't like you driving alone.'

They went back into the office and he opened the side door into the yard and there was Frisky waiting for her. Her father took hold of the bridle and led him out, then helped Lydia into the trap. 'Now don't loiter, because I think we'll have rain, but don't rush either,' he said. 'Just take it steady. Off you go!'

'I will, Papa. Don't worry – I'll be fine.' She gave him a wave and was off with a great gust of breath. Worrying about me getting safely home will stop him being anxious about what the project might be, she thought; he'll question Mother, of course, but she knows nothing. I'm grown up, Papa – a woman, in case you've forgotten. I have to make my own judgements about my life.

Grey cloud was rolling over. She hoped it wouldn't rain, though the sky was darkening ominously.

'Come on, Frisky,' she called, touching the pony's back with the tip of her crop. 'Come on, stir up a bit.'

'*Stir up*,' she murmured. 'Where did I hear that?' She clicked her tongue and Frisky kicked up his heels. Ah, I remember. It was Alice telling Mary to stir up. She laughed. Out of the mouths of babes and— Goodness, the clouds are really racing in.

She heard a distant roll of thunder as they pulled out of town, passing the lane where her parents' house was and leaving the street lights behind. Turning on to the lane leading to Cherry Burton, Frisky kicked up his heels. Lydia was sure he didn't like the low rolls of thunder; he picked up speed. It was becoming even darker as copses and tall trees shut out the remaining daylight.

'Oh,' she breathed, 'we're going to get soaked!' In the distance she could see her cottage chimneys. 'Not so far. Come on, Frisky!' She tipped the crop again on the pony's back, though really there was no need, she chastised herself: he's as anxious as I am to get home before the rain begins.

Ahead of her she thought she saw a wavering light. It's near my house, she thought, but what is it? I can't make it out. There aren't any other dwellings; it must be someone caught unexpectedly, but who would be out in such weather? Another crack of thunder came right above her head and Frisky whinnied and skidded.

'Steady,' she called. 'Steady there.' She saw the flicker of light again, well ahead of her still but closer than her own house and coming towards her. Who was it? She was beginning to feel anxious. Did I leave the gate open? Can we drive straight in? Come on, Lydia, you wanted to become a countrywoman. Did I? she asked herself.

The light was still moving towards her and easier to see

now. Frisky gave another loud whinny and a voice shouted back, 'Lydia! Lydia! Slow down. There's running water. Slow down! Slow down!'

'Oh, Matthew! Thank the Lord!' She drew back on the reins, and Frisky responded as if he knew the voice and whinnied again.

She saw Matthew's tall figure as he held the flaming torch high in front of him and she drew again on the reins. He walked towards her, talking quietly now to the pony, who slowed to a walk and allowed Matthew to lead him in through the open gate and towards the stable door.

The rain was pouring down as he helped her down from the trap. 'I'll see to 'hoss,' he said. 'You go inside – you'll catch your death out here.'

'So will you,' she shouted, but headed for the door.

She fiddled with the key, as her fingers were cold and trembling, but eventually turned it and stepped inside. She felt the warmth and was glad that she had added some coal to the fire before leaving. Bending to unlace her boots, she stepped out of them and shook off her wet coat, letting it drop to the floor. In the sitting room, she moved the fire screen and fumbled about on the hearth for the tinder box where she kept a flint and candles. Happily, a low fire was still burning in the grate, and she took out a candle to light a lamp and then dropped more coal on to the fire. 'Oh, I'm exhausted,' she breathed. 'Morning excursions only from now until spring. Poor Matthew. Will he come in?'

She went to the front door, her hair still dripping wet, and met Matthew returning from the stable. 'They were glad to be inside,' he said as she urged him to come indoors. 'I've rubbed them both down with 'sacks that were hanging up on 'wall to help them dry off, and there's plenty of feed. They get on well together, don't they? No arguing over dinner!'

'No,' she laughed. 'But what about you? Let me get you a towel before you catch a chill too. Come into the kitchen – it will be warmer in there.'

'No, thank you. I've left Alice with 'bairns, but I'm never sure about 'lads. Ben will get it into his head to come and look for me if I tek too long.'

'Do they know where you are? Where you were going?'

'Aye,' he said. 'It was Ben who said there was no light showing in your house and he wanted to come and look for you. I told him that mebbe you'd stopped over in Beverley once it began to rain, but he was having none of it. He put on his coat, and then I started to worry too. I guessed you'd be careful, but then there was a thunderous crash and lightning, so I lit the flare and came out. I told Ben that he was in charge of 'young uns and that settled him.'

'I'm so sorry to have been such a nuisance,' she said. 'My father was worried too; it wasn't raining then, but it was getting dark so early. So go home and don't let them be anxious about me. They'll be worried enough about you if you've been out long.'

He bent down and kissed her cold wet cheek. 'Go and get those wet clouts off,' he said softly. 'Don't want you catching a chill. I'll let myself out – you put a hot brick in your bed and get warm.' He turned for the door. 'I'll see you sometime tomorrow. Take a few hours off from 'children and have a morning in bed.'

'Thank you, Matthew,' she said, feeling tearful because

she had caused such anxiety. 'Bring the children in the afternoon.'

But she felt something else too: the kiss from this kind caring man who thought of others before himself had lit a glowing warmth inside her, even though she was wet and cold from her fingertips to her toes.

CHAPTER TWENTY-EIGHT

She had two stone water bottles to heat the beds, one for Nicholas's use on winter nights and one for hers. She lifted the kettle on to the range. I'll use them both, she thought, but not the warming pan. The long-handled copper pan would hold hot coal or cinders, but she was always afraid of burning the sheets, or even herself.

She thought about Nicholas and where he might be. Would he be sharing someone else's bed? She doubted it, for after sleeping in the same bed on their wedding night and honeymoon in the Dales, he had told her that he would prefer it if they had separate beds in the future as he couldn't sleep in a shared one.

When they had arrived back at their new house, which so delighted Lydia that she instantly called it home, he took the smaller bedroom with its two single beds, which had been bought with the thought that the newlyweds might have guests to stay at some time – at least, she considered now, that was what *I* had thought – and she had been left with the larger room, which held a bigger wardrobe and dressing table, a comfy chair placed next to a small table for having a cup of tea whilst admiring the view from the window, and a large bed which had been made for two.

She didn't mind too much, as she had expected he would still come to join her, but he rarely did. It wasn't a discussion she thought she could instigate, for on the rare occasions when he did climb in beside her and she waited for something to happen, apart from a cold hand on her hip nothing ever did.

Trying a little persuasion of her own with her fingers under his nightshirt, but not really knowing what was down there and receiving no instruction apart from a sharp intake of breath, she thought that perhaps it was something that took time to learn.

She had tried without success to coerce Emily into giving away secrets; she searched out books, but none of them gave her a single clue. It was as if the reader was meant to know the basic facts; she didn't even know what the terminology meant.

Three years had passed in the same manner, and she had begun to wonder if she could live in this situation for the rest of her life, without love or warmth or even much conversation. But where was he now? Had he felt the same way, and, realizing their mistake, had decided to leave and make another life?

But now, as she slid down between the flannel sheets warmed by the stone water bottles, she felt a heady glow from the kiss given to her in friendship. She was fairly sure it had been no more than that, to show the relief Matthew had felt because his neighbour was safely home, but she felt gratitude for his kindness, and deep in her heart there was a longing that there might be more. That was impossible, she knew. He had lost a loving wife, the mother of their children, and he would remain forever faithful to her memory. That was the type of man he was.

And as for me, I am married to a man without compassion, and without much love either, or else why would he have taken his departure without saying goodbye? Did he look in her bedroom before he left? Would he have paused had she been awake?

No, she didn't think so. She turned over and slipped her hand beneath her cheek and closed her wet eyes. No point in thinking about it when she was so tired. Tomorrow she would give it some consideration.

She slept all night long and woke to sunshine. She climbed out of bed feeling refreshed and unwilling to think about anything yet, and putting on her dressing robe went downstairs to make tea which she brought up on a tray and placed on the table near the side window. Drawing back the curtain, she could see the window of Matthew's cottage, and the tall brick chimney where a curl of smoke wound its way into the bright blue sky. She looked at her clock, and wondered if her father would drive over to see her. He had been concerned about her journey home in the dark; perhaps more anxious now that she was living alone, and it would be of no use explaining that she had a considerate neighbour, for he was a man and that would bother her father even more. She hoped he would come so she could explain what her plans were and why she had been into the bank. She would also tell him that Dawson approved of her plan for a dame school. Perhaps the banker had children too.

She heaved a breath. The Children's Academy. It was a

grand name for an extension built on to her home; did she need permission? If so, from whom? It wasn't intended as a replacement for the village schools, but as an academy for children from different backgrounds.

Children such as Matthew's, perhaps; maybe Emily's when they were old enough. Not infants, but those of five and upwards. It might take some time to build, and was there even enough room to put on an extension?

I must speak to Matthew. He will know, and he'll be sure to know a builder. She was suddenly galvanized into action. Finishing her cup of tea, she washed and dressed, put on her indoor shoes and made her way downstairs, feeling like a different woman from the one she had been yesterday on discovering the empty wardrobe which confirmed Nicholas's departure.

Someone rattled the door knocker, which made her jump. She unbolted the door and turned the key, hoping it would be Matthew, but it was her father. She hadn't expected him so early, if he came at all. There was a hackney waiting outside the gate, and her father signalled to the driver; they had obviously made some arrangement, for the horse moved on and she guessed that the driver would turn round further up the road and come back to wait.

'Come in, Papa, do. I'm just about to make coffee – would you like a cup?'

He came in, taking off his top hat and undoing his coat. 'I would,' he said. 'I've barely slept, I was so worried about you. Your mama, too – she said I should have insisted on you staying with us, but I don't suppose you would have agreed.'

'You were right, Papa. I wanted to get home, but the weather was atrocious. The storm came so suddenly, but fortunately I was almost here when I caught up with a very kind neighbour who helped me by putting the animals in the stable and giving them some feed and dry bedding whilst I unlocked the door.'

'Animals!' he barked. 'Why? How many have you got? I thought you only had the pony?'

'No,' she said. 'I bought a donkey to keep Frisky company. He seemed lonely on his own. They get on very well,' she added.

'What stuff and nonsense,' he said. 'Animals don't have the same feelings as we do! Come on then, lead me to the coffee. I can't stay long.'

He watched as she made a jug of coffee and set some milk to warm in a small pan on the hob. 'I must reassure your mother that she needn't worry about you. You're clearly quite capable of managing on your own, but tell me about this neighbour of yours.'

They sat down at the table to drink their coffee, and he didn't seem to notice that they were in the kitchen and not in the sitting room. She told him about teaching the Wade children to read and write, about her ambition to open a children's academy, and finally of Matthew Wade and the joinery business which would enable him to look after his family at home.

He sat quietly as she talked, nodding his head now and again as if in agreement whilst sipping his coffee. Extraordinarily, he topped up his own cup from the jug, and then offered to top up hers, a thing she had never known him do before.

'Well, the fellow is to be complimented,' he murmured when she stopped speaking. 'There are few who would have managed. Men generally don't know how to cope under such difficult circumstances; you know, if he ever wanted to take out a loan to expand his business, I know several people who would oblige such an enterprising fellow.'

'That's a very generous offer, Papa,' she said quietly. 'And I'll tell him, but I'm quite sure that it wouldn't be accepted. I can't see him going into any kind of debt.'

'It wouldn't be considered as a debt, but as a loan,' her father replied. 'That's how business works.'

'Really?' she said. 'That's interesting.'

Her father looked up, startled. 'That's how it works for men,' he said sharply. 'I don't say it would work for ladies.'

She sighed. 'Why doesn't that surprise me?'

Her father shook his head. 'I do understand your frustration, Lydia, but change is coming. Women are beginning to want the same rights as men, and so many of them are standing up and demanding it that I'm inclined to think that one day it will come.

'So, your school or academy,' he went on, changing the subject. 'Do you think this house is big enough? I doubt that you could take in enough pupils to make it pay, or indeed enough teachers; they couldn't all teach in one room.'

'I was thinking of adding a long room, divided into units, to run from back to front.' Have I got my thinking wrong? she wondered. Will it ruin the house that I love so much as it is? It took me an age to decide how I wanted it when we first came here; Nicholas told me to do as I wished. It was as if he didn't really care as long as there was somewhere to lay his head – alone!

'If you found sponsors, then you could see if there's

anywhere in the district that might be suitable,' her father suggested. She was astonished that he was taking her vision seriously. 'How many children does this neighbour have, did you say? Those who are school age, I mean?'

'Four. Another one is about two, and there's an infant, not yet twelve months.'

He blew out a breath. 'And he looks after all of them himself?'

'He has a young woman who, erm, took care of the baby after his birth,' she said. 'But the other children look after each other. The baby will soon be walking, and the toddler is very sweet. Ben is a proper country boy, and the oldest is Alice, who is eleven. She's lovely, and talented, and does most of the caring of the others. Lastly there are twins, a girl and a boy. Now that their father is earning he has a woman who comes in to clean the house.'

'Great heavens,' Mr Davenport spluttered. 'I've never heard of such a family! But I do believe that people in such circumstances help each other, whilst people with easier lives, like us, don't notice.' He heaved a great sigh. 'Or maybe we don't care.'

She didn't reply. She didn't know what to say, for she had never in her life had such a conversation with her father. If anyone had asked her to describe him, she would have said that other people's lives didn't touch him at all, and clearly she would have been completely wrong.

CHAPTER TWENTY-NINE

Lydia was astonished that her father approved of her plan; he didn't ask her how much it might cost, but said to be sure to consult him on such things as contracts or agreements. He asked her how she would contact possible teachers for the project, saying she should find out who might be interested in joining her before looking for a suitable property if she decided not to use her own home.

'The thing is, Lydia – and I'm not speaking as a businessman, because I'm not one, I'm a lawyer – I have seen men come unstuck in business only because they haven't thought everything through beforehand. If you want your academy to attract the right kind of teachers as well as parents, it must look as if it *is* one, rather than looking like a house with an extension built on the side. Do you understand what I'm saying? The building must look like a school with professional staff.'

'Yes, I do, and you're right. I was already planning to bring in some professional women teachers. Perhaps men too, if they will come, for boys need better education than I can give.'

He patted her arm as he got up to leave. 'Don't think you are incapable of doing this, Lydia; you have good organizational skills as well as a belief in your project. The teachers you bring in will know how to teach – that is what they have trained for – but they need someone to lead them, and you can do that. I have no doubt about it.' He nodded his head as if in approval. 'You always knew what you wanted to do when you were small. You would never be put off if someone said you couldn't do it. *But I want to,* you would say, and do it you would! Well, now I must be off.' He rose from the kitchen chair, and was just putting on his coat while Lydia held his hat when someone rattled the knocker on the door. She was immediately nervous: it could only be one person, she thought, opening the door.

Matthew was standing there, smiling at her. By his side was Ben, and behind him stood Charlie and Lily. 'Beggin' your pardon for disturbing you, Mrs Mercer.' He touched his forehead at her father. 'Good morning, sir. Matthew Wade. I won't keep you, for I see you have a carriage waiting, but 'children have been anxious about Mrs Mercer after last night's storm and wouldn't settle until I agreed we could call and ask if she was all right.'

Lydia opened her arms to them, and first Lily, then Ben and then Charlie came for a hug. She kissed the tops of their heads, and stroked their cheeks. 'I'm fine, thank you,' she told them, 'but I was very grateful to your father last night, because he had opened the gate for me, and brought the donkey in from the paddock.'

To her astonishment, her father leaned forward and put out his hand to Matthew. 'Thomas Davenport,' he said. 'My daughter has been telling me about your help last night. I came especially this morning to enquire if she had arrived safely home; her mother and I were very worried. I'm much obliged to you for your concern whilst she is presently here alone.'

Matthew smiled. 'Don't worry unduly, sir. Children are allus on 'watch.' He turned to them. 'Happy now? Come on then, you young peazens; let's have you home and you can give 'good news to 'others.'

'I understand you have more children?' Lydia's father didn't seem in such a hurry to leave. His voice had dropped to a murmur. 'My condolences on your loss.'

Matthew nodded his thanks. 'Three more, sir, including 'youngest. All healthy and growing up fast. I'm blessed indeed.' He turned to leave, but Ben tugged on his sleeve. 'Ah, yes. Mrs Mercer, could Ben first check on 'blackbird's nest? See if it's still intact after last night's storm?'

Lydia nodded. 'Of course. Ben, you know you can come any time.'

Ben pressed his lips together. 'Thank you,' he said, and then gave a cheeky grin. 'I told Da you'd said I could, and he said best to check if you had company.' He looked up at Lydia's father. 'Are you company, sir?'

Thomas Davenport raised his eyebrows, but his lips twitched. 'In a manner of speaking, I suppose I am, but if my daughter Mrs Mercer says you can come at any time, then you can.' He put his hand out for his hat, which Lydia was still clutching. 'Must be off. Pleasure to meet you, Wade, and thank you again.' He patted Lydia on the arm. 'Take care, Lydia. I'll tell your mother she has no need to worry about you. You're perfectly capable of looking after yourself, and you have good neighbours.'

'Thank you, Father.' She felt emotional, not having previously thought that either of her parents would worry about her: was it only since Nicholas's departure, or had they always been the same, but never shown it?

The children had all run off to the back of the house to look for the blackbird's nest. Lydia waved goodbye to her father as the carriage departed, and let out a huff of breath. 'Why am I always nervous about what my parents might think?'

Matthew smiled. 'We all want our parents to think 'best of us. I was 'same, with my father in particular. Our ma – we allus knew she thought 'sun shone out of us, me and my brothers.'

'Your brothers? I didn't know you had any brothers!'

'I don't. Not any more. They were twins, and left for Australia when they were sixteen. Broke my mother's heart. When she was near to death, I told her that I'd received a letter from them to say they were well and happy and would be coming to see her soon.' He heaved a deep breath. 'Onny lie I've ever told, but she died happy. My da didn't believe a word of it, so I told him it was a lie. We never did hear anything from them.'

'And what happened to your father?'

'Pneumonia, two years later. He was never 'same after Ma died and didn't take care of himself, but he'd already made sure I'd be all right. Apprenticed me to a joiner when I was fourteen, so I would allus be able to earn a living.'

'I'm so sorry,' she whispered. 'But then you met Mary?'

He nodded. 'I was living in lodgings in Pocklington district, and once I'd finished 'apprenticeship I thought I'd move on. Make another life. Tried several places and finished up round here, and then I met Mary.' He took a deep breath. 'I haven't talked about any of that – about my ma and da or my brothers – in years.'

'I didn't mean to pry,' she murmured, and he shook his hand to show that he didn't mind; and then they heard running feet and the children turned the corner, whooping to be the first to say the nest was still there. 'I need to discuss something with you, Matthew,' she said when they'd run off again. 'My father has given me food for thought—'

'Meat pie? Apple crumble?'

She laughed. 'No, neither of those! I have a project in mind, but after discussing it with Pa I think I've been heading in the wrong direction. I can take a better route.'

'All sounds very mysterious,' he said. 'Is it something I can help you with?'

'I hope so,' she said softly, and wondered if she was being over-ambitious. For one thing, she would need money: a loan? If she spent all she had in the bank, how would she manage? She would have bills to pay; and Maggie and Cook, could she afford to keep them? Food to buy, coal for the fire – she had never in her life had to think about such things. For all her ambition to do good, was this just another dream?

'Alice said she wants to ask you something, but not in front of 'others.'

She raised an eyebrow, but he shook his head. 'Don't know,' he said. 'Something private, I suppose; that's what little girls are like, I think.'

She nodded. 'Yes, we like secrets, especially when we're growing up, but sometimes we share them with people we trust. I'm flattered that Alice has chosen me.' And perhaps it is something personal, she thought. Young Alice is growing up, and that brings pressure of all sorts. 'She can come over this afternoon. We'll have a cup of tea together, and a slice of cake.'

'Hmm. Perhaps you'll invite me sometime? There's nothing I like better than tea and cake!'

'Well, now that you've met my father and he's decided you're a safe neighbour, on a purely formal basis, Mr Wade, you may come for a cup of tea. But you must take a chance on cake!'

He smiled and called the children to come. 'I'll do that!'

CHAPTER THIRTY

'Miss Lydia.' Alice was pale-faced when she arrived. 'I'm sorry, I didn't want to bother you, but I'd forgotten what my ma told me and so I wasn't ready for it.'

'Ready for what?' Lydia knew what she must mean, but didn't want her to think there was any stigma in talking about the normal changes a woman's body went through. 'Do you have a question and don't know how to ask it?'

Alice nodded. 'Ma said not to talk about it except to her, and she would explain.' She pressed her lips together. 'But Ma's not here now,' she said tearfully, 'and I can't ask Da.'

She probably could, Lydia thought. Matthew would think it was a perfectly normal thing for a motherless young girl to ask her father about, but he wouldn't want her to be embarrassed. 'Are you feeling unwell?' she asked quietly. 'Headache, or tummy ache?'

Alice nodded and looked away. 'I wish Ma was here.' Her eyes filled with tears. 'But she's not.'

Lydia took hold of both her hands. 'Let's go upstairs and I'll explain. It happens to all women,' she said quietly, 'young and older. But I have everything here you need for now, and next time I'm out shopping I'll get a stock for you. And I have an idea – would you like to stay here tonight? Then you wouldn't have to explain to anyone that you don't feel very well, or have a tummy ache or headache, and we can talk. You mustn't worry – it's perfectly normal, and girls just have to accept it. It's all part of growing up and becoming a woman, and isn't that a wonderful thing?'

'Oh, yes, it is,' Alice said, smiling shakily through her tears. 'I just didn't realize it would be yet.'

Lydia took her upstairs to her bedroom and showed her where everything she needed was kept, then took her into what had been Nicholas's room. 'I thought you could sleep here tonight if you'd like, Alice – it's my husband's room but he won't be needing it for a while, if at all.' She tapped her finger against the side of her nose to indicate a secret. 'I'm going to get someone to redecorate it and then I'll ask your father to carry a chair upstairs for me, and we'll bring cushions, and lace doilies for the chest of drawers, and maybe I'll put up some pretty curtains too. And it's such a very plain wallpaper; we'll change that, don't you think? Something flowery might be nice. I'll get some pattern books to look through.'

Alice took a deep breath. 'May I look at them with you? I love colour and flowers too.'

'Then you can help me choose. Next time I'm in Beverley I'll call at the wallpaper shop and ask them to send a collection of pattern books so that we can pick one.' She took a box of matches from the mantelpiece and bent down to the grate, which was laid with screwed-up paper, sticks and coal.

'I think as a special treat you should have a fire, even though it's not quite winter.'

As the paper caught, and then the sticks and the coal, she placed a fireguard in front of it. 'Now, would you like a warm bath? I think you'll find one very soothing at this time of the month. I have nightgowns and dressing gowns, too – they'll be rather large for you, so do be careful that you don't trip over the hem.'

Alice came downstairs half an hour later, in one of Lydia's shorter dressing gowns, pink-faced from the warm bath which Lydia had filled for her. Alice found her in the sitting room, setting out a small table with plates and cutlery. 'That was lovely,' she said. 'It was so kind of you to think of it, Miss Lydia. I feel very, erm . . .'

'Relaxed? Yes, I thought you would. We're very lucky to have hot water – it's heated by the kitchen range and piped upstairs. Come and sit down. I thought we'd sit in here to have our supper – it's so nice and warm by the fire. Cook made a bacon and egg pie this morning, and there's cold ham, or a potted liver paste of Cook's that is one of my favourites. We'll finish with fruit scones and apple pie, with the apples from my tree. Would you like a cup of tea or cocoa with them?'

'Oh, cocoa please. Am I being too greedy?'

'Of course you're not,' Lydia assured her. 'You're my guest, after all. I invited you, Alice, and it's my pleasure!' She bent towards the girl and kissed her cheek. 'Snuggle up under the blanket by the fire and I'll bring the tray through.'

Lydia went back into the kitchen where she had already

filled the tray, but she paused for a moment before putting the milk on to heat. That dear child, she thought. Her mother not here when she needs her most; when she's on the cusp of womanhood. I can't recall how I felt the first time. My mother was there, but it was one of the young maids who told me what to do. 'Get on with it,' I recall her saying. 'We all have to put up with it, and it's a blessing after all.'

She gave a wry grimace. A blessing. Not for me it isn't. Something's gone awry somehow. Parhaps I will speak to Mrs Bower after all, since I have a husband who doesn't seem to care one way or another.

After supper Alice had drunk her cocoa and gone upstairs again by seven o'clock, having bidden Lydia a shy goodnight. 'I'm ready to climb into that lovely warm bed.' Lydia had already filled one of the stone bottles and put it into the bed to warm it. There were warm flannelette sheets too, as she had asked Maggie to strip off the cotton ones when she knew Nicholas had gone.

She sat for a while and then got up to take the tray into the kitchen. She gave a deep sigh. *This has been a lovely day. My father here, then Matthew and the children, and then Alice, such a sweet child.* She put the remains of the food into the larder, and piled the crockery into the sink and filled it with cold water to let them soak. I'll see to those later, she thought, and sit down again to make the most of the last of dusk. I love to see the sun go down. It really has been such a lovely day. I feel quite content.

She sat by the window and looked up the lane at the trees edging the fields; the sun, sinking down behind the trees, was a deep fiery orangey red and lit them up so that they held shades of flickering flame, orange and crimson. She gave a start as a figure walked past her fence towards the gate before realizing it was Matthew. Of course; he was coming to collect Alice. He didn't know that she'd invited her to stay the night.

She invited him in. 'I'm sorry, Matthew, but I've kidnapped your eldest child. She's already in bed.'

His eyebrows rose. 'She's not ill?' he asked anxiously.

'Not at all,' she reassured him. 'She's on the brink of womanhood and didn't know what to do, so came for some reassurance, that's all. Nothing to worry about. But I invited her to stay the night in case the other children asked her why she had come. She has the usual headache, and tummy ache, but otherwise she's fine. We've had supper and a chat by the fire and now I would guess she's fast asleep. Would you like to go up and see her?'

He hesitated and glanced upstairs.

'She's in the smaller bedroom, not in mine,' she said softly. 'I assume she's used to sleeping alone?'

He smiled. 'That's 'expectation, but there's always one or another in bed with her 'next morning. Yes please, if I may.'

She led the way upstairs and quietly opened the bedroom door; the low fire was still flickering, sending shadows around the room, and there was no movement from the bed. Matthew leaned over Alice and gently moved a stray fair hair from her face. He nodded. 'Fast asleep,' he murmured, and turned away.

Lydia quietly closed the door behind them. He didn't speak, but she felt he was battling some emotion, and put her hand on his arm. 'She's safe,' she whispered. 'She won't come to any harm whilst she's with me.'

He nodded and swallowed. 'I know.' He pressed a finger and thumb against his eyes and she knew that he was weeping. 'My poor baby,' he murmured. 'My firstborn, trying to take her mother's place. Thinking that she's an adult, but yet she's still a child. How can I do right by her and 'other bairns?'

Gently she patted his arm. 'No one could do it better, Matthew,' she murmured. 'Your children think the sun shines out of you, just as your mother felt about you and your brothers. They believe in everything you do. Come.' She put her arm about his shoulder. 'Let's go down and have that tea and cake.'

He turned to her, his face wet with tears, and she guessed that it wasn't only his children that he was weeping for, but their mother too.

'Lydia,' he said, and then he bent his head and kissed first her left cheek and then her right. 'It's as if your love and kindness towards my children has brought me back to life.' He gazed down at her, and then with one hand he lifted her chin and kissed her mouth. 'Thank you,' he breathed. 'From my heart. Thank you.'

CHAPTER THIRTY-ONE

They sat by the sitting-room fire without speaking for a few minutes, but then she rose from her chair to go into the kitchen to make tea, and he looked up. 'I must go,' he said quietly, getting to his feet. 'I don't want to leave 'other bairns too long. They know I've only come here, but I don't like to leave them on their own, not without Alice to supervise them.'

'I understand,' she said. 'But let me give you the cake to take home. There's enough to share!'

He nodded. 'And we'll have that conversation soon; it's about 'schooling, I suspect. Is it proving too much for you?'

'Oh, no! Not at all,' she assured him. 'Quite the opposite, in fact. I have spoken to my father about my scheme, and he hasn't decried it, and neither has the bank manager.'

'You've spoken to 'bank manager *and* your father?' he said incredulously. 'And yet you want to discuss 'subject wi' me? You overestimate my ability, Mrs Mercer. I'm onny a working man and haven't 'learned education you need.'

She smiled. 'I need your common sense, Matthew, and

knowledge of – well, several things – but I will need others who might be useful in a different way as well.' He followed her into the kitchen, where she put a whole cake into a paper bag. 'It's very rich,' she said, 'so perhaps just one slice tonight?'

'Young Mary and Aaron will be asleep,' he said, 'so theirs will keep till 'morning.'

'Is Aaron eating cake?' she asked in astonishment. She was rarely there at meal time.

He laughed. 'Pobs, their ma called it. We gave them bread and milk mashed up when 'bairns started teething. Cake will taste even better.' He took the bag from her, and kept hold of her hands. 'Thank you, Lydia,' he said quietly. 'I hope I didn't offend you with my tears and kisses?'

She shook her head. 'The sweetest kisses I have had in a long time,' she said softly, 'except for those from your children.'

He nodded, and said, 'I'll come again tomorrow after I've finished 'job I'm working on. Alice can make her own way home in 'morning when she's ready.' He kissed her cheek. 'Thank you again, dearest friend,' he said softly, 'for all you do and have done.'

Lydia sat by the fire, meditating. So much had happened that day: her father coming to make sure she was all right after her journey in the storm, then Matthew coming too and meeting him; there had been some kind of connection between them, she thought, though she couldn't put her finger on what it was. But her father was impressed by him, she could tell; perhaps it was his work ethic, or the way he was with Ben.

More than anything, she thought of her own explanation to Alice about how her body was changing, and that what was happening was perfectly normal as she slowly emerged from childhood into womanhood. 'Like a caterpillar into a butterfly?' Alice had whispered.

'Exactly like that.' Lydia had smiled. 'That's the loveliest explanation I've ever heard,' she'd said softly. 'It's a transformation,' but then she'd laughed. 'But we live a lot longer than a butterfly.'

And then there was the kiss from Matthew; not the friendship kiss on each cheek but the one on her lips, which was totally unexpected, and, as she had confessed, the sweetest kiss she had ever had. The kiss that she would like to think of as given in love. 'But no. Don't pretend, Lydia,' she told herself as she sat by her fire. It was given in friendship; he had said, hadn't he, *dearest friend.* How could it have been given in any other way? He is a widower and I am an abandoned wife.

She slept badly, disturbed by jumbled thoughts on the day, and it seemed as if she had only just fallen asleep when she was woken by a soft tap on the bedroom door. It was opened awkwardly by Alice, who was holding a tray with two cups of tea and a plate of biscuits.

'Good morning, Miss Lydia,' she said as she came in, closing the door with the heel of her shoe. 'I thought you might like a cup of tea in bed this morning.' She placed the tray on the table by the window and picked up a cup and the biscuit plate and brought them across to the bed.

'Oh, how lovely,' Lydia said, pulling herself into a sitting position. 'What a treat! I think I'm going to adopt you, Alice!'

Alice laughed. 'I don't think my da would be very happy about that. And besides, all my brothers and sisters would want to come too, especially if there were biscuits and tea in bed.'

'Oh, and crumbs too. Can you imagine?' Lydia took the teacup and put it on a side table, then pulled back the covers on the other side of the bed. 'Are you coming in?'

Alice collected her own cup and sat on the edge of the bed. She took a sip of tea, and then, looking shyly at Lydia, lifted her legs and covered them with the sheet and blankets. 'I've never done this before,' Lydia said softly. 'I was an only child, with no one to share beds with.'

'Until you got married?' Alice asked, raising her eyebrows. 'I expect you did then, with Mr Mercer. Ma and Da did and we couldn't go in without knocking first, in case they were asleep, Da said, but they never were. They allus got up early.'

Lydia laughed. 'Yes, of course, I expect they did. There's so much to do with a family to look after.'

'I think I'd better go home as soon as I'm dressed, Miss Lydia. Da will want some help with 'other bairns – especially Aaron. He throws food and milk all over 'place if he's not watched, and Mary has to be watched too or she'd be out of 'door afore we knew it.'

'You have a lot to do, Alice. What a brave, kind girl you are. Your father came to see you last night. He wanted to check if you were all right. You were fast asleep when he came up and you looked very cosy.'

'It was kind of you to let me stay,' Alice said shyly. 'I hope I wasn't a bother.'

'No bother at all,' Lydia told her. 'I enjoyed your company.

You must come and stay again, and not only when your monthlies come round, but any time you want some time to yourself.'

'Oh, yes, I'd forgotten that it comes every month,' Alice said. 'When does it stop?'

'Not for ages yet,' Lydia murmured, 'but that's for discussion another time.'

They had breakfast and then she waved Alice off home and said she'd see her later. Cook arrived as she was leaving and then Maggie came in and another day began. Lydia took a notebook and pencil upstairs so that she wasn't in the way, and asked Cook if she would make a few more scones than usual.

She wrote down notes about what she would need if her project began. She was pondering the whys and wherefores, and how she would begin, when the children arrived for their reading lesson. Alice brought them, but didn't stay for the lesson. She had some jobs to do in the house, to save her father from having to do them, she said, but Lydia guessed that she probably needed time for herself too.

Near to lunchtime, as Maggie and Cook were getting ready to leave, she spotted Mrs Bower's dog cart heading towards the house and hurried outside. 'Mrs Bower,' she called. 'Mrs Bower?'

The midwife drew up. 'Yes, Mrs Mercer? Summat up?'

'Not exactly, but . . .' How do I say this? she wondered. 'Could you spare me ten minutes? Not right now, as the Wade children are here; but later this afternoon if you have the time? I need your advice.'

'I could come round this afternoon, Mrs Mercer. I'm

attending one of my mothers at about three, so mebbe three thirty or four o'clock?'

'Perfect,' Lydia said, feeling nervous and foolish.

She couldn't concentrate on anything else that morning, so she set the children to painting or crayoning on any subject they wished before giving them a lunch of ham and potted beef with fresh bread that Cook had made that morning, followed by a cup of milk and a slice of cake. When Matthew came to collect them he apologized again for his earlier behaviour, but she shook her head. 'Don't apologize too much, Matthew,' she said, smiling. 'I haven't had as much as a kiss on the cheek for a while, except from my father, so please don't regret it!'

He smiled back. 'I won't,' he said. 'And I don't, as long as I didn't offend you. That's 'last thing I'd want to do.' He looked up. 'Here's Mrs Bower stopping.' He gave a little frown. 'We'd better be off. Thank you again for looking after Alice. She's been worried, I think, and now she's not. Come on, everybody. Let's leave Miss Lydia in peace.'

Lydia waved them off and invited Mrs Bower in. She asked if the midwife would like refreshment, but she declined. 'I'd as soon get off home, thank you. How can I help you, Mrs Mercer?'

'It's rather embarrassing, Mrs Bower, and I don't know who to ask, apart from Dr Tennyson, and I really don't want to ask him.'

Mrs Bower nodded. 'He's used to women's problems, Mrs Mercer, so no need to be shy. But tell me by all means, if you'd rather.'

'Well, I would, Mrs Bower, and you might be surprised by what I'm about to ask you, but I need to know.'

'Doubt it, Mrs Mercer,' the midwife proclaimed. 'I've seen and heard many things in my lifetime, and it's not likely that I'll be shocked. So tell me, and then mebbe we'll have that cuppa tea and a chat after all.'

CHAPTER THIRTY-TWO

Mrs Bower says I must seek advice if I want to end my marriage.

Lydia sat by the sitting-room window, looking out as the midwife drove away. She hadn't been shocked, Lydia considered, but rather startled to hear that we have been married for so long and hadn't realized sooner that something wasn't right. She had often been called upon by young brides with innocent young husbands, she had told Lydia, but not by a woman with three years of marriage behind her.

I do want to end my marriage, and now Mrs Bower has confirmed that it isn't a proper marriage at all; it is a sham. But what if it should get out? Will my parents be embarrassed about it? And although I'm sure my father could arrange an annulment on my behalf, would he want to be embroiled in something so controversial and scandalous? I don't know how I can bear the shame.

She blew her nose; tears were very close. Perhaps I should go away, she thought; somewhere no one knows me. Effie Gray, Millais's wife, caused a scandal by suing her previous husband for divorce because theirs wasn't a real marriage either, Mrs Bower told me. I don't remember it at all.

How can it be discussed? 'Say it out loud, Lydia,' she told herself. 'My marriage is unconsummated. I must visit Dr Tennyson. There will have to be proof and he will advise me. Mrs Bower said she would come with me. I can't visit him alone, but who else would I ask?'

Immediately, Emily's name came to mind. *She would come with me. She wouldn't be afraid to, nor would she be embarrassed, but she would be shocked. But where is Nicholas? How can someone be called to court if he has disappeared?*

It was fate, it seemed, for she heard the letter box clatter and then saw the postwoman going out of the gate. Second post. A butcher's bill, she thought. I know I owe him.

She rose reluctantly from her chair. The children had gone home, Alice back to her normal self but with an additional air of cofidence, Lydia thought, as she embraced her new reality, and they had all had a good reading day.

The envelope bore a London postmark. 'Do I know anyone in London?' But then she saw the twirl on the capital M and her heart began to hammer. It had to be from Nicholas. And it was; she sat down again as she opened it. *Does he want to come back? Do I want him to? Would he behave differently? Where has he been, and what has he been doing for money?*

Her fingers shook as she spread open the single page. There were apologies first, but then her eyes opened wide. She read that he was leaving London for Liverpool immediately and sailing to America in a week's time. 'I'm sorry if I have hurt you by my actions, but you already know that I am not cut out for marriage. I will release you from ours if you can find a way to end it.'

She sighed as she read it again. 'I do know now, and he

must always have known,' she breathed, 'but we never discussed it. So why did he go through with our marriage? What advantage has there been in it?' She sat with the letter in her hand. 'Find a way to end it? Does he not realize – does this make it easier for me or not?' she wondered.

The door knocker made her jump. She wasn't inclined to greet visitors just now, not that she had many apart from Matthew or the children. But it was Emily on the doorstep, without the children, and Lydia broke down in tears when she saw her.

'What's this?' Emily didn't wait to be invited but stepped inside. 'Are you alone?'

Lydia nodded, too overwrought to answer, so she handed the letter to her friend, went back into the sitting room and sat down. Emily followed her.

'I'm not crying because I miss him, because I don't. But oh dear, Emily, what a tale I have to tell! Two tales, in fact, but I'll start with the letter from Nicholas. Read it,' she said, getting up from the chair again, 'and I'll make coffee.'

'He says he's going with a group of travellers,' Emily commented a few minutes later, following her into the kitchen. 'But divorce? Does he have money? Or perhaps one shouldn't ask? Have you visited your bank recently?'

'Yes, I have, and the manager is aware of the situation . . . or some of it; certainly not all.' Lydia snuffled, took a handkerchief from her pocket and blew her nose, then rinsed her hands and went back to making coffee.

'But what about you?' Emily asked, aghast at the situation. 'He's going without you? He's not digging for gold, is he? I would have thought that most of it must have gone by now.'

Lydia snuffled out a laugh at the idea of Nicholas digging for gold, and shook her head. 'He doesn't want me with him. Nor would I go, though I suppose I would be expected to if we'd had a normal marriage.'

Emily looked blankly at her. 'A normal marriage? What's that supposed to mean? Isn't that what we all have, a marriage with ups and downs?'

'Not mine. But never mind that for now. I want to tell you what else I've been considering, especially now that Nicholas is leaving – indeed, has left.'

'But to divorce you! On what grounds? It's scandalous!'

'Laws are changing, Emily, and without a husband I will be able to decide for myself what I want to do with my life. I might not have the education or learning to actually fulfil my ambition, but I know others who have.'

She took a deep breath. Reaching for a cloth to pull the steaming kettle off the hob, she said, 'I'm going to open a school – an academy, to be called the Children's Academy.' Pouring hot water on to the coffee grounds, she went on, 'I couldn't tell you before, as I hadn't sorted it out in my mind, but I've spoken to the bank manager and my father and have their approval. There *was* a stumbling block, but now that the stumbling block is going abroad, well, I will have to earn a living, won't I?' She gave a shaky smile. '*I* am going to make a divorce claim against *him*, and there will be proof!'

She thought for a minute, stirring the coffee with a long-handled spoon. 'He will have left the country by the time my claim goes to court, but that doesn't matter – I am not wreaking vengeance upon him. But my father will not make it easy for him to enjoy the fruits of my labour if the school should be a success, and I'm determined that it will be.'

'Lydia, I don't know what you're talking about!' Emily said impatiently.

'Well,' Lydia said, 'people often say the law is an ass, and they are possibly right, but you do know, don't you, Emily, that if a married woman makes any money in a profession or any kind of work her husband can claim it and put it in his name?'

'No, I didn't know that – or perhaps I did but didn't take much notice because it didn't concern me. But now I think about it, that's not fair, is it?'

'It's not in the least fair. There are many women scientists and doctors with the same qualifications as men who are not allowed to claim the same salary.'

'So if you own a school and charge fees . . . I don't understand, Lydia. I thought you were on the side of the people who *hadn't* any money for schooling their children.'

'I am,' Lydia said, pouring the coffee into two white cups and bringing out biscuits and milk. 'My idea is to attract patrons with money who would give something towards the education of children whose parents can't afford to.'

'People like us,' Emily said, raising her eyebrows.

'Exactly.' Lydia smiled. 'And I want all the children to dress the same. The school will provide the uniform. Grey-striped dresses for the girls, with a red-buttoned cardigan for colder days, and dark red jumpers and grey trousers, long or short, for the boys, so no one will know the social standing of anyone else.'

'You've done a lot of thinking, haven't you?' Emily sat on a stool to drink her coffee.

'I have, over several weeks,' Lydia confessed. She pushed a plate of biscuits towards her friend. 'But there's a lot more to think about, and I've had several changes of heart. At one time I thought of adding an annexe on to my house' – she saw Emily frown – 'and now I am considering a different building entirely, but have yet to start looking for one, and where will I find a suitable place? Most importantly, how do I attract patrons, and could I get a loan?'

'I don't know,' Emily said. 'But you mustn't use your lovely house, Lydia, because it must look like a proper school. Gideon might know of an empty building. Where would you want it? Are you thinking of the villages, or Beverley?'

'Definitely the villages,' Lydia told her. 'Beverley has schools already, but the children of the villages don't always attend them, because they can't get there alone. Besides, the national schools are often closed.'

'And won't that be the same with your proposed school?' Emily asked. 'There's a lot to think about.'

'There is, and I haven't yet thought everything through. I wondered whether, if the school had a pony and trap, we could hire a driver to collect the children and take them safely home too?' She sighed. 'It's a big undertaking, I know, and it seems to get bigger and bigger. But I want to do something useful, and I have loved teaching the Wade children to read. What's more, I have seen the difference it has made to them.'

'Have you discussed it with your Mr Wade?' Emily asked cheekily.

'He's *not* my Mr Wade, Emily, as you very well know. No, I haven't, but he knows I have a project in mind. I haven't told him what it is, but I will; he's very straight-thinking and level-headed; from what I can gather he's made that way and wouldn't ever take unnecessary risks.'

'Probably because he's always had to work hard for a living, and has a family to think of,' Emily suggested.

'Yes. I'm so pleased that you called, Emily. And as it happens, I was going to ask you if you would do something for me. Will you come with me and Mrs Bower . . .' she hesitated, and took a shallow breath, 'to see Dr Tennyson on a very delicate but important mission? It could change my life.'

CHAPTER THIRTY-THREE

Emily drove Lydia to the doctor's surgery, which he held at his own home. 'Don't worry about it,' she said. 'Believe me, it's nothing to worry about.'

'Well I am worrying,' Lydia muttered. 'It's so embarrassing.'

'We'll be on the way home in ten minutes,' Emily said. 'If you were having twins, that would be worrying!'

Lydia breathed out: she realized she'd been holding her breath. She wished Mrs Bower was there, but the midwife had said that if Mrs Horner was going with her there was no need for her to go as well, because she had already given Dr Tennyson the details. Lydia had groaned. How humiliating!

Emily pulled up outside the doctor's house. 'Now then, are you sure you want me to come in with you?'

'Yes please,' Lydia whispered. 'I might run away if you're not there.'

Emily shook her head. She hadn't at all understood what the fuss was about until they'd had a chat, but then she had realized that Lydia was an innocent in comparison with herself, who had four children and a husband who adored her. Lydia hadn't had anything to compare with that love, just a man who had probably only wanted a father-in-law who could offer him a step up the ladder of the law, but he had obviously been disappointed, for Thomas Davenport gave little away unless it had been worked for.

'Come on then, let's get it over with.' Emily jumped down and fastened up the pony and waited for Lydia, who was still pondering in the trap. 'We'll be no more than ten minutes,' she urged her. 'I'd take a bet on it, if I were a betting type of woman.'

Reluctantly, Lydia got down and went up the steps to the doctor's door. After a moment, she lifted the knocker. A young maid dipped her knee and invited her in. 'Is it Mrs Mercer?' she asked.

'It is,' Lydia croaked, and Emily gave her a little nudge from behind.

She was invited to follow the maid, who told her that Dr Tennyson was ready for her. Emily followed her. 'Told you it would be all right, didn't I?' she whispered.

Dr Tennyson got up from his chair as the maid knocked, opened the door and announced her. 'Good morning, Mrs Mercer. Ah, and Mrs Horner too, I see. Now don't tell me you require my services as well, Mrs Horner?'

'I most certainly don't, Dr Tennyson, thank you. I am simply accompanying my friend, who is a trifle nervous about being here, even though I have told her that there is nothing to be worried about.'

'Indeed there is not,' he said affably. 'Won't you both take a seat?' He shuffled some papers about on his desk, sat down again, and leaned towards Lydia.

'I understand from Mrs Bower that you wish to divorce your husband on account of your marriage being unconsummated. You have been married for . . . how long?'

'Three years,' she croaked.

'And how old were you when you married?'

'Just twenty.' It seems a lifetime ago, she thought. What a waste of those years. I wonder what I might have done with them?

'And how old is your husband?' He was making notes as he spoke.

'He will be twenty-nine next month.'

'I see.' He put down his pen. 'Old enough to know about life, one would think.' He was talking to himself, she thought, and made no reply. 'So six years older than you?'

'Yes.' She nodded. I thought Nicholas seemed so knowledgeable and mature when we were introduced. How wrong I was! He knew nothing, either about women or about life; he just sailed through the days, and I wonder now whether he knew anything about anything. He was oblivious of most things. But, she thought, ignorance of life doesn't add up to divorce.

'Well, Mrs Mercer,' the doctor sighed, 'it seems to me that there is no bar to annulment here. There are no children to consider, for the obvious reason; there is no union between you, and you wish to step aside from the marriage.'

'Yes,' she said firmly. She took out the letter she had received from Nicholas and handed it to Dr Tennyson. 'And it appears that so does he.'

He read through it, pursing his lips. 'Well, it seems to me that he is of no use here, but I think we can use this letter as extra ammunition if we should need it, so I shall keep it here. I will write you a letter to say I think you should be allowed out of this marriage, the reasons being exactly as Mrs Bower directed, given her vast experience, and I will forward the details to your barrister if you will send me his name and address.' He put all the paperwork into a folder and stood up. 'Perhaps choose one from out of town,' he suggested. 'Maybe York, or London, where you are unknown, and then no gossip should accrue.'

Lydia stood up too. Was that it? she wondered. Nothing else required from me, then?

'Thank you so much, Dr Tennyson. I appreciate your advice.'

'I am pleased to be of assistance,' he told her. 'And I hope the outcome will lead to a happier phase in your life.' He paused. 'Is there a chance that you might enter a more fruitful union? You are still young enough, providing that the lawyers don't take too much time over such an important issue, straightforward as it should be.'

'Sadly there is no one at present, Dr Tennyson,' she said after a moment. 'But I have plans that will keep me occupied for some time to come. I am looking forward to acting as an independent woman, with no one to answer to.'

They drove back to Lydia's house. Emily didn't question her friend or expect her to chat about indifferent topics, and Lydia was glad, as she was quite shaken after her ordeal, but relieved that there had been no invasion of her privacy. Dr Tennyson had the details provided by Mrs Bower, and it seemed that had been enough.

'Once I've asked my father to find me an out of town

barrister, I can begin to look for a suitable property to adapt into a school,' she said when they turned down her lane, and she glanced across at the Wades' cottage and joinery shop. Emily noticed the direction of her gaze.

'Mr Wade is keeping busy, is he?' she asked curiously.

'I believe so,' Lydia answered. 'I rarely see him for a chat, for he never lingers when he drops the children off, but I do sometimes take them home to save him time. Emily, will you come in for a cup of tea? I really do want to say thank you.'

'Oh, my dear girl,' Emily said. 'I have done nothing but drive you there and back, so I don't need any thanks. You would have done the same for me had our circumstances been reversed.'

'Of course I would, except that you are more worldly wise than I am, and wouldn't have been as unaware as I was. I was just waiting for things to improve! How ridiculous is that?' She began to laugh; at her innocence, her discomfort in speaking of bedroom encounters, and her embarrassment about speaking to her husband on the subject, and then Emily laughed too.

'Lydia,' she said as they approached her gate. 'Throw your hat in the air!'

So she unpinned it, took it off and threw it as high as she could, and it came down and landed on the gatepost.

'Well done,' Emily laughed. 'Now all we have to do is find you another husband!'

Lydia got down to rescue her hat and open the gate, and looked up at Emily. 'I don't think so,' she said. 'Not yet, thank you very much, and in any case I might be stuck with this one for a while yet.'

*

'I could throw you a party,' Emily said. 'I'll try to find some eligible rich men.'

They were having a quiet celebration with red wine, at Emily's suggestion. 'Please don't,' Lydia implored. 'They might decide I'm a scandalous woman and not want to come near me. I'll concentrate on my school; it could take a long time for it to come to fruition. What you *could* do is ask Gideon if he knows anyone with a building to sell or rent that could be converted into a school; and as I said, I'll need sponsors, Emily. Who do you know?'

Emily groaned. 'I knew there would be a catch. Pour me another glass, Lydia. I can think much better then.'

CHAPTER THIRTY-FOUR

After Emily had driven off, Lydia took off her shoes and rolled down her stockings, then went upstairs to take off her corset. 'I don't like this,' she muttered. 'I am not in need of anything to squeeze in my flesh. Why should I wear it? Begone!' she crowed. 'I'm free to wear what I like and do what I like, or at least within reason, and *definitely* within the law.'

She threw the offending garment on to the bed and took the pins and combs out of her hair to let it down. It settled below her shoulders in thick unruly waves.

Now, she considered. What I need is an office of sorts, or even just a chest of drawers to keep paperwork: one drawer for my school plan, and a separate one for the paperwork regarding Nicholas and the divorce. I know, I'll use the one in Nicholas's bedroom – no, *not* Nicholas's room. He's gone – it's the guest room now.

Somehow the pressure to conform, to behave as a wife – a woman without any right to do anything without deferring first to her husband – should behave had dissolved, and she felt free, freer than she had ever felt during the last three years. She wandered in to look around and ascertain what she should move and what she would need.

A sharp rap on the back door made her jump. Who was that? Those who knew her came to the front door, except for Cook who always came to the back. Maggie too came to the front door if she thought it might be unlocked.

She looked out; she could only see the top of a boy's head, taller than Ben or Charlie, and a pair of feet clad in working boots. Sighing, she headed down the stairs and through the kitchen to open the back door. It was Matthew and a youth, who looked older than his own children, maybe thirteen or so. Matthew had Mary on his shoulders, and she looked as if she'd been crying.

Matthew's eyebrows shot up, she supposed in surprise at the manner of her dress, but he touched his forehead, and the boy did the same. 'Sorry to bother you, Mrs Mercer, but I promised to look out for a lad to do general jobs for you.'

'Oh, so you did, Mr Wade.' She'd forgotten; with all the other things crowding her mind she hadn't given his offer a thought, even though she really did need someone.

'I've brought Jim,' he said. 'He's 'son of Ted, a former fellow worker from Stephenson's who's going to be working with me. Is it all right for him to look around to see what needs doing?'

She blew out a breath. 'Oh, yes, of course. Hello, Jim. Would you care to look in the stable first, and then in the coal and wood store? There's plenty of wood, thanks to Mr Wade's giving me offcuts, for which I'm very grateful, and it needs cutting or splitting.'

Mary was leaning from her father's shoulder to reach her, and she lifted her arms to take her from him. 'Why, she's so hot! Is she feverish?' She held the toddler close. 'Poor darling, are you not very well?'

Mary clung to her, her arms around her neck, and began to wail. 'You'd better come in, Matthew,' Lydia said, giving up on propriety, and after giving the boy some instructions about the animals in the field he followed her into the kitchen.

'Alice has been looking after her,' he said, taking his daughter back from Lydia, who picked up a small pan and poured milk into it before putting it on to the warm hob, then reached into a cupboard. 'I brought her out with me to see if she would settle,' Matthew continued, 'but clearly she hasn't.'

'I'll give her a powder and some warm milk,' Lydia said, indicating that he should sit down. 'Has Alice given her anything?'

'No, she just called me in.' He shook his head. 'It's a worry! I've been so lucky with my bairns: they've never ailed except for colds in winter, and they've soon shaken them off.' He gently rocked Mary, soothing her as he spoke. Alice became Mary's surrogate mother at far too tender an age, Lydia thought. I recall so well the day their mother died giving birth to Aaron, and now little Mary can run around without any help at all.

'You can leave Mary with me for now, Matthew – I'll look after her, but I'd like to speak to you later, please, if you have the time.'

'I'll always have time, Mrs Mercer . . . Lydia.' He smiled. 'Something is different about you today. I saw you and Mrs

Horner drive by earlier, and hoped you were having a day out.'

She laughed. 'Not exactly. Our outing didn't take long, but the outcome was tremendous.'

'Today has been a good day for me too, apart from Mary being unwell.' He kissed the little girl's cheek. 'Her middle name is June; I'm wondering whether to use it. Not that I ever want to forget her ma, my Mary, and I never will, but it might help 'children to think of *this* Mary as Mary June. But that isn't what I meant by a good day.' He took a deep, satisfying breath. 'Young Jim's father worked alongside me at Stephenson's, and now he's been dismissed as well cos he wasn't able to work 'extra hours Stephenson wanted. He came to me yesterday and asked if I'd any work he could do! He has three bairns – Jim is 'eldest – and I said yes, as I'd already been considering that I could do with somebody else. Work is rolling in!'

'Really? That's wonderful! I'm so pleased for you, Matthew.' She patted his shoulder and he closed his hand over hers.

'It started with you, Lydia,' he murmured. 'I might never have begun without you, I was at such a low ebb.'

She nodded. He was. And who wouldn't have been, losing his wife and his job and with six children to bring up. She bent over to take Mary June, who was falling asleep on her father's knee, and they swapped places, she taking the chair with the toddler on her lap and he pouring the warm milk into a cup over some small pieces of bread and stirring the powder into the pobs before handing the cup to Lydia.

'Well,' she said quietly, 'there might be even more work coming your way, but at the moment everything needs talking through. And something even more momentous could be happening too.'

'Which is?'

'I can't even speak about it yet. I can only say that I must consult a lawyer, and not my father, but someone unknown to me. The action will change my life if it is successful.'

He shook his head. 'I've no idea what you might be talking about.'

'And I can't tell you yet, but I think I could say I have been through stage one today.'

'You look different,' he commented. 'Relaxed, more at ease, and – lovely,' he murmured, 'with your hair loose about your shoulders. I didn't realize it was so long.' He reached out as if to finger a strand and then straightened up, begging her pardon, and turned for the back door, murmuring that he'd see what Jim was up to. She reflected that though it might be considered unseemly of Matthew to behave in such a manner, she had enjoyed the sensation and knew she had a smile on her face.

Whilst she fed Mary June, who kept opening her mouth for another spoonful, she pondered on what her next steps would be. Tomorrow she would ask to see her father professionally, if he was in the office and not with a client; then she'd call to see Dawson at the bank, and finally visit her mother and tell her about Nicholas and her probable divorce, though perhaps not every aspect of it. She would tell all of them that her husband had left the country permanently.

Mary June was falling asleep. Lydia carried her into the sitting room, took a shawl from the back of a chair and wrapped her in it, then gently lowered her on to the sofa, resting her head on a soft cushion and covering her with a warm blanket which she often used herself whilst reading in the evening.

She heard Matthew, and she thought Jim too, coming back into the kitchen and went in to speak to them. 'Mary June is asleep,' she murmured, and Matthew smiled at the name and nodded in approval. 'I think you should leave her here,' Lydia went on. 'She can sleep with me tonight, and I'll make sure she's safe.'

'Thank you, Mrs Mercer,' he murmured, using her surname for Jim's sake, she was sure.

She turned to the boy. 'What do you think, Jim – can you tackle what needs doing? Looking after the animals and keeping the stable clean – I know it has been neglected? Are you willing to bring in coal and chop wood and sweep outside if it needs it?'

'Oh aye, I can do all o' that. I know how to chop wood, and I'm all right wi' animals. When can I start?' he asked eagerly.

'Tomorrow at eight? It would be wonderful if you could come every day but Sunday and check if the coal hods need filling, make sure there's enough firewood for the day each morning, feed the animals and put them in the field, and any other job that needs doing, and I'll pay you every Saturday. How does that sound?'

'Sounds good, Mrs Mercer.' He touched his forehead. 'Thanks very much. And thanks for recommending me, Mr Wade. Me ma and da will be right chuffed.'

'You're welcome, Jim,' Matthew said. 'I'm sure Mrs Mercer will be pleased with you. Now it's time you were getting off home, but I believe you wanted a word wi' me, Mrs Mercer?'

'I do, if you're not in a hurry. I won't keep you long; you'll be anxious to get home too. Goodbye, Jim, I'll see you in the morning. If I'm not about, you'll probably find Cook and Maggie here already, so just tell them that I've employed you and start on your jobs.'

The boy touched his forehead again and was gone, and they heard him whistling as he went out of the gate, fastening it securely behind him.

'Just briefly, Matthew,' she said, 'I want to tell you, as a friend and neighbour, that Nicholas has written to tell me that he has left me and – and is not considering returning.'

'What!' Matthew's forehead creased in consternation. 'Does he expect you to follow him? What's his destination? Has he said?'

'I believe that he's bound for America.'

'But he didn't ask you to go with him?'

'No. Not that I would have done in any case.'

'But you're his lawful wife, and if he hasn't asked you to follow him, then he's deserted you. What are you supposed to do? How are you expected to survive?'

'I don't think that even crossed his mind. I suppose he thought that my father would take responsibility for me.'

'That's shocking!' Matthew said vehemently. 'To leave his wife and tell her in a letter. Not man enough to do it face to face! Does he consider himself to be a gentleman?'

'Oh, I expect so,' she answered mildly. 'That is how he will portray himself. But don't worry, Matthew. I'll manage well enough. I have a plan that I want to unfold, and this is what I wanted to confide in you. I've loved teaching your children to read and write, but I'm not a professional teacher: I don't have any qualifications, and in any case married females are not allowed to teach in national schools, only in private ones, dame schools and suchlike, where they can.'

'But who can afford those? Not the average parents; not people like me!'

She lifted a finger. 'Sshh! Listen, Matthew. I want to open a school, and if you will bear with me, I will explain.'

CHAPTER THIRTY-FIVE

She hadn't wanted to rush into telling Matthew her plans, though she thought she had intimated at least some of them to him; she hadn't formulated them completely for herself yet, and realized that she must speak to her father first. He would, she knew, view her plan professionally, whilst she was thinking emotionally, especially now. Would being an abandoned wife make the prospective plan more difficult?

I must write down what I hope to achieve: a school for how many? Boys as well as girls, in equal numbers? And where*? Where will I find a building suitable for renovating into a school?*

Mary June had fallen asleep again, and the tip of her thumb was slipping from between her lips; Lydia covered her more closely with the shawl and blanket, her thoughts continuing. And what about a nursery for children of Mary June's age? Could that be possible? She rose from her chair and went to stand by the window. I mustn't bite off more than I can chew, but it would be good to catch them whilst they're young, so also give young mothers a short break in their busy days.

She leaned sideways to watch Frisky and the donkey,

standing by the fence and looking over it into the drive. Perhaps I'll bring them inside, she thought. Dusk is descending. I don't like to be in the stable once it gets dark. She glanced at Mary June, who was still fast asleep, then making sure that the fireguard was in place she tiptoed into the hall and reached for an old gardening coat that she kept for visits to the animals.

They both followed her when she opened the gate and headed into the stable. Jim had already tidied and swept the floor and filled the hay bags with fodder, and it was with a sigh of relief at being spared a job that she closed up the stable doors and turned back to the house. Sunset was beginning to drop and she drew in a deep breath; she loved to watch the ending of daylight, and it had been a meaningful day: she felt less frazzled than she had at the start of it, calmer and more positive. Going to the front window she looked inside; Mary June was still fast asleep, breathing steadily, and she smiled. The toddler was such a sweet child.

She turned round and gazed up at the sun sinking towards the horizon. It had been a fine bright day, with fluffy clouds, and the few wispy trails that were left were tinged with colour: gold, rose and vermilion. 'How lovely,' she breathed. 'Such an incredible day.' So much better than I expected, she mused. In fact, I hadn't known what to expect; the visit to see Dr Tennyson had been looming over me, and it proved to be neither embarrassing nor invasive, as I had expected, but an opportunity to begin a new life.

She looked about her. The lane was quiet, as it usually was at this time; there was little passing traffic of traps or milk carts or whistling butcher boys, unlike early mornings. She could hear a thrush singing its goodnight song; she recognized a blackbird, and the throaty coo-coo of doves somewhere high in the treetops.

A rabbit loped across the paddock, followed by another, and both paused to nibble on the grass. She watched them for a minute and then turned to make her way back to the kitchen; she must find some food for supper. There would be fresh soup in the larder, and bread baked this morning. *What else might Cook have left? She has free rein to make and bake; she knows my likes and I have few dislikes.*

Onion soup was a favourite, and she brought a pan of it out of the larder and put it on one hob to reheat, laying a slice of bread on the other to toast. She could still see the sunset from the front kitchen window and the paddock from the side ones, and saw that the rabbits were still nibbling the grass. *Good thing I haven't any vegetables growing there; they'd be gone before I had a chance to pick them.*

Looking down to the other end of the paddock, she pondered whether she could have a glasshouse there. *But would I have time to tend one when I begin the school?*

Pausing for thought, she remembered the soup and rushed to lift it from the hob, just as it began the rise to overspill. She shook her head to clear it, stirred the soup, and poured it into a mug with a handle rather than a bowl. She put the toasted bread on a plate and carried both across the kitchen to lay them on the wide windowsill whilst she gazed out over the paddock. 'Crazy woman,' she mumbled. 'Why didn't I think of this before?' She opened the back door and looked out.

How much acreage do I have? It's a very large paddock, a field really. I must keep Frisky, he's essential for getting about, and the donkey, too – she's so gentle and calming. Janet! Wherever did that name come from? The bottom end could be . . . and there would still be space for a playground as well as a—

What am I thinking, she admonished herself. Who do I know who could advise me? Matthew. He must be tired of me asking him for advice. Oh, soup. Must eat.

She sat down to enjoy her soup and had just finished when she heard Mary June – the name came so easily to her now – call out for her father. She hurried into the sitting room, calling, 'I'm coming, love.'

The child was sucking her thumb, the shawl still draped over her. 'Want Da,' she said, and put up her arms to be picked up. Lydia obliged and sat down with the toddler on her knee. 'Da's at work,' she said, thinking that might well be the usual answer. 'Are you hungry? Want some soup?'

Mary June nodded, then slid down on to the floor. 'Alice?' she said, and Lydia got up too and took her hand. 'Come on. Soup first, and then we'll look at the rabbits! I have had such a splendid idea,' she told the little girl as she put warm soup into a bowl and then lifted her up to a chair at the kitchen table. She looked about for an apron to fasten beneath Mary June's neck, and pulled up a chair next to her, giving her a spoon. 'Shall I tell you about it?' she said. 'You'll be the first to know.'

Mary June opened her mouth to take the soup that was being offered and then put her own spoon into the bowl as well, spilling soup down her front as she attempted to feed herself. Lydia laughed. 'Though I'm going to ask your da for his advice before I begin,' she went on, 'and then my father. You don't know him, though you might have met him.'

She managed to feed Mary June most of the bread and soup and have a rather one-sided discussion of the possibility of building a school next to the house, but nothing about how big or small it might be. Mary June considered very carefully, her eyes wide but blinking sleepily, and finally asked again, 'Alice?'

'Shall we try out the bed?' Lydia suggested.

She picked her up and took her to the sink to wash off the remains of the soup, drying her face with a kitchen towel. 'I think that a bath in the morning will do,' she went on. 'I can't find the energy to fill a tub of water tonight, but what I can find for you is my very special dolly. She's soft and cuddly and likes to be in bed.'

'Door!' There was no mistaking the command from Mary June. The knocker had been wielded gently, and Lydia called out, 'Who is it?'

'Matthew!'

'Come in!' Foolishly, she hadn't locked the door as she usually did.

'I'll fit a chain,' Matthew said as he stepped inside.

'For me?' Lydia asked mildly.

'For the door!' he said firmly. 'You shouldn't leave it open for anyone to just walk in!' He held out his arms, and Mary June struggled to get down. Lydia set her gently on the floor and she ran into Matthew's embrace.

'I didn't think you were coming back. I told you she could stay.' Lydia was disappointed.

'I know – I'm sorry. It was a unanimous decision taken by 'other bairns – I wasn't given an option.' He grinned. 'They all said they wouldn't sleep if she wasn't at home.'

'Aaron's talking already then?' she suggested wryly.

'Except for Aaron,' he added quickly. 'I was voted down.'

'I was about to put her to bed. She's had a sleep, and I've given her some bread and soup, and we've come up with a plan.'

'Not another plan!'

'Can I explain now or would you rather wait? It might take some time.'

'I'll wait, I think. Is it to do with 'other plan?'

'Replacing the other one, but I still have to speak to my father and the bank, which I will do tomorrow after the children have finished their lessons.'

'Do you want to give 'bairns a day off? They can entertain themselves and I'll be able to keep an eye on them now that Ted's working with me. Not that they're any bother. They're good bairns on the whole.'

She paused for only a second to think. 'Yes,' she said. 'I'll be able to catch my father if I go in early. It's imperative that I speak to him first.'

Matthew gave a frown. 'You'll mention Mercer, won't you? Not just this plan?' He didn't give Nicholas his full name; it was as if he had taken up cudgels against this errant husband. 'You'll tell your da that he's cleared off abroad?'

'I will, Matthew; and I'll also tell him that I'm going to sue for divorce.'

'But . . .' He seemed confused. 'I thought women couldn't do that? Thought they were stuck wi' . . .' He paused. 'I won't say what I'd call him for leaving you in 'lurch.'

'I could guess,' she said, smiling. 'But it seems that there are some circumstances where women can sue for divorce;

precedents have occurred, with good results for the wife. I'm going to try, at least.'

'People might turn against you,' he muttered.

'Well, then I'll know who my friends are, won't I? Anyway, the court case might be held elsewhere, perhaps in London? The newspapers won't be interested in Yorkshire gossip.'

Matthew shook his head. 'You are a brave lady, Lydia. My admiration knows no bounds.'

'I'm not brave, Matthew, but I can't let what Nicholas has done ruin my life. Things are changing for women – there is a chance that they will be able to leave unhappy marriages and not be left without a home. They might even be allowed to set up in business under their own names, not their husband's or their father's; *and*,' she went on, 'one day young women will be able to work for a university degree just as their brothers can.'

'Do you believe that, Lydia?' he asked quietly.

'I believe *in* it,' she said. 'Whether it will happen in my lifetime, I don't know.'

CHAPTER THIRTY-SIX

Cook and Maggie arrived as she was bringing Frisky out from the stable. 'I have several appointments in Beverley,' she told them. 'I doubt if I'll be back before you finish, so will you lock up as always, please? Oh, and I've taken on a young lad. I expect he'll be here at any minute; he's called Jim and seems very willing. He'll fill the coal hods and bring them in, so will you tell him where to put them, please, Maggie? He's going to chop wood too, and do the stable work. He'll sweep the drive of leaves as well. I'm sure you'll find him useful. Will you tell him if there's anything else you wish him to do?'

'Master still away, is he, Mrs Mercer?' Cook asked. 'Shall I just do 'cooking and baking for one?'

Lydia nodded. 'For some time yet,' she answered, thinking that she would tell them soon that he was working abroad. She knew they were not gossips, but she didn't want to give them the full picture. 'The butcher's lad has been,' she went on. 'There's meat in the larder. I could quite fancy a lamb stew if you would, please, Cook. Oh, and maybe some cheese scones. The ones you make are so delicious.'

Not too taxing, she thought as she drove away; it was a relief to know that they were so reliable. It was a good arrangement, she thought: they were happy not to live in, they were not overworked, and she was glad to have them.

As she drove into Beverley she saw her father walking to the office and drew up to offer him a ride. 'You're out early,' he said, climbing in beside her for the short journey.

'I wanted to be the first to catch you,' she said, and suddenly felt nervous. 'I also need to speak to Dawson at the bank.' He turned to look at her: had there been a sudden inflection in her voice that had alerted him?

'Something cropped up?' he asked.

She pulled into the office yard. 'Yes, as it happens, something has. Who else is in the office?'

He shrugged. 'Everybody, I expect.'

'Could we sit here for a minute while I give you the bare facts?'

He nodded. 'Nicholas?'

'Who else?' Her voice croaked.

'What else would make you so nervous? It's not me, is it, my dear? I don't make you nervous? You can tell me anything, Lydia, and I'll be on your side.'

She could feel her throat close. Yes, of course he would be. He was her father; he would always defend her in every way, not only in law.

'Nicholas has left me,' she said baldly, taking the letter from her pocket and giving it to him.

He read the few lines. 'What! The—' He swore; she had never in her life heard her father swear. She was sure that it was the same blasphemous word that Matthew would have used if he hadn't stopped himself. Gentlemen both, she considered.

'When did you receive this? We could stop him from sailing.'

'Actually, I'd rather you didn't,' she said, her voice breaking and her eyes welling with tears. 'I'd sooner he was gone. It's probably too late in any case.' They sat in silence for a few minutes, and then she said, 'I want to apply for a divorce – or rather an annulment of our marriage, Papa.'

He didn't seem shocked. Had he switched into his lawyer role? 'Difficult for women,' he murmured, 'although in some rare cases it can happen. He hasn't any reason to divorce *you*, though he could have claimed that you'd been unfaithful. It's lucky that you haven't any children, because he could have claimed them if he'd wanted to.'

She shook her head. 'But *I* have good reason to divorce *him*, and he'll be embarrassed by the inference everyone will draw.'

He glanced sharply at her. 'What inference?'

And so, in the plainest of words, she told him. No beating about the bush, just the barest of facts, and the only response he made was to take hold of her hand and give it a tender squeeze.

When he left her to go into his office and absorb what she had told him, she walked away to her usual coffee shop. She was shaking, and needed something to steady her. She didn't go into the café where she had met Hannah. She didn't want to speak to anyone, just to clear her head before she called at the bank, but in particular she did not want to speak to

Hannah, who with her sharp acuity would know at once that there was something amiss.

She ordered cake and sipped a cup of strong sweet coffee. She had not been looking forward to the discussion with her father, but he had listened to her without speaking, and she had seen his eyebrows rise a few times and heard a drawing in of breath. As he'd turned to enter the office, he'd paused. 'Of course I'd heard of Effie Gray and Ruskin,' he'd commented quietly. 'It made headline news at the time, but it's mostly forgotten now. We'll take the case to London,' he'd added. 'Don't even think about it, Lydia. I'll see to everything. I know a few people.'

And so I must leave it to him. He'll do the best for me and shelter me from publicity. I'll speak to Mama; I must tell her at least that Nicholas has left the country, but need not add any more. She doesn't read newspapers so is not likely to read any salacious gossip, and I know that my father won't discuss anything with her.

She walked slowly from the café to her bank and hoped that Mr Dawson would not be too busy to see her. Several people were forming a small queue at the counter, so she bypassed them and went to ask a reception clerk if Mr Dawson would be available today, and whether she might request an appointment.

'In about half an hour, Mrs Mercer,' she was told, and she thanked him and left, promising she would come back in good time.

She wandered along Toll Gavel, looking in windows, and then into Wednesday Market. A few stalls were set up, though not many as it wasn't market day, and she noticed that the woman who had bought Alice's baby items was there. She had various items on display, but none of them Alice's.

Mrs May recognized Lydia and called out a good morning, beckoning her to come forward. 'Is 'knitter still in business?' she asked. 'I sold all 'garments I bought from her friend. Any chance of some more? I've got customers waiting.'

'I, erm, I don't know,' Lydia said. It was true; Alice hadn't mentioned her knitting lately. 'I'll ask when I next see her. What kind of things were you thinking of? Infant clothing, blankets? I believe she will knit to order.'

'I can sell owt she knits. Bairns' jumpers, leggings, pram blankets, cardigans. Whatever she's got. I'd be obliged.'

'Very well. I'll be out in her district tomorrow, so I'll ask if I see her.'

She didn't want to appear too eager; nor did she want to overburden Alice. She walked back towards the bank and called in at a shop that sold knitting wool and needles. Noticing some needles that were twice as thick as the ones Alice normally used and a pile of thick cream wool sitting next to them, she bought a pair of needles and a reasonable quantity of yarn.

Half an hour later, Mr Dawson was available, and the clerk beckoned her forward to take her into his office. Seeing her come through the door, the banker rose to his feet and smiled. 'So very nice to see you again, Mrs Mercer. I hope you are well?' He drew out a chair for her, and she noticed the file that was on his desk.

'I'm quite well in health, thank you, Mr Dawson, but a little down in spirit.'

'I'm sorry to hear that. Is there no further news from your husband?'

'There is indeed news of him,' she said, trying to keep her

voice steady. She took off her gloves and put them on the desk. 'But it is not good, I'm afraid.'

He sat down opposite her and clasped his hands together. 'Mmm, I did wonder, as there was some movement in your account. I was surprised, but not concerned; it was, I thought, quite legitimate, and your dowry is unaffected.'

'And relating to . . .' she murmured.

'Relating to . . .' he opened the file in front of him, 'a payment to a steamship company in Liverpool. The payment was made before we had finalized the change of account name.'

She nodded slowly. So he has gone, she considered. When he wrote to me he had already booked his passage. 'I received a letter from my husband, Mr Dawson, to say he was leaving for America. This is proof that he has indeed departed.'

'I think that is probably correct.' He hesitated for a second. 'And will you be following him in due course? Is that on the cards?'

Slowly she shook her head. 'I am not a gambling woman,' she said. 'And America has nothing to offer me that I can't find in my own country. It is a relief to know my situation at last. So,' she said brightly, 'what about the accounts? How do we stand?'

He shook his head, smiling. 'Transferring money abroad is extremely difficult, Mrs Mercer, and as America is apparently awash with it, I think we can safely say that Mr Mercer won't be needing any of yours.'

CHAPTER THIRTY-SEVEN

She collected the pony and trap and set off to visit her mother on the way home. She felt steadier, calmer now than previously, as if difficulties had been removed or handed over to others; she could rely completely on her father to attend to things she couldn't, such as the divorce, and she trusted Mr Dawson to keep her money safe.

My money, she thought, and not Nicholas's, because he had made the decison to remove himself from her, their marriage and his country. It wasn't easy to assimilate these facts, she admitted; through no fault of her own she had found herself in an unsuitable situation, which now appeared to be resolved.

She tied Frisky's rein to the fence; there was no room for the trap on the drive of her parents' house. She saw her mother at the front window and gave her a cheery wave and a smile. I must show an aura of happiness despite feeling as if I have been embattled, she acknowledged, for Mother will sense any suspicion of anxiety or unease.

'My dear!' her mother greeted her at the door. 'How lovely to see you.'

'Are you lunching out?' Lydia asked her, for her mother looked very smart and fashionable, which rather gave the game away. 'I've only come for half an hour or so, so if you are I won't hold you up.'

'Oh, you must always drop in, my dear, it's always good to see you. Shall I ring for coffee?' She hovered as if about to ring the bell for the maid.

'Thank you, but no. I have had one already, at a nice quiet little place near the bank – do you know the one I mean?' She sat down on the sofa. 'Who are you meeting?'

She let her mother give a short account of the friends she would be seeing, and because her mother was so smiley and happy Lydia decided that she wouldn't talk about Nicholas. It would ruin her afternoon.

'I had to go to the bank,' she said, 'so I dropped by to see Papa. Mama, can you guess what I'm planning? It's so exciting!'

Her mother shook her head. Lydia saw her glance at the clock on the wall, and said quickly, 'Well, it might take too long to explain now, especially as you're ready to go out, so maybe we'll discuss it another time. I want to ask your opinion.'

'*My* opinion!' Her mother laughed. 'No one asks my opinion, my dear, especially not your father, so I dare say it's not worth a pinch of salt. But I'd like to know, when you have the time.'

Lydia got up from the sofa and kissed her mother's cheek. 'All right. I'd better fly and let you get ready. Enjoy your lunch, and give my regards to your friends.' She picked up her handbag. 'I'll let myself out – I'll see you again soon.'

Frisky kicked up his heels and set off in the direction of home. 'It was ever thus,' she sighed. Mother was always busy socializing and didn't ever think her opinion was necessary or of any worth, which isn't true.

Arriving home, she went inside and took off her hat and coat and slipped into an old jacket before going back outside to put Frisky in the paddock, where donkey Janet was waiting. 'Poor donkey,' she murmured, giving her a pat. 'You don't go anywhere, do you, just stuck in this paddock all day.'

To her surprise, Janet put her nose up against her and just stood there. 'What is it then?' she murmured. 'Have you been lonely without us?'

The donkey stood perfectly still whilst Lydia ran her hands over her head and ears and felt a calmness flowing through her own body. Frisky came over and stood next to them and waited patiently; when Lydia looked up, Matthew was standing inside the gate watching them. Ben was with him, watching too.

'Hello,' she called, and the spell was broken.

'We wondered how you were after your morning in Beverley?' Matthew said as he and Ben walked towards her. 'We've been sent to invite you to lunch.'

'Really? At your house?'

'Alice has made scones,' Ben told her. 'She wouldn't let us try 'em 'til you came. What were you saying to 'donkey?'

'I don't think I was talking to her – I think *she* was telling *me* something.'

'Donkeys can't talk,' Ben objected.

'No, they can't,' she agreed, but she knew that donkey Janet had been offering her some kind of comfort.

She locked up the house and the three of them set off to walk back to the Wade cottage. 'Not working today?' she asked Matthew.

'I was,' he said, 'until I was sent to deliver the invitation. Alice said we shouldn't wait for a special day to invite friends to lunch. I can't think who is putting such ideas into her head,' he said wryly, looking straight at Lydia. 'But I told her I could only stop for an hour.' He grinned. 'I've got another big order – came in this morning from your friend Gideon Horner. It's not for him, but someone he knows.'

'That's wonderful, Matthew!' She tucked her arm into his. 'News soon spreads, doesn't it?'

'It seems that it does, and now that I've got Ted working for me I can accept more. I'm thinking of getting an apprentice.'

She was proud that he was doing so well. 'Stephenson will be rueing the day he sacked you,' she said, and then could have bitten off her tongue. It was also the day Matthew's wife Mary had died. She clutched his arm. 'I'm sorry,' she breathed. 'I'm so sorry. I didn't mean to—'

He put his hand over hers. 'It's all right,' he said softly. 'It's a day I shall never forget, but I can't expect people to remember every tragedy that occurs. I have Aaron to remind me constantly, but 'other bairns, apart from Alice, are beginning to forget.'

She thought of the memory book that she had suggested the children should write of their mother, but gradually, as time passed, they had begun other projects. I must bring that up again. Catch them before their childhood races away, and their memories too.

'But tell me, Lydia.' Matthew's voice broke into her thought. 'How are you coping with *your* problems and tragedies?'

She was silent for a moment, her eyes following Ben, who had jumped over a ditch into a copse. 'I'm all right,' she said softly. 'I wasn't to begin with, but I realized some time ago that Nicholas and I were not a good match – we had nothing in common, and he must have felt the same, but there were things that he should have told me: major concerns that would ultimately concern me too.'

Matthew turned to her, frowning, not understanding issues she could not possibly discuss. She tried to lighten her tone. 'But not tragedies, Matt, just mistakes in our choice of marital partner, and if I'm honest I'm glad that he's gone away. If . . . if all goes well and our marriage is dissolved, then I can get on with my life. I'm not old . . .' Her voice trailed away. As they approached the Wade cottage, she wanted to say that she hoped to find love, for she certainly hadn't found it the first time round, but somehow she just couldn't find the words.

'Miss Lydia, Miss Lydia!' The children rushed to greet her, all but Alice, who, flushed from the heat of the oven and wearing an apron, was standing in the doorway with a tray of scones in her hands. Lily and Charlie, who had been trying their best to put a cloth on the table, dropped it into a heap and ran to hug her, and Lydia fell to her knees to reach the two youngest, picking up Aaron to keep him out of harm's way and blowing a kiss to Mary June. She looked up to see Matthew gazing down at her with a smile.

'What?' she said.

He shook his head. 'Nothing. Just that you look so happy.'

'I am,' she said softly. 'Happier than I have been in a long time.'

To her surprise, he too dropped to the floor, tucking his

long legs underneath him. 'I'm glad,' he said. 'I've often thought that you seemed unhappy and lost somehow. But – Nicholas? Do you not miss him at all?'

'Not in the least,' she told him. 'He was the reason I was unhappy. He behaved as though he didn't care a jot for me – I'd guess that he realized I wasn't the wife he desired after all. I wish I could tell you more, but I can't. There's no shame, none on either part, except that he should have spoken. But perhaps he couldn't,' she murmured, more to herself than to Matthew. She shook her head. 'But it's done with now – or soon will be.'

Matthew got to his feet – how lithe he was – and put out a hand to take Aaron. Then he gently patted her cheek, as if he were comforting one of his children after a fall.

Lydia shook the now creased cloth and laid it on the table so that Alice could put out crockery and cutlery, pork pie and mustard, and arrange the plated scones and a pot of jam in the middle. 'Lottie's ma brought us 'jam,' Alice said. 'She said she'd made it herself from last year's apples and blackberries.' Then she frowned, and looked at the old clock ticking on the wall. 'This isn't really lunch, is it? Is it afternoon tea?' she asked Lydia.

'It can be anything you want it to be, Alice.'

'Well, we used to call it dinner,' she said. 'Didn't we, Da?'

'Aye,' he said. 'It's our betters who call it lunch, Alice. Isn't that right, Mrs Mercer?'

She nodded. 'You could be right, Mr Wade, and when you've made your fortune you can call it whatever you like! For instance, when I called to see my mother today, she was about to go out for lunch with friends, and she won't be eating anything better than we are having now.' Which wasn't quite true, she considered, but the company in this cosy little cottage was perfect.

When they'd finished eating and Aaron, sitting in the new high chair that his father had made for him, had thrown most of his scone on to the floor after first licking off all the jam, Lydia thought that it might be just the right time to make an announcement.

'I have something to tell you,' she said. 'Something that I think you will like.'

All but Mary June and Aaron looked up at her. 'Is it a treat?' Charlie asked.

'Not exactly,' she answered. 'But I think you'll be pleased.'

She glanced at Matthew, who had an enquiring frown on his forehead. 'It began when you all came to my house to learn to read. I really enjoyed that time, teaching you, and you all seemed to enjoy it too; and I thought how wonderful it would be if you could learn about other subjects too.'

'What's subjects, Miss Lydia?' Charlie asked.

'It's other *things*,' she answered. 'Like numbers, and knowing how to add them together or take them apart; like adding up how many scones we've eaten or how many days there are in the week.'

'Seven,' Charlie shouted out.

'And it's about history,' she continued, 'and learning about what happened in the past, and geography too, and learning about the world. So I thought that what we needed was a proper school – an academy where many subjects could be taught.'

'I'd like that,' Ben said, crossing his arms. 'Finding out why birds sing and rabbits don't. So where is it, this school?'

'It isn't built yet. We have to get permission before we can start building, so we'll need to find a builder, and someone to put down floors, and build a roof and put in doors and windows. Such a lot to do, and where are we going to put it?'

From the corner of her eye she saw Matthew's lips turn up at the corners and she turned her head slowly to see his full expression. 'Is this your plan?' he asked quietly, and she nodded.

'I've spoken to my father and the bank manager to see if it's feasible.'

'And is it?'

'They both agree that it is.'

'And where will you put it?'

She looked towards the children, who were chattering to each other about what they were going to learn first, except for Alice, who seemed to be waiting for more information, and then back to Matthew.

'I have a very large field, haven't I? Enough room for a few sheep or cows, but I don't want either. I'm not a farmer. Will you measure up for me, Matthew, and tell me if it's feasible as a building plot? It won't be a large school, but big enough for local children between five and maybe twelve. A Children's Academy. And when it's built I shall find qualified teachers, I hope mainly married women, and they'll teach things children need to know.'

He leaned forward and took hold of her hand. 'Well done,' he murmured. 'Very well done indeed, Lydia.'

CHAPTER THIRTY-EIGHT

Lydia eventually told her mother that Nicholas had left her and gone abroad to live, and that she wasn't expected to follow and didn't want to.

'I don't understand.' Her mother was visibly upset. 'Nicholas was always so charming. I can't think why he would choose to do that; he had a good career ahead of him, a beautiful wife, and a lovely home. What else could a man want?'

'I have no idea, Mama,' Lydia answered, 'but whatever it was he obviously didn't find it with me. But,' she added carefully, 'it means that I am free to do whatever I want to do, and what I want to do is—'

Her mother broke in. 'But Nicholas wouldn't have stood in your way, Lydia dear, he would have allowed you to do whatever you wished, and given you his help and advice, as your father does for me.'

But you don't *do* anything, Mama, she wanted to say. Her mother loved the social life, the tea parties and suppers – some of them to raise funds for charity, it was true – but Lydia was sure there was nothing in her heart that roused her, that gave her the wonderful sense of herself that she had felt when teaching the Wade children.

Mother was brought up as a lady, Lydia thought, even though her parents were penniless, funded by others in the family who were able to finance them; and so she didn't tell her mother the full extent of her future plans, hoping that perhaps her father might do so. But she had told Alice that she was now living alone, because she was sure that Alice, being the bright intelligent child that she was, would have already noticed the absence of Nicholas, yet had never mentioned it, having been taught not to ask personal questions that were nothing to do with her.

'Are you lonely, Miss Lydia?' she asked, after Lydia had explained the circumstances. 'I did realize that something might have happened, when I came to stay with you. You can always come to us, you know, if you're feeling sad, and we'll cheer you up – like you did with us when our ma died.'

Lydia was touched by Alice's kindness and the child's instinctive realization that her life had changed, but in a totally different way from her own, a fact that was borne in on her when the girl went on to ask further questions.

'You'll still be able to come to us, won't you? And you'll still teach us our lessons as well as being – being . . .' She hesitated, as if not knowing how to express what she wanted to say.

'Being a friend?' Lydia prompted, and Alice nodded vigorously.

'And being our da's friend too? He does need you, Miss Liddy. He needs a grown-up friend as much as he needs his bairns.'

Lydia felt her eyes fill, and she blinked the tears away. 'Of course; I hope your da and I will always be friends, Alice. It doesn't always happen with grown-up people – not between men and women, at least – but I do hope our friendship will continue.'

Alice pressed her lips together. 'I hope so too,' she choked. 'Because you allus reminds us of how our ma loved us.'

'Of course she did, as your father does – and as I do too. I feel as if you are *my* family, *my* children, even though you're not.' She put out her arms and Alice slid into them, tears running down her cheeks. 'You can come to me at any time – you do know that, don't you?' She smoothed the girl's hair away from her face, and kissed her forehead. 'And you know now that every month there's a time when we women often feel sad about something – or so angry that we don't understand why we want to throw something across the room!'

Alice gave a sound between a sob and a laugh which sounded like a snort, and Lydia gave her a hug. 'Now,' she said. 'About this school, this academy – it might take some time to organize, because I might have to obtain permission to start, but on the other hand maybe not – I don't know yet. I do know that women can teach at home – dame schools, those are called – and the women who teach in them are not necessarily qualified. I am not either, but the teachers I want will be able to teach at my school – my academy – even if they can't teach at national schools because they are married.'

'Why does that mean they can't teach?' Alice asked.

'Because the positions have to be kept open for single women who need to earn a living. Married women are expected to rely upon their husbands for their income.'

Alice frowned. 'What if their husbands don't want them to?'

'Then, my dear, they're stuck, and their knowledge goes to waste.'

'Will I be able to come to this academy, or will I be too old by 'time it's built,' Alice asked, after a thoughtful pause.

'I see no reason why you shouldn't.' Lydia smiled. 'In fact, as you might well be older than the other children I would probably make you head girl, somebody the younger children could come to if they were a bit nervous about asking questions of the teachers.'

Alice gave a huge smile. 'And I could teach them to knit, too!'

So much to think about, Lydia considered. Matthew was looking around at various builders and Gideon Horner had asked an architect friend of his to visit Lydia to discuss her plans, whilst her father was contacting professional people who dealt with divorce.

She had no forwarding address in New York for Nicholas, if indeed that was his port of arrival, and she therefore couldn't tell him she was suing him for divorce. It won't be easy for him, she thought, if the story somehow follows him to America. His reputation will be in tatters, as mine might well be too. Am I being vindictive? I don't mean to be, but I want a life of my own. I want to be happy, and not to be known just as an abandoned wife.

The year moved on. November was cold and the weather got colder as December came in with its occasional sharp frosts. She continued teaching the Wade children and knew that this was still what she wanted to do; she loved the eagerness in their eyes when they read a page from a story book aloud or painted a picture from their imagination – perhaps a flower (this was Lily), or an indeterminate bird sitting on a tree branch (Ben). Charlie would bring her something he had made in his father's workshop, and Mary June, too young to construct anything, still knew how to bring down a tower of wooden building blocks with one fell swoop of her chubby hands.

She walked the first half of the road home with them, holding Mary June's hand, and then they all gave her a kiss before setting off to walk the latter part, Mary June skipping happily between Alice and Ben. She gave a wave to Matthew waiting outside the Wades' gate with Aaron lifted in his arms so that he could see his sisters and brothers, to whom he would sometimes wave. And as she turned round and retraced the route home, she gave a great sigh and felt the weight of sadness of going into an empty house.

'It is all quite doable, Mrs Mercer,' architect and surveyor agreed when they came to look at the site. 'A separate building from your house; it need not be of any great size. Boys and girls to be taught together, you said, and indeed why not? Maximum of twelve to fourteen, so I would suggest two rooms for teaching, an activity room, and a small quiet room with books to read. And did you say a nursery? I would suggest large windows to let in plenty of light, perhaps set fairly high so that the children don't get distracted by what is going on outside, and an outdoor play area. Two of the usual outdoor privies, and two inside for bad weather. Yes, I think that might do, but did you say there was something more?'

'A kitchen,' Lydia repeated, 'so that the children aged, say, ten years or more can learn basic cooking.'

'Mm, well, that follows my thinking.' The architect, Joseph Robson, rubbed his chin. 'What if we have a short corridor or passageway, say of brick and glass, leading from the school building to your back door and into the present kitchen, which could be enlarged easily enough, and the whole building' – he swung his arms wide to encircle it all – 'though attached, will be seen as separate from your present house!'

Would Cook be all right with that, Lydia wondered. She's only here in a morning, so it shouldn't be a problem, or she might even like to teach the children to bake, though there would have to be strict rules about clearing up afterwards.

She was so excited that plans were moving on. I hope there will be enough money to pay for it all, she thought. I must start to ask around for sponsors and explain that we'll need trustees to set it up; I'll ask my father if he would agree to be one, and then find responsible teachers to teach.

Oh, I just can't believe that it is actually going to happen!

CHAPTER THIRTY-NINE

Her father suggested a meeting at her house and said he would bring along a couple of people he thought might be interested in being trustees.

'It won't be taken out of your hands, Lydia, but we must follow the rules. Will you ask your neighbour – Wade? – if he would attend? He's the down to earth, no nonsense type of person just right for this project, and he knows what children need, as he seems to have several of his own.'

Of course she was delighted to do so, and to see that Matt was very pleased to be asked. He had come in to collect the children, who were staying later as their father got busier, weeks were moving on, and dusk was falling earlier.

'You're changing my life, Lydia,' he murmured. 'I'll be getting too big for my boots.'

'Then you must buy some bigger ones, Matthew,' she replied, laughing. 'Business is good, isn't it? You can afford a new pair.'

'I can!' He reached out and caught her by the waist and swung her round, her skirts flying. 'I have money in my pocket and I'm going to buy 'bairns some new clothes for winter!'

The children all rushed up. 'Swing me, Da,' Lily shouted.

'Me, me,' Mary June cried out, and clapped her hands. Lydia gathered her up, held her under the arms, and swung her around until she squealed.

Ben and Charlie just watched, Ben folding his arms across his chest as if to show that he was too big for such frivolity and Charlie, who had reached the stage of copying his brother as closely as he could, did the same.

'What are you cooking tonight?' Lydia asked, when she'd caught her breath. 'Is it your turn?'

Matthew had decided that on at least one night in the week he would cook their evening meal to save Alice having to do it, but occasionally, if he was busy – as he often was with so many orders coming in – he would forget and they would have to eat eggs: omelette with cheese, or simply fried with bacon. 'Beef stew; been cooking all day,' he said now. 'You can come if you'd like to – there's plenty. I'll walk you home afterwards; 'nights are getting dark.'

She took only a minute to say yes. Eating alone, she often made do with something simple such as toast and ham, even though Cook had left food in the larder for her. 'I'll just get my coat,' she said, and went to take it off the coat stand. Picking up a cake from the larder, she wrapped it in cheesecloth, locked the back door, and joined them outside. I need to tell him something anyway, she excused herself.

They could smell the stew as soon as they opened the cottage door, and everyone drew in a breath. Matthew tasted it and remarked it was his best stew ever; Alice raised her brows and sighed dramatically, then set the table and brought out bread. Lydia undressed Aaron and Mary June and put them into their bedtime clothes, before fastening old but clean serviettes beneath their chins. Serviettes that had seen better days at her house, but were perfect for catching the drips and splodges of food that the two youngest children would scatter.

Mary June looks so sweet, she thought, with her curls brushed, her hair the same dark auburn as her father's. Lily and Charlie were both as fair as their mother had been, and Alice and Aaron both had straight blond hair. Such a handsome family, Lydia considered. I wish they were mine. But she was happy that they all gave her a hug or a kiss when they greeted her in a morning, and again when leaving her after their lessons.

Matt served up the stew. He fed Aaron, whilst Lydia helped Mary June so that Alice could eat hers in peace. 'It's lovely, Da,' she said when she had tasted it. 'Much better than I can make.'

'Oh, I don't know about that,' he said. 'Aaron seems to think otherwise.' Aaron was blowing bubbles and spitting out small shreds of meat and potato. 'I think he might prefer vegetables. I didn't make a pudding,' he added, 'I ran out of time.'

The boys groaned, until Lydia said, 'I brought cake,' and then they all cheered. Everyone loved Cook's cakes, and Lydia had noticed that since she had got to know the Wade children, after Cook had filled the cake tin ready for the oven there was always enough mixture left to shape a few extra buns.

Aaron and Mary June were put to bed soon after the meal was over, and Lydia gathered her coat and scarf in preparation for going home before kissing everyone goodnight. 'Sleep tight, darlings,' she said. 'See you tomorrow.'

Lily put her arms round her, and then Charlie did too. Ben hung back, and then, as if making up his mind about kissing, held up his cheek for Lydia as well. At the door, Lydia stretched out her arms to Alice, who whispered, 'I wish you could stay.'

'You must come and stay with me one weekend,' Lydia whispered back, 'and we can go shopping. Did I tell you that Mrs May is eager to sell more knitting from you?'

'I haven't had time to do much,' Alice said quietly. 'There's always something else to do.'

Lydia nodded, and decided to have a word with Matt as he walked her home about Maggie coming to the Wades' once a week to do the housework and give Alice some time back. But she knew she must be careful not to interfere; Matt was keen to be independent and not seen as a helpless male.

'I won't be long,' he told the children. 'Lads, you're on your honour not to fight, not to touch 'fire under *any* circumstances, to wash your hands and faces, and be ready for bed when I get back.'

'Aw, can't we talk?' Ben asked.

'Of course you can talk,' their father smiled. 'Choose a subject, and mebbe I can join in when I get back. Alice, leave 'dishes and everything, and I'll do them.'

'A subject!' Charlie said. 'I know what that means. What shall we choose?'

'A painting,' Lily told him. 'We've got a book with pictures in it. Let's choose which we like best.'

'Lovely idea!' Lydia agreed, and blew them a kiss. 'See you tomorrow!'

She took Matt's offered arm as they stepped into the lane. It was almost dark, a pale moon partially hidden in the cloudy sky. 'Did you leave a light on at home?' he asked.

'No, I didn't, though I built up the fire in the sitting room. I'll start lighting the outside lamp now that it's getting darker, although I rarely get any callers.'

'Only me, and I generally carry a paraffin lamp.'

She drew in a breath. 'I have something to tell you,' she said.

'What?' His voice was suddenly tense. 'About 'school?'

'No. That's moving along. Surveyors and builders are meeting tomorrow. If all goes well, they'll begin soon after Christmas if the weather is right.'

She heard Matthew gasp, as if he'd forgotten about Christmas and what it might mean for the children, but he said nothing, just waited for her to continue.

'It's about the court case I'm bringing against – against Nicholas. It's to begin in London in just over a week's time. I have to be there, but thank goodness my father will come with me, even though he won't be involved unless he's asked to give a character reference, as he knew Nicholas. But he's very angry; he blames himself for introducing us, which means he's biased, so I don't understand why he thinks they would ask him anything.'

Matthew cleared his throat. 'Wear a veil,' he said, 'even though no one there will recognize you, only your name. Are you nervous about giving evidence?'

'Yes,' she murmured, 'I am. It's shaming.'

'Not for you it's not, onny for 'worthless beggar who brought this down on you!'

She could hear the anger in his voice, and she remembered it from when she had told him about his wife, and he had run like the wind to get home in time. The anger, she was sure, was because he knew that he could do nothing about this either.

'Did he – at any time – ask you to go with him?' he asked in a low voice.

'No,' she said. 'And I would have refused if he had. I had discovered we were incompatible quite early in our marriage.'

Her house was in darkness, apart from a glow from the sitting room where the fire was still burning, which she was pleased to see as it was a chilly damp night.

He took the keys from her and unlocked the door, then gave them back to her. 'I'll see you tomorrow,' she murmured, turning towards him. 'Thank you for supper, and your company.'

'My pleasure, Miss Lydia.' He gazed down at her. 'I'll *never* again call you Mrs Mercer. Will you go back to your maiden name after . . .' His words trailed away and he put his hands on either side of her face and bent towards her. He kissed her on each cheek, on her forehead, her nose, and then her lips, leaving her breathless.

'I'm . . .' she croaked.

'Don't speak,' he whispered. 'I'm sorry. I shouldn't have . . . not when you have so much to think about – not at all – it was wrong of me,' but he bent again to kiss her lips before he pulled away. 'Go inside. Lock your door, don't let me in. *Please*, don't let me in, not under any circumstances.'

More than anything she wanted him to kiss her again, but his family was waiting for him; children who would worry if he was late home. 'I won't,' she murmured, and stepped inside. Turning, she put her fingers to her lips, and as she began to close the door she reached out and pressed them to his mouth. He caught hold of the fingers and kissed the tips and gently pushed her hand back inside, pulling the door towards him and closing it.

Details were being finalized with the architect and surveyors with regard to the academy. Builders were there to give their verdict: a brick building to blend with Lydia's own house and the brick and glass corridor linking the two. A play area in front of the building for the younger children, with wooden swings and a roundabout. A fence to be put halfway across the paddock, the space nearest to the building for the children's sport and the top part for donkey Janet and Frisky to graze.

The boy, Jim, looked on with interest, wondering if he might be able to earn a copper or two clearing up after the builders came to prepare the site. Matt got the contract for fitting floors and cupboards and all things wood, apart from the desks and chairs which would be ordered from specialist furniture shops.

'I can't believe it's going to happen,' Lydia told Emily when she called the day before Lydia and her father were due to travel to London. Lydia was going to stay the night with her parents in Beverley, where they would catch the early train to Hull and then go on to London.

'And I still can't believe that you have to go through this annulment procedure,' Emily declared. 'I'm so sorry, Lydia.

It seems so unfair and dreadful that Nicholas should not have considered what impact it would have on your life when he told you to end your marriage if you could. It was very unkind . . . even cruel. Married women are so vulnerable when husbands can act in such a manner. I hope he cannot claim a penny from your dowry or your home.'

'In his defence, he hasn't touched the dowry,' Lydia told her. 'And apparently he could have, as the bank manager explained to me that a dowry is money meant for sharing. And Papa cleverly put the house in my mother's name before we got married.' She gave a little laugh. 'I don't think Mama knows about it, or she might have bought a frock or two and a few baubles on the strength of it.'

She was being flippant, but it was her way of coping with what lay ahead: with having the details of her most private life discussed in front of officials, judges and the general public, just as the infamous Effie Gray and Ruskin had had to and were still remembered for it. *It won't ever go away. I don't know if I can cope with the sordid details which will be talked about, and newspapers will try to find out where I live, and – and how will my mother cope with the scandal of it if they find out whose daughter I am?*

She didn't say any of this to Emily, for she too might have to face questions about her, and what – *what* of Matthew and the children and the academy? Would he draw away and maybe not let her see the children again, which would break her heart? She hadn't given him any details except that Nicholas had left her and gone abroad. *Who will send their children to be taught at a school run by a divorced woman like me?*

Tears ran down her cheeks as realization hit her, and she

held back a sob, but Emily heard her and turned. 'What? Would you like me to come with you? I know your father is going to accompany you, but if you wanted I would come to support you, Lydia, don't ever think that I won't!'

Lydia shook her head. 'No! I couldn't ask you to do such a thing. You would be tarnished too. I'm alone with this, Emily. Totally alone.'

CHAPTER FORTY

She did wear a veil, as Matthew suggested; she borrowed one from her mother, having finally explained to her that as Nicholas had effectively abandoned her, she was suing him in his absence for a divorce. She didn't mention the annulment, as she was sure that her mother would ask what it meant and she didn't want to explain the detail.

She had also led Matthew to believe that it was separation she was seeking, as he knew that women had no rights whatsoever in the matter of divorce, and couldn't apply. An annulment was possible, but only if a woman was brave enough to ask for it.

She wore a grey coat and a hat to which she had attached a black veil which covered her face to the lips as she and her father entered a private carriage on the train to London. She took off the hat once the train was en route to the capital with no changes scheduled, and when it stopped to take on refreshments halfway she took out a fan to cover her face in case anyone should look in the window.

Her father took care of everything, his face like thunder

because he was still blaming himself for not realizing that Mercer was an out and out villain, as he described him. Once or twice Lydia attempted to defend him, but her father was having none of it.

'He gave me details of his education in law, and it was a fairy tale. I checked recently with all the contact names he gave me and not a single one of them knew him.' His face was red with anger, knowing that he was partially responsible. 'It all seemed legitimate, and because of that I didn't make adequate checks when he first came to us. That will *never* happen again.'

She decided to leave well alone. The advocate her father had chosen to represent her had the details; how much she didn't know, and neither did she ask.

Her father had booked rooms at an hotel close by the courts, or rather Hannah had booked them, and Lydia had drawn in a breath at that information and hoped the secretary didn't have any other details of her case. 'Bad behaviour and desertion is all she knows,' her father told her, 'nothing more,' and Lydia drew in a breath of relief, even though she wondered if that description would be considered true. Abandonment, she thought, would have been the more accurate charge to cite.

What her father hadn't explained until now was that her case would be heard in a family court. 'One of the things you should know, Lydia, is that until only three years or so ago you wouldn't have been able to apply even for annulment. This new Act of Matrimonial Causes opens doors to many women who will now have the right to divorce brutal husbands. An Act well overdue, in my opinion.'

The bed in her hotel room was very comfortable, but she didn't sleep. She rose feeling wretched and ate no breakfast, drinking only tea whilst her father tucked into bacon, eggs and sausage and washed it down with a full pot of coffee. Fortunately, her case was to be held that morning and they were due at the court to speak to the advocate at nine thirty.

They were early, and Lydia was glad of her veil, as there were many people circling in the entrance hall. Her father spotted a clerk holding up a paper with *Davenport* written on it, and he signalled that he was that person.

'This way, sir, madam,' the clerk said. 'Samuel Burniston, your advocate, is already here.'

Burniston was a middle-aged man, though probably younger than her father, Lydia thought, and she hoped that that indicated he was well versed in law and knew how to handle all kinds of matters. Surely, she thought, there would be many more women seeking freedom from unsuitable husbands now that the law would allow it.

The three of them sat down together at the far side of the room to talk before the hearing, and Burniston, glancing first at Lydia's father and then at her, took several sheets of printed paper from a folder. 'We have more news, sir, and madam,' he said, turning to Lydia. 'I hope you won't find it too distressing. We always do our own searches when a person is said to have absconded from these shores, and as I understand it, Nicholas Mercer was thought to have taken ship to America from Liverpool.'

Both Lydia and her father nodded. 'There is a letter,' Lydia said, looking at her father. 'From my husband, saying he was leaving for America. We sent a copy, did we not, Father?'

'Yes, yes.' Her father too opened up a leather briefcase and brought out a paper. 'It says here quite clearly that he has booked a passage, and adds that his wife may file for divorce, which as we know is practically impossible for women.'

'There is no dispute over that, sir, none whatsoever. The difficulty is that we can find no trace of the said Nicholas Mercer on any ship leaving Liverpool for America on any days of that or the following week.'

Lydia sat staring at him. No trace of him? Did he change his mind? And why?

Her father was furious. 'What other ships were sailing during that time?'

'Many, sir, and we checked them all. There wasn't a single name that bore any resemblance to Nicholas Mercer. The passengers listed were mostly families and commercial travellers.'

'He said he had a ticket booked,' Lydia whispered. 'He drew out money to pay for it.'

'Villains can say anything they want, ma'am,' Burniston said wryly. 'It doesn't mean that what they say is true.'

'So where does that leave me?' Lydia asked. She had found her voice, and needed to know.

'I'm going to speak to the judge and ask his opinion, ma'am. He is in court just now, so if you will excuse me I will go and wait.'

Lydia and her father sat across from each other as Burniston left the room. Lost for words, her father shook his head. 'What is he trying to achieve, Lydia?' he asked after a moment.

'I can't imagine,' she told him. 'It's as if I've never known him. How could he be so elusive, so baffling? I have never known him to be so . . .'

'Shifty,' her father said. 'He's playing some kind of game.'

But what game, she wondered, and why?

They waited more than half an hour before the door opened again. Burniston cleared his throat. 'Judge Bennet will see you now, ma'am. Alone,' he added as her father rose to his feet. 'It is unusual, sir, I realize that, but if we don't continue now, then the case will have to be heard on another day.'

Lydia adjusted her veil and stood up. 'Don't worry, Father,' she said in an assured voice, which in no way indicated the turmoil in her mind. 'I want this over and done with.'

Her father sat down again, his hand covering his mouth, and nodded. He was upset, she knew that, but she was determined to do this, and make him proud. She had sounded more positive than she felt as she followed Burniston down a dark corridor – behind the court room, she assumed – where he knocked briefly on a door, opened it to let her in, and closed it behind her.

Judge Bennet was sitting at a desk with a pot of coffee in front of him and a large cup in his hand. He signalled for her to come forward. 'Mrs Mercer, do take a seat.' He indicated a chair next to him, not in front of the desk. 'I would offer you a coffee, my dear, but I'm afraid there are no extra cups. Most remiss,' he mumbled.

She shook her head. She couldn't have drunk anything even if he had had cups, and sat down, folding her hands in front of her to stop them trembling.

He leaned towards her. 'May I be permitted to ask you to

lift your veil? There is no one else here to see you.' She took off her gloves, lifted the veil and folded it back. He nodded and gave a gentle smile. 'I understand why you would wish to hide your face, Mrs Mercer. A face such as yours would make headlines in the newspapers. You are young, I think?'

'I am twenty-three, sir,' she whispered.

'And married at twenty, I understand?' he said, glancing down at a pile of papers. 'Well, I have looked at all the details here, and I think that you and your so-called marriage have been used as a hideaway by a man who had a quite different agenda, though it is not for us to speculate on what mischief he might be up to. It seems that he is masterly in hiding the real person behind the name, and it is possible that he has been married previously. Was he courteous and polite?'

'Yes,' she whispered. She had to admit that he was, mostly.

'And he didn't disturb your sleep?'

She took in a breath. Now the questioning was to begin, and it would be mortifying. 'No.' She shook her head. 'Only occasionally did he come to my bed, and when he did he would say he couldn't sleep, the mattress didn't suit him, and get out again.'

Judge Bennet nodded and looked away. 'And so your marriage was never consummated?'

She felt the tears begin and blinked to stop them. She mustn't fail now. 'No sir. Never.'

'And you didn't think it odd?'

'I didn't know what to think, and it wasn't a question I could ask anyone else.'

He sighed. 'Young maidens should be taught what to expect in a marriage,' he mumbled, then added, 'in my opinion, for what it's worth.' He drew a sheet of paper towards him and wrote a paragraph, signing it with a flourish, then stamped it with a rubber stamp and wrote his initials over the top. He handed it to her without looking at her. 'The marriage might or might not have been legitimate, but that is not my concern now. Here I have certified an annulment due to non-consummation of marriage. The marriage was null and void and in legal terms did not happen. You are free now to live as a single woman, or find a man who will love you.'

Now he looked across at her and smiled. He looked grandfatherly, she thought; kind but with a no-nonsense attitude. 'I think the latter will suit you best.' Tears began to slip down her cheeks, and he reached for her hand and patted it. 'Put it all behind you, my dear. Begin again and find love.'

He rose from his desk, and that was her cue to realize that it was over and she could leave. 'Thank you,' she said. 'From the bottom of my heart.'

He nodded, putting his hand to his chest and giving a short bow, then walked to the door to open it and let her out into freedom.

CHAPTER FORTY-ONE

'A new life, Father,' she told him as they travelled home. Once more they were in a private carriage. 'The marriage did not happen in law, Judge Bennet said. He seemed to think that Nicholas Mercer' – she paused and swallowed. *I must think of him as someone who has – had – nothing to do with me* – 'had other schemes.'

'I believe he was probably right,' her father said. 'Mercer might well have been hiding in plain sight. He had some knowledge of the law and was therefore able to pass himself off as a would-be lawyer.' He gave a grunt. 'Fooled me, at any rate.'

'All of us, Papa, not just you. But now we can forget about him. I, at least, can start thinking about the academy project again.'

'How will you feel about living alone?'

She took a deep breath. 'I have been living alone for most of my . . . time with Nicholas.' She had almost said *marriage*, but according to Judge Bennet that did not happen. 'I love my home, and the Wade children visit me every day.' She didn't mention Matthew, though she wanted to. 'My friend Emily calls regularly, and Mama comes to tea sometimes, and when the academy is ready and open I hope I shall be busy. What I must concentrate on now is garnering sponsors and trustees to help me run it.'

Her father gazed at her. 'I often thought that I would like a son,' he said quietly, 'but it didn't happen, and I realize now that I have the best thing of all: a lovely daughter who is as clever and intelligent as any son could have been, and has made me proud.'

She was happy. It was as if the world had shifted and she had taken her rightful place as a woman of her time.

Although it wasn't late, darkness was falling when they arrived back at Beverley rail station, and her father wanted her to stay the night with them in town. But she said no, she really wanted to be at home, where she could put her mind in order.

He seemed to understand her mood, and at the station he called over to where the hackney carriages were waiting and asked a driver he knew to drop him off and then take his daughter home. 'I know it, Mr Davenport, sir,' the man said. 'I've taken Mrs Davenport there a time or two.'

'Good man. Stay with her until she's safely inside, will you?'

The driver tipped his bowler and said he would.

Lydia felt tiredness overcoming her. She had so many mixed feelings on her mind that she just wanted to sleep and hoped that she could. The driver, true to his word, stopped outside her house and stepped down to open the carriage door and help her out. He handed her overnight bag to her, and opened the gate. 'Somebody's lit 'lamp for you, ma'am,' he noticed.

'Oh, how thoughtful!' she said. A flickering oil lamp hung beside her front door. 'I have good neighbours who look out for me.'

Through the window she could see low lamplight in her sitting room, and for a second she had the shivers at the thought that Nicholas might be there, but no, she had taken his key inside. I must have new locks fitted, she thought.

She thanked the driver, who had already been paid by her father, and he closed the gate behind her and waited until she had unlocked the door and stepped inside.

Such peace, she thought, opening the wooden box where she kept lucifers and candles. She lit two, bringing light into the hall. 'Home,' she sighed. 'How sweet the word!'

In the sitting room a small fire was burning low in the grate, and she added some twigs from the log basket to liven it, laying a small log and a piece of coal on top. Had Maggie been back to light the fire? It surely couldn't have been in all afternoon. She lit the lamps from one of the candles, and thought that if anyone was looking from the Wade cottage they would see the light and the smoke from the fire.

She took off her coat and hat, reminding herself that she must unpick the veil and give it back to her mother, and went into the kitchen, taking the candle with her. Her parents had gas lamps in their house, for the supply had been brought to many street lamps and some households in Beverley, but it had not yet been introduced into the nearby countryside. She lit the oil lamps from the candle and looked about her: Cook had left cold chicken and fresh bread beneath cheesecloth on the table.

'How lucky I am,' she murmured, and went to the sink to fill the kettle. 'I'll make a hot drink to have with the bread and butter and cold chicken, and put a hot water bottle in my bed to warm it, and then – oh, such bliss – I will have an early night.' It was only just after eight o'clock but she felt exhausted, what with the rail travel and the trauma of being at the court, even though the result had been good, and now she wanted only to relax and, she hoped, sleep.

Someone tapped on the front door, making her jump, and she walked slowly into the hall, holding the candle. It could only be Matthew, but she called out 'Who is it?' nevertheless.

'Matthew and Ben. Just checking that you're safe home.'

'One moment.' She smiled as she put the candle down. Still ever careful about her reputation, always bringing a child with him even though there would be no one about to see him. She drew back the bolt and turned the key. 'Come in, do.'

They stepped inside the hall. 'Where've you been, Miss Liddy?' Ben asked spontaneously. 'We wondered where you'd gone!'

She gave a big sigh. 'I've been to London, Ben. It was a last-minute arrangement, all done in a hurry. I'm sorry. I hope you weren't worried?'

'A bit,' he said. 'Da said you'd had to dash off somewhere.'

'I was with my father, so I was perfectly safe. You've met him, haven't you?'

'Oh, yeh! That's all right then. I'll tell 'others – well, Charlie and Lily, anyway. I think Alice might know, though she said she didn't, but Mary June's been crying for you!'

She looked up at Matthew who was standing with his arms

folded as he waited for Ben to finish, and he nodded. 'Come on, then, now that we know that Miss Liddy's all right. We'll come and see you tomorrow, Miss Lydia. I don't suppose you've looked out of 'kitchen window?'

'I've been home a mere ten minutes – just enough time to put wood and coal on the fire. How on earth has it kept in so long?'

'Maggie. She was bothered that you'd come home to a cold house, and as we didn't know when you'd be home I came to meet her here at four o'clock so we could build up 'fire in case you came home today.'

She took a deep breath, and sighed it out. 'Everything was completed. There was no reason to stay in London.'

He gazed at her, moistening his lips. 'Done?'

She smiled. 'Yes! Completely.'

'Right. Good. Well done!' He looked down at Ben. 'In that case we'll get off, and we can all have a good night's sleep!'

'That's what I'm looking forward to,' Lydia told him. 'But what did you mean about looking out of the kitchen window?'

'Nothing that won't keep 'til 'morning, but do be sure to look. And you might hear workmen here early, so don't be worried by any noise, and young Jim'll see to 'animals as usual.'

'Oh, I'd forgotten about Jim. I think I need to pay him.' But she couldn't help but add, 'And now I'm going to bed. I need to ponder on my new life!'

She couldn't see anything except a stack of bricks and ladders and various piles of something covered over with tarpaulin when she looked out of an upstairs window before she climbed into bed. The window that was in what had been Nicholas's room, which she intended to change completely. Now she was free, she would do as she pleased: she would buy another bed, or maybe two so that Matthew's children could stay overnight if they wanted to; she would have the room completely redecorated, with fresh bright wallpaper and curtains, and would buy another fireguard so that a fire could be lit in winter to make the room cosy. *And I must ask the builders if maybe the loft could be converted into a third bedroom and a staircase made up to it. Or perhaps an annexe could be built.* Her mind ran wild with opportunities as she lay in bed, sleepless even though she was so tired, overcome by the emotion of the last few days. *What have I said to Matthew? Have I explained the details? No. How could I when Ben was there, and what would I have said anyway? He would have been supportive, of course he would, but why would he need to know? Except, except – when he kissed me and insisted that I didn't let him in the house. What did he mean?*

She fell asleep and was beset by dreams, tossing about, waking, and then sleeping again until the sky lightened and she heard men's voices and realized that a new day had begun. She went into the other bedroom – she was going to call it the children's room, she decided – and looked out of the front window to watch the workmen coming through the gate and leaving it open, and then moved to the side window, above the kitchen.

A large square concrete base was partially covered by sheets of something, she couldn't make out what: some kind of woven cloth. Bricks were piled up neatly by the paddock fence, and Frisky and donkey Janet were standing looking over it as if supervising. Then she saw Matthew appear and begin measuring, and she remembered that the field was to be halved with a fence across it, so that the paddock would be at the top end, and a play area would fill the bottom. She went back into her bedroom and looked at the clock. It was nine in the morning, she had slept after all, and she must get washed and dressed and ready to begin the day. Were the children coming today, and would they be able to concentrate with all the construction work going on?

Going downstairs fully dressed, she heard the letter box open and saw an envelope being pushed through. She picked it up, saw *Mrs N. Mercer* in Nicholas's handwriting, and opened the door. 'Postie,' she called, 'I don't want this. Can you return it, please?'

On the back of the envelope she saw *Nicholas Mercer* and *Liverpool,* but no house address. She picked up a pencil from the chest, and crossing out her name with a thick black stroke wrote, *Not known at this address. Return to sender.*

She was curious, of course she was, but as far as she was concerned this sender was nothing to do with her. She felt a sense of intense satisfaction as the postwoman took it, gave her a funny look, and pushed it back into her post bag without saying a word. It's done, she thought. At last.

CHAPTER FORTY-TWO

'I need to talk to you, please, Matthew, when you have some time to spare,' she said when she saw him outside the house. 'Where are the children? You haven't brought them with you?'

'I thought you'd need some time off after . . . after—' He broke off.

'No,' she said. 'I want to do what I always do; I don't want to think about what has happened, not yet. I want to get used to my new life of being unmarried again, but so much of it is a jumble. You said last night that I'd see you today, and I assumed that you'd bring the children. Who's looking after Aaron and Mary June?'

'Lottie. She still comes sometimes; she hasn't any money so I pay her for watching over 'young uns.'

'Oh yes, of course. I'm sorry. Does she bring her little girl?'

'Usually leaves her with her ma, I think.'

'Did she marry her young man?'

'She did, but he's lost his job. I give him a few things to do, but he's not all that bright, so they're struggling. Drat,' he said, hesitating over a fencepost. 'I've lost count.' He gave a deep sigh. 'I'd better get on, Lydia. By the way, what will you call yourself?' He looked at her. 'Your surname, I mean?'

She shrugged. 'Davenport, I suppose. It's – I mean, I haven't told you what happened yet.'

'No, but you don't have to.'

'I know I don't, but I'd like to, only not yet. I haven't, erm, absorbed the knowledge myself yet. All I can think is that I'm no longer married; that has simply melted away as if it never happened.'

He looked at her for a long moment. 'I don't see how a marriage can be just swept away, even a short one.'

She saw another workman arriving. 'Can we talk later? Inside? Not out here!'

'Yes, of course.'

'I think I'll stroll up to see the children. Is that all right?'

'Of course it's all right. Why wouldn't it be?'

Something's wrong; he's never irritable. Something's upset him. But what? She turned back to the house, but not before she saw him pick up a piece of timber and sling it under the far hedge.

THE END

After lunch the children arrived, brought by Alice. Matthew seemed to have disappeared.

'He's working,' Ben announced. 'He's got a lot o' work on. That's what he said, and he said we hadn't to be any bother.'

'You're never a bother, not to me,' she said. 'But where is Mary June? Why isn't she here?'

'Lottie's come to look after Aaron, so Da said Mary June might as well stop with her as well,' Ben said. 'She didn't want to; she wanted to come wi' us.'

'*With* us,' Lydia said vaguely. Alice didn't say anything, but sighed.

'All right. Ben, will you get the memory books out, please? Alice, can I have a word?'

Ben charged off into the sitting room, and Lydia looked gravely at Alice. 'I hope you weren't worried about me, were you, Alice?'

'Not really,' she answered in a low voice, 'but I did wonder why you'd gone away without telling us. I hoped you were coming back.'

'Of course I was coming back!' she said gently, putting an arm round the girl's shoulders. 'It was important that I went, but it was a grown-up thing, Alice, and not something I could explain to you.'

Alice pressed her lips together. 'Was it about Mr Mercer? You're not going away as well, are you?'

'No, Alice, I am not.' She bent and kissed her cheek. 'If I tell you that I went to London with my father to end my marriage to Mr Mercer, can it be private, just between you and me? I don't want anyone else to know.'

'Oh, yes.' Alice's face lit up. 'I swear I won't tell anyone. But Da knows, doesn't he?'

'He does, but no one else at present, except for my parents. Now, can you be in charge and get the others working on their memory books, whilst I slip up to see your father and collect Mary June?'

'Oh, yes, I can.' Alice put her arms round Lydia's waist. 'I'm so pleased you've come back to us.'

Lydia looked down at her, and stroked her hair. 'I'm not going anywhere, Alice. This is home.'

'I was worried that you'd gone looking for Mr Mercer to bring him back here.'

Lydia smiled. 'No, quite the contrary, and I don't know where he is in any case! He's gone for good and I'm unmarried once again.'

'Does that mean you can get married again if you want to?'

'Yes, if I found someone special who wanted to marry me, then I could. And I would.'

Alice heaved a breath. 'Oh, good,' she said happily. 'I hope you find someone like that.'

Lydia put on her coat and slipped out, hearing the children chattering about what they would write in their memory book and Alice telling them that Miss Liddy had gone to fetch Mary June. 'I like that name,' she heard Lily say.

It was a bright sunny day and she hoped that it would stay like that for a while whilst the builders were doing their preparatory work. She took some deep breaths: it was good to be outside in the cold fresh air, and she thought how wonderful it was to be living in the countryside. She'd loved her house as soon as she'd set eyes on it; Nicholas hadn't been so keen and would have preferred to live in a house in town. 'I'm not used to the country,' he'd said. 'I'm a townie really.'

'So where else have you lived apart from London?' She didn't think he sounded like a Londoner.

'Everywhere. I've been around a lot,' he'd said.

She put her hand to her forehead the better to see against the bright sky. Someone was coming towards her. It looked like – yes, it was Matthew, with a child on his back. She waved and he lifted a hand in greeting.

'Where are you going?' he said, turning his back so she could hold Mary June as she struggled to get down.

'I've arrived,' she said, giving the little girl a hug as she set her gently on the ground and tried to hold on to her. 'It was to see you and collect this darling little girl.'

'She's not been a darling little girl,' he said, 'she's been a mithering monster.' He gently squeezed Mary June's cheek. 'Want Liddy,' he said in a squeaky voice. 'Don't want Dada, want Liddy. I should be working,' he added flatly. 'I've got a big order coming up: fences, window frames, storage boxes . . . I'm going to have to employ more carpenters.'

'No!' she said, a big smile on her face. 'How dreadful for you!' She looked up at him. 'If you won't give me at least one of your children, will you marry me and share them all with me?'

He blinked. 'What?'

'I said—'

'No, I heard what you said. You're just divorced; why would you want to marry again?'

'I only want to marry you, not anyone else. I had the idea that you were fond of me, and when I saw you last time – or maybe the time before, or it might have been the time before that – you begged me not to let you inside the house, and I thought it was because . . . because you wanted to tell me something . . . and besides, I'm not divorced, because the judge said it had been an unlawful marriage all along and therefore null and void. I'm unmarried. A single woman.'

'What?' he breathed.

'He said—'

'No, no, I heard you.' He leaned towards her and kissed Mary June in her arms and then tenderly kissed her. 'Why would you want to marry *me*? I'm just a working man who happens to love you desperately, but what . . .' he swallowed, and she saw that his eyes were moist. 'What would my wife – my Mary – think?'

She shook her head, and then gently stroked his face. 'You don't have a wife, my darling Matthew. You did have, a wonderful one, and I'll *never, ever* take her place. Mary will stay in your heart for ever *and* in the remembrance of your children, who are right now writing a book of memories of her so that they never forget either.'

Tears ran down his face, and hers too. 'I loved you the very first time we met on that most dreadful day,' he said, 'and I thought I would never live through it. But I knew that I must, because of the bairns.'

'You were so brave,' she whispered. 'So kind with the children, who didn't understand what was happening; after Mary they were the most important beings in your life. I saw that. You were the kindest person I had ever met.'

There came a sound from behind them, the clip-clop of hooves and rattle of carriage wheels, and they turned together, arms around each other and Mary June.

'Good day to you.' Dr Tennyson lifted his whip, smiling at them both. 'Lovely morning!'

After a frozen moment, they both laughed. 'Shall we go home?' Lydia suggested. 'My home – and yours, if you'll have it. You can spare half an hour, can't you? But I think we're missing somebody. Have you counted your children?'

'Aaron!' he said, and Mary June clapped her hands. They went back into the cottage and collected Aaron, and Matthew paid Lottie for her time, then told the joiner working in the shed – now called the Wade Workshop – that he wouldn't be long.

At Lydia's house, the men in the paddock were busy measuring and pacing, and merely looked up and nodded as the couple went inside to find the children, who were studiously drawing and writing on sheets of paper under the supervision of Alice. They all looked up and then continued what they were doing, apart from Alice, who kept very still.

'Anybody want to come to a wedding?' Matthew said. 'It'll mean new frocks for 'girls, and smart pants and shirts for 'boys.'

'Yes!' Alice screamed, and hurled herself at her father and then at Lydia. 'Can I be a bridesmaid?'

'Me as well!' Lily jumped up, and the boys almost cottoned on. 'Whose wedding is it?' Ben asked.

'Mine,' his father said.

'And mine,' Lydia added. 'If that's all right with you.'

'If you're getting married at this wedding, you'll have to share with Da,' Charlie said solemnly, looking at Lydia, 'cos we won't have enough beds.'

'You could share with me,' Alice said, 'but we'd be better coming to your house.'

'And we'd be nearer to school,' Lily said studiously. 'If it's ready in time.'

'If we had a bigger trap we could all get in it and use Frisky and donkey Janet to take us to Beverley for our new clothes,' Ben remarked some days later.

'Hm, yes, possibly,' Matthew said thoughtfully, 'I'll look into that,' and turned to Lydia. 'Janet? That's an odd name for a donkey, isn't it? Especially for a male.'

'Oh! Is she? He? I hadn't noticed.'

'Castrated,' he said, and grinned, 'and don't look at me like that!'

They married in St Mary's church in Beverley the following spring, the sacred venue being allowed as she was an unmarried woman and not divorced. Her proud father gave her away for the second time, and her mother cried.

The reception was held in the Horners' garden at their invitation, and the children, including Aaron and Mary June, were invited to stay overnight with the family, for they had plenty of staff to look after them all, and a midnight picnic in bed was planned for the older ones, who mostly fell asleep instead, worn out with the excitement.

Matthew and Lydia decided that instead of a honeymoon they would take a holiday at the seaside in the summer, and all the children could come too.

Lydia was nervous on her wedding night; after all, she deliberated, her first so-called wedding night wasn't worth thinking about, as she had virtually slept alone. She had thought that Nicholas would teach her about love between two people, but it seemed he didn't know about it either.

But she already loved Matthew, and his children too, and he was so tender, so loving, treating her as if she was the most treasured woman on earth, that he brought her to a point of ecstasy that she had never known. Then he whispered a question in her ear and she asked what he meant.

'You were married for three years,' he murmured. 'Why are you . . .'

'I don't know what— do you mean . . .' she whispered, running her fingers across his lips, 'what the judge said? That it was an unconsummated marriage?'

He leaned on one elbow and looked down at her, and nodded. The glow from candles and lamps sent flickering lights over her hair and face. 'Didn't I say that?' she said softly. 'Didn't I tell you that?'

'No. No, you didn't tell me that.' He laughed. It was a joyous sound and he ran his fingers over her eyebrows, her eyelids, her throat, and kissed her lips until she shivered with anticipation, and she wasn't in the least disappointed.

*

The academy took a further year to complete, and by then they had a waiting list of girls and boys aged from five to twelve. They also had a list of young and middle-aged teachers hoping for a place, almost all of them female and married. There was one young man, Mr Hawthorn, who in the interview said he'd like to teach fitness, sport and natural studies. His main interest was in ornithology, and so they took him on.

Ben was his star pupil and bound for further education. Charlie was still set on working as a joiner with his father so that he could have his name put on the sign hanging outside the workshop, and be one of Wade and Son.

Alice was destined to set up in business selling her knitwear and teaching other young people to knit, whilst Lily said she was going to be an artist, but wasn't going to art school as she already knew how to draw and paint and she'd make a studio in what had been Alice's bedroom in their old house.

Lydia put her role as director of the Children's Academy on hold and took an executive position, bringing in the very efficient and enthusiastic Hannah, who said she was tired of dealing with men, to manage all other aspects of running the academy. Lydia, meanwhile, looked after the youngest children, Aaron, Mary June, and little Flora, who arrived twelve months after her marriage.

She heard nothing more from Nicholas Mercer, and dismissed him from her mind. For many years, on Aaron's birthday, they went to the chapel as a family to say a prayer for Mary and lay flowers on her grave. Matthew stood solemnly and gave thanks to her for her enduring love and for their children, and as the years rolled on Alice, Ben, Charlie and Lily together took flowers on her birthday and on their return looked in their memory books to remind them of her. To Aaron and Mary June, Lydia was their known mother, as she was to Flora, and then Toby when he came along.

'You know what?' Matthew said one day. 'I think we'll extend the house, like your ma wants. There's a huge space up in 'loft. What do you think, Charlie? Could we tackle it?'

Charlie nodded. 'Aye,' he said. 'I reckon we could.'

AFTERWORD

It was early morning, still dark, with a hazy fog lingering over the dockside; the man trod carefully, shuffling alongside crates and storage huts. He had heard a church clock strike two about an hour ago and decided that it was safe to continue his journey.

He had arrived by the last train at Liverpool's Lime Street Station and hung around in a doorway as if waiting for someone. He wasn't noticed; there were always men around, seamen and dockers mostly, who were dressed like him in shabby coats and well worn boots, with sacks over their shoulders to carry their belongings. The only item that marked the man out was the top hat. It had seen better days, and anyone noticing it would have thought he had stolen it from some other down-and-out fellow.

He shuffled on. Things had changed since he was last here; the docks were even busier by the look of the many more ships he could see, and he took a turn to bring him out into the dark and narrow streets. Here he must take even more care as the police – the peelers as they were commonly known – were always on the lookout for those who shouldn't be lingering near the docks.

Taking several turns he easily found the narrow street and the house that he wanted. He dared a knock on the door that he hoped wouldn't wake the neighbours, but he was careful: it was such a rotten-planked door that a hard fist could have broken through it. It was after three o'clock, but he knew she was a light sleeper, and sure enough, after his second knock, he heard her voice and raised a smile. He was home.

'Clear off, you beggar. There's nothing 'ere that you'd want.'

He knocked again; three sharp knocks, a pause, and then two more.

'Who is it?' The voice was nearer.

'It's me, Ma.'

'Who's me, you beggar?'

'Your favourite son, Ma. Who else?'

The door opened a crack and he saw her, her hand holding a thick stick, a shillelagh, brought from Ireland by her own mother.

'Hello, Ma. Are you going to let me in?'

'You beggar,' she growled, and unhooked the stout chain to unfasten the door.

He stepped inside. 'Huh,' she grunted. 'Peelers came lookin' a time or two. They had posters up for Top Hat Jack for more'n eighteen months. Told me you were probably dead. Who've you been this time?'

'Nicholas Mercer.' He grinned. 'A gentleman,' he said. 'A lawyer, no less.' He sighed. 'Or almost. It's good to be home.'

ACKNOWLEDGEMENTS

I would like to thank the Transworld team once again: editors Sally Williamson and Lara Stevenson, long-standing copy-editor Nancy Webber and production editor Vivien Thompson and the whole Transworld Penguin Random House team for bringing the book together, not forgetting Marianne Issa El-Khoury for creating the lovely cover; nor my faithful local Divine Clark PR team who guide me through the terrors of social media and publicity.

For the encouragement and support of friends and family, I thank you all.

ABOUT THE AUTHOR

Since winning the Catherine Cookson Prize for Fiction for her first novel, *The Hungry Tide*, **Val Wood** has become one of the most popular authors in the UK.

Born in the mining town of Castleford, Val came to East Yorkshire as a child and has lived in Hull and rural Holderness where many of her novels are set. She now lives in the market town of Beverley.

When she is not writing, Val is busy promoting libraries and supporting many charities. In 2017 she was awarded an honorary doctorate by the University of Hull for service and dedication to literature.

Find out more about Val Wood's novels by visiting her website: www.valwood.co.uk